LEEDS COLLEGE OF BUILDING
T07315

HOUSES AND HISTORY

Other books by the author

THE ENGLISH FARMHOUSE AND COTTAGE
THE HOUSE AND HOME
EUROPEAN TOWNS: THEIR ARCHAEOLOGY AND EARLY HISTORY
LINCOLNSHIRE AND THE FENS

HOUSES AND HISTORY

by

Maurice Barley

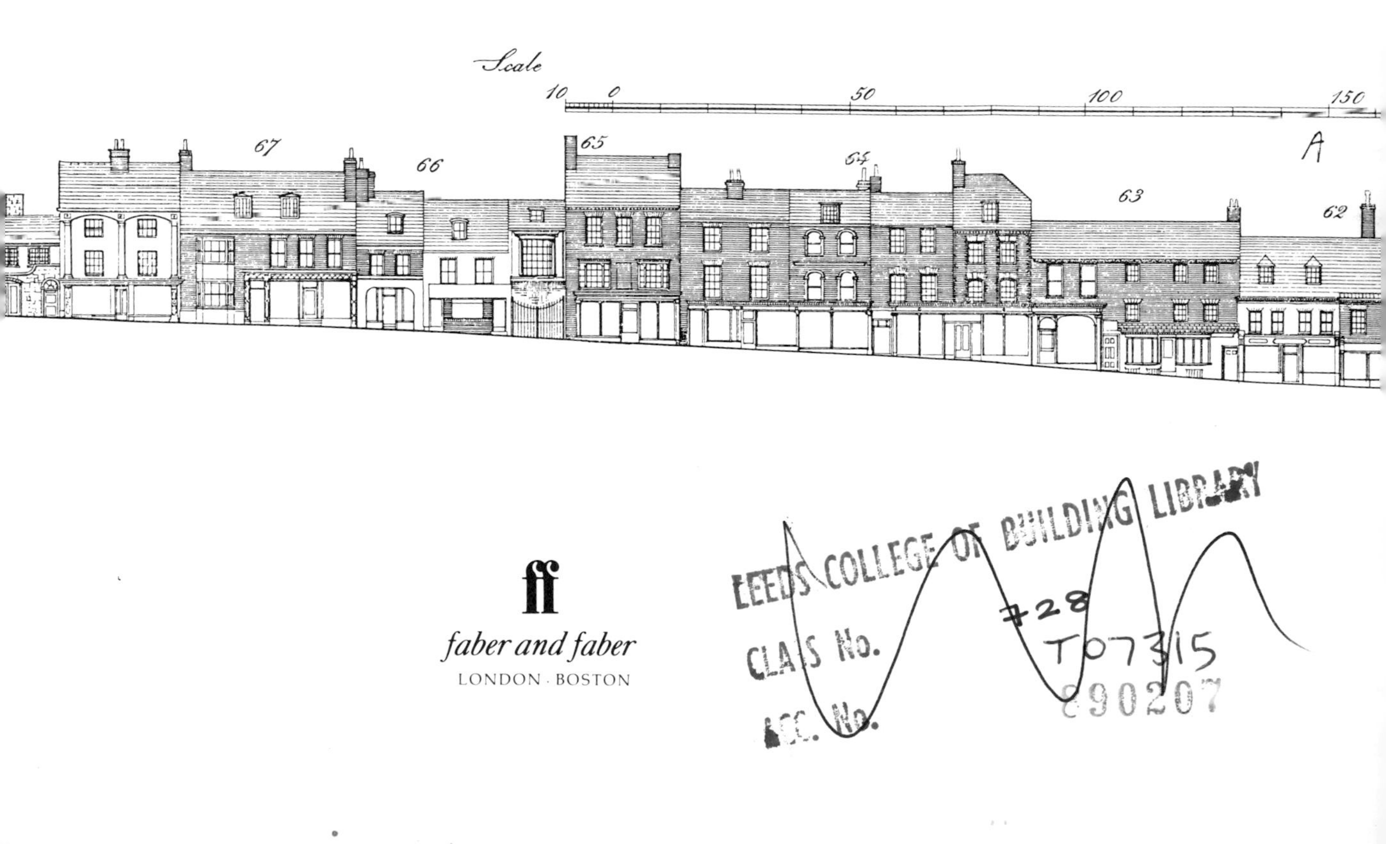

ff
faber and faber
LONDON · BOSTON

First published in 1986
by Faber and Faber Limited
3 Queen Square London WC1N 3AU

Printed in Great Britain by
Butler & Tanner Ltd, Frome, Somerset

British Library Cataloguing in Publication Data

Barley, M.W.
Houses and history.
1. Architecture, Domestic——England——
History
I. Title
728'.0942 NA7328

ISBN 0-571-13631-1

Contents

Preface

The study of historic houses has long been one of my principal interests. At first I concentrated on the small houses of the English countryside; not the sort open to the public but those which it is fashionable to call vernacular. Eventually I found that understanding them involved the study of the houses of the richer classes who could afford to employ master masons and architects rather than jobbing builders to design their houses, which can be labelled Norman, Gothic, Classical and the like. A distinctive feature of English society is that its class structure has long been fluid, and that men have been able to rise in the world and acquire new wealth and new houses to mark their success. Inevitably, such men have copied the houses of their betters. I hope that this attempt to describe houses of all classes, in town and country, and to explain their development will make a coherent and credible story.

The attempt to paint so broad a picture could not have been made without the advantage of seeking enlightenment from colleagues in other disciplines within a university, and without participation in those conferences, research groups and seminars which are part of the academic world. Including chapters on town houses would have been impossible without the help of the Historic Buildings Division of the Greater London Council, and of archaeologists working in historic towns on sites threatened by redevelopment. Formal acknowledgement of drawings and photographs provided, in the captions to the illustrations, is a bald but sincere expression of gratitude. Illustrations unless otherwise acknowledged are by the author. Recognition of help and encouragement is due to the staff of the Royal Commission on the Historical Monuments of England and its National Monuments Record.

Dr N. W. Alcock, Professor P. D. A. Harvey and Mr Eric Mercer read some chapters in typescript and helped to make them clearer and more accurate. Many friends were consulted in compiling the map [89] of surviving medieval peasant houses; I hope they will feel that its speculative character is justified. The Cambridge University Press has allowed the use of several drawings originally prepared by me for volumes of the

Agrarian History of England and Wales. Mr Adrian Gibson drew the perspective views of medieval open halls; he and Dr Patrick Strange prepared the isometric drawings of Coningsby and Quaintree House. Mr David Taylor, with guidance from Dr Philip Dixon, devised the analytical diagrams of Harlech Castle gatehouse and Bolton Castle; he also redrew Dr Mark Girouard's reconstruction of Holdenby which the latter has kindly allowed me to use. Mr Gavin Simpson and Dr Chris Litton provided the illustration of dendrochronology. Last but certainly not least, thanks are due to the photographic department of Nottingham University, and to Mrs June Knight and Mrs Marjorie Dawson for turning a messy manuscript into typescript.

Nottingham M. W. Barley

Abbreviations

Agr. Hist.	*Cambridge Agrarian History of England and Wales*, ed. Joan Thirsk, vols, IV, 1500–1640 (1967), and V, 1640–1750 (1985)
Ant. J.	*Antiquaries Journal*
Archaeol. J.	*Archaeological Journal*
BAR	*British Archaeological Review*
BE	BE preceding italicized county names indicates volumes in Nikolaus Pevsner's *Buildings of England* series (Penguin)
CBA	Council for British Archaeology
EFC	*The English Farmhouse and Cottage*, M. W. Barley (1961)
EVH	*English Vernacular Houses*, Eric Mercer (1975)
House and Home	*The House and Home*, M. W. Barley (1963)
HMSO	Her Majesty's Stationery Office
J. Brit. Archaeol. Ass.	*Journal of the British Archaeological Association*
King's Works	*The History of the King's Works*, H. M. Colvin (general ed.) vols. I (1963) to IV (1982)
Med. Archaeol.	*Medieval Archaeology*
NMR	National Monuments Record
PRO	Public Record Office
RCHM	Royal Commission on the Historical Monuments of England
Turner and Parker	*Domestic Architecture of England and Wales*, 3 vols. (1851–9)
VCH	Victoria County History of England
YAT	York Archaeological Trust

NOTE: Historic counties are used to locate places, rather than the new counties (Avon, etc) to which they may now belong, since that makes it easier to pursue references to them in printed sources such as BE and in record offices. The NMR archives have been rearranged under modern counties.

Introduction

Any old building, whether a church, a castle, a mill or a house, is likely to have been altered at times to suit changing needs within a particular function. It may indeed have been converted from one function to another. If we are to observe and interpret changes of that sort which happened centuries ago, we need in each case to ask several questions. Such a series of questions has been formulated[1] as follows:

1. What was the original form of the house in terms of plan and use of rooms, and when was it built?
2. What sort of person lived in the house, and was it a typical dwelling for such a person?
3. Are there any structural features which are peculiar to that period of building?
4. Are there any decorative forms or features peculiar to that period?
5. How, when and why was the house altered?

The answers to these questions will bring us closer to those who built the houses; but we shall then wish to identify individuals or, if that is not possible, to establish the status of the persons responsible. Hence the plan of this book, with chapters devoted to social classes, from kings, barons and bishops to peasants and the working classes of industrial England. Not all houses will fit convincingly into such a scheme. Class distinctions are fluid and do not always correspond to the realities of personal life. Even if categories of house overlap at times and their status cannot be precisely defined, it is possible to recognize links between personal wealth and status and the form of a house, and the emergence of new families and social classes. At some periods and in some regions, houses provide clearer evidence of social conditions and changes than any other sort of evidence, as will be seen from Chapter 8.

When first conceived, this book was to have been entitled *The Archaeology of the House*. The main reason for discarding that title was to avoid the impression that it is only about the buried remains of the past. If in fact it reads like social history, then the archaeological evidence used and the archaeological principles adopted will have served a proper purpose. Since the past thousand years constitute a historic period, not a *pre*historic one, the archaeologist's closest links are with the historian, and he in turn depends on documents and archivists. The subject matter of archaeology is all the material remains of the past, whatever their age: they are collected, classified, arranged in typological order and dated. The method is just as applicable to buildings as to pottery or other portable objects; indeed, houses are so numerous that they cannot be handled, and interpretations of them offered, in any other way. The book comments at first or second hand on many houses; it aims to encourage the reader to fit his own knowledge and observations into the pattern. It also uses the evidence of excavation, in that limited sense of archaeology, particularly in Chapter 1, since no houses built before about 1200 still stand, and the account would be less coherent if Anglo-Saxon houses were not included.

There is, for the purposes of the book, only a technical difference between a house abandoned or demolished and one standing. Investigation of the former calls for a spade or a trowel in the first instance, the latter only for a tape measure and a drawing board. In between is the house worth investigating but about to be demolished or in need of drastic restoration. There the student needs not only his tape measure but also hammer, chisel and possibly pickaxe, in order to carry out if not a controlled demolition at least a thorough examination of what is concealed under paint, wallpaper and plaster.

The archaeologist will provide the most comprehensive answers to the questions posed on page 11, and he will be just as interested in answers to the last question about changes in the house as in answers to the first about its original character. The original design may be a proper subject for architectural history, a new discipline conveniently exemplified in the forty-odd volumes of Nikolaus Pevsner's *Buildings of England* (Penguin). They are frequently cited here, but ninety-nine houses out of a hundred are beneath the notice of an architectural historian. They are called 'vernacular' by those who specialize in studying them, but the expression 'vernacular architecture' is avoided in this book, because its meaning is not altogether self-evident, and using it sometimes obscures the social context of a house.

The fact that a good half of the book is devoted to the Middle Ages – that is, the period from 1200 to 1550 – may seem to need justification. The reason is simply that England and Wales together possess far more small houses built before about 1550 – or significant remains of them – than any other country in western Europe, and that we now know far more about them than we did a generation ago. The Welsh heritage has been superbly presented in Peter Smith's *Houses of the Welsh Countryside*

(HMSO 1975). The English heritage is still being explored. The word heritage, properly relating to an individual, is now used to imply that the remains of the past belong to all of us. As far as houses are concerned, that is not much of an exaggeration; the vast increase recently in the proportion of houses owned to houses rented makes many more householders responsible for a bit of our heritage.

A generation ago, the danger was decay and neglect. Now it is rather the converse – too many people wishing to restore or improve an old property, and able to afford to do so, impelled by mass advertising and current fashions. These are only transient aspects of processes of change which have always gone on. The historian and the archaeologist, thinking they best appreciate the past, may feel obliged to join a conservation group or ask to be consulted before changes are approved; but in the last resort their common desire is to understand the past and to convey their understanding (or interpretation) to a wider public. This must depend on whether a record (measured drawings and photographs) is made of what is altered or pulled down. Apart from contemporary building contracts, accounts and the like, the book draws on such records. Since 1970, archaeological units have sprung up, funded mainly by central and local government, to excavate sites threatened by urban redevelopment or intensive exploitation of the countryside. The natural public interest in totally new discoveries has obscured the fact that buildings of all sorts, from cathedrals, colleges and country mansions to mills and working-class houses, may at times be altered without the same sort of concern for recording what is done. These words are being written at a critical point in public affairs of this kind, for government responsibility has been handed over to the new Historic Buildings and Monuments Commission for England. Finding a better balance between recording the buried and the standing remains of the past and presenting the results to the public will be one of its most important tasks.

Note

1 By R.W. McDowall in the introduction to *Recording Old Houses* (Council for British Archaeology, 1980).

I THE MIDDLE AGES TO 1550

1 *Anglo-Saxon Houses*

The oldest houses of which there are remains still standing were built in the centuries following the Norman Conquest. To start this history of the house at 1066, however, would be to leave out the emergence of the social classes found in medieval England and therefore of the types of house which those classes needed, as well as the earliest evidence of building crafts. Houses of medieval kings, nobles and peasants can be linked both in plan and construction with those built before 1066, abandoned later and excavated by the present generation of archaeologists. A search for origins is one of the most fascinating aspects of historical and archaeological research. We must begin, then, with the contribution of archaeologists to the earliest phase of England's written history.[1]

When Anglo-Saxon kings adopted Christianity in the seventh century, they were persuaded that stone was the proper material for churches. The missionaries who led the campaign of conversion thought they were reviving the glories of Rome. Building houses was, with very rare exceptions, the business of the carpenter, whether the house was for a king or a peasant. There are a few references to houses in Anglo-Saxon sources. Bede in his *History of the English People* reports a speech made in AD 627 by one of the chief men of Edwin, king of Northumbria, when the possibility of adopting Christianity was under discussion.[2] He likened the life of man on earth to the swift flight of a sparrow through the king's hall on a winter's day: in through one door, past the comforting fire and out at the other into the wintry world again. The *Anglo-Saxon Chronicle* records that in 978 during a meeting of the king's council in his house at Calne (Wiltshire) 'the leading councillors of England fell down from an upper storey, all except the holy archbishop Dunstan, who alone remained standing on a beam.'[3] The stories fit our expectations: Edwin's hall open to the roof and heated by a central hearth and Edward the Martyr's at Calne either raised on the first floor or with a gallery at one end. We may add the description of the hall called Heorot in the epic poem, *Beowulf*, written perhaps soon after AD 700: built of timber, lofty, with a steep gilded roof.[4] The gilding, possibly on oak shingles, is beyond

1. Aerial view of BARTON-ON-HUMBER, LINCOLNSHIRE, showing St Peter's Church (Anglo-Saxon) and beyond it the fifteenth-century manor house (L-shaped). There must have been a manor house on that site as long as there was a church. *Cambridge University, Committee for Aerial Photography.*

our expectations. King Alfred when he translated Christian authors such as St Augustine and Boethius from Latin into Anglo-Saxon introduced some vivid metaphors from his own experience; he wrote about taking wagons to cut and carry timber for building, and he saw that a ruler, like any craftsman, depended on his tools and his materials.[5] What his metaphors meant, in detailed and practical terms, only the archaeologist can tell us.

We are nowadays encouraged to take a gradualist rather than a catastrophic view of the change from Roman Britain to Anglo-Saxon England. Both had highly stratified – indeed, class-conscious – societies; the Germanic leaders are likely to have taken over existing Romano-British estates in the fifth and sixth centuries with some of their native population rather than to have occupied a virtually empty land. To this mixture of peoples the later Scandinavian conquest and settlement added another ethnic contribution, like the others of unknown scale. The medieval village, we have been taught, consisted of houses clustered round a church and a manor house and surrounded by its open fields [1]. In those counties where nucleated villages became characteristic, they did not begin to develop with their open field system until late Saxon times. Virtually all that we know of houses of the period 450–1066 comes from sites deserted as a result of this development. In the last fifty years more than 200 Saxon sites have been excavated, a few of them totally. They include two royal palaces, a few houses of lesser landowners and four villages, as well as small sites with a few buildings. For towns, the evidence is inevitably more scrappy, and the archaeologist is most likely to encounter, even in London, a dark layer of earth overlying Roman levels, with no trace of structures, as if towns were largely deserted.[6] The only remains of buildings are usually a few sunken huts set in the spaces between derelict Roman buildings as at Canterbury or, in London and York, those dating from the later Saxon centuries when town life was unquestionably reviving. The amplest evidence has come from York, where, on a site in Coppergate outside the Roman walls, waterlogged conditions have preserved remains of houses and workshops constructed c. 970 and later.

Palaces
Yeavering

The affairs of kings and bishops dominate the written history of this period and the outline of a picture of their residential establishments has begun to emerge. Documents tell the archaeologist where to look for them and aerial photography may then pick up distinctive crop-marks of large timber buildings. Such sites will, in present circumstances, be excavated only if threatened and so qualify for the use of government funds. Several sites known from aerial photographs have not yet been touched.

Excavations of the palace at North Elmham (Norfolk) of bishops of the East Angles, abandoned following the Danish conquest of 879, revealed the character of the complex – three separate buildings in an enclosure – but little in detail about their function. Yeavering (Northumberland) was identified as the site of a palace of kings of Northumbria by combining the documentary evidence and air photographs; it was excavated in 1962–3 before destruction by quarrying for sand.[7] The palace flourished mainly under kings Æthelfrith and Edwin (592–632) and was abandoned later in the seventh century in favour of *Maelmin* (now Milfield), 2–3 miles away. Both sites eventually returned to the plough. The Yeavering buildings stood alongside a palisaded enclosure which may have served as a cattle-corral, or a market, or perhaps a place for collecting food-rents on the hoof. The eight buildings (not all standing at one time) were dispersed in three groups, the furthest some 140 m (150 yds) apart. They were not immune from attack and were twice extensively damaged or destroyed by fire: it was calculated hostility rather than accident.

In its most flourishing phase, the main group comprised the largest hall [2], a smaller hall and a wooden theatre where as many as 320 people could be assembled before their king. These buildings were in an east–west line, their orderliness reflecting the ceremonial of the court. West of the theatre were five buildings serving diverse purposes. One of them is thought to have been originally a pagan temple later converted to a Christian chapel. Bede tells us that the missionary Paulinus 'accompanied king Edwin and his queen to the royal residence at Gefrin' (Yeavering). If the building did have an ecclesiastical function, it stands at the head of that line of private chapels which were, for more than twelve centuries, to be an essential part of a landowner's establishment, from the royal palace down to the manor house; thousands of such

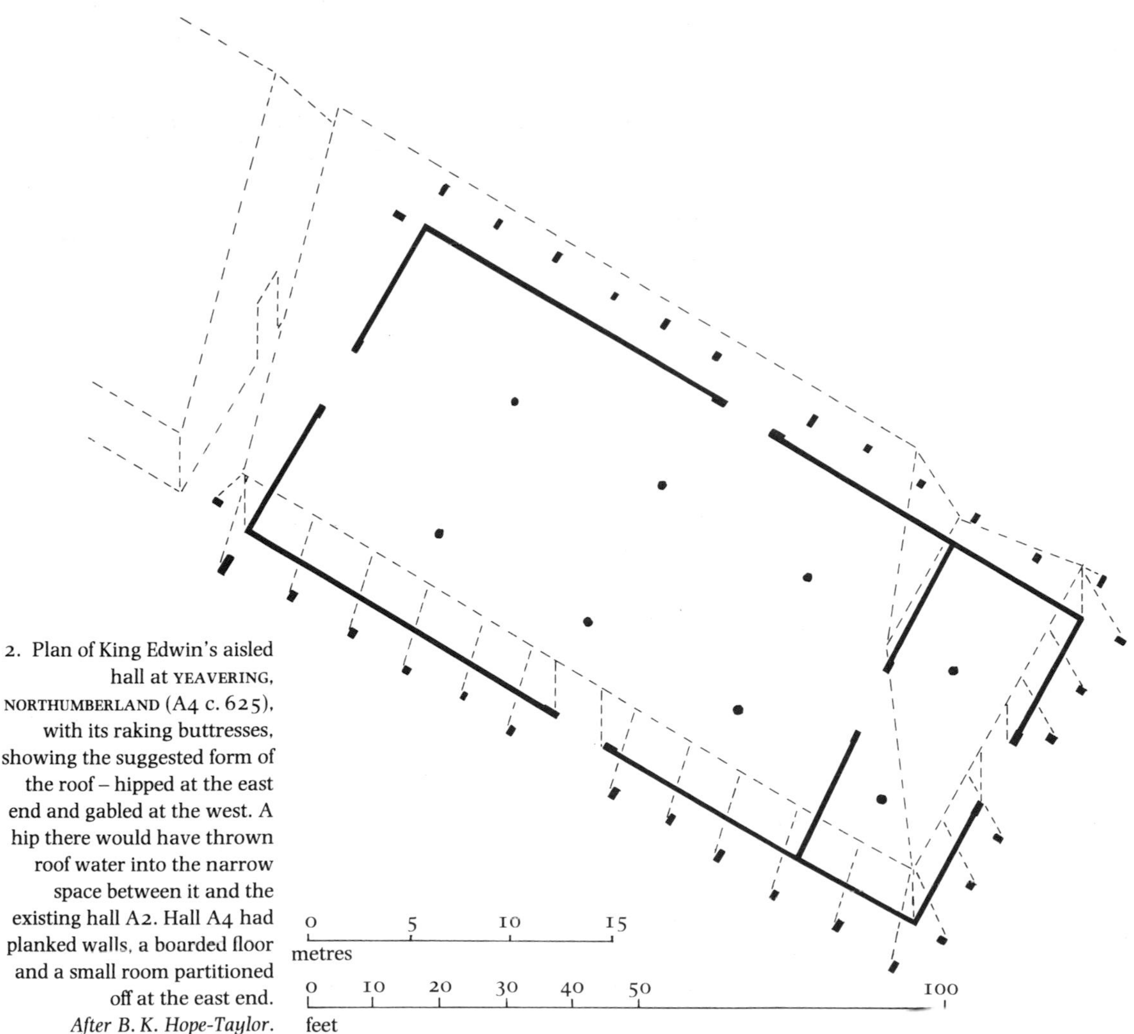

2. Plan of King Edwin's aisled hall at YEAVERING, NORTHUMBERLAND (A4 c. 625), with its raking buttresses, showing the suggested form of the roof – hipped at the east end and gabled at the west. A hip there would have thrown roof water into the narrow space between it and the existing hall A2. Hall A4 had planked walls, a boarded floor and a small room partitioned off at the east end. *After B. K. Hope-Taylor.*

chapels became parish churches as the parochial system took shape [1]. Not far from the Yeavering chapel was a large sunken house with two hearths which may have been the kitchen; certainly no other building in the complex fits that need. There was also a group of four buildings strung out in a line north-west from the great hall and up to 110 m (120 yds) from it. The furthest was a sunken house and may have served for weaving; the other three were for domestic use, to judge from the scatter of pottery and animal bones.

Is it possible to people these buildings and to say more than that they served a 'domestic' purpose? The great hall was aisled in form, and had an arrangement of post-holes which suggests a throne facing the central hearth and in full view of nobles seated or lying on the boarded floor of the aisles. The three smaller halls may have been the family homes of leading members of the royal household, or they may have been allocated to unmarried men and women serving the royal family. Other than *hall*, the Anglo-Saxon language had only one word, *bur* (bower), for a domestic building; literary allusions show that it might also mean an inner room especially for sleeping, or a lady's chamber or women's quarters. We have no way of estimating the size of the royal household in AD 600, either in peaceful times or when the king's war-band was assembled. In spite of such uncertainties, we now have material evidence of buildings which, in their scale and in their finish if not their decoration, match the account of the hall in *Beowulf*.

Cheddar At Cheddar (Somerset) excavation has revealed part of a royal palace of the kings of Wessex established in the ninth century and remaining a royal property into the twelfth century.[8] Land next to Manor Farm earmarked for a new village school was suspected to be the site of a palace known from documents, and no other location was suitable for the school; the site was therefore excavated for ten months during 1960–2. Ironically, the school was eventually built further south and west so that the outlines of the Anglo-Saxon buildings could be marked out on an open space; even so, the new building may well have buried – and preserved for another generation of archaeologists – a further part of the palace. Within the available area, the complex proved to be defined on two sides by its bank and ditch, and there were two large halls, three smaller buildings (possibly bowers), a privy and a curious building thought to have been a poultry house with a store and a dwelling for the poultry keeper. None of the Cheddar buildings was subdivided, and their size points to accommodation for a large gathering on formal occasions; the king's council met there three times in the mid-tenth century. Nonetheless, we look in vain for a kitchen and the other buildings needed by thirty or so dignitaries and their scores of retainers.

It could scarcely be expected that from a pattern of post-holes the archaeologist could deduce a first-floor hall of the sort familiar in royal palaces on the continent from c. 800 onwards and common in palaces and manor houses in Britain after 1066. The account of the mishap at Calne in 978 and the illustration of Harold's manor house at Bosham (Sussex) in the Bayeux Tapestry – designed and worked in England – leads archaeologists to look for evidence, and the Long Hall at Cheddar [3] has been interpreted as a first-floor hall; it had sloping posts internally which may have supported an upper floor, but it seems more likely that they were for a boarded floor at ground level. Some Yeavering buildings may have had a loft or gallery at one end of an open hall, rather than a separate room. A western gallery reached from the tower is not uncommon in late Saxon churches, similar in purpose to the gallery in the palace chapel at Aachen where Charlemagne's throne still stands. It may be, then, that royal and other superior persons separated themselves from others, on both religious and secular occasions, by sitting in a gallery.

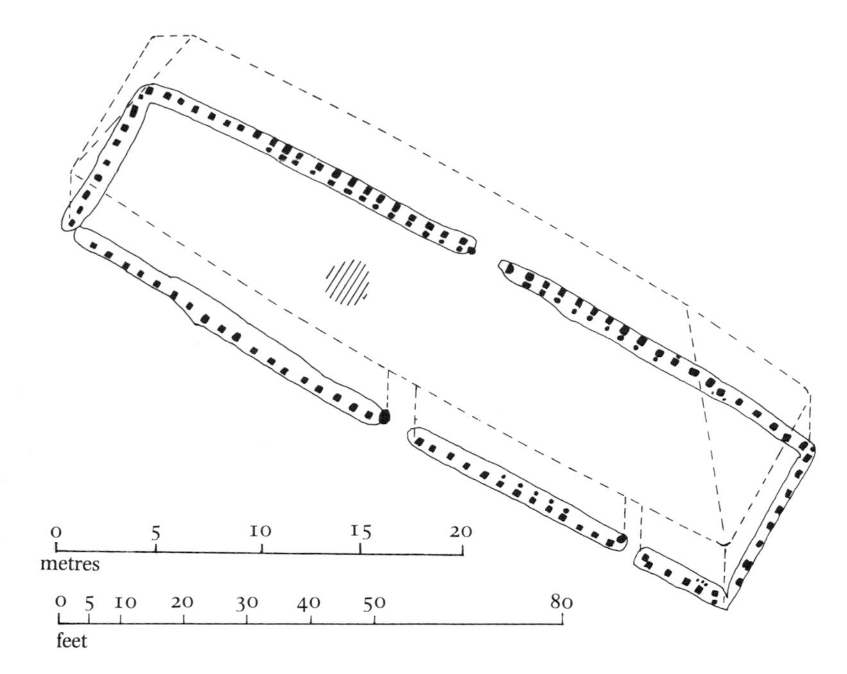

3. The Long Hall at CHEDDAR, SOMERSET, built c. 875 with squared wall-posts set in a trench, the spaces presumably filled with wattle and daub. The hall was long and low, the inner line of post-holes probably supporting a boarded floor. It was slightly wider in the middle than at the ends and so the ridge was correspondingly higher there. Traces of a hearth imply an outlet for smoke above it. *After P. A. Rahtz.*

The Anglo-Saxon manor house

The excavations illustrate the process by which retainers were rewarded with grants of land and a class of manorial lord came into existence. When first recorded the name of Goltho (Lincolnshire) was *Golthawe*, the second element being derived from the Anglo-Saxon *haga*, an enclosure; the whole probably meant 'the enclosure where marigolds grow'.[9] Place-names with *-haga* are not uncommon in the midlands and north; the equivalent in the south is *-burh*, as in Bloomsbury, and the laws of Wessex assumed that every person of noble rank would have a *burh*. At Goltho a palisaded enclosure was banked round late in the tenth century and the bank was enlarged when the manor house was rebuilt for the third or fourth time in its history. It was meant to provide only a modest degree of security, and soon after 1100 a new owner converted it into a small but strong earthwork castle. The earth shifted then served to bury the remains of earlier buildings and to preserve them for excavation.

Goltho [4] gives us the earliest picture of what, from later buildings and from documents, we expect a manor house to be: a group of separate buildings, evidently in one ownership, serving the range of functions required in a household of superior status. How such buildings eventually coalesced within one building is the essence of the story of such houses. There is no barn within the *haga*. We expect a hall, and there it is with a hearth in the middle of one half; we can safely regard the small room partitioned off at one end as a private chamber for the owner to sleep in. Two small buildings west of the hall are identified respectively as a kitchen and a *bur* – the women's room. A larger building some 18 m

4. Saxon manorial hall at GOLTHO, LINCOLNSHIRE, built c. AD 1000. Its large post-holes, for a building about 23 m (75 ft) long, can be distinguished from the holes and trenches of later buildings behind the hall and overlying it at a different angle. *G. Beresford.*

(60 ft) south of the hall is thought to have been a weaving shed. In a tenth-century rebuilding both kitchen and bower were shifted nearer the hall and another building was put up; a century later the complex was rearranged yet again.

The Saxon hall at Sulgrave (Northamptonshire) was found during excavation of the earthwork castle there, part of a research project into the origin of castles.[10] The story remains incomplete because resources have not been available to carry the research further. The earthen castle was constructed shortly after 1066 and buried a large timber hall built about AD 1000. It had a kitchen near one end and a bower near the other, both of timber, and a stone building of unknown purpose. The hall had a central hearth and an end room for services; beyond it was a cobbled porch. In the developed medieval manor house, entrance to the hall is by opposed doorways at the end nearest the services; Sulgrave carries this feature back two generations before the Norman Conquest. The hall also had a bench down one side, either for sitting or sleeping. This bench is a rare hint that in the manor house there were retainers or servants to be fed and housed, as well as rents in kind to be stored and horses to be stabled.

Anglo-Saxon villages

Goltho grew into a nucleated village with a tiny church and peasant houses. Excavators of such sites find that later buildings, superimposed, have usually destroyed the remains of the earliest houses; even in villages deserted in Saxon times the archaeologist finds only fragmentary remains of them [5]. West Stow (Suffolk) was eventually covered with blown sand, but only after centuries of ploughing had bitten into the fifth- to seventh-century levels.[11] It is a matter of interpreting a pattern of holes

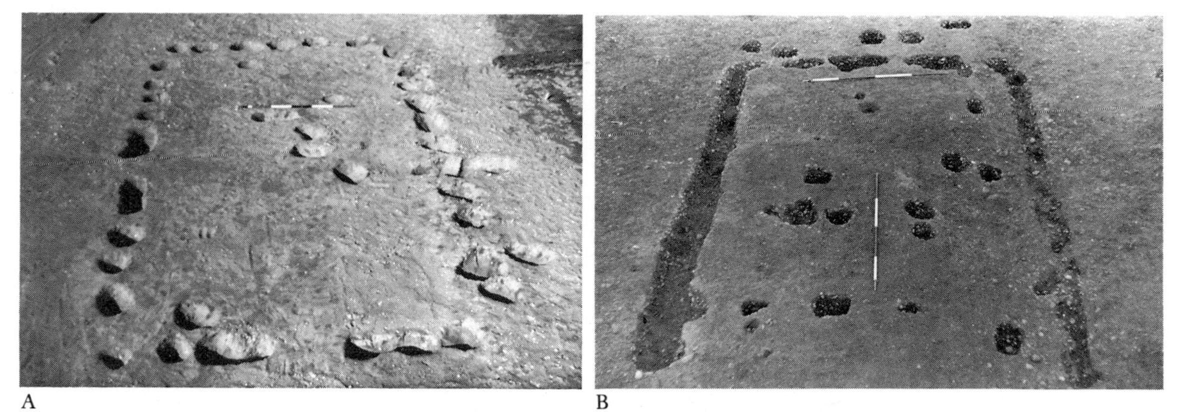

A B

5. Excavations of Anglo-Saxon peasant houses. A. WEST STOW, SUFFOLK, with posts in separate holes (6 ft scale). *S. West.* B. CATHOLME, DERBYSHIRE, with posts set in a trench (2 m scale). *S. Losco-Bradley.*

and trenches for earth-fast posts and those rectangular hollows which were sunken huts.

Four villages have been more or less completely excavated and the following table summarizes the results.

Place	*Date*	*Post-buildings*	*Sunken huts*
Catholme	C6–C10	60	17
Chalton	C6–C7	60	4
Mucking	C5–C8	50 (?)	213
West Stow	C5–C7	7 (?)	50

The hollow of a sunken hut (the *Grubenhaus* of German archaeology) was the first sort of Anglo-Saxon domestic building to be discovered, but we no longer need regard it as the only one. The four villages totally excavated vary so much in size and variety of buildings that none can be regarded as typical; Catholme (Derbyshire), strung along a gravel terrace in the Trent Valley, has the best claim if only because it lasted the longest.[12]

Both there and at Chalton (Hampshire)[13] it is possible to pick out a group of buildings surrounded by a fence or ditch, as if one was a house and the others barns or cowsheds; Catholme may have consisted in all of eight or nine farmsteads. If there was a typical house [6], it shows up most clearly at Chalton and at Mucking (Essex); it was a building twice as long as wide with doorways in the middle of each side and a small store-room partitioned off at one end with its own entrance in the gable end. The type is represented by the smaller halls at Yeavering. Groups of four or six post-holes represent granaries; four posts round a small pit were privies.

The sunken hut measuring about 3 × 4.5 m (10 ft × 13–16 ft), was a utility building, simple and cheap to put up and serving a variety of purposes. It was clearly used, from finds in the filling, for domestic crafts such as weaving, spinning and working bone. It may have served as a makeshift dwelling, or slaves' sleeping quarters. It varied in the elaboration of its

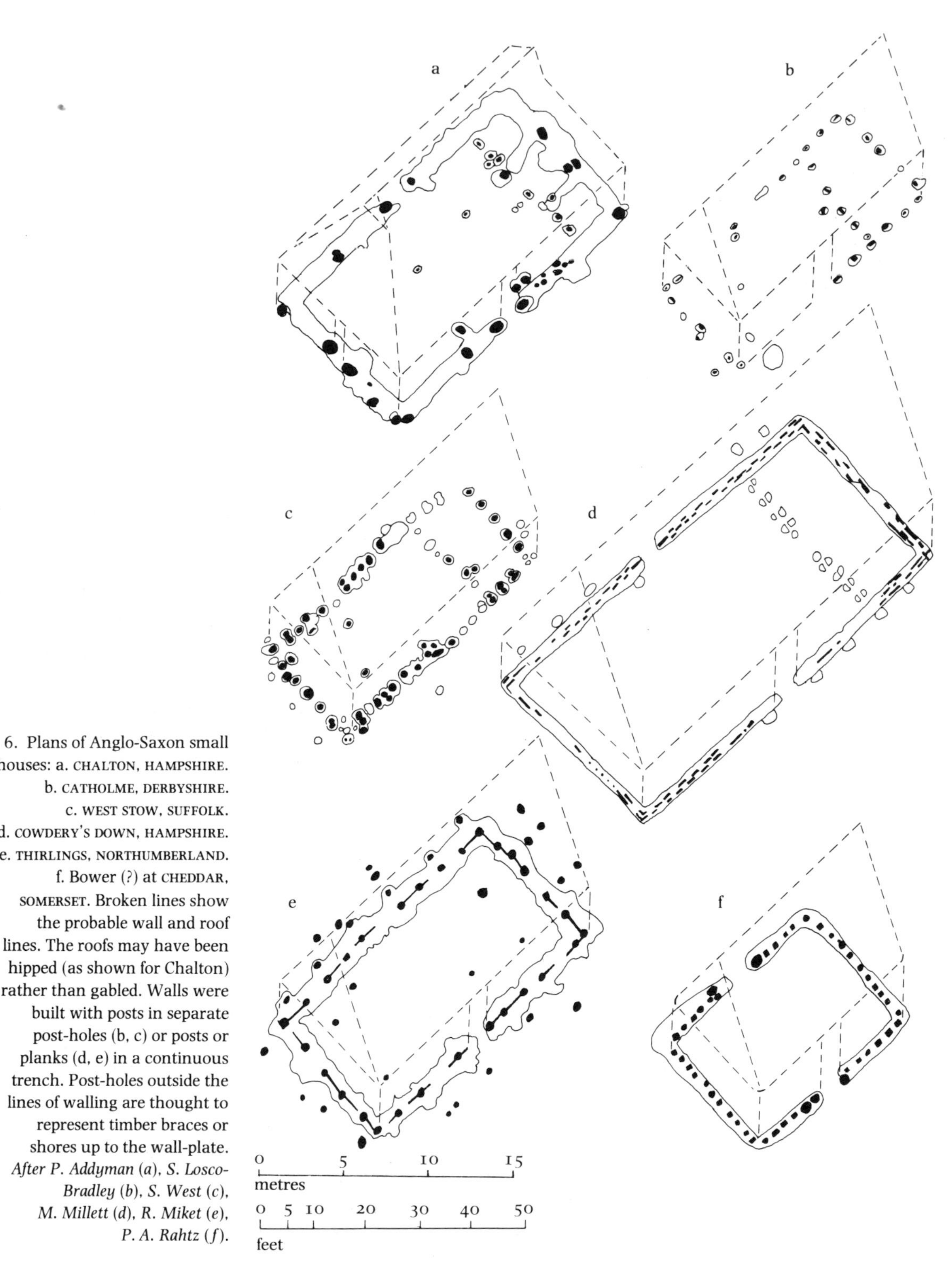

6. Plans of Anglo-Saxon small houses: a. CHALTON, HAMPSHIRE. b. CATHOLME, DERBYSHIRE. c. WEST STOW, SUFFOLK. d. COWDERY'S DOWN, HAMPSHIRE. e. THIRLINGS, NORTHUMBERLAND. f. Bower (?) at CHEDDAR, SOMERSET. Broken lines show the probable wall and roof lines. The roofs may have been hipped (as shown for Chalton) rather than gabled. Walls were built with posts in separate post-holes (b, c) or posts or planks (d, e) in a continuous trench. Post-holes outside the lines of walling are thought to represent timber braces or shores up to the wall-plate. *After P. Addyman (a), S. Losco-Bradley (b), S. West (c), M. Millett (d), R. Miket (e), P. A. Rahtz (f).*

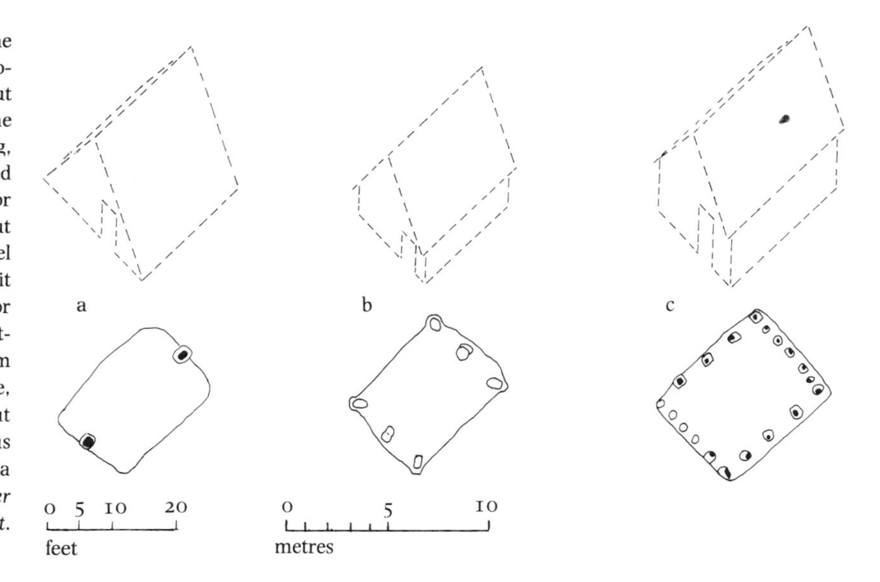

7. Plans of three of the commoner types of Anglo-Saxon sunken-floor hut (*Grubenhaus*) showing the suggested form of the building, based on examples excavated in CANTERBURY, KENT. The floor was sunk to a depth of about three feet below ground level and the sides of the pit retained with wattling or something similar. Two post-holes (a) in the bottom indicate a tent-like structure, and six post-holes (b) a hut with low side walls; numerous post-holes (c) may suggest a raised and boarded floor. *After Canterbury Archaeological Trust.*

construction; in some the sides of the hollow were lined with wicker or boards, post-built walls rising above ground level, a carefully-fitted plank floor laid in the bottom or a raised wooden floor over a sort of cellar. Such huts have been found in cities (London, Canterbury, York, etc.) as well as in the countryside. The sunken hut may have contributed to the development of building two-storeyed houses, especially in towns, but not to the main stream of domestic planning [7].

On the continent the dominant type of peasant house from prehistoric times onward and persisting through medieval into modern times was essentially different in design and function from these English houses: aisled in form (the 'three aisled hall house' of continental archaeology) and dual-purpose, with a single-roomed living end and a larger end housing animals. The long house for family and livestock under one roof has not been found in any excavation in lowland England of a site of this period.

The Anglo-Saxon builder

In the highland zone of Britain, adequate shelter could best be provided by using stone slabs or rubble for each face of a thick wall, the core being filled with turf, soil or small rubble. Such houses have been found, one in a tidal inlet on the north Cornish coast, a few on the Isle of Man and one in the Pennines. A house at Ribblehead[14] in north-west Yorkshire, standing at an altitude of 340 m (1115 ft), had walls 1.5 m (5 ft) thick [8]; its plan with gable-end entrances resembles Scandinavian houses in Shetland (Jarlshof) and Orkney (Birsay), and at Ribblehead four coins of about 860–70 were found. Only excavation of other nearby sites visible on aerial photographs would show whether Ribblehead belongs to an intensive Scandinavian settlement or to an older tradition. On Dartmoor,

8. Viking stone-walled house on Gauber High Pasture, RIBBLEHEAD, INGLETON, YORKSHIRE. *Alan King.*

houses rebuilt in stone in the thirteenth century replaced houses with walls of turf stacked between rows of stakes, showing rebuilding several times; the earliest must go back before 1066.

The pattern of post-holes of a timber house can be read to show both the form of the house and also the carpenter's degree of skill and the diversity of his techniques.[15] He was rarely called on to put up an aisled building, but if he did so it was with wooden rather than stone walls, and at Yeavering and Thirlings (Northumberland) the halls had external braces as well.[16] The halls at Yeavering were laid out with absolute precision using a standard foot of 11.05 inches; the walling consisted of studs set in a deep trench, tongued and grooved together, caulked with clay and finished with plaster; there was a boarded floor. Buildings at Thirlings were smaller and less regularly laid out but also had planked filling between posts. There was a degree of uniformity in the Chalton buildings, as if the preparation of timbers had been supervised by one carpenter. Of the sixty buildings there, only one was aisled and it does not resemble a house in plan. Whether the wall between posts consisted of planks or wattle and daub we do not know.

The clearest evidence of wall construction, after Yeavering, comes from Cowdery's Down on the outskirts of Basingstoke,[17] and York [9]. The size of the Hampshire houses and their quality suggest aristocratic rather than peasant owners. Upright planks clasped horizontals; more planks outside braced the wall-plates; wattle and daub made the buildings weather tight. Soil had accumulated on the site after the buildings were abandoned and so preserved these telling traces after the timbers had decayed. Only in the York buildings, originally sunk in the ground, have the timbers of such walls, as distinct from their ghosts in the soil, been preserved and that to a height of a metre or more.[18] Thus a hamlet on the Hampshire downs and an area of downtown Jorvik both suggest that planked walls were a feature of the most substantial houses. In the later Middle Ages when outer walls were framed or built of stone, internal partitions were often formed of alternate thick and thin uprights tenoned into a frame (stud or muntin and plank); this must represent the persistence of an ancient tradition.

Reliance on rigid walls, adequately tied together across the building, distinguishes English houses most sharply from those on the Continent. A royal carpenter was capable of building a hall as much as 23.6 m (76 ft) long at Cheddar, as a unitary structure under a single roof, and it might be half as wide as long. The archaeologist plotting his post-holes looks particularly for pairs accurately opposed across a building; when he finds them he deduces that they carried tie-beams holding the wall-plates by means of dovetail joints. They were probably planted on every pair of posts rather than at the larger intervals of 2 to 5 metres normal in the later Middle Ages. Wall timbers may be placed in a continuous cutting rather than in separate holes, or else on a beam laid in a slot in the ground; this must represent precision in preparing and setting main posts and may imply planked walls. Cheddar had one aisled hall and two with wall-posts. Of the latter, the Long Hall of c. AD 930 had squared posts set in a trench, but the West Hall, which stood for over two centuries with two major reconstructions, had heavy posts set in pits up to 2.3 m (8 ft) apart and up to 1 m (39 in) deep.

There was no sign at Cheddar of how the walls were finished, and the choice lies between planking and wattle and daub. The same difficulty of interpretation arises with hundreds of post-built structures of this age, for traces of daub, unless a building was fired and the clay baked, are rarely recovered. Buildings with wattled walls, without posts or planks, have shown up most clearly on waterlogged sites in Dublin and York [9]. The Dublin building was wattling woven *in situ* (as distinct from prefabricated panels) to make them rectangular on plan with rounded corners; such buildings would certainly support a roof, as anyone would agree who has tried to crush a basket, and wattled walling had a long subsequent history in Ireland. The York buildings, put up c. 900–70 and earlier than the sunken huts, had slightly rounded corners; all three on the street front had hearths and so were presumably houses. It is possible that on rural sites, where only the deepest features can be observed, wattled buildings have disappeared without trace.

What is the archaeologist to make of this diversity? The buildings cannot be fitted into a clear typological sequence, demonstrating progressive improvement in technology over five centuries; variations cannot be ascribed to particular ethnic groups. One form of house not so far mentioned is that with bowed side walls and hence with a ridge rising

A

B

9. Houses in COPPERGATE, YORK. A. Post-and-wattle walling of c. 900–70. B. Partially sunk building with post-and-plank walling. *York Archaeological Trust, M. Duffy.*

like a hog's back. It was thought to be Viking in origin, because of parallels in Scandinavia and the resemblance to hog-back tombstones found in northern England, but it is also known from sites in Germany (Warendorf) and Holland (Dorestad). Examples in England include the Long Hall at Cheddar, the hall of c. 875 at Goltho and smaller buildings both urban and rural. Bowed walls must be a technical device, possibly to resist wind pressure, but if so it brings us back to the carpenter, whose skills were not a matter of his racial or cultural background. The principal timber joints – the mortice and tenon, the dovetail and the lap – had been known and used, in Britain and on the continent, for thousands of years and were part of everyday life in town and country, whether under a Roman provincial governor or an Anglo-Saxon king. The corpus of Anglo-Saxon timber houses represents the range of work of specialists in building, of carpenters for whom a house was a change from making a plough or a harrow, and of peasant farmers for whom building or repairing houses had to fit in with growing crops and tending livestock. Any attempt to make a model of a house or to draw a reconstruction ought to assume dressed timbers jointed together rather than undressed trunks and branches lashed together with rope or withies.

Notes

1 There are two general accounts, by P. V. Addyman, 'The Anglo-Saxon house: a new review', in *Anglo-Saxon England*, I (1972), 273–307; and Philip Rahtz, 'Buildings and rural settlement', in D. M. Wilson (ed.), *The Archaeology of Anglo-Saxon England* (1976), 49–98.

2 Penguin Classics (1968), bk. 2, ch. 13, 127.

3 D. Whitelock, *English Historical Documents*, I (1955), 210.

4 Rosemary J. Cramp, 'Beowulf and archaeology', *Med. Archaeol.*, I (1957), 57–77.

5 Whitelock, op. cit., 844–6.

6 J. Schofield, *The Building of London* (1984), 19, 23.

7 B. Hope-Taylor, *Yeavering* (1977).

8 P. Rahtz, *The Saxon and Medieval Palaces at Cheddar: excavations 1960–2* (1979).

9 G. Beresford, *The Medieval Clay-land Village: Excavations at Goltho and Barton Blount* (Society for Med. Archaeol. Monograph Series no. 6, 1975).

10 B. K. Davison, 'The origins of the castle in England', *Archaeol. J.*, 124 (1967), 208–9; *Med. Archaeol.*, 17 (1973), 147.

11 S. West in *Current Archaeol.*, 4 (1973–4), no. 10.

12 S. Losco-Bradley in *Current Archaeol.*, 5 (1975–6), no. 59.

13 P. V. Addyman *et al.*, 'Anglo-Saxon houses at Chalton, Hants.', *Med. Archaeol.*, 16 (1972), 13–32.

14 Alan King, 'A Viking age settlement at Ribblehead', in R. A. Hall (ed.), *Viking Age York and the North* (CBA Research Report 27, 1978), 21–5.

15 P. Dixon, 'How Saxon was the Saxon house?', in P. J. Drury (ed.), *Structural Reconstruction* (*BAR* British Series 110, 1982), 275–87.

16 *Med. Archaeol.*, 19 (1975), 226.

17 M. Millett, 'Excavations at Cowdery's Down, Basingstoke, Hampshire, in *Archaeol. J.*, 140 (1983), 151–279.

18 R. A. Hall, 'A late-pre-Conquest urban building tradition', in P. V. Addyman and V. E. Black (eds.), *Archaeological Papers from York* (1984), 71–7.

2 *Building and Materials 1066–1550: Mass Walling*

In Britain, as part of the temperate zone, timber was the most plentiful and natural material for walls. Roman rule brought with it the art of mass walling in stone, equally natural for the Mediterranean zone. Fortresses, town walls and public buildings such as basilicas and temples of stone became the most evident mark of imperial rule; they set an example to the native aristocracy and provided a training ground for native masons. In the fifth and sixth centuries, stone buildings even in decay must have been a source of wonder to Germanic immigrants. In the years after AD 597, Augustine's mission to convert the English revived Roman methods and standards. By 875 substantial cathedrals and monastic churches of stone were to be seen all the way from lowland Scotland to Hampshire and from Essex to Gloucestershire; none of the cathedrals stands, but a few abbey churches and some private chapels survive. In some cases the quality of the building and in a measure its survival is due to the fact that Roman fortresses and town walls served as quarries for second-hand stone or brick. How the skills in using such material were revived we can only speculate. The missionaries were immediately able to have churches built in Canterbury of second-hand Roman bricks and flint laid with hard lime mortar, and new concrete floors were laid in *opus signinum* (a sort of concrete). It seems likely that the monks sent back to Rome for building workers, as Benedict Biscop is known to have done. Missionaries have always had to be practical men and our image of Anglo-Saxon bishops and abbots as saintly, learned and single-minded men ought to include a capacity to recruit and train selected personnel of both sexes for a great diversity of tasks. The use of stone for fortifications where it was readily available has a long ancestry in prehistoric Britain, as revetments for ramparts; the one new ingredient in Anglo-Saxon mass walling, a Roman legacy, is a lime mortar, as distinct from clay or earth, both between courses and for rendering the surface of rubble walling. The only contribution from excavation to knowledge of building techniques in this age has been the recent discovery in the middle of Northampton of several mechanical mortar-mixers.[1] Large quantities of mortar or plaster were stirred and mixed in a shallow bowl, 2–3 m (6½–10 ft) across, by means of paddles hung from a rotating beam, turned perhaps by a horse. They must have served a large stone building; mortar hardens fairly quickly and mixing in such quantities implies a large force of masons.

By the time of the Norman Conquest much prospecting for building stone had gone on; the best oolitic limestone had been located and could be carried as much as 70 miles either overland or by coastal and inland waters.[2] Kings, bishops, abbots and nobles owned quarries and could recruit masons without necessarily going far afield to do so but of course only for religious buildings. We can put names to only two craftsmen, both in royal service: one Leofsi may have been Edward the Confessor's master mason at Westminster Abbey, and the king gave an estate in Shepperton to Teinfrith, his 'church-wright' – a reminder that a church might well be built entirely of timber, rather than of stone with a timber roof.

The effect of the Norman Conquest

To understand the England of 1200, the earliest time at which we can trace surviving houses, it is essential to appreciate the enormous amount of building in stone generated by the economic expansion which followed the Norman Conquest. Even by 1100 there were two stone castles, in London and Colchester, far more massive and lofty than any Roman building, and several others such as those in Exeter and Richmond already had a stone gatehouse and perimeter walls. In the course of the next century, many royal and private castles originally of timber were progressively strengthened with stone keeps and walls. Each of the seventeen cathedrals was built new or rebuilt; of the 650 or so monasteries which eventually marked the landscape of England and Wales all but about thirty were founded after 1066 and most of them before 1200. That leaves uncounted the number of churches newly built or rebuilt in town and country.

Of the men involved in this operation, we may first list the skilled trades and the semi-skilled and unskilled labour force supporting them, recorded in building accounts, such as those of King Henry III for Dover and Winchester Castles and Westminster Abbey, surviving from 1221 onwards and the earliest such accounts in Europe.[3] The work force comprised quarrymen, stone-dressers and masons; diggers (*fossatores*) to dig for moats, vaults and foundations, or for mining and siege-works in wartime. There were carpenters for scaffolding and roofs, for the timber of castle gates, bridges and superstructure; in wartime they built siege-engines. By the thirteenth century if not before, sawyers working in pairs used the long saw to prepare timbers for ceilings, floors and roofs. The building industry has always been labour-intensive but the numbers employed in the twelfth and thirteenth centuries, at least seasonally, must have formed a far higher proportion of the adult male population than today. The number employed on rebuilding Westminster Abbey reached 433 in July 1253. Men in such numbers can be thought of in another way: as local tenants whose labour services in return for land might be used to dig ditches and make moats for castles and manor houses; as monks and particularly lay-brothers flocking to new monasteries to serve God by helping to build; lastly as tradesmen and labourers working for a daily wage.

Royal building involved the sheriff, who had to account for expenditure on a castle or a house in his shire, and the laymen called in to view the work and certify that it had actually been done; it involved the constable in charge of a castle and clerks appointed as keepers of works, as administration evolved towards an office of works. Kings, barons and bishops were constantly on the move; Henry II is said to have worn out his household, and John in 1204–5 stayed in nearly a hundred places, and so with their entourage must have known well their castles, manor houses and monastic guest-houses. There must have been talk, after dinner, of master masons and carpenters as well as of matters of state and the success of the day's hunting. The key figures in this explosion of new building were the master masons and carpenters who found continuous employment with the crown or with wealthy ecclesiastics such as Alexander, bishop of Lincoln, who in 1123–48 built three castles and founded three monastic houses and a leper hospital; he was no doubt responsible for other buildings on his manors, in stone or timber, of which we know nothing. Who Alexander employed we do not know, but the career of one master carpenter in royal service demonstrates the mobility of men of his class. Nicholas de Andeli may have worked on the castle, Château Gaillard, built at Les Andelys in Normandy by Richard I. John brought him to England after the loss of Normandy and between 1207 and his death in 1245 he worked at several castles and royal houses.

By 1200, then, grand buildings of stone were a familiar sight in every county and a significant proportion of the population had had a hand of some sort in their erection. Regional variations in design – for instance in church towers in East Anglia and Lincolnshire – had begun to emerge by 1066; they suggest that while a king's mason might be sent from Dover to Newcastle, most masons as they followed building contracts could find work without moving great distances. The architectural historian and the archaeologist face the task of tracing two threads in the pattern of building: the work of master masons and that of local tradesmen. The largest building operations drew on the widest field; the obvious example is Edward I's programme, from the year 1277 onwards, for seventeen castles in north Wales, for which skilled and unskilled labour was conscripted from every English county except Cornwall.[4] Of the

3,500 men employed at Beaumaris in the summer of 1295, some no doubt settled in Wales; others returned to England to an old or a new home with old skills reinforced or new experience acquired. Building workers on the move are only one aspect of a mobile society: kings, barons and bishops were constantly travelling and their tenants engaged in supporting them; raw materials and manufactured goods were transported over distances great and small; and there were the journeys implied by the pattern of local market towns and of annual fairs of international importance at, for instance, Stourbridge (on the outskirts of Cambridge) and Boston in Lincolnshire.

10. Stone-walled house of c. 1200 in QUEEN'S STREET, KING'S LYNN, NORFOLK, demolished 1977. *Norfolk Archaeological Unit, C. Shewring.*

The most highly regarded materials such as Caen stone from Normandy were moved great distances; Purbeck marble from Dorset was used not only for the cathedral at Lincoln but also for the piers of the bishop's aisled hall. The choice of materials in houses for the great is not always to be explained in simple terms of available materials or site conditions. At Hereford, the first Norman bishop built his palace chapel of stone, and a century later a new hall entirely of timber was built by one of his successors. Nevertheless, the use of stone had begun by 1200 to extend from strictly fortified residences to rural manor houses on more or less open sites and to merchants' houses in towns. The manor houses at Burton Agnes (East Yorkshire) and Boothby Pagnell (Lincolnshire) [61] have survived mainly because they had stone walls and a vaulted undercroft.[5] The remains of bishops' rural residences include some with stone buildings, often the chapel alone but sometimes a hall and a solar as well. Throughout the Middle Ages the great majority of town houses were built of timber, but stone was used in some places for two-storey houses. By 1200, merchants in King's Lynn were beginning to build stone houses facing the river Ouse [10]; a dozen have been recorded, most of them now demolished.[6] Stone was used mainly for vaulted undercrofts intended for storing wine; they are known in the largest numbers in London (along the waterfront), Winchelsea, Southampton, Bristol, Gloucester [33] and Chester.[7] In York, apart from one stone house with a first floor supported on timber posts (like the two twelfth-century houses at Lincoln), stone was used only for the ground-floor walls of two guildhalls and a few private houses, the rest of the buildings being framed. The same is true of many of the Chester houses over vaulted cellars. Stamford has one undercroft of the thirteenth century, one vault built later and a few houses with fragments of stone building before 1300, yet a great deal of stone was quarried in the medieval town from ground clear of buildings. Vaulted undercrofts had a high rate of survival compared with houses with rubble walls or with stone footings for timber.

Excavation of deserted village sites has suggested that 'in almost all stone-producing areas buildings with timber walls were being replaced during the late twelfth and thirteenth centuries by walls built of stone'.[8]

If this is true it was the rural consequence of locating more deposits, opening more quarries and training more men to extract and use stone for churches, castles and houses of the wealthy. It was not an enduring consequence at all social levels; in the later Middle Ages the fashion for framed building seems to have reasserted itself for manor houses. The excavator is usually unable to deduce, from the volume of material found, the original height of stone walls, since rubble may have been removed for use elsewhere or to clear a site for cultivation. The more critical question is whether he is dealing with the remains of walls, usually 0.6–0.9 m (2–3 ft) thick or with stone footings, usually less than 2 ft wide, for a framed building.

In the course of the Middle Ages every local material from soft sandstone to cobbles, boulders and flint was brought into use for buildings of one class or another. The resourcefulness of medieval builders at a humble level can be observed in village churches, but the variety and combinations of material have not been plotted, as Clifton-Taylor has pointed out.[9] Collaboration between geologists (to identify stones) and archaeologists (to provide dates), especially in counties not blessed with first-rate stone, would show how village communities managed to find materials and how far they could be transported. Those who examine closely buildings of the twelfth century onwards, whether religious or secular, have to take into account the possibility of finding reused stone. At Wharram Percy (East Yorkshire) where chalk for walls was quarried behind the house sites, as was limestone in Stamford, excavators also found fragments quarried 3–4 miles away and used by peasants after being discarded from the church or manor house during rebuilding.

11. Mud walling of the early thirteenth century at WALLINGFORD, BERKSHIRE. *R. D. Carr.*

Mud and turf walling

The earliest observed instance of the use of earth alone for walling belongs to the early thirteenth century; excavations within Wallingford Castle [11] revealed a large building with three rooms, its mud walls preserved to a height of nearly 2 m (6 ft), built soon after 1200 and buried when the ditch was deepened and the material used to raise the level of the inner ward.[10] Though a unique discovery for its period it is enough to prove that where no sort of stone was available the skill and confidence to build mass walling of mud or cob – clay with organic material to bind it – had already developed and may then have been ancient. It was the cheapest kind of walling, and manorial accounts contain many unenlightening allusions to mud walls either as parts of farm buildings or as boundaries.[11] We may be sure that when peasants built a mud wall round a manorial yard, they were doing for the lord what they were used to doing for themselves. Cob was much used in Devon for houses of yeomen [12]; the earliest standing examples date from around 1300.

A B

12. Cob-walled house, ST CYRE'S, LANGFORD, DEVON. A. General view which reveals nothing of its age. B. Back doorway which proves that the house is fifteenth century. *N. W. Alcock.*

Turf or sods may have been more widely used than we can now know. A sod house at Jurby in the Isle of Man was photographed in 1897. Rows of stake-holes found below thirteenth-century stone houses on Dartmoor [13] are interpreted as retaining walls of turf, and in the Isle of Axholme fourteenth-century peasants claimed the right to cut turf for walling as well as for fuel.[12]

Tile and brick

Compared with other aspects of medieval archaeology, the study of bricks has been neglected. It requires several disciplines, including geology and chemistry, and unlike the examination of other ceramic products such as ridge-tiles of a distinctive form, the results are less likely to contribute to a chronology for other buildings. The only piece of general research has shown how many factors need to be considered, such as size, colour, stony inclusions and microscopic particles.[13] Dating bricks will continue to depend on such external factors as the documentation for a building or on architectural and stratigraphic evidence. The earliest bricks, such as those in Little Coggeshall Priory (c. 1150) were made from fine-grained silts and were so fired that they have a black core: that is, the iron compounds were not oxidized. By the end of the Middle Ages, brick-makers chose clays containing enough iron to produce red rather than cream bricks, and improved firing techniques eliminated the black core.

13. Plan of excavated house at HUTHOLES, DARTMOOR, DEVON, showing the post- and stake-holes of several turf-walled houses eventually rebuilt in stone. *G. Beresford.*

Inferior or intractable stone, suitable only for straightforward lengths of walling, called for something better for quoins and openings. In counties where only flint occurred, it was worth while to ransack Roman sites for the tiles used for bonding courses, and churches still stand in Canterbury, Colchester, Dover and St Albans built partly or entirely of reused Roman materials. It is not surprising that the revival of the pottery industry in late Saxon times was accompanied by the manufacture of floor-tiles which are known from a few important ecclesiastical buildings.[14] Though churchmen were able occasionally to engage tile-makers to produce polychrome tiles for the sanctuary of a great church, there was as yet no continuous activity. When the Cistercians in 1148 took over Coggeshall (Essex), they were able to recruit brick-makers, no doubt enrolled as lay brothers, to ensure a speedy building programme on a site where there was no good local stone. Bricks of various shapes were made for quoins, piers and openings, with flint for walling and tiles either plain or glazed for flooring and benches.[15] The brick-makers may have come from a Cistercian house in Spain or the Low Countries and returned home afterwards. Several Cistercian houses in Yorkshire had elaborately tiled pavements at about the same time.

Floor-tiles are increasingly common from the thirteenth century onwards, but are almost confined to ecclesiastical buildings.[16] A fashion adopted by Henry III for his palace at Clarendon (Wiltshire) was followed by very few laymen. Excavations in Winchester have produced, from a house in Lower Brook Street which may have belonged to a rich merchant, tiles similar to those made for Clarendon.[17] Clifton House at King's Lynn, the home of a wealthy merchant with a wharf on the Ouse, had tiles in two rooms, laid early in the fourteenth century; another house in Norfolk Street had tiles made nearby at Bawsey. Maxstoke Castle (Warwickshire) had in 1346 a tiled room in the Lady Tower.[18]

The layman, if he did not aspire to a floor of patterned tiles, saw the sense of having plain tiles for the hearth and back of a fireplace in a framed house, and for its roof. The London fire regulations of 1212, banning thatch and prescribing tiles as an alternative to shingles, boards, lead and even plastered thatch, prove that tiles could be bought in the capital.[19] Archaeology has begun to show that they were occasionally used for walling – that is, as wall-tiles – by the time of the Norman

Conquest if not before; they have been found below the castles at Oxford and Ludgershall (Wiltshire). At Goltho (Lincolnshire) the cellar under the motte of c. 1100 was lined with bricks of poor quality, and the hall of c. 1150 had a tiled roof.

14. LITTLE WENHAM HALL, SUFFOLK, with brick-walling of c. 1270 above a stone base.

Little Wenham Hall (Suffolk), built c. 1270–80, is the best preserved house of the thirteenth century, and the materials are as significant as the design [14]. The foundations and base courses are a mixture of septaria (a local conglomerate) and flint; limestone was brought from Northamptonshire for dressings, but the walls are of bricks made locally. The first firings produced pinkish bricks, but higher up the walls are uniformly yellow, evidently the desired colour. There are yellow bricks of a similar date at Allington Castle (Kent) for vaulting and dressings, and in Antony Bek's work at Eltham in the same county.[20]

The brick industry must have been stimulated by imports from the Low Countries. They were a convenient form of ballast for ships returning from the Low Countries, and the fourteenth-century undercroft in Clifton House, King's Lynn, is built of large yellowish bricks, probably imported. By the next century they were certainly being made there for warehouses and two guildhalls. Flemish tiles, as they were called, were imported for the Tower of London in 1278 in such enormous quantities that they must have been used for walling.[21] In the Humber basin, brick-making started before 1300; the vaults of Beverley Minster are filled with bricks, and some were used in St Mary's church there in 1327. The Carmelite Friars of York were able to sell wall-tiles to the Merchant Adventurers for the ground-floor walls of their hall in 1358; in the next century the vicars choral at York made a substantial income from bricks and roof-tiles made in their kilns.[22] By then, brick-making was a major undertaking in the whole of the Humber basin, from Thornton (Lincolnshire, Priory gatehouse) and Barton-on-Humber (the manor house, Tyrwhitt Hall), up the Trent to Gainsborough (Old Hall) and the Ouse to Cawood (archbishop's palace), and to York itself. Municipal enterprise was also active, for town walls and gates at Hull, King's Lynn and Yarmouth. The Cow Tower at Norwich, with brick walls 3.3 m (11 ft) thick and 15 m (50 ft) high, was being built in 1378, and the North Bar at Beverley was built in 1410 with bricks from the town's kilns.

During the fifteenth century and increasingly in the second half, the crown and lay lords joined ecclesiastics in using bricks for their projects. Kilns at Slough provided millions of bricks for Henry VI's college at Eton in the 1440s and 1450s, though the chapel was built of stone.[23] If we could still see Lord Cromwell's college at Tattershall, which was going up at the same time as Eton (and Tattershall Castle), it would seem equally impressive.[24] William Waynflete, bishop of Winchester, was executor to Cromwell and finished the Tattershall undertaking; he was Eton's first provost, he built a brick school at Wainfleet (his Lincolnshire birthplace) and used brick at his palaces at Esher and Farnham. Thomas Rotherham, successively bishop of Lincoln and archbishop of York, founded a college at his Yorkshire birthplace and enlarged his residences at Buckden (Huntingdonshire) [58], Bishopthorpe and Cawood (Yorkshire), all in brick. Bishops were also responsible for the earliest known instances of brick used for walling which was then faced in stone: the timber spire of Norwich cathedral, after more than one fire, was rebuilt in brick with stone cladding by Bishop Goldwell (1472–99), and at Canterbury the upper part of the central tower, Bell Harry, was added while John Morton was archbishop (1486–1500) in the same combination of materials.

It is possible sometimes to infer the stages by which bricks came into use for houses as well as for colleges and palaces. Norwich still has far more brick undercrofts [34] than any other medieval town, built before c. 1600 for houses of the wealthy minority of inhabitants. A cheap alternative was unfired bricks as much as 60 cm (2 ft) long and more than 30 cm (1 ft) wide, large enough to be handled after no more than drying in the air.[25] The use of 'clay lump', as these unfired bricks are called, is familiar in later East Anglian houses and excavations in Norwich have shown that they were being used there in the fifteenth century, possibly as footings for mud and stud construction.[26] This particular practice is not found elsewhere. In the Humber basin the manor house (Tyrwhitt Hall) at Barton-on-Humber, next to the Anglo-Saxon Church of St Peter, was built in the fifteenth century with brick infilling for its close-studded walls. Such infilling for timber-framed walling is often taken to be renewal; it would be surprising if it was not sometimes original.

In the countryside it is sometimes possible to trace the influence of a grand building which was the first and for a time the only building in this new material. In addition to Tattershall castle and college, Lord Cromwell built a brick hunting lodge nearby, Tower on the Moor; he had a kiln at Boston and building accounts show that bricks were used as footings in a timber-framed house built for him at nearby Skirbeck.[27] The owner of one of the two brick houses near Boston with a solar tower (Hussey Tower) was associated with Cromwell in public affairs. At Coningsby, one mile north of Tattershall, the rectory has a wing cased in brick in 1463, according to an inscription in the glass of the parlour window. This was the work of the then rector, John Croxby, of the same surname as Cromwell's clerk of works in the 1440s.[28] Whether it is a matter of one Croxby or two related men, the Coningsby bricks from their appearance came from the Tattershall kilns. This is only the earliest of many instances of bricks from a private kiln sold or given away for other building projects, and is inherently credible. Proof is another matter. The itinerant brick-maker, carrying at most his moulds and frequently needing new ones, cannot be traced from one building to another as can the tile-maker, producing tiles with unique patterns and sometimes taking his moulds to distant projects. Common ownership may suggest a link, as in the case of Bradgate House and Groby Manor House (Leicestershire), two miles apart, both built of brick, c. 1500, by Thomas Grey, marquis of Dorset; neither building has been properly examined. Brick-making on the scale required for Eton and Tattershall and permanent brickyards at Hull and Norwich taught many men how to temper brick-earth and mould bricks; it was bound sooner or later to lead to what has been called household production;[29] that is, firing a few thousand bricks in a clamp or temporary kiln. This may have started in rural areas in the fifteenth century, though it is proved by documents only in later centuries.

Notes

1 J. Williams, 'The early development of the town of Northampton', in A. Dornier (ed.), *Mercian Studies* (1977), 140–5; and RCHM, *Archaeological Sites and Churches in Northampton* (1985), p. 42.

2 E.M. Jope, 'The Saxon building-stone industry in southern and midland England', *Med. Archaeol.*, 8 (1964), 91–118.

3 H.M. Colvin (ed.), *Building Accounts of King Henry III* (1971); *King's Works*, I, 62–3.

4 A.J. Taylor, 'Castle-building in Wales in the later thirteenth century' in E.M. Jope (ed.), *Studies in Building History* (1961), 104–17.

5 M.E. Wood, *The English Medieval House* (1965), 19, 83.

6 H. Richmond, R. Taylor and P. Wade-Martins, *East Anglian Archaeol.* 14 (1982), 108–28.

7 J. Schofield, *The Building of London* (1984), 77; P.A. Faulkner, 'Medieval undercrofts and town houses', *Archaeol. J.*, 123 (1966), 120–35; BE, *Sussex*, 632; *Med. Archaeol.*, 26 (1982), 166–8; RCHM, *City of York*, 5 (1981), 91–2.

8 M. Beresford and J. Hurst, *Deserted Medieval Villages* (1971), 93–5.

9 A. Clifton-Taylor, *The Pattern of English Building* (1972), 26–8.

10 *Med. Archaeol.*, 17 (1973), 160–1.

11 L.F. Salzman, *Building in England down to 1540* (1952), 88, 187.

12 *House and Home*, pl. 199; *EFC*, 36; *Med. Archaeol.*, 23 (1979), 116–17.

13 R.J. and P.E. Forman, 'A geological approach to the study of medieval bricks', *Mercian Geologist*, 2 (1967), 299–318.

14 *Proc. Suffolk Inst. Archaeol.*, 35 (1981), 20–6.

15 *J. Brit. Archaeol. Ass.*, 18 (1955), 19–32.

16 M. Eames, 'Decorated tile pavements in English medieval houses', in *Rotterdam Papers*, 2 (1975), 5–16.

17 M. Biddle, 'Excavations at Winchester 1964', *Ant. J.*, 45 (1965), 248.

18 V. Parker, *Making of King's Lynn* (1971), 77; *Archaeol. J.*, 135 (1978), 213.

19 Salzman, 223.

20 BE, *West Kent*, 129; *Med. Archaeol.*, 21 (1977), 229.

21 Salzman, 140–1.

22 RCHM, *York*, 5, xcvi.

23 *King's Works*, I, 286.

24 *Med. Archaeol.*, 12 (1968), 168–9.

25 Clifton-Taylor, 292.

26 *Norfolk Archaeol.*, 36 (1977), 297–8.

27 T.P. Smith, 'Hussey Tower, Boston ...', *Lincolnshire History and Archaeol.*, 14 (1979), 31–7.

28 M.W. Barley *et al.*, 'The Medieval parsonage house, Coningsby, Lincolnshire', *Ant. J.*, 49 (1969), 346–66.

29 D. Peacock, in A. McWhirr (ed.), *Roman Brick and Tile* (BAR International Series 68, 1979), 6.

3 *Building and Materials 1066–1550: Timber*

Despite the twelfth-century expansion in the building industry, and the consequent wider range of choice of materials for houses, building in timber was still an attractive proposition in many circumstances. It was probably quicker and cheaper; if a building became redundant it could be taken down and re-erected elsewhere; if it had to be rebuilt, timbers could be used again. For a meeting of Parliament at Westminster in 1397 the hall could not be used and a temporary timber hall was put up. A year later it came down and all the materials were sold; some of the timber went to a royal manor house at Sutton, Surrey. Another temporary timber hall was erected in the middle of Leicester in 1414 for a meeting of Parliament; it measured 36.5 m (120 ft) each way and was built in less than a month.[1] These instances, known from state records, can stand for what happened lower down the social scale. Royal hunting lodges, in forests or castle parks, were commonly built of timber throughout the Middle Ages, for they were only for occasional use. It was not unknown in the later Middle Ages for new royal apartments in a castle or manor house to be timber-framed: for instance at Sheen in 1367–8, using second-hand materials from a house at Byfleet, or at Eltham in 1400. New apartments in Nottingham Castle were built in timber for Edward IV.

Timber resources

Royal forests were the main source of timber for royal building, and it was no problem to send it by sea from Essex for Dover Castle in 1222, or from Hampshire, Surrey and Hertfordshire to Westminster in 1394–1400 for the new roof of Westminster Hall, the largest medieval timber roof in northern Europe.[2] It was also possible to find timber merchants in London, and no doubt in provincial towns as well, or to buy Baltic boards at Boston and King's Lynn. For a landowner, finding timber was not a matter of plunging into virgin forest but of inspecting woodland for the desired combination of timber and underwood (in the forester's terms): timber being trees that had been allowed to grow to great girth and so were suitable for dressing to produce main beams, and underwood being younger trees for rafters, joists and braces. A small Suffolk manor house (Grundle House, Stanton), with a hall and two cross-wings built about 1500, used some 330 trees which might have been produced once in six years from 50 acres of managed woodland. Of those trees about forty were large and the rest were no more than fifty years old. West Suffolk then had woodland capable of producing seventy such houses each year.[3] The evidence for management of woodland has been collected mainly from south-eastern counties where late medieval houses are most common; in western counties and in Wales, timber building tends to use more massive material as if management of woodland was less intensive.

Grundle House contained about 20 per cent elm, a reminder that other species than oak were used in medieval buildings of all sorts. Some contracts for houses, especially in the fifteenth century, specify oak; there is one instance of a builder being sued for using alder and willow where he should have used oak; cruck blades of poplar and elm have been observed and they would have been satisfactory if not exposed to the weather. The use of sweet chestnut for roofs has often been suggested but very rarely proved. For peasants, ash was probably the most useful since it grows fast and straight, especially if coppiced, and coppicing as a form of management was practised from prehistoric times. Manorial custom often entitled a tenant to some rights in his lord's woodland, but disputes about such rights very rarely get into records so that we do not know how much or little they meant. It was not normally a lord's affair to look after his peasants' houses. When Merton College, Oxford (founded 1274), was given the manor of Cuxham as part of its endowment, the warden and fellows immediately repaired some cottages, presumably because they were run down; the expenditure did not recur.[4] In the later Middle Ages things were different for the peasant and on balance to his advantage. Manorial records refer increasingly to peasant buildings out of repair, presumably because one peasant might have more than one holding and so some redundant buildings, but labour was scarce and fines for dilapidation were ineffective. In the circumstances, lords were sometimes ready either to repair or to provide timber for a tenant to carry out work for himself. The bishop of Exeter repaired houses from 1374 onwards on one of his Devonshire manors; he did not do so on other manors. The bailiff's accounts of 1453–4 for Northamptonshire manors belonging to Ralph Lord Cromwell include repairs to tenants' houses, mainly to roofs (rafters, thatch, slates etc.), as well as to a manor house and to a bailiff's own house. Evidence of the same sort comes from manorial accounts for Bedale and Snape (Yorkshire).[5] These cases are a measure of either desperate or enlightened management, mostly the former, on the part of wealthy lay and ecclesiastical landowners whose records have survived; one can only assume that lesser men might do the same. Evidently there was no longer a land shortage.

15. Timber windows.
A. 9 QUEEN STREET, SALISBURY, WILTSHIRE, C. 1306. B. FLORE'S HOUSE, OAKHAM, RUTLAND, C. 1375.

Medieval carpenters

The men who designed the timber buildings, or the roofs of those with stone walls, ranged in status from Master Alexander, who with a master mason was in 1256 (at Winchester Castle and Westminster Abbey) chief master of the king's works, and Hugh Herland who in 1393–7 was responsible for a new roof for Westminster Hall,[6] to the workers who in manorial accounts repaired a lord's buildings and occasionally put up new ones. Buildings and documents together show a transformation of the carpenter's craft both in skills and in the numbers of men who possessed them. The wright was a fairly humble member of medieval society, because his raw materials were plentiful, his tools in widespread ownership and his work diverse: for that reason wrights would not belong to craft guilds; they made or repaired carts, wooden utensils, harrows, ploughs, and 'other works' according to a fifteenth-century tale. Diversity of work meant diversity of status; throughout the Middle Ages and later there were men, especially in woodland regions, who worked part-time on the land and were engaged otherwise in satisfying the demands of rural communities for wooden products, but an increasing number was able to find work for wages on major buildings and to develop appropriate skills [15]. In 1278 Edward I ordered sheriffs to recruit 300 carpenters and sawyers from Derbyshire alone and 120 more from Cheshire.[7] A bishop or baron had his own office of works with master carpenters travelling from one estate to another and directing local men. When we read that the bishop of Durham's tenants at Bishop Auckland had to build him a hunting lodge with a hall, buttery, chamber and chapel, we should assume that they worked under the orders of a master carpenter.[8]

Dating timber buildings

It is not unfair to the antiquarians and architects who by the nineteenth century had worked out the history of medieval architecture, and given us the terminology we still use for the phases of its development (Early English, Decorated, Perpendicular), to say that they took for granted the carpenter's role. They were certainly not very interested in buildings entirely of timber. In cathedrals, abbeys and grand churches, on which their history was based, the carpenter's work, apart from fittings such as stalls and screens which followed the mason's styles, was confined to roofs hidden above stone vaulting. The first book on English cathedral carpentry was published only in 1974,[9] although Victorian architects did produce measured drawings of open roofs. When a German scholar, Friedrich Ostendorff, published in 1908 a history of timber roofs in western Europe[10] he was able to include a chapter with illustrations on the English *open* roof, so called to distinguish it from typical continental roofs. The earliest drawing of the open hall of a Kentish yeoman's house with its central hearth was published by Sir Reginald Blomfield in 1887;[11] it appeared in an art journal and marks the romantic approach to such houses represented by several books published by B.T. Batsford early in this century. Since 1947 – a date worth quoting as marking publication of the first volume of *Monmouthshire Houses*[12] – there has been an explosion of interest in such houses. It was essentially an aspect of the growth of archaeology, in that it took the form of collecting data and arranging them in typological order of development.

Medieval timber-framed buildings very rarely carry an integral date such as an inscription.[13] Documents occasionally provide circumstantial evidence. For instance, several houses in Salisbury can safely be ascribed to rich wool merchants in the town known by name;[14] they include William Russell's house in Queen Street [15], now a shop in which his hammer-beam roof and windows of 1306 can comfortably be viewed (without any obligation to purchase). Another was Balle's Place, built by a John Ball (d. 1387); it was demolished in 1962 but not before its hammer-beam roof had been recorded. There is no reason to doubt that Coningsby rectory (page 143) was built by a rector who held the living in 1335–75; integral evidence (a stained-glass window with an inscription) shows that it was improved by another in 1463, but a stage of enlargement between is undated. Documents may provide the names of two generations of owners, as they do for Flore's House at Oakham [15, 37], with a date-span of fifty years; a house called Tickerage at West Hoathly (Sussex) was almost certainly owned by three generations of carpenters named William, Simon and Richard Tickerage.[15] In these cases one can only propose one man or another as builder according to

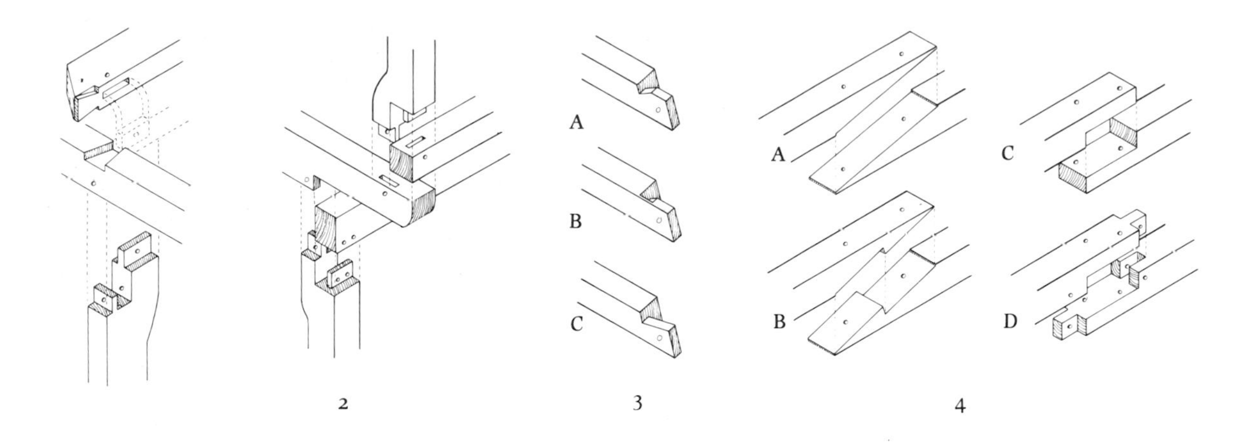

16. Medieval methods of jointing timbers. 1. At the top of a framed wall. 2. In a framed building with a jetty. 3. Joining timbers such as braces or collars other than at right angles: A. a notched lap; B. a secret notched lap, only to be detected by probing; C. half dovetail. 4. Forms of scarf joint: A. through splay; B. splayed and tabled (*trait de Jupiter*); C. edge-halved; D. edge-halved with bridled butts.

notions of the place of a particular form of roof in a typology. Contingent evidence such as a contract or building accounts may show that work was done at a known place without identifying certainly the building in question or the part of it. The dates quoted in the following pages are therefore probable rather than exact.

One recent development which has attracted widespread interest is the proposal that timber buildings incorporate a progressive improvement in the types of joint used and that these joints must be accurately identified [16] because they provide a more precise chronology than forms of construction.[16] The theory was derived originally from a study of Essex buildings but was later extended; it was supported by perspective drawings of remarkably impressive quality and accompanied by a very complex terminology for joints. It has certainly made investigators notice joints but it has not convinced them that the chronology works everywhere, or even that it works in Essex with the precision originally suggested. The elaboration of particular forms of joints seems to depend on the status of the building and the skill of the carpenter employed. His problems were to devise rigid joints for timbers at right-angles to each other, or at acute or obtuse angles, or else to join timbers in continuous lengths. The first problem was encountered in framed buildings with vertical wall-posts, transverse tie-beams and longitudinal wall-plates. The lap-joint for braces in a rafter-truss was elaborated so as to resist not only lateral movement but also withdrawal: the notched lap. For a wide and lofty roof over a manor house of high quality such as Cogges near Witney (Oxfordshire), built c. 1260–70, the rafters usually had to be scarfed; that is, made up of more than one length of timber, and so did purlins and wall-plates in a building more than about 6 m (20 ft) long. The most elaborate scarf-joints are found in south-eastern counties.[17]

As the technique of radio-carbon (C14) analysis developed it was naturally applied to a few medieval buildings, but it was soon abandoned,

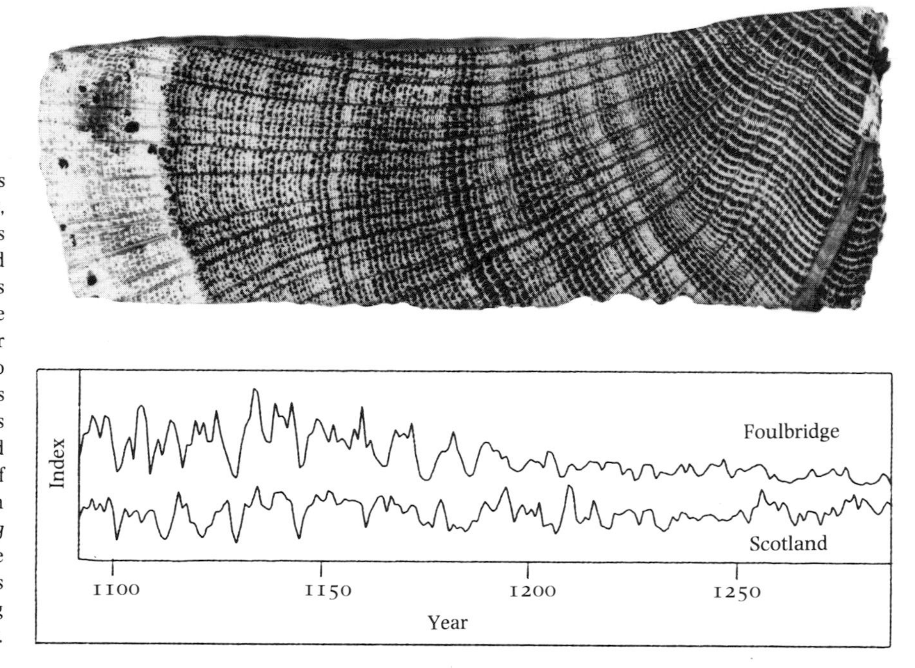

17. Dendrochronology. Graphs representing tree-ring widths, here called indices. The years are plotted horizontally and the indices vertically. Indices are used rather than the widths as they represent better the variations from year to year. The Foulbridge graph is an average of several samples and is to be compared to, and dated by, a master sequence of indices of ring widths from Scottish oaks (*Tree-ring Bulletin*, 37, 33–44). The sample in the photograph is one of those used in making the Foulbridge graphs.

since the dates produced have a margin of error (100–200 years of 95 per cent confidence) too great to be useful for buildings later than say 1200. It has now been proved that tree-ring dating (dendrochronology) [17] may in favourable circumstances provide accurate dates in the British Isles.[18] Research is being done in several universities; success depends on the statistical quality of the results, which in turn depends on a number of samples with a large number of rings. Fortunately, results tend to support so far the views based on typology.

The time and energy being spent by the present generation of professional and amateur archaeologists in collecting data is producing a mass of material which cannot yet be summarized; it is dispersed in national and local repositories and in private hands; the size of the accumulations, their dispersal and their disparate quality has made it impossible to use computers to bring them to accessible order. The one exception is the computer-based study of the one form of construction easiest to identify: cruck building.[19] Otherwise, attempts to arrange types of timber construction in an orderly development are represented by articles in journals, stimulated originally by work on roofs of ecclesiastical buildings in France, earlier in date than surviving examples in Britain.

The earliest timber houses

The oldest upstanding remains of construction entirely in timber are of aisled halls, built by royal carpenters in Leicester castle and by an episcopal office of works for a bishop of Hereford. They were built on a bay system which is as old as the Neolithic age; it had been taken over from

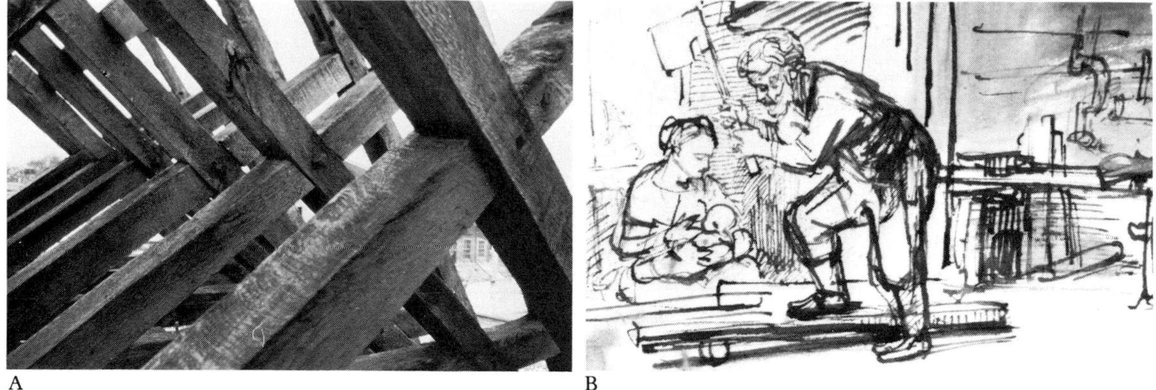

A B

18. A. The roof of the BEDERN HALL, YORK, c. 1350, showing scissor-braces halved across each other and across the collars (lower right). *York Archaeological Trust, M. Duffy.* B. Rembrandt drawing, *Joseph in the Carpenter's Shop.* There are no English illustrations of a carpenter dressing timber with an axe. This drawing shows Joseph adopting a no doubt normal method. *Courtauld Institute, University of London.*

carpenters by medieval masons building great churches so that whatever the materials or the size of the building, the structural load is collected at points on stone columns and buttresses or on posts with tie-beams and braces. Timber houses built before c. 1350 have usually had their walling renewed or altered, or even replaced in stone, so that attention inevitably concentrates on forms of roof. Archaeologists are satisfied that the oldest form is the coupled-rafter roof [19A] which must have depended on tie-beams; the oldest roofs of this type are over churches with stone walls. In the Mediterranean region the covering of a stone vault might rest directly in the vault. In the temperate zone, the climate called for a separate timber roof over the vault. Carpenters therefore evolved the steep-pitched roof whose stability depended on doubling rafters or multiplying cross-braces [18] in one way or another. A further characteristic of these roofs is that their members are reduced, by sawing or dressing with an axe, to uniform dimensions, another practice derived from large-scale operations such as building cathedrals. Such a system of roof-trusses was prevented from 'racking' – that is, collapsing like a pack of cards – by the laths nailed on rafters to carry the covering of thatch, oak shingles, clay tiles or stone slates. Buildings identified by this form as early in date – that is, before c. 1350 – are of superior status and found mainly in south-eastern counties. Some of them are aisled halls and barns. It has been assumed that the Normans brought with them carpenters and this form of roof, as well as masons and a new style of architecture.

The problem of longitudinal stability was solved by introducing members into the length of the roof, either a plate in the centre underneath the collar to each common rafter truss, or a purlin at the side in the slope of the roof.[20] The earliest English roofs, on ecclesiastical buildings, show a variety of solutions, reflecting experiment by carpenters and their mobility. Some roofs closely resemble those in northern France. These systems made it possible to reduce the number of tie-beams and so to economize in the use of timber. By c. 1250 English carpenters had found, for themselves rather than by picking up a French idea, the solution they

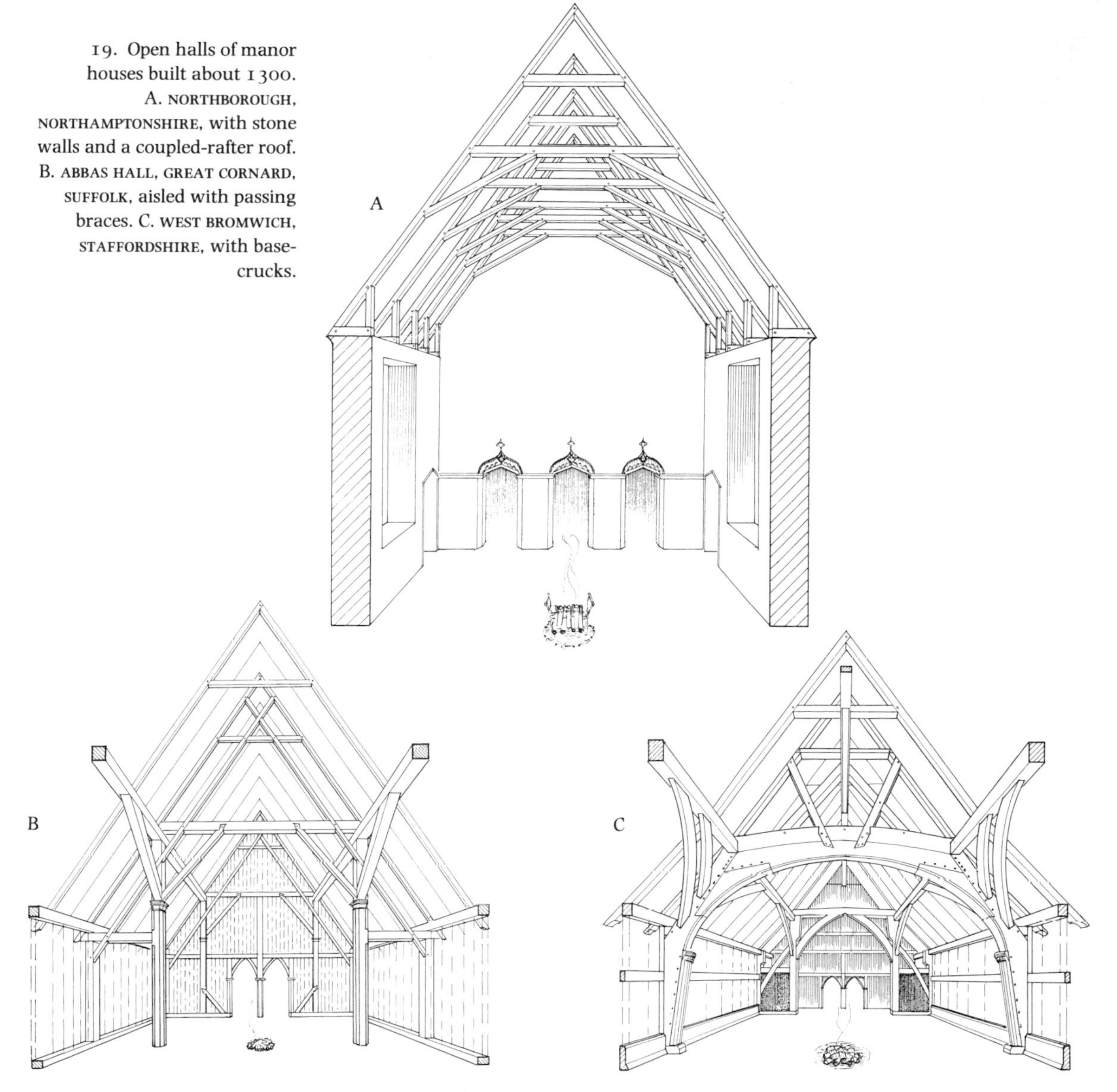

19. Open halls of manor houses built about 1300. A. NORTHBOROUGH, NORTHAMPTONSHIRE, with stone walls and a coupled-rafter roof. B. ABBAS HALL, GREAT CORNARD, SUFFOLK, aisled with passing braces. C. WEST BROMWICH, STAFFORDSHIRE, with base-crucks.

came to prefer for its appearance: the crown-post roof with a central crown-plate [20B]. It is so common in south-eastern counties in churches and in houses of both lords and yeomen that no one has yet tried to count how many there are or to map their distribution.

Carpenters carried it to the midlands and the north, especially for town buildings. Its simplicity of design and economy of materials gave it a life of about three centuries; the only heavy timbers were the wall-plates and only the crown-post and its braces varied in design. All the earliest examples are over buildings with stone walls; from the early fourteenth century it was used over houses with framed walls, implying the integra-

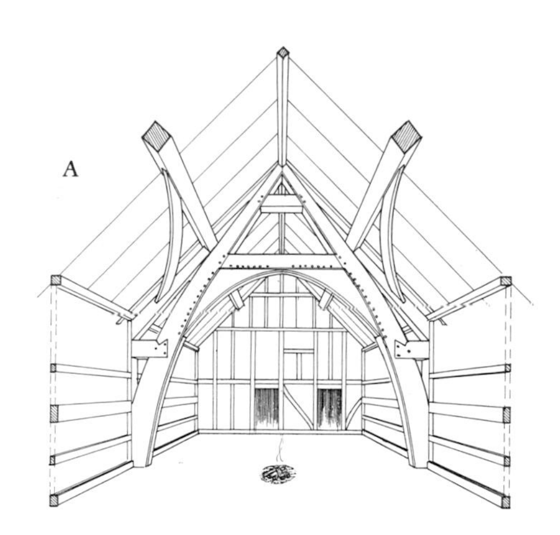

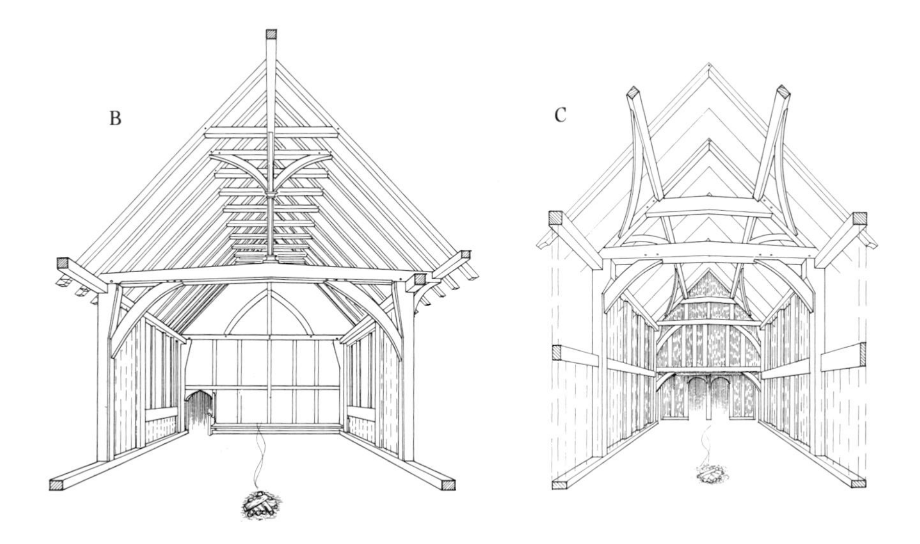

20. Open halls of peasant houses. A. BOX TREE COTTAGE, DEFFORD, WORCESTERSHIRE, fourteenth century, with crucks. B. Wealden house at WILLINGTON, KENT, early sixteenth century. C. House in HIGH STREET, COLESHILL, WARWICKSHIRE, with clasped side-purlins. Above the twin service doorways the chamber is jettied out over the hall.

tion of walls and roof in a progressive mode of erection, with cross-frames reared at intervals and then locked into position by longitudinal members.

Cruck building

The bay system can most easily be observed in cruck building. The form of construction is superficially so simple that it seems primitive. Pairs of substantial timbers, straight or curved, stretch from the ridge down to the ground; they support a ridge-piece, side-purlins and wall-plates and thus rafters and wall-posts [20A]. This is a simplified definition; there is in fact so much variety of detail that the system is certainly not primitive and shows how skilfully and ingeniously carpenters could employ a particular principle. It is also so distinctive that it has proved possible to compile a catalogue of more than 3,000 buildings (mainly houses) in England and Wales and to use a computer to produce distribution maps of them and of some of the variations.[21] The catalogue and the accompanying discussion of it make a contribution unique in western Europe to the archaeology of timber building. The oldest cruck buildings belong to the thirteenth century on the evidence of C14 dating and the earliest documentary references to crucks begin shortly before 1200.

It seems likely that cruck building originated with carpenters working in the West Midlands for the upper classes; a few buildings such as the hall of Stokesay Castle (Shropshire)[22] and a manorial barn at Leigh Court (Worcestershire) support the possibility. They show that crucks could be used to span a building more than 9 m (30 ft) wide, but its greatest convenience was for houses and barns no more than 6 m (20 ft) wide put up for small landowners, parsons and, most of all, peasants. Crucks cannot be dated closely, except by dendrochronology. Most in the southern half of England must have been built before 1500 or 1600; they were unsuitable when the new demand was for houses with two full storeys. Cruck building went on after that in northern England, but references to it in manorial records show that distinct local concentrations, as on the North Yorkshire Moors, had developed by the fifteenth century.[23] The total absence of cruck buildings in eastern England has defied explanation, especially for counties such as Norfolk where there are no surviving peasant houses of the alternative form with crown-post roofs.

The open hall

The open hall, however large, was most conveniently heated by a fire on a central hearth, the smoke escaping from a louvre on the ridge of the roof [21], but in the course of the century from c. 1275 onwards, English carpenters found more than one way of clearing away the rows of posts of an aisled hall for those clients for whom the distinction between nave and aisles had no practical convenience.[24] One solution was to support the upper part of the posts (and so the roof) on a tie-beam; what is called raised-aisle construction. It was being adopted before 1300 for manor houses in Essex, where carpenters were most experienced in building aisled halls. Another solution was the hammer-beam roof, in which in effect both the lower section of the posts and the middle part of the tie-beam were eliminated. Pilgrim's Hall, Winchester, was built by the dean and chapter about 1290; it is a long range of six bays divided into two rooms, one of which has hammer-beam trusses. In the fourteenth century this construction was used for a few manor houses, and for inns and large houses in Salisbury; it was elaborated in scale and ornament for royal palaces (Westminster, Eltham). When Henry V decided in 1419 to build a royal palace at Rouen he used French masons and English car-

A

21. Louvres. A. Crown-post roof at PIERCE HOUSE, CHARING, KENT, showing two rafter trusses made good after removal of wooden louvre. *E. W. Parkin*. B, C. Pottery louvres made in a kiln at LAVERSTOCK, WILTSHIRE (*Salisbury Museum*) and recovered in a NOTTINGHAM excavation (*Castle Museum*).

B

C

penters,[25] no doubt because he wanted a hammer-beam roof. It also became the glory of East Anglian churches in the later Middle Ages. Some carpenters evidently specialized in church work; hammer-beam roofs are unknown in East Anglian houses, but on the other hand a group of Devon carpenters built the Guildhall in Exeter and three houses in and near the city, early in the fifteenth century, with elaborately carved hammer-beam roofs.[26]

Midland carpenters working for the landed classes – barons, bishops, abbots and lords of manors – found yet another way of clearing an aisled

22. Axonometric drawings of the fourteenth-century roofs of FIDDLEFORD MILL, DORSET. Note the arched braces to collars with cusped struts above and two tiers of cusped wind-braces. *RCHM.*

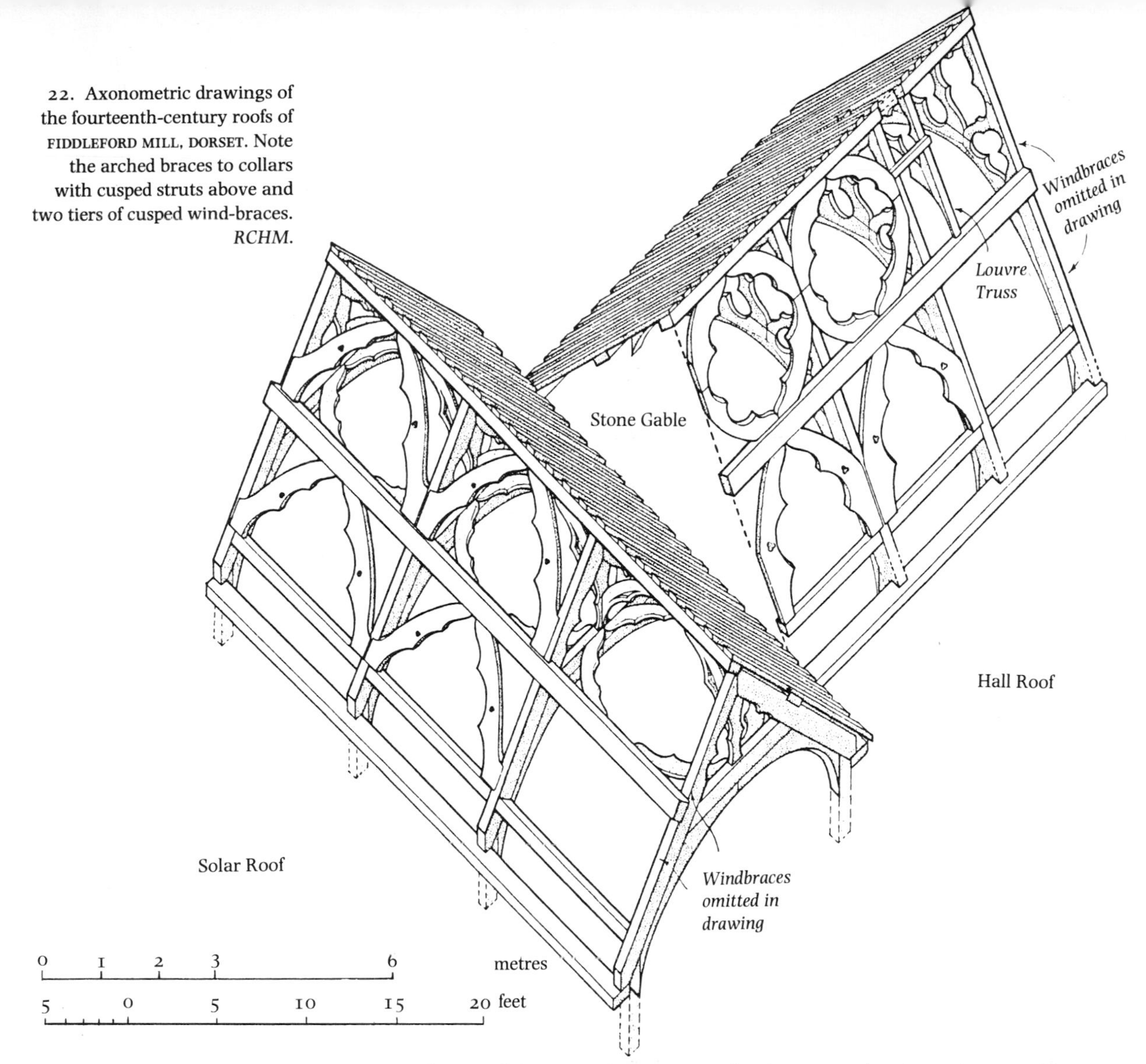

hall or a barn of free-standing posts: the base-cruck. Curved posts like cruck blades planted on the line of the walls rise to support the arcade plate.[27] Since this form of construction was first noticed in the 1950s more than a hundred examples have been recorded, the earliest of them built before 1300 and nearly all before 1400. Pilgrims' Hall, Winchester, is of special interest because it has both hammer-beam and base-cruck trusses in the one building and contemporary. Both forms have been found, used at least as much for visual effect as for practical convenience, in small halls with only one aisle.

The arched roof All classes shared, as far as their means would allow, a desire to have cross-members lifted above the level of wall-tops and to give them an arched form [22]. In parts of the continent where oak was less plentiful than in Britain this was often done by building a series of stone arches (diaphragm arches) to carry purlins and rafters. There are a few halls in England with such arches:[28] the archbishop of Canterbury's palace at Mayfield (Sussex); Battel Hall, a house of c. 1330 at Leeds (Kent) and Ightham Mote (Kent), built at about the same time. At Conway Castle, the timber supports for the hall roof were replaced in 1346–7 by eight stone arches. In stone-walled houses, the arched effect could be achieved by rearing principal trusses at bay intervals, the principal rafters carrying side-purlins held by collars with arched braces up to them. In cruck buildings, the tie-beam was not essential to an open truss because the wall-plate could be supported on what is called a spur-tie [20A], and an open truss could then have arched braces to the collar. With stone walls, height in a cruck building, convenient in a barn and visually impressive in a hall, could be increased by planting the cruck trusses above ground level – the raised cruck. In Somerset and Devon local carpenters devised an economical form of cruck construction, as lofty as was desired, by making up cruck blades from two pieces of timber jointed together.

With a crown-post roof, the tie-beam could not be dispensed with. The effect of a flat arch could be achieved with a cambered tie-beam and curved knee-braces to it from wall-posts, but visual interest focuses in the centre of the roof space and on the crown-post and its braces. The crown-post roof ceased to be used after c. 1350 in great houses and was hence a virtual monopoly of carpenters working for the yeoman class. If longitudinal stiffening was provided by side-purlins, in the slope of the roof, the roof space was opened up and this came to be preferred. The widespread adoption of the principal-rafter roof with side-purlins is the most significant development of the later Middle Ages, and it is not surprising to find that it cannot be traced to a single source. It must have had advantages in the rearing processs. Slender side-purlins were used by carpenters working, before 1300, for a bishop of Chichester on the cathedral and for a bishop of Winchester on his palace at Bishop's Waltham (Hampshire).[29] Side-purlins were always part of the cruck system.

The hierarchy of roofs

The diversity of open-hall roofs of all classes in the centuries 1350–1550 can be set out as a hierarchy, from the cheapest to the richest and the earliest to the latest, all aiming at an arched effect. The buildings may be in stone or in timber-framing, the latter with box-frame or cruck construction.

1. *Number of bays:* from one (with no open truss) to several, with division in the grandest halls into primary and secondary trusses.
2. *Tie-beam:* straight or cambered, with knee-braces from wall-posts curved to suggest a flat arch.
3. *Collar:* straight or cambered with arched braces from principal rafters or cruck blades.

4. *Mouldings:* to wall-posts, crucks, braces, wall-plates, side-purlins; crown-post plain or moulded with capital and base.
5. *Cusping:* to arched braces, collars, struts to principal rafters or to cruck blades.
6. *Multiplication:* of side-purlins with curved wind-braces, plain, cusped, paired to form arches, grouped in fours to make circles.
7. *Openings:* within trusses filled with Perpendicular-style openwork panels.

The one element that such a grading cannot convey is the diversity of status found for one design in different regions. Crown-post roofs are standard in late-medieval York but are invariably plain;[30] division of a roof into primary and secondary trusses may be found in a five-bay hall at Boughton (Northamptonshire) [76] and in a two-bay hall at Amberley Court (Herefordshire). This contrast between size and quality is most marked in north Wales, where two-bay halls are superbly designed and richly moulded and cusped.[31]

Wall-framing

The external timber walls of medieval houses have had much less chance of survival than roofs; there is little evidence before the fourteenth century and few examples can be confidently dated before c. 1450.[32] The material used to fill panels formed by vertical and horizontal members is even more likely to have been renewed.

The main distinction in late-medieval wall-framing is between panels, large or small, and close-studding [23]. Small panels, using shorter lengths of timber, are more common in the west, especially for smaller houses.

23. GREAT FUNTLEY FARMHOUSE, WICKHAM, HAMPSHIRE. Two-storeyed house, c. 1525–50, with continuous jetty.

Large panels required a solid base for daub. Close studding is more common in the south-east; it only appears to be characteristic there because expensive houses are more numerous. In close-studded walls, pieces of rubble, stone or tile, wedged in grooves in the studs and plastered over, gave a durable result; where bricks were available, as in the Humber basin, the brick infilling is original and the same may be true elsewhere.

24. DRUMBURGH CASTLE, CUMBERLAND, C. 1518. The king-post roof preferred by northern carpenters in the late Middle Ages. *P. W. Dixon.*

Some sixteenth-century houses with stone walls, especially in the south-west and in Wales, have partitions at the superior end of the hall consisting of vertical studs tenoned into a head-beam and grooved to take planks between them:[33] the stud-and-plank or plank-and-muntin partition of technical literature. We see a hint of an unbroken tradition, sustained from late Saxon to modern times by carpenters working for well-to-do clients, of finishing walls with vertical timbering.[34] Traces of such walling, in the form of a groove or close-set mortices under a wall-plate, have been noted in a few early Sussex houses, among them the Old Rectory at Warbleton, built c. 1300. Close-studding would then appear to be a somewhat cheaper and perhaps more lasting form with stone or brick, daub or plaster, instead of planks [32].

Jetties Although timber-framed houses in French and German towns differ from British in the details of their construction, they have in common the use of jettying for upper storeys, and this may be one case where continental influence is responsible for an insular development, starting in the fourteenth century. If so, its principal purpose, whatever its technical advantage, was to provide somewhat more space on the first floor; there can

25. Excavated house in the BEDERN, YORK, showing in centre padstones or bay-stones at regular intervals to support main posts. *York Archaeological Trust, M. Duffy.*

be no other explanation of jettied houses in narrow lanes in Venice, where they must represent German influence. The jetty was adopted as an integral part of the design of the Wealden house and in Essex the cross-wings flanking an open hall were often jettied, but the variety of its use – at the front only, or front and one end, or front, back and end – seems to reflect fortuitous decisions by builders or householders. If we knew more about the make-up of medieval Kentish houses, how many servants lived in and where they slept, we might understand why houses with an end-jetty are common there and possibly earlier than Wealden houses. Houses with two storeys appear first in the south-east [23] and they are easy to distinguish by the fact that they have a continuous jetty at the front. That form of building was adopted first for terraces in towns [41–4]. Single houses with a continuous jetty appeared first in towns c. 1500; they may demonstrate that by that time, if not before, the urban housewright was beginning to dominate his trade.

Excavated houses

Excavation ought to complement the evidence of standing houses and so it does, with important limitations. Where stone was available at least for foundations if not for walling, plans of houses may be recovered but not methods of using timber for walls or roofs. Deserted rural settlements in Britain have been a matter of intense and systematic interest but some obvious questions are as yet unanswerable. There have been no excavations of such sites in south-eastern counties where small houses of c. 1350 and later are so numerous; it must be that the pattern and density of settlement has long been stable, or has expanded, and so the Kentish peasant's house of the earlier Middle Ages is quite unknown. In regions where stone was not readily available, excavations have at least shown that by the later Middle Ages prefabricated timber buildings were the norm in town and country. In York, sites long occupied with a deep subsoil called for either piling with single substantial timbers or clusters of small ones, or else stone pads. Deserted villages on clay are the most informative.[35] At Goltho (Leicestershire) and Barton Blount (Derbyshire) the most sophisticated houses and barns had stone pads regularly placed for wall-posts. Manorial records for North Yorkshire villages include payments for searching for bay stones [25] and for raising houses and barns.[36] Evidently prefabrication was already practised, and this is an important contribution to knowledge of areas where no medieval small houses still stand; whether this work was supervised by estate carpenters we do not know. Yorkshire references to cruck construction show that even before 1550 it was concentrated in the North Yorkshire Moors. If houses there were not cruck built, they probably resembled those buildings described in terriers of c. 1600 and later, especially in the East Midlands, as being of mud and stud. They had a simple frame with uprights (studs) too far apart for panels to be filled with wattling, so laths were nailed to them as a base for mud applied to the outside. Instead of framed trusses resting on a continuous timber sill, they had separate lengths of sill interrupted by the uprights on their padstones. It is likely that the roofs were hipped.

Other excavations on clay land have revealed a yet more primitive mode of construction as late as the early fourteenth century in date, indicated by postholes varying in diameter, not regularly aligned along a wall and not paired with posts on an opposite wall: that is, not built on a bay system. It has long been a challenge to archaeologists to reconstruct a building on this evidence. The best explanation is that the posts formed a core to a clay wall thick enough to compensate for any misalignment in the posts. This compound wall need not be as thick as mass walling with mud alone but could carry a wall-plate and a simple roof. In no case have the actual timbers been preserved, but timber less durable than oak or ash would have served, protected as it was by clay. Building timber-laced walls (as they have been called) of this sort for houses or for the minor buildings in a manor complex may have been the work of peasants too poor to employ a carpenter to prepare and erect cruck and box-framed buildings.

Notes

1 *King's Works*, I, 532, 703, 1004; 764, 996–9.
2 Ibid., 521.
3 O. Rackham, 'Grundle House ...', *Vernacular Architecture*, 3 (1972), 3–8; idem, *Ancient Woodland* ... (1980), 146–7, 160–4.
4 P. D. A. Harvey (ed.), *Manorial Records of Cuxham, Oxfordshire, c. 1200–1359* (1976), 252, 165.
5 N. W. Alcock, 'The medieval cottages of Bishops Clyst', *Med. Archaeol.*, 9 (1965), 146–53; H. B. Sharp, 'Some mid-fifteenth century small-scale building repairs', *Vernacular Arch.*, 12 (1981), 20–9; B. Harrison and B. Hutton, *Vernacular Houses in North Yorkshire and Cleveland* (1984), 4–6.
6 H. M. Colvin, *Building Accounts of King Henry III* (1971), 9; *King's Works*, I, 164.
7 A. J. Taylor, 'Castle building in Wales in the later thirteenth century', E. M. Jope (ed.), *Studies in Building History* (1961), 106.
8 W. Greenwell (ed.), *Bolden Buke: a survey of the possessions of the see of Durham ... 1183* (Surtees Soc. 25, 1852), 24, 29.
9 C. A. Hewett, *English Cathedral Carpentry* (1974).
10 *Die Geschichte des Dachwerks* (Leipzig and Berlin, 1908).
11 Reproduced in K. Gravett, *Timber and Brick Building in Kent* (1971), 2.
12 Sir Cyril Fox and Lord Raglan, *Monmouthshire Houses* (1947), pt. 1.
13 D. P. Dymond, *Archaeology and History* (1974), 148–53.
14 RCHM, *Salisbury*, I (1980), 85–8 (no. 132), 135–7 (no. 351).
15 *Trans. Leics. Archaeol. Soc.*, 50 (1974–5), 38; R. T. Mason, *Framed Buildings of the Weald* (1964), 52.
16 C. A. Hewett, *English Historical Carpentry* (1980), particularly the appendices.
17 *Oxoniensia*, 37 (1972), 177–83; *Med. Archaeol.*, 22 (1978), 107–11; *Vernacular Arch.*, 12 (1981), 30–6; *Oxoniensia*, 47 (1982), 78–80.
18 Lists are published in *Vernacular Architecture*.
19 N. W. Alcock, *Cruck Construction: an Introduction and Catalogue* (CBA Research Report 42, 1981).
20 J. Munby *et al.*, 'Crown-post and king-strut roofs in south-eastern England', *Med. Archaeol.*, 27 (1983), 123–35.
21 Alcock, *Cruck Construction*.
22 R. A. Cordingley, 'Stokesay Castle', *Art Bulletin*, 45 (1963), 91–107.
23 B. Harrison and B. Hutton, ch. 1.
24. J. T. Smith, 'Medieval aisled halls and their derivatives', *Archaeol. J.*, 112 (1955), 76–94; idem, 'Medieval roofs: a classification', *Archaeol. J.*, 115 (1958), 120–2; J. Crook, 'The Pilgrims' Hall, Winchester', *Proc. Hants. Field Club*, 38 (1982), 85–101.
25 *EVH*, nos. 119, 128, 463; RCHM, *Dorset*, 2, ii (1970), 301–2; *King's Works*, I, 461.
26 *Archaeol. J.*, 114 (1957), 138, 161.
27 N. W. Alcock and M. W. Barley, 'Medieval roofs with base-crucks and short principals', *Ant. J.*, 52 (1972), 132–61 (1981), 322–6.
28 M. E. Wood, *The English Medieval House* (1965), pl. 3; BE, *West Kent*, 346, 374; *King's Works*, I, 352.
29 *Med. Archaeol.*, 27 (1983), 130–1.
30 RCHM, *York*, 5 (1981), lxviii–lxxix.
31 P. Smith, *Houses of the Welsh Countryside* (1975), figs 45–72.
32 *EVH*, 115.
33 *House and Home*, pl. 43.
34 B. Meeson, 'Plank-walled building techniques ...', *Vernacular Arch.*, 14 (1983), 29–35; *Historic Buildings in E. Sussex*, (Rape of Hastings Archit. Survey, 2, 1981), 40–4.
35 G. Beresford, *The Medieval Clay-land Village* ... (1975), figs 9, 16, etc.
36 Harrison and Hutton, ch. 1.

4 *Houses in the Medieval Town*

The towns of Norman England were transformed by having castles planted in them, either within the built-up area or so close as to dominate them. Some of these new fortresses had a short life, so much so that their sites cannot always be located. Only earth-and-timber castles later rebuilt in stone left enduring remains. London and Colchester had stone keeps from the first, London because of its importance and Colchester because of the scale and quality of the remains of Roman buildings: the Colchester keep, larger in area than the Tower of London, stands on the podium of a Roman temple. Royal palaces were not usually built within a medieval walled town.[1] At Gloucester and at Westminster, where William Rufus built a stone hall which at the time (1097–9) must have been the largest stone hall in England and perhaps in Europe, the royal residences lay outside the Roman walls. Lesser royal residences at Coventry (Cheylesmore), Guildford and Oxford (Beaumont) were also outside those towns. Bath had for a time a royal residence within the abbey precincts, so that monarchs could use the King's Bath, but it was given up in 1275; Portsmouth, a naval base from 1194, had a royal residence in the town but it too was abandoned less than a century later. There was a royal residence at Aylesbury, the site of which is perpetuated in the name Kingsbury for the open space east of the church, but it did not outlast the twelfth century.

Bishops' palaces

In more than a dozen Norman towns, most of them of Roman origin, the wealthiest individual was a bishop, often busy building a new cathedral or rebuilding an old one. In all but one (Carlisle) he built a residence alongside the cathedral; no other domestic buildings of like scale and quality were ever put up in medieval towns and only a few urban castles, mostly royal, could rival them. We know them as palaces, and the name deserves comment. *Palatium* in later Roman times meant the residence of an emperor; by the twelfth century it began to be used of bishops' residences, both on the continent and in this country. The first English usage occurs at Winchester.[2] The building of Henry de Blois, a nephew of Henry I

26. Reconstruction of the archbishop's Great Hall at CANTERBURY, KENT, seen from the outer court. *Canterbury Archaeological Trust, J. Bowen.*

and a younger brother of Stephen, was described in 1138 as *domum quasi palatium*: the annalist chose the analogy because of Henry's royal connection or because of the grandeur of the house, or conceivably for both reasons. In the course of the Middle Ages this word came into increasingly general use, especially for the palace alongside the cathedral but by the sixteenth century for bishops' rural residences as well. In Scotland, but never in England, it came to mean a first-floor hall, as distinct from a tower house.[3] Of all the buildings of English bishops – and including their castles and rural manor houses some 200 can be identified from documents – their palaces alongside their cathedrals were the earliest to be built of stone; they were so substantial that their medieval character can be seen or deduced, even if they fell into ruin after the Reformation or were altered by bishops in modern times. Only London, Coventry, Lichfield and York lack significant remains of the first palaces, though the evidence at Norwich is limited.

Throughout the Middle Ages, the residences of the great had to serve both private and public functions, and bishops' palaces like the residences of lay lords (and royalty) invariably had the most private accommodation (chambers and chapels) on the first floor. The strength of that preference is emphasized by the fact that in at least seven cathedral cities, bishops started by building a hall on the first floor, and three Norman bishops who built castles in towns included such a hall in them – Hugh de Puiset (or Pudsey) at Durham, William Giffard of Winchester at Taunton, and Alexander of Lincoln at Newark. The bishop of Durham was the wealthiest prelate after Canterbury and Winchester and enjoyed royal powers in his palatinate of Durham. The first stone buildings in the earthwork castle at Durham, built by William I in 1072 and handed over to the bishop, included a public hall; Hugh de Puiset before 1195 built a private hall in the north range with a doorway of opulent splendour and over it a room lighted by a range of windows looking on to the bailey. That room, now called the Norman gallery or Constable's Chamber, was really the bishop's private chamber, the constable and his staff being housed in the gatehouse or the keep. There is no other instance of a private chamber above a hall though it is a feature of later medieval residences in France. Giffard's palace in the London suburb of Southwark had a first-floor hall.[4] Thirteenth-century bishops built such halls (or rebuilt earlier ones) at the new city of Salisbury (c. 1220), Wells (1230–50) and Worcester (c. 1271). The last in the sequence is at St David's, where Thomas Bek (1280–93) built one first floor hall and Henry de Gower (1327–47) another. St David's is unusual in that even the kitchen, built c. 1350 to serve both halls, is on the first floor.

The second hall at St David's belongs to a second phase of palace building, when some bishops built a grander hall for more public and ceremonial occasions. The aisled halls at Lincoln (c. 1224), Exeter (1224–44), Canterbury (before 1243) [26], Wells (1272–92) and Norwich (1318–25) represent the grandest aspect of the episcopal way of life; households, entirely masculine, must in the case of the wealthiest bishops have amounted to a hundred or more. All bishops except Carlisle, Rochester and the Welsh bishops held their lands by military tenure, their assessments ranging from sixty knights for Canterbury and Lincoln to two for Chichester; their entourage therefore included knights as well as clerics of every grade. In the fifteenth century, when there is detailed evidence of the style of archbishops of Canterbury, accounts show that two daily meals were served in the palace and that the company in October 1459 averaged seventy-four for dinner (*prandium*) and sixty-two for supper (*cena*); since they were divided into gentry and others, the gentry probably ate with the bishop in his private hall and the others in the larger hall. An account roll of the bishop of Hereford for 1289–90 suggests that the *others* got a less elaborate meal.[5]

The remains of the palace at Lincoln show that by the beginning of the thirteenth century the hall and its supporting services had been integrated in a manner which in the course of the Middle Ages was widely adopted down to the level of the yeoman farmer: to one end of the hall a two-storey block was attached, containing on the ground floor two service rooms, buttery and pantry, with a chamber over them [27]. This has been called the end-hall plan[6] and can be seen in castles (Oakham c. 1190, Ashby-de-la-Zouch, early thirteenth century), in abbots' lodgings (Wenlock Priory, thirteenth century) as well as in secular houses.

Another particular feature appropriate to the largest households but rare before c. 1300 was a passage between the buttery and pantry to a kitchen beyond.[7] The earliest example is in the royal palace of Clarendon (Wiltshire, probably 1176–7); the hall at Oakham Castle had it c. 1190

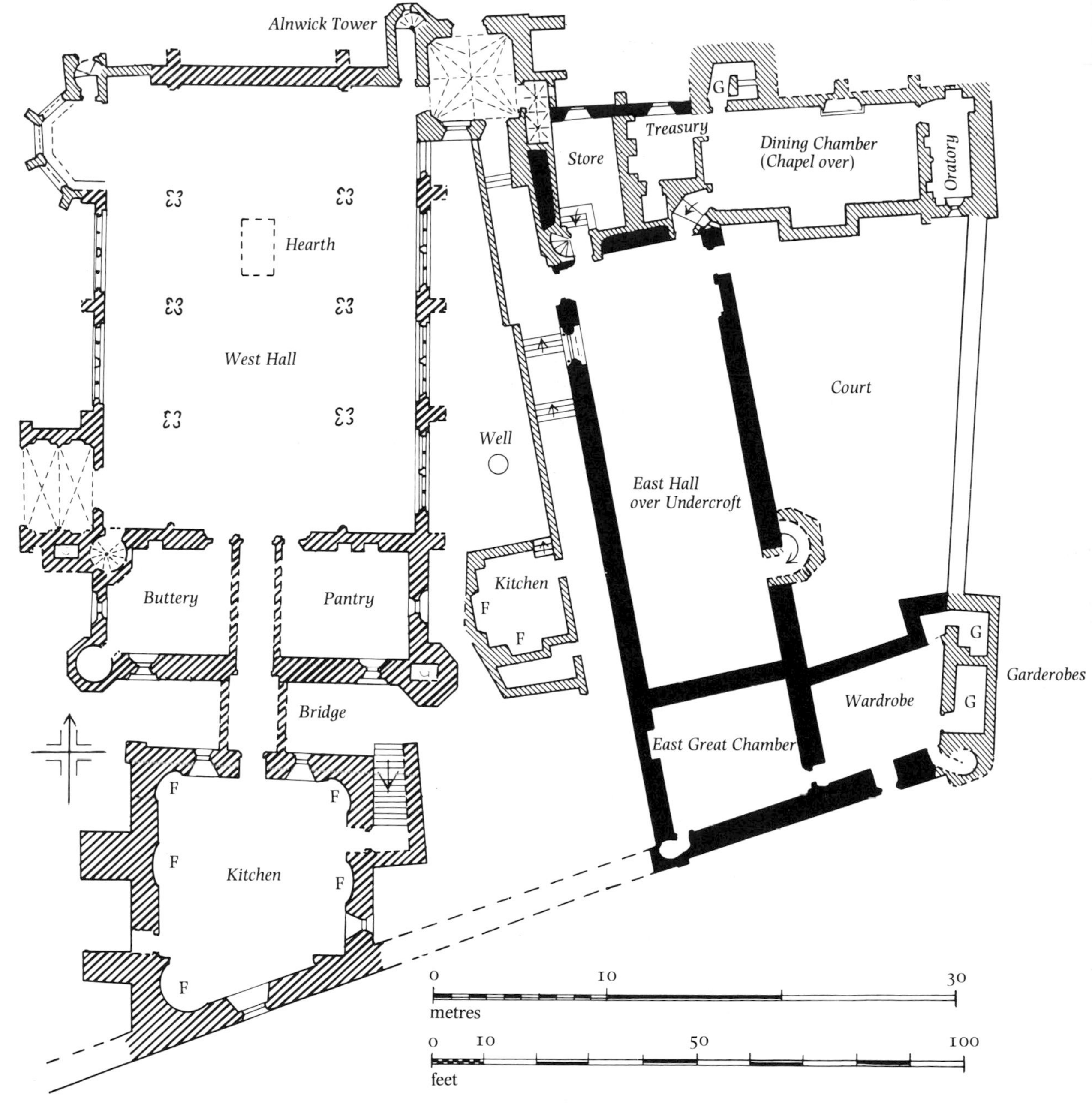

27. Plan of the bishop's palace, LINCOLN, showing the phases of its development. The East Hall was built first with chambers at its south end, all over vaulted undercrofts. The West Hall was built next, mainly by Hugh of Welles (1209–35), with a chamber over the service rooms and a kitchen reached by a bridge, since the site slopes down to the south. William Alnwick (bishop 1436–49) added the third element: private quarters with a dining chamber, a chapel over it and a solar tower containing his chamber, and a privy kitchen. He also added garderobes to the East Hall and an oriel window in the West Hall. *After P. A. Faulkner.*

A

B

28. THE OLD PALACE, LINCOLN. A. Aisled hall of c. 1225 showing service doorways, responds of arcading (close to modern drain pipes), blocked doorway to bishop's chamber over services, and entrance from porch. B. Private dining parlour of c. 1440, showing buffet (left), bay window (foreground), and jambs of fireplace (back wall).

and so had the palace at Lincoln a generation later [28]. The Oakham kitchen is known only from excavation but the remarkable kitchen at Lincoln survives, built up on the slope over a vaulted basement. Bishop Burnell's aisled hall at Wells (c. 1280) has a closely similar plan, but the kitchen has disappeared.[8] Although the hall (*aula*), service rooms and a private chamber (*camera* or *solarium*) from the twelfth century had been integrated into one structure (the end-hall house), the kitchen was detached and remained so in the grandest houses mainly because of the scale of its operations. Some forty medieval kitchens survive to show how cooking for large numbers was organized, in palaces, castles, large manor houses, monasteries and colleges. The earlier examples are uniformly square on plan, as they are on the continent; that was equally convenient when there was one large hearth in the centre, which was no doubt the earliest form, and when in the more elaborate thirteenth-century kitchens there were several fireplaces on side walls. The bishop's kitchen at

Chichester has a form of hammer-beam roof and was probably built shortly before 1300; it had only a central hearth.[9] At Lincoln (c. 1224) there were five fireplaces, backed with tile. The roof has gone but was probably octagonal and covered with lead. These differences correspond to the fact that Chichester was one of the poorest bishoprics and Lincoln one of the richest.

It is tantalizing that no urban palace shows us where the members of the bishop's household slept. Documents imply that in rural residences there were private chambers for a few, but squires and even knights and clerks and certainly yeomen, grooms and pages must have shared chambers like dormitories; presumably they did so in town palaces. In Norman Canterbury, officers of the archbishop's household had their own houses in the town;[10] presumably the same is true in other cities, and the provision of ranges of lodgings, as at Southwell, is a later development, particular to places where the staff could not be expected to find their own accommodation because they were only intermittently resident.

Some urban palaces show another development in the fifteenth century which was of wide significance in later times: the withdrawal of the bishop yet further from the busy public life he was obliged to lead. When the great aisled halls were built, the earlier hall became a private hall, but eventually that degree of privacy was not enough. The complex at Lincoln includes a small dining hall, with a stone sideboard at one end and a new chapel over it; the dining parlour would not have seated more than about a dozen, and was probably built by Bishop Alnwick (1436–49). A new kitchen and a solar tower for his private use were built at the same time. Bishop Bekington of Wells (1455–66) did exactly the same and his third hall (or dining room), with a parlour and a second kitchen, still survive.[11]

Involvement in national affairs of church and state obliged bishops from the twelfth century onwards to acquire a residence, usually called an inn, in London; they can be located from documents, but all have vanished except for remains in Southwark of Winchester House, and the chapel (St Etheldreda, Ely Place) of the palace of the bishops of Ely.[12] The latter had been bought by a bishop from his private means and given to the diocese – a not uncommon origin for such houses. Ralph Neville, bishop of Chichester (1223–45), built a residence on what is now the site of Lincoln's Inn and as the king's chancellor gave his title to Chancery Lane. Hereford bought an inn in Old Fish Street in 1234 and gave it to the diocese; Lichfield's residence was in Temple Bar (1304), Salisbury's in Fleet Street (1335) and Worcester's in the Strand.

Sanitation

A cathedral palace, even if used only occasionally, for instance for ordinations or diocesan synods, must have served as a model for the houses of the clergy and wealthier laity. It might be expected that while the bishop was in residence with a large household, of men and boys and sometimes women guests, elaborate sanitary provision would have been needed. The earliest privies were no doubt timber structures over pits and detached from the stone buildings; there is no parallel in palaces to the monastic reredorter with its row of seats over running water; perhaps since palaces were not occupied continuously, pits could be emptied and privy chambers aired when the household had departed. Henry III was most particular about sanitation in royal residences and when in 1251 he proposed to stay in the archbishop's palace at York, he ordered in advance a privy chamber twenty feet long 'with a deep pit' to be constructed next to the chamber he was to occupy. When c. 1220 Hugh of Welles completed the west hall at Lincoln begun by his predecessor, he had a stone-walled garderobe built as an attachment to the solar at the end of the hall.[13] Another bishop (perhaps Henry de Burghersh c. 1330) when Newark Castle was partially rebuilt had garderobes incorporated in the thickness of walls, with chutes to the outside, in the manner normal in castles. Privies were incorporated in the design of a palace with thinner walls, as at Southwell late in the fourteenth century, buttressed out like fireplaces. Southwell has the unique feature of a corner turret, adjacent to what is thought to be the bishop's private hall, with four privies arranged round a central shaft.[14]

Cathedral dignitaries

Round the new Norman cathedrals where the establishment was secular and not monastic, houses were required for the principal dignitaries (dean, precentor, treasurer and chancellor) and for the canons who made up the rest of the chapter. Some of these houses survive for the same reasons as do palaces; they were built in stone and have remained the property of the chapter. This was at first a matter of private enterprise and documents show how members of the chapter bought or built houses; by c. 1300 chapters retained control of houses left or given to them and embarked on an active policy of purchase. Of all the closes of secular cathedrals (Chichester, Exeter, Hereford, Lichfield, Lincoln, Salisbury, Wells and York) only the buildings at Lincoln, Salisbury and York have been comprehensively examined and even these are not all published. Three minsters in the diocese of York, cathedral-like in scale and collegiate in organization, were surrounded by canons' houses comparable with those of cathedrals, but their chapters had only a dean or provost at the head; at Southwell the canons' residences can be located, though they were largely rebuilt by lessees in recent centuries.[15] Unlike bishops' palaces, these houses were entirely private in purpose and resemble manor houses; they usually stood back from the street front and they only needed one hall. The late fifteenth-century deanery at Wells still has its gatehouse, outer court and the house built round an inner court; at Lincoln the Chancery [29], which has been on its present site

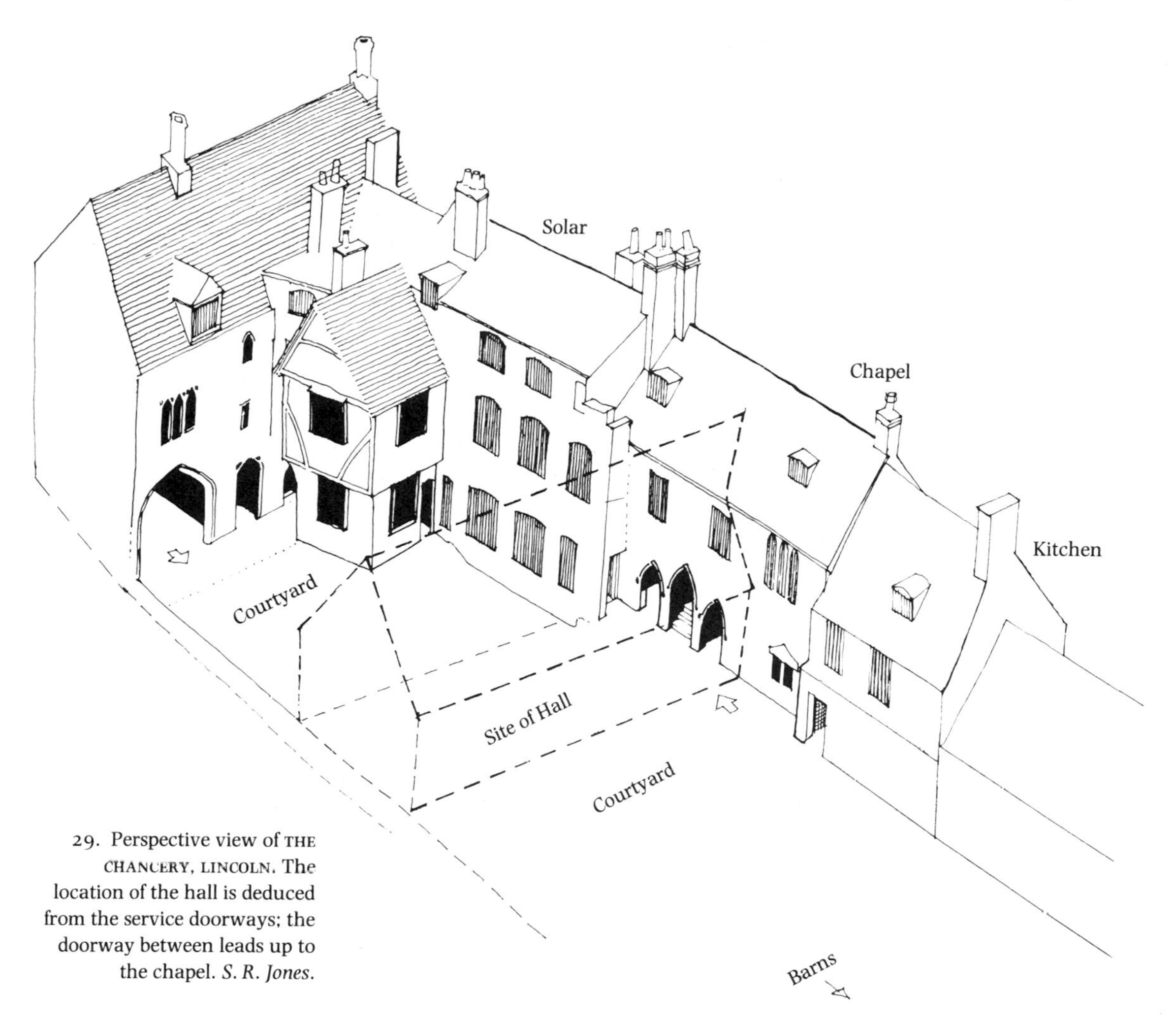

29. Perspective view of THE CHANCERY, LINCOLN. The location of the hall is deduced from the service doorways; the doorway between leads up to the chapel. *S. R. Jones.*

since 1321, has a carriage entrance below a chamber range of 1480–94; the hall separated an outer from an inner courtyard.[16]

From these buildings a composite picture can be put together of the house of a wealthy dignitary; as well as a grand hall (Salisbury) with appropriate fittings (Lincoln) there might be a private chapel (Lincoln) and a handsome great chamber with more chambers for guests or personal staff (Lincoln, Wells). Investigation in 1959 of the Old Deanery at Salisbury, which was threatened with demolition, showed that so much survived of the building of 1258–74 that it was reprieved and the hall restored.[17] Its original character, in spite of later alterations, could be seen or accurately deduced: a grand open roof, gabled windows rising above eaves level (as at Stokesay), three service doorways but no fixed screen to form a passage, a central hearth and a dais at the upper end.

It was big enough for generous hospitality, for the hall measured 9.4 m (31 ft) by 15.2 m (50 ft), and a survey of 1440 shows that it then had seven tables, the three largest being 5.5–7 m (18–23 ft) long, each with their benches. The Treasurer's House at Lincoln (known since the nineteenth century as the Priory) was built at about the same time, on a more modest scale. When the cathedral close was walled in 1285–1318, the circuit was slightly extended to include the house, and the service end was rebuilt as a tower on the wall, leaving the treasurer his buttery and pantry and giving him his only chamber on the first floor of the tower.[18] At the same time a stone buffet or sideboard with a carved side was installed between the service doorways. At Salisbury the deanery had from the beginning a cross-wing at the upper end with a great chamber over it.

The deaneries at Salisbury and Wells and the Lincoln chancery show the kinds of change common in the later Middle Ages in houses of this class, and similar at a more modest level to the change in palaces. The ground floor or cellar of the cross-wing at Salisbury was in the later fifteen century converted into a parlour by the insertion of a handsome fireplace and new windows. At the same time a small timber-framed parlour was added to the Lincoln chancery and a splendid great chamber, of brick with a stone oriel window, was built along the frontage of the site. The rebuilt deanery at Wells included the open hall, a parlour, a great chamber with oriel windows, and over it, unusually, a second floor with three guest chambers. Variations of terminology – between second or third hall in a palace and parlour in a dignitary's house – conceal parallel social changes of the same sort; the elaboration of the plan so that owners and their intimates could distance themselves from the rest of the masculine household. We shall see changes of the same sort in family homes.

At Lincoln, documents make it possible to locate canons' houses but no significant medieval remains now survive. At Salisbury, planting a new cathedral city involved a unique element of planning in the close. Land was of course allocated for the bishop's palace; plots were also set out by 1222 on the other three sides of the close, for 'fair houses of stone' for members of the chapter.[19] No sites were earmarked for particular dignitaries; we have seen how a dean gave to the chapter the house he had built facing the west front of the cathedral. Only at Southwell were particular houses round the minster tied to prebends named after the villages where lay the land forming their endowments.

One other form of residential building in cathedral cities needs to be mentioned, if only to indicate changing standards. Canons in secular cathedrals had originally lived a common life, like monks, though not subject to a rule: by the thirteenth century, as we have seen, they expected to occupy private houses. At the same time a body of vicars choral was emerging to deputize for canons at services, and from c. 1250 colleges for them began to be founded. In some cases no doubt this represented only a change of occupants of the same site. At York,[20] where a college was founded in 1252, and at Beverley and Ripon, the institution was known as the bedern, or house of prayer; elsewhere it was simply called a college of vicars choral. It contained a hall and kitchen, a chapel and separate rooms (cubicles at York) for the vicars. At York, the hall, built soon after 1248, survived and has recently been restored [18A]; the chapel also stands, though roofless. At Beverley, recent excavations have shown that the bedern south of the minster had an aisled hall, first with earth-fast arcade posts and later rebuilt with stone foundations. At Lincoln, the college was established c. 1310 in the form of a courtyard; the hall and kitchen have gone but the two storey lodgings on the south range are little altered; each vicar had one heated room with a garderobe or privy.[21] At Wells, the college was founded in 1334 on a long narrow site north of the cathedral; the existing buildings belong to the fifteenth century. It was developed as a street rather than a courtyard, closed at one end by the gateway with a first-floor hall and at the other by a chapel; each side of the street has two-storey buildings, in which each vicar had a heated ground-floor hall with a fireplace and over it a chamber with a privy, making forty-two dwelling units in all.[22] At Southwell buildings of the vicars' court with stone ground-floor walls and framing above are known from Grimm's drawing of 1775; the courtyard was rebuilt in 1787 in brick as a large house for the one residentiary canon, flanked by two pairs of semi-detached houses for vicars choral.[23] The vicars' closes at Chichester and Lichfield were each timber-framed originally [32].

Merchants' houses

So far we have been concerned with houses built by individuals of clearly identified status, many of them known by name. We now turn to houses of laymen who can rarely be identified; in later times they were associated at Southampton with kings John and Cnut and elsewhere with known members of the Jewish community. The one certainty is that stone houses of distinctive design were being built in medieval towns in the twelfth century; all had the living accommodation on the first floor, in most cases over a vaulted basement. Those who built them could afford to employ experienced master masons. The burgesses of Colchester built a moot hall c. 1160 (demolished in 1843) and obtained the services of a sculptor who also worked at Rochester cathedral and Dover priory.[24] The mason who designed the two Norman houses in Lincoln in c. 1170–80 [30] left no such individual mark on his buildings but had the original

30. JEW'S HOUSE, STEEP HILL, LINCOLN. The stonework of the side wall shows that it was two rooms deep.

31. GREEN DRAGON, WATERSIDE NORTH, LINCOLN. Large merchant's house of the fifteenth century on the river bank, now an inn.

idea of combining the head of the ground-floor doorway with the buttress for the fireplace in the hall upstairs. The Lincoln houses are important in the evolution of the house in that both were double piles – that is, were more or less square on plan and two rooms deep. Other double-pile houses of stone have been identified in Southampton and Stamford.[25] The wealth and importance of such Jews as Aaron of Lincoln and Jurnet

32. The rear of VICAR'S CLOSE, LICHFIELD, STAFFORDSHIRE.

of Norwich make it tempting to accept a Jewish origin for these stone houses but it cannot be proved in a single case and is probable only for Jurnet's House in Norwich.[26] Canterbury, Lincoln and York had the largest Jewish communities. We know that at Canterbury Jews were part of a group of men combining goldsmithing, the minting of currency and lending money; among those known to have lived in stone houses only one bore a Jewish name.

The status of a house with its first-floor rooms marked by decorative treatment went along with the convenience of having space at street level for a shop, workshop or warehouse. Surviving evidence often consists only of walls below street level, sometimes no doubt for an undercroft with timber posts (called samson posts) for joists and a boarded first floor. Recent research has shown that in a few towns vaulted undercrofts were numerous. Low-lying places like Hull, King's Lynn, Salisbury and York had none or very few; it is surprising that they have not been found in Exeter. Some undercrofts were at the level of the street, others sunk partly below ground; both forms may have been built in the twelfth century, at Colchester and Gloucester for example [33], but in later centuries they were more usually sunk below ground.[27] They were numerous in Coventry and according to documents were used mainly as taverns; that may have been their commonest function everywhere. Norwich still has more than sixty brick undercrofts [34], the earliest built c. 1350; they were primarily platforms on sloping sites for timber-framed houses to stand on.[28] Most were reached directly from the street and so could have been used separately from the house; some with an entry away from the street and from a ground-floor service room must have gone with the house. There were many elaborations in the size and plan

33 34

33. Ribbed barrel vault of stone, c. 1200, under 74–6 WESTGATE, GLOUCESTER. *NMR*.

34. Ribbed brick vault (late medieval) under 4 TOMBLAND, NORWICH. *Centre of East Anglian Studies, University of East Anglia.*

of undercrofts and variants in construction such as the use of timber for a front wall and side walls above ground; there must have been as many variations in use, including show room, stock room and craftsman's workshop. In Nottingham, standing on sandstone, it was not a matter of building but only of cutting cellars, rubbish pits and privies in the sandstone; a thousand years of such activity has left the rock below the medieval town riddled with caves of great complexity. One group was certainly used for tanning. While the sunk undercroft might form one tavern or shop, the raised ground floor might be used as another. At Chester this split-level development with access to both levels from the street led to the creation of a raised footway at the upper level (the Rows). Whether they were planned following a fire in 1278 or were a piecemeal redevelopment over centuries is still uncertain.[29]

In twelfth- and thirteenth-century town houses we can see the beginning of an insular tradition: halls on the ground floor. On the continent the lowest storey at ground level, often with an open arcade to the street, continued to be used for making and selling goods; living accommodation on the first floor was augmented by adding one or more floors above the *piano nobile*. In late medieval towns in this country the first-floor hall became rare, though more examples have come to light since Margaret Wood listed them in 1965.[30] The best known is the fourteenth-century house at Norwich which is now the Bridewell Museum; others include Vaughan's Mansion at Shrewsbury (c. 1300–50), Stone House in Much Park Street, Coventry, with a vaulted undercroft and the former Fox Inn, Low Petergate, York (fifteenth century, demolished 1956). The town

35. Drawing by H. O'Neill, c. 1825, of an aisled hall of stone in BALDWIN STREET, BRISTOL, being demolished. *Bristol Museum and Art Gallery.*

house continued to incorporate a hall open to the roof even when parts of it might have two or three storeys. It has been suggested that this represents a transfer to the town of a rural type of house, and certainly the growth of towns in medieval and modern Britain depended more on a flow of labour, skills and enterprise from the countryside than on natural growth of population. This explanation must not be pressed too hard. There are no true crucks in towns though there are some base-crucks; the aisled hall was common for manorial lords and ambitious freemen, but only one urban example can be named; Cogan House, Canterbury, was built c. 1200 with timber arcading; and Colston's House, Bristol (demolished 1961), had originally a stone hall with one aisle [35].

The fortified town house forms no part of this English development. The bishops of Lincoln and Salisbury got licences to crenellate their palaces, as did the dean of York for his house there; otherwise the list of licences includes only a few London instances: two episcopal inns, one residence of a royal valet and five merchants or citizens. This is a contrast with the towers of medieval Italian towns, and the tower houses of the Rhineland. Dutch and German towns such as Utrecht and Cologne have many houses of the fourteenth and fifteenth centuries of three storeys of brick or stone, finished with a parapet rising above the eaves and defensible in appearance if not in fact.[31] Most of the known tower houses in Scottish and Irish towns were presumably built in the sixteenth and seventeenth centuries, like those in the countryside. Boston's two fifteenth-century houses with solar towers (page 121) are located outside the borough. Houses in Bristol and Salisbury show that successful townsmen preferred an elegant and imposing interior to a formidable exterior; witness the hammer-beam roof of Balle's Place, Salisbury (page 44), and the later roofs of Canynge's and Colston's houses in Bristol.[32] The strong carpentry tradition of the west of England made possible these displays of mercantile success. In other provincial capitals, Norwich and York, no such expression was attempted. In Norwich, roofs such as those of Stranger's Hall (built by a merchant c. 1450), Suckling Hall and Dykerell's House are in the simpler tie-beam and crown-post idiom of eastern counties. In York the most splendid roofs are those of public and institutional buildings such as the Merchant Adventurers' and the Merchant Taylors' Halls; domestic roofs are even plainer than in Norwich.

Urban plans The planning of a town house depended on the size of the burgage plot: that is the area of land allocated for rent by the lord of the town, or by the burgesses themselves. At Oxford, plots in the main streets were 6–9 m (20–30 ft) wide and sometimes 60–90 m (200–300 ft) long; in the planned town of Ludlow the plots were of similar width and went back to service lanes midway between the main streets. There was variation in King's Lynn from widths of a mere 4 m (13 ft) up to 15 m (50 ft). In most towns, whether their layout was planned or an organic growth, burgage plots had a narrow frontage to the street but this varied from town to town and over time. The study of individual houses shows cases of plots divided into two or more, and of adjacent plots combined. It is impossible to find a single town house whose ground-floor plan has not been altered at some time; elucidation of the plan depends mainly on features away from the frontage and at upper levels. Very often identifying the former hall, from the character and extent of a roof that has survived alterations, is the key to the plan. The most extended plan was the courtyard form. In Salisbury the planned grid of streets of equal width, with few back lanes, meant that many merchants could live in courtyard houses filling the frontage and entered by a carriage way [36]. Elsewhere, the courtyard plan is more likely to be the result of accretion, as it is in Hampton Court, King's Lynn.[33] In either case, the plan links

36. Courtyard house in CRANE STREET, SALISBURY, WILTSHIRE, late fifteenth century.

the wealthy merchant's house with rural manor houses and with such institutions as colleges and monasteries. Differences arise in exploitation of a street frontage at ground level for shops and of a back range for warehouses and the like. Inns, such as the New Inn, Gloucester (1457), the White Hart, Newark-on-Trent (c. 1475), and the Saracen's Head, Southwell (c. 1500), naturally had a courtyard plan for access to stables. Courtyard houses were easily converted to inns in the later Middle Ages, and there are three such instances in Salisbury.

37. FLORE'S HOUSE, OAKHAM, RUTLAND, c. 1375, house at right-angles to the street.

Within the complex, the hall might be placed along one side of the courtyard (Hampton Court, King's Lynn) or occasionally between a first and a second yard (Courtenay House, Exeter and Suckling House, Norwich), a plan more common in the country and of the highest status. A hall in the front range on the street, as in 47 New Canal, Salisbury,

38. ABBOT'S HOUSE (so-called), BUTCHER'S ROW, SHREWSBURY, SHROPSHIRE, with houses over shop units. *NMR*.

39. GOVERNOR'S HOUSE, STODMAN STREET, NEWARK, NOTTINGHAMSHIRE, a merchant's house which had originally a carriage-width entrance (behind right-hand female figure). The first floor at the front (presumably over a shop) was one grand chamber with painted beams; the hall was behind it. Dendrochronology has now shown that this front range was built c. 1474.

suggests an owner who could forgo the advantage of letting shops.[34] In most cases the demand for shops [38] must have precluded using the frontage for a hall; there were as many as 200 shops in twelfth-century Canterbury, often tiny lockups or permanent stalls set beside the streets.[35] The halls of these houses are for the part most readily identified among later changes by lofty windows of high quality, a cross-passage, service doorways or a spere truss, but most clearly from the roof. Timbers blackened with soot are sometimes a matter of argument but when certain they imply a hall with an open hearth. It might be thought that on restricted urban sites, designing a house with a hall heated by a fireplace and chambered over would have become popular in the late Middle Ages, but examples are very rare; one[36] is Marshall's Inn, Cornmarket, Oxford, and another is the Governor's House, Newark [39]. Locating the hall in the plot may then show whether the solar or best chamber was over the service end or over a parlour at the upper end of the hall. A kitchen in these courtyard houses can rarely be identified, since it was detached and not part of the nuclear plan.

The vast majority of medieval houses were built on narrow plots and vary so much that no comprehensive classification of their plans has yet been produced. The width of the frontage is not a precise guide to the status of a house. William Canynge, the great Bristol merchant and ship owner (d. 1474), lived in Redcliff Street in a house of high quality occupying a frontage of only 8.5 m (28 ft), but the plot extended back more than 60 m (200 ft) to the riverside.[37] His three-unit house had a shop or service room at the front with a hall about 6.7 m (22 ft) wide and 10 m (33 ft) long behind it; not large, but with a splendid roof and heated by an open hearth, for the roof had a louvre. Beyond the hall, the third room had a fine tiled floor – perhaps the parlour. The house, 'by a deplorable piece of vandalism' was demolished in 1937 for road-widening; the floor-tiles are now in the British Museum. The house was well recorded, for it had long interested local historians, antiquaries and artists; William Worcestre (1415–85) described the tower or lodge on the riverside built by Canynge and there are good nineteenth-century drawings of the house in the Bristol City Art Gallery.

Whatever the position and plan of the house, such narrow-fronted properties were usually entered by a passage along one side under the front range of building leading to open space behind [39, 40]. There was great variety of choice in placing the open hall, provided it could be lit.

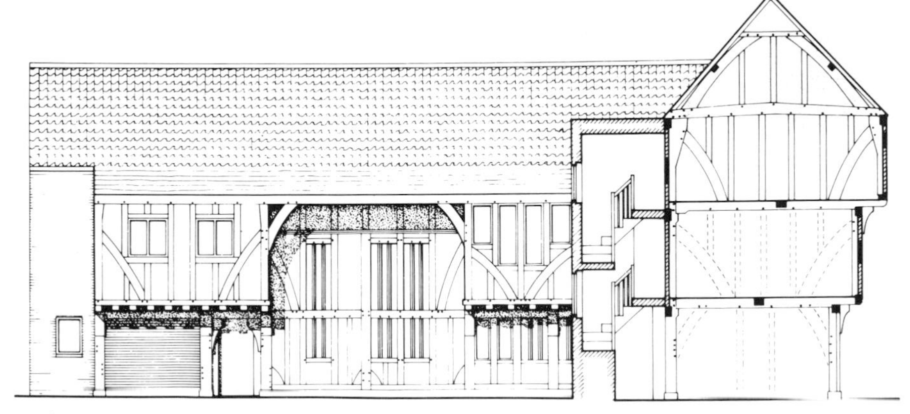

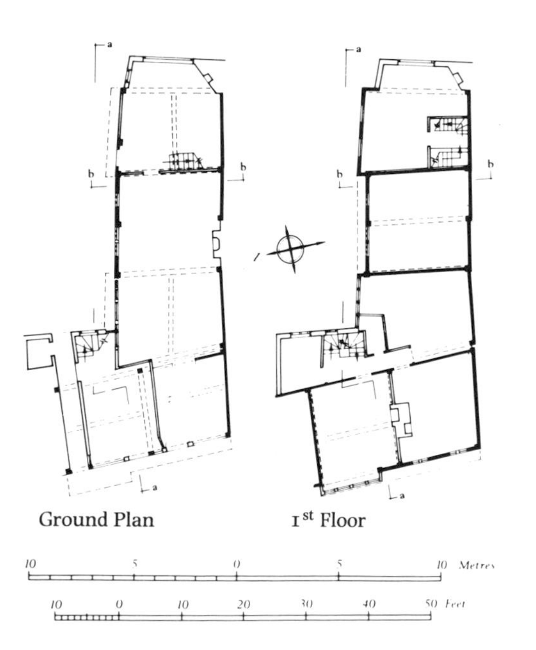

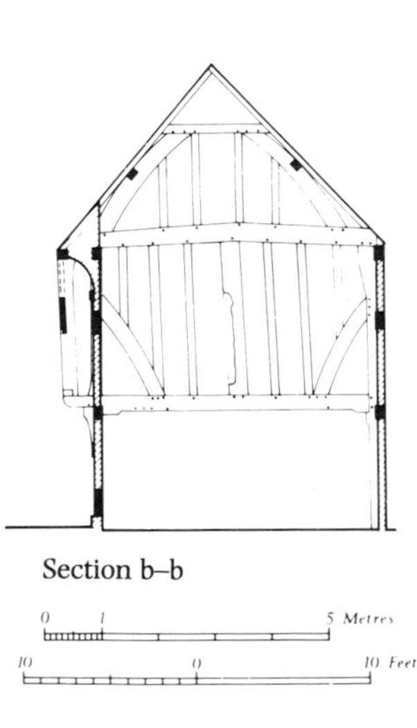

40. Section of 49, 51 GOODRAMGATE, YORK, showing three-storey front range and Wealden-type hall range behind it, reached by a side passage. *RCHM*.

It was rare for a hall to be placed along the street frontage with the entrance from a passage at its lower end, but there were examples in Coventry (Spon Street and Much Park Street) and elsewhere; the inference must be that the builder or tenant did not need a shop. The Spon Street houses [43] formed a terrace built in the fifteenth century to let, and are an ingenious adaptation of the Wealden design.

If the building was roofed parallel to the frontage, a convenient plan was to place a hall in a second parallel range behind, lighted from the yard, with a solar or chamber over the shops. Tackley's Inn (now 106–7 High Street, Oxford) was built thus in 1291–1300 by the parson of Tackley, an Oxfordshire village; it became later the first home of Oriel College. There were originally five shops on the ground floor with a passage through to the residential part.[38] Double-pile plans like this were not uncommon. The twelfth-century examples are widely dispersed but later ones are most common in the Midlands and about ten have been recorded in Coventry, dating from the fourteenth to early in the sixteenth century; three of them still stand in Spon Street.[39] Another common arrangement was for the hall to be placed behind the front range and along the side of the plot, so that lighting came from the yard. Structurally this might take the form of a simple rectangular block with a gable to the street; alternatively, the street range, roofed parallel to the frontage, formed a cross-wing to the hall. Carpenters eventually found more complex solutions to the demand both for an open hall and maximum accommodation; for instance, a third-storey range on the front, or a hall in which a chamber projected over part of the room, leaving not much more than a space for the smoke to escape from an open hearth [40, 42].

Medieval terraces

In the later Middle Ages the demand for small houses produced speculative development both by religious institutions and private individuals [41–4]. The rows and semi-detached pairs of Wealden houses in Coventry – twenty-eight have been identified – were presumably built by private enterprise, either to let or for sale [43]; the Holy Trinity Guild may have been involved.[40] At York the survival of records makes the role of the church quite explicit.[41] In 1316 the parish church of Holy Trinity was authorized to build a row of houses in the churchyard [41], the rents to be used to endow a chantry in the church. Though altered, Lady Row still stands, the oldest timber-framed buildings surviving in the city. Each house consisted simply of a ground-floor room, presumably to be used as a shop or workshop, with a chamber over; neither room had a fireplace. Twenty years later, four other parish churches promoted similar developments in part of the churchyard: All Saints Pavement, St Martin's Coney Street, St Michael Spurriergate and St Sampson Newgate. Of those, the houses built by St Sampson survive in part; there were originally ten or twelve, also consisting of one up and one down; the row was jettied on

41. Medieval terrace, LADY ROW, GOODRAMGATE, YORK, c. 1316. *York Archaeological Trust, M. Duffy.*

the street side and towards the churchyard. Fifteenth-century terraces of two-storey houses (i.e. shop and solar) have been noted in King's Lynn; at Salisbury there is a row of three in St Thomas's churchyard [44], and there is a contract of 1497 for a row of four in Canterbury.[42] Such houses must commonly have been the homes of independent craftsmen.

42. CHURCH STREET, TEWKESBURY, GLOUCESTERSHIRE, early sixteenth century.

In addition to infilling of churchyards, market places were encroached on as stalls assumed a permanent form with residential accommodation. This process can be observed at St Albans, for instance, where some of the buildings are three storeyed and jettied. In Shrewsbury, Greyhound Chambers in Butcher Row have lost their original shop openings to the ground floor, but the Abbot's House in the same street, wrongly said to have been the town house of the abbot of Lilleshall, is a similar development retaining its shops [38]. The rows of twenty-four small timber-framed houses built by an abbot of Tewkesbury [42] on a strip of land outside the precinct wall have a heated hall behind the shop,[43] but some of these terraces and market buildings have no trace of heating. The

43. Restored Wealden row in SPON STREET, COVENTRY, WARWICKSHIRE.

contract for St Martin's Row in Coney Street, York, refers to louvres, but the Holy Trinity Row had no fireplaces. There were plenty of cookshops in medieval towns, to judge from borough regulations forbidding them from selling warmed-up meat and fish; it is possible that poorer inhabitants as well as market-traders depended on them for an occasional taste

44. Three houses in SILVER STREET, SALISBURY, WILTSHIRE, built in 1471 as endowment of a chantry in the cathedral.

of cooked food. In Coventry, 'where the cooks lived' described the area at the central road intersection, and there is a Cooks Row in All Saints Churchyard at Bristol.

Neither existing buildings nor documents provide an adequate account of the housing of the poorer element in the town. Clothmaking was the most important industry in towns such as Lincoln, Salisbury and Stamford, and weavers came low in the social scale. In Winchester a row of four houses in Lower Brook Street, a part of the town where cloth was finished, consisted of one-roomed dwellings with mud walls; each had a hearth in one corner and a small sleeping-area screened off in another. On the fringes of Salisbury were tenements which may have held cottages with open ground (rack-closes) where cloth was laid out to dry.[44]

Studies of town houses have paid more attention to large boroughs with a regular system of burgage tenements than to small towns where a lord obtained a licence for a market and only occasionally sponsored a degree of planned development. A list of places in Sussex with a degree of urban status and function would include some now regarded as villages, such as Cuckfield, Midhurst, Pulborough and Robertsbridge. Where their houses have been surveyed, they are found to have a notable number of Wealden houses, as at Robertsbridge; the abbot of Battle built a row of Wealden houses in the little market town outside his gates.[45] In the seaports of Hastings and Rye the Wealden type predominates; they are tall in Hastings, because the central area was small with narrow plots; in Rye some of them are very small and built of poor timber. One Wealden there is only 4.2 m (14 ft) wide and in some the open bay of the hall is no more than 4.8–5.5 m (16–18 ft) long. Three-quarters of the men were involved with the sea and did not need work-space in the house. Inland, the cloth industry probably contributed most to the widest prosperity of Sussex towns in the later Middle Ages. The lord of the manor of Castle Combe (Wiltshire) in 1409–59 was Sir John Fastolf, the soldier-landowner who built Caister Castle (Norfolk) (page 101), and he was able to clothe his troops in red and white cloth made there. His agent, William Worcestre, made a list of the more than thirty houses built there by clothiers moving into the town,[46] but it has never been examined closely to see whether any of the houses can still be identified. The picturesque Arlington Row at Bibury (Gloucestershire) consists of seven cottages dating in their present guise from the seventeenth century, but a survey has shown that they represent the conversion of a medieval building connected perhaps with the cloth industry. To attract clothiers to his village of Wells (Somerset), an abbot of Glastonbury laid out a street leading to the church, and two rows of more or less uniform houses were built c. 1470; they await detailed examination.[47]

There was a yet lower stratum of urban society, men with no fixed employment, about whose housing we know nothing: porters at Lincoln waiting to carry goods up the hill from the riverside; men engaged occasionally to clean out ditches and privies. To a landlord they might be squatters, called 'unthanks' in twelfth-century Canterbury; in a tax assessment for Colchester in 1296 and 1301 they are shown to possess no goods worth taxing.[48]

Notes

1 *King's Works*, I, 48; II, 896, 898.
2 *Ant. J.*, 52(1972), 127, n. 3.
3 W.M. Mackenzie, *Medieval Castles in Scotland* (1927), ch. 5.
4 BE, *London 2: South*, 583.
5 F.R. du Boulay, *The Lordship of Canterbury* (1966), 260–1; J. Webb (ed.), *A Roll of the Household Expenses of Richard de Swinfield ...* (Camden Soc. 62, 1855).
6 P.A. Faulkner, 'Domestic planning from the twelfth to the fourteenth centuries', *Archaeol. J.*, 115 (1958), 163–80.
7 M.E. Wood, *The English Medieval House* (1965), 124.
8 *Archaeol. J.*, 131 (1974), 340–4; 107 (1950), 108–9.
9 W. Horn and E. Born, *The Plan of St Gall* (1979), I, 276.
10 W. Urry, *Canterbury under the Angevin Kings* (1967), 173.
11 H. Chapman *et al.*, *Excavations at the Bishop's Palace Lincoln* (1975), 11; *Archaeol. J.*, 107 (1950), 110.
12 F.M. Stenton, *Norman London* (Historical Association, 1934), 26–32; J. Schofield, *The Building of London* (1984), 65, pls 62, 74.
13 H. Chapman, 13.
14 N. Summers, *A Prospect of Southwell* (1974), 50–3.
15 Summers, ch. 6.
16 *Archaeol. J.* (1950), 110–11; Stanley Jones *et al.*, *Survey of Ancient Houses in Lincoln* (1984), 23–32 and fig. 19.
17 N. Drinkwater, 'The Old Deanery, Salisbury', *Ant. J.*, 44 (1964), 41–59.
18 Jones, 1–14.
19 C.R. Everett, 'Notes on the ... houses in the Close of Sarum', *Wilts. Archaeol. Mag.*, 50 (1944), 425–45.
20 RCHM, *York*, 5, 57–61.
21 Wood, 180.
22 *Archaeol. J.*, 107 (1950), 113; L.S. Colchester, *Wells Cathedral, a History* (1982), 215–7.
23 Summers, pls XL, XLIII.
24 P. Crummy, *Aspects of Norman and Anglo-Saxon Colchester* (CBA Research Report 39, 1981), 63–7.
25 P.A. Faulkner, in C. Platt and R. Coleman-South, *Excavations in Medieval Southampton 1963–69* (1975), 56–124.
26 V.D. Lipman, *The Jews of Medieval Norwich* (1967), 27–32.
27 P.A. Faulkner, 'Medieval undercrofts and town houses', *Archaeol. J.*, 123 (1966), 120–35.
28 *Ex inf.* Alan Carter of the Centre of East Anglian Studies, University of East Anglia.
29 *J. Chester Archaeol. Soc.*, 45 (1958), 1–42.
30 Wood, ch. 2.
31 C.L. Temminck Groll, *Middeleevwse Stenen Huizen te Utrecht* (The Hague, 1963), 169–72.
32 RCHM *Salisbury*, I, 135–7; I.L.L. Foster and L. Alcock (eds), *Culture and Environment* (1963), 470–8.
33 Foster and Alcock (eds), 448–55.
34 *Salisbury*, I, no. 177.
35 Urry, 170–1.
36 *Med. Archaeol.*, 6–7 (1962–3), 223.
37 Foster and Alcock (eds.), 470–3.
38 W.A. Pantin, 'Medieval English townhouse plans', *Med. Archaeol.*, 6–7 (1962–3), 217–9.
39 M.W. Barley, 'The double-pile house', *Archaeol. J.*, 136 (1979), 254–5.
40 S.R. Jones and J.T. Smith, 'The Wealden houses of Warwickshire and their significance', *Trans. Proc. Birmingham Archaeol. Soc.*, 79 (1960–1), 24–35.
41 RCHM *York*, 5, 143–5, 171, lxxiii; *Archaeol. J.*, 137 (1980), 86–137.
42 V. Parker, *Making of King's Lynn* (1971), 66; L.F. Salzman, *Building in England* (1952), 554; D. Portman, *Exeter Houses 1400–1700* (1966), 3.
43 *Country Life*, 26 October 1972.
44 *Ant. J.*, 48 (1968), 261, 265–6; *Salisbury*, 1, xlii-iii.
45 *Historic Buildings in Eastern Sussex* (Rape of Hastings Archit. Survey, 1, 1977), 3–5.
46 J.H. Harvey (ed.), *William Worcestre Itineraries* (1969), 405–6.
47 *EVH* 157–8; *Med. Archaeol.*, 3 (1959), 150.
48 *EFC*, 18–19; Urry, 171.

5 *Royal and Aristocratic Houses in the Countryside*

The houses of the greatest and wealthiest of the land are the best documented and were the best built; their remains are therefore the easiest to identify, to date and put into their social context. They served as a model for lesser men both in their planning and in their use of particular materials, either for display or for technical reasons. We are concerned with the residences of those whose territorial possessions were numerous and extensive, and who as a matter of course kept up more than one house. They had castles, as well as fortified manor houses, and also manor houses not evidently fortified at all; these classes of residence shade into one another.

The History of the King's Works for 1066–1485 contains accounts of 150 royal castles and eighty-six royal houses.[1] Of the castles, only about twenty-six remained for long in the king's hands and were continuously maintained. Some such as Odiham and Rockingham became part of the dower of a medieval queen or like Otford were granted away into private hands. Others retained by the crown in the later Middle Ages were thought to have no military value and were allowed to decay. The royal apartments at Winchester were not rebuilt after a fire in 1302 destroyed them, and of such apartments in other provincial castles, none survives to a comprehensive degree except at Portchester (below, page 93). Castles in county towns such as Cambridge, Colchester, Hereford, Leicester and Oxford were used for meetings of the shire court and contained the county gaol and a house for the sheriff.

Of the eighty-six royal houses, most were short-lived. They were primarily hunting lodges and many were built of timber; if a monarch's liking for a particular forest or its house was not inherited by his successor, the house might be given away or allowed to decay. Henry III and Edward I had twenty or so houses; by 1485 the number was reduced to four (Clarendon, Clipstone, Havering and Woodstock), though twenty-five other houses had been in royal possession for short or long periods. Already during the Middle Ages the houses most remote from Westminster such as Feckenham (Worcestershire) and Burstwick (Yorkshire) were

45. Pentice in the cathedral precinct, CANTERBURY, KENT. A very rare survival, fourteenth century. *Canterbury Archaeological Trust, P. Blockley.*

abandoned in favour of nearer residences. Even so, of all the royal houses only Eltham [53], originally in Kent and now in greater London, still preserves one of its buildings, the hall built in 1479–83; at Guildford, not much further from Westminster, even the site of the royal house cannot be clearly identified. Some palace sites have recently been excavated in part: Cheddar (Somerset), Clipstone (Nottinghamshire), Greenwich, Writtle (Essex) and King's Langley (Buckinghamshire). Two – Havering (Essex) and the Castle at Hertford – are known from Tudor surveys; the buildings have since disappeared. In a few more instances, the site is known from surviving earthworks: Hall Yard, east of the church at King's Cliffe (Northamptonshire), Moat Bank near Gentleshaw church (Staffordshire) and the site of a hunting lodge called Radmore in Cannock Chase. It is clear that royal castles and other residences were at least as likely as those of ordinary men to be abandoned or rebuilt.

Henry III's personal interest in architectural matters left behind a wealth of documentary evidence, unique in its detail; the buildings themselves have largely vanished. He spent large sums on seven residential castles; apart from Windsor, only his ceremonial aisled hall (1222–35) at Winchester remains. He was equally busy at Westminster, at his manor houses of Clarendon, Guildford, Havering and Woodstock, and at several hunting lodges. He was mainly concerned to provide more chambers, wardrobes and privies for himself and his family; to see that they were insulated with wainscotting and glazing and suitably decorated, and to ensure that passing about a haphazard multiplication of buildings would be done in the privacy and shelter of alleys and pentices [45]. Such tasteful but unprofessional initiatives were inconsistent with domestic planning.

Bishops' rural residences

Medieval bishops are known to have had more than 150 residences;[2] in Henry VIII's time Leland often described them as palaces (see page 60), whether rural manor houses or residences adjacent to a cathedral. As a group, bishops' houses are easily identified from diocesan records, from which itineraries of episcopal journeys can be compiled; unlike a king or a lay magnate, a bishop could not dispose of the endowments of his office, so episcopal manors constituted an unchanging group of properties from early Norman times until Tudor monarchs and magnates seized many of them. In a few instances a bishop acquired a manor and built a residence from his private means and then gave it to his diocese: Grey, archbishop of York, bought Bishopthorpe in 1241; Bourchier, archbishop of Canterbury, bought Knole in 1456. At some time the bishop of Carlisle bought the manor of Horncastle (Lincolnshire) although he had a residence at Melbourne south of Derby, much more directly on a route to London from his remote diocese. Two important residences of medieval bishops, Somerton Castle (Lincolnshire) and Acton Burnell Castle (Shropshire), were private and not diocesan.

Partly because of continuous ownership, partly because of the wealth of the builders, something remains of nearly half these residences. Those of the bishop of London situated in what is now greater London or Essex have disappeared except for Fulham and Much Hadham (Hertfordshire). Of the bishop of Chichester's four, three survive in some measure (Amberley Castle, Cakeham and Chichester), while Aldingbourne has vanished; of the bishop of Lichfield's seven, something survives at Beaudesert and Eccleshall. Three of the bishop of Worcester's houses (Bishops Cleeve, Ripple and Withington) became parsonage houses in modern times. A large diocese required a large number of residences for the bishop to be able to oversee diocesan affairs, and so Lincoln had at one time or other seventeen, including three castles. Winchester and Worcester each had a similar total number, reflecting in Winchester's case the great wealth of the bishopric, to which belonged Taunton Castle and manors in Somerset. To judge from itineraries, bishops used more of their rural manor houses in the thirteenth century than later. The bishop of Lincoln ceased after the thirteenth century to stay at Louth (Lincolnshire), and Fingest (Buckinghamshire) disappears from his itineraries; Spaldwick (Huntingdonshire) was also abandoned, no doubt because it was near a favourite residence, Buckden. Bishop Bransford of Worcester (1339–49) made use of fifteen manor houses; by c. 1450 his successor spent money only on nine, including the palace at Worcester, Hartlebury Castle and an inn in the Strand.[3] The poorest bishops had only four (Chichester and Rochester) or five (Carlisle) residences, and Rochester in fact used principally two, Halling and Trottiscliffe.

If kings in the later Middle Ages preferred to make most use of residences within easy reach of London, medieval bishops were less free or inclined to spend their time and energies with the confines of a diocese, for they were heavily involved in affairs of state. In addition to an inn in London, some found it convenient to have a manor house to be used on journeys to and from the capital: Worcester at Hillingdon (Middlesex), Salisbury at Sonning[4] and Exeter at Faringdon (both Berkshire).

Travelling as they did with large retinues, some bishops chose sites where they could move provisions and staff by water. Salisbury's manor house at Sonning was on the bank of the Thames; Ely's house at Fen Ditton (Cambridgeshire), licensed for crenellation in 1276, stood in a moated enclosure of 5 acres (recently destroyed) near the Cam, and a fragment of the house still stands; there is evidence of Thomas Arundel (1353–1414) moving baggage there by water.[5] Durham had a manor house at Howden (Yorkshire), and another at Riccall only eleven miles away, both on the Ouse; Riccall was rebuilt as a farmhouse in the eighteenth century. Part of the stone hall at Howden survives, long neglected but recently repaired. From Riccall, the next village up stream is Cawood, where York had a fortified manor house of which a fine gatehouse remains, built in Tadcaster stone by Kempe (1426–51), and alongside it is a two-storey range in brick, perhaps originally lodgings for staff. At Laneham (Nottinghamshire), a Trent-side village where York had a manor house much used in the thirteenth century, there is no trace of a moat but the Georgian manor house stands on the very bank of the river.

Bishops preferred, when affairs took them to their cathedral cities, to stay a few miles away. Most of them found themselves at one time or another at loggerheads with the canons or monks who ruled in their cathedrals, so York acquired Bishopthorpe, Lincoln Nettleham and Norwich Thorpe. Wells preferred Banwell and Exeter Bishop's Clyst; the bishops of St David's developed Lamphey, less than four miles from the cathedral and its grand palace, and made there a park of 144 acres.[6] The palace at Hereford was said to be in ruins in 1404, and so cannot have been much used.[7]

York had three ancient minsters in his diocese, Ripon, Beverley and Southwell, and there had been houses alongside each minster since before the Conquest; the archbishop in the thirteenth and early fourteenth centuries preferred to stay at Laneham when he was in Nottinghamshire and at Bishop Burton, three miles west of Beverley, when he was in the East Riding. Neither at Laneham nor Bishop Burton is there now any trace of the archbishop's manor house, and his Southwell house [46] was rebuilt late in the fourteenth century (pages 86, 98). A bishop, like a king, could afford to indulge personal preferences, and so the pattern revealed by itineraries changes from age to age.

In most cases the remains of these houses are fragmentary but there is enough evidence – topographical, documentary, architectural – for a composite picture. The rural manor house stood next to the parish

46. ARCHBISHOP'S PALACE, SOUTHWELL, NOTTINGHAMSHIRE, looking south from the tower of the Minster. His hall (remodelled in 1908 as a residence for modern bishops) was to the right of the camera, his second hall in the opposite (south-east) corner, his private apartments in the east range with a chapel in the north-east corner.

church, in a few cases evidently built by the bishop himself, as at Bishop's Canning and Potterne (Wiltshire) in the diocese of Salisbury; at East Meon (Hampshire) Henry de Blois, bishop of Winchester, not only built a splendid church but equipped it with a marble font, like the one in his cathedral, imported from Tournai. Beyond the manor house, often enclosed by a moat, lay the bishop's park, for some rural residences such as Bishop Auckland (Durham), Scrooby (Nottinghamshire) and Stow (Lincolnshire) started as hunting lodges; the opportunity for hunting evidently remained an appropriate amenity. At Beverley and Southwell the existence of a park from at least the twelfth century still influences the topography of those places; at Southwell the archbishops eventually made two parks in the parish [47] and at Beverley and Ripon, parks (in the plural) are still marked on the map.[8] In some villages such as Blockley (Gloucestershire) the location of a park is now the only hint of where the manor house stood. At Lyddington (Rutland) part of the bishop of Lincoln's manor house still stands, converted into almshouses in 1602 by Lord Burghley; there is a battery of fishponds nearby and the park was on the edge of the parish.[9]

No surviving manor house shows how a bishop could shelter the size of household he is known to have maintained. Alexander, bishop of Lincoln 1123–48, never travelled 'without so vast a band of followers that all men marvelled'; in 1179 pope Alexander III decreed that no bishop on a visitation should have a retinue of more than forty or fifty men, and canon law later reduced the number to thirty. The will of bishop Swinfield of Hereford in 1289 contained legacies to nearly sixty persons, William of Wykeham's (d. 1404) to one hundred and fifty, and

47. Map of the parish of SOUTHWELL, NOTTINGHAMSHIRE, belonging to the archbishop of York, who had two parks there (and two others in adjacent parishes). The inset shows the Minster with the palace (1) and the park south of it. Land north and west of it was allocated to prebendaries, all of whose houses can be identified; there were also colleges of vicars choral (2) and chantry priests (3). The small market town grew up north of the Minster, with a narrow market place (5, now built over). The Saracen's Head (4) is a large courtyard inn built c. 1500.

Thomas Brenton's of Rochester (d. 1389) to twenty-nine. Thomas Arundel's household while he was bishop of Ely (1373–88) numbered nearly eighty, but he did not always move with such a number; when he was at his London inn in Holborn he left some of his household at Totteridge.[10] A rural manor house may have been used more by estate officials holding a manor court, auditing accounts or seeing to repairs of farm buildings. The bishop of Winchester's small manor house at Rimpton (Somerset) was used on journeys to Taunton by the bishop's steward, by the constable of the castle and occasionally by the bishop himself.[11] The liberty of Hexham (Northumberland) belonged to the archbishops of York, who built there a tower house for the use of the steward and also a prison.

Robert Grosseteste, soon after he became bishop of Lincoln in 1235, composed a set of rules for the management of a large estate and the household of its owner;[12] his rules evidently met a widespread need, for they exist in a dozen copies made before c. 1350. He prescribed how his officers were to dress and behave, what their duties were in the hall, how the company was to be seated and served. As for the lord or lady, 'order that your dish be so refilled and heaped up, especially with the light

48. The bishop of Chichester's manor house at CAKEHAM, SUSSEX, with part of a thirteenth-century first-floor hall and a brick solar or watch tower of c. 1520.

courses, that you may courteously give from your dish to right and left at high table and to whom else it pleases you.'

The few remains of bishops' residences of the twelfth and thirteenth centuries suggest no more than a hall and chamber plan, sometimes with a first-floor hall (Amberley and Cakeham [48] (West Sussex), West Tarring (Canterbury)). At Norham Castle (Northumberland) the first stone building may well have been a first-floor hall (like that at Richmond Castle), later absorbed in a stone keep. Norman bishops of Durham built aisled halls at Bishop Auckland and Howden, and Grosseteste of Lincoln another at Buckden (Huntingdonshire) before 1254. There were two halls at Saltwood Castle (Kent) after archbishop Courtenay began in 1382 to make it his principal residence and at Lamphey where bishop Gower built a second hall in 1327–47. When William Rede in 1377 got licence to crenellate Amberley [49], the original first-floor hall and chamber block were retained for his private apartments, and a new hall placed to separate an outer from an inner or private court.[13] Similarly at Sonning (Berkshire), bishops of Salisbury retained a thirteenth-century two-storey block with its first floor hall or chamber at the end of a new hall.[14] A bishop of Worcester in c. 1250 built a stone manor house at Bishop's Cleeve (Gloucestershire) which has survived because it became the

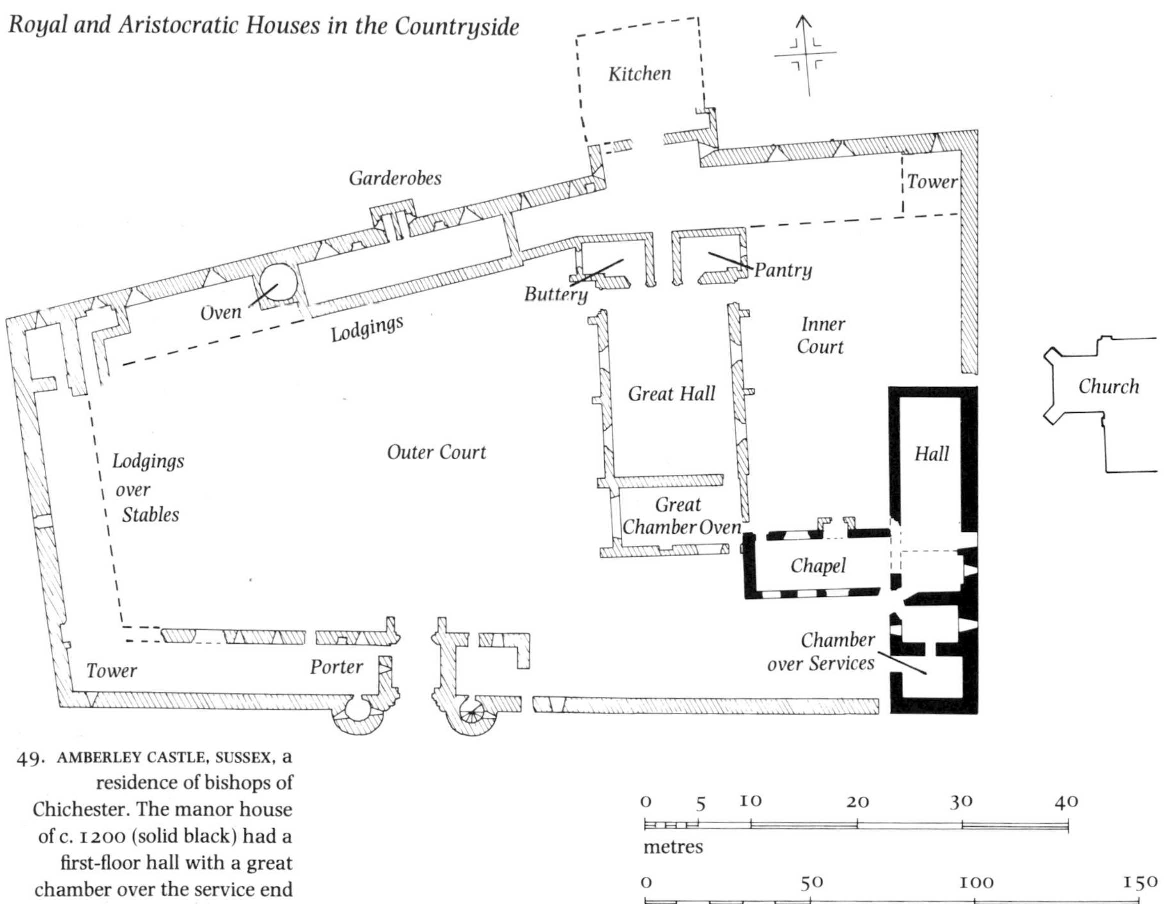

49. AMBERLEY CASTLE, SUSSEX, a residence of bishops of Chichester. The manor house of c. 1200 (solid black) had a first-floor hall with a great chamber over the service end and a chapel. Bishop William Rede obtained in 1377 a licence to crenellate it and built (hatched) a courtyard castle with gatehouse and corner towers, lodgings (no doubt timber-framed) over stables. A great hall with a solar was built to divide the outer or lower court from an inner, private court. The parish church stands about 7.6 m (25 ft) east of the earlier hall. *After W. D. Peckham.*

parsonage house after the Reformation. Bishop's Cleeve belongs to a different world from the buildings of Robert Burnell, a king's clerk who became chancellor of England in 1274 and bishop of Bath and Wells a year later. He built a great new aisled hall for the palace at Wells, together with a new chapel; on the family manor at Acton Burnell (Shropshire) he built what is known as a castle, and indeed obtained in 1284 a licence to fortify it. It was in fact a crenellated manor house, not a castle.[15]

Castles as residences

It is impossible to quantify in a similar way the residences of lay grandees. Castles with mottes (i.e. built before 1216) have been counted (741) and mapped but the large number reflects the 'overriding necessity for speedy fortification and digging in' following the Norman invasion, and then the anarchy of Stephen's reign, rather than any aspect of housing.[16] The stone keep or donjon evolved out of the first-floor hall within a fortified enclosure and was certainly designed for residential use; plans of more than sixty are illustrated in *Norman Castles in Britain*. Very few of them still present a clear picture of the residential accommodation. Compared with the years 1066–1216, few entirely new castles were built in the later Middle Ages. To an extent rarely recalled, the great castles and fortified houses of later times represent a rebuilding. At Caernarvon, Edward I's castle, begun in 1283, incorporated in the upper ward the motte of a Norman castle built by Earl Hugh of Chester before 1100 and levelled since 1870.[17] Recent excavations at South Wingfield (Derbyshire) have shown that Ralph Cromwell's fortified house of 1440–50 replaced a manor house built after demolition of a motte and stone buildings. At Haddon (Derbyshire) there was a house in 1170, but the present structure is basically of the mid-fourteenth century.[18]

It is usual to think of medieval castles as private fortresses (though they were rarely put to a military test) which incidentally contained residential quarters, described in contemporary records as the houses within the castle; that is, the term houses referred indiscriminately to residential as distinct from military constructions. Two royal palaces, Westminster and Clarendon (Wiltshire) and especially the latter, present a picture of royal residences of the twelfth and thirteenth centuries as a random assemblage of buildings[19] 'like unrelated counters tossed at random onto a board', but there is a group of royal and episcopal residences, all within castles, in the form of courtyards more or less closed, and built within a century (c. 1107–1204). No such houses are to be found in the rest of the thirteenth century; they are therefore an aspect of Norman and Angevin castle building. Whether, like the stone keep or donjon, the courtyard house in the castle was a Norman import is at present unknown; stone towers of the tenth and eleventh century are now recognized in France, not only in Normandy but as far south as the Loire, but no courtyard houses of comparable date have been found.

Except for the latest of them (La Gloriette at Corfe) these early courtyard houses were built by a group of men related by blood or closely connected by affairs of state:[20] Henry de Blois, bishop of Winchester, nephew of Henry I and younger brother of Stephen, built Wolvesey Castle at Winchester (c. 1130–40 and c. 1170) and Bishop's Waltham Castle (c. 1135 and c. 1170–80). Roger of Salisbury, bishop of Salisbury 1107–39 and Henry I's principal minister, built the courtyard house within the inner bailey at Old Sarum while the castle was in his custody (before 1135) and it closely resembles in plan the house he had built for himself in his castle at Sherborne. Alexander, bishop of Lincoln 1125–48, was the nephew of Roger of Salisbury; his castles of Banbury, Newark and Sleaford may well have had similar courtyard houses. At New Windsor, where William I had built a motte and bailey castle on a chalk cliff commanding the Thames valley and taking its name from a Saxon royal estate nearby, the 'King's houses' in the upper ward were the work of

Henry II; they lay round a courtyard or herb garden.[21] There was usually a pentice or covered walk round the interior. John's building of 1201–4 in the inner bailey at Corfe was known from at least 1280 as 'La Gloriette' (pavilion) and was an elegant and sophisticated house, entered by a tower-porch, with all the principal rooms on the first floor; only the location of the chapel remains uncertain.

In all these royal palaces, the courtyard house represented a degree of withdrawal from the public life of the court, focused on William II's great hall at Westminster or the 'king's house' of Henry I in the outer bailey at Corfe. They reflect the fact that the bureacracy of government was evolving out of the business conducted in the chamber where the king slept and the wardrobe next door where his clothes hung. The king was beginning to duplicate the accommodation designed for himself; La Gloriette had a chamber and a parlour for the queen, and at Windsor Henry III built another courtyard complex in 1235–41 for the queen and the royal children.[22] He had then just completed a new set of apartments for himself, in the outer ward, alongside the existing great hall and also planned round a courtyard; its south range was occupied by a new chapel and the courtyard survives as the cloister of the collegiate church of St George, rebuilt by Edward III in 1348. Henry III spent well over £10,000 on building at Windsor.

The aristocratic household

The households of the greatest tenants of a feudal king – barons, bishops, abbots – resembled those of the king himself; they were formal and highly organized masculine institutions managed by officers often bearing the same titles as his. The most explicit evidence comes not from the buildings but from charters.[23] In 1215 a dispute between the abbot of Westminster and one of his tenants, Ivo of Deene (Northamptonshire), was resolved in a fashion which shows both the burden of entertaining a superior and the life style of a great abbot. The latter had to give a fortnight's notice of his intended visit; on the day,

> seven servants of the abbot shall precede him, to whom shall be given charge of seven departments of the house; namely, to the seneschal the charge of the hall, to the chamberlain the custody of the chamber, to the pantler the custody of the dispense and the bread, to the butler the custody of the butlery and the drink, to the usher the custody of the door, to the cook the custody of the kitchen, to the marshal the custody of the marshalsea [stables].

Ivo and his men were to receive honourably the abbot and the men coming with him and to find food, drink and other necessaries proper to honourable entertainment, and at the end Ivo was to tip the seven servants; if the abbot wished to stay more than twenty-four hours, he was to buy 'at a just price' whatever he had. The larger of the guest houses at Fountains, built in the twelfth century in the form of a first-floor hall about 22 m (72 ft) long by 7.3 m (24 ft) wide with an attached garderobe (i.e. latrine) block, shows that an abbot at home could house his guests as he expected to be housed when travelling.

These residences of the greatest in the land had to accommodate not only the owner, whether a king, a bishop or a secular magnate, but what may be called a compound household, varying in size but invariably large, each of the principal officers having his own official and personal staff, requiring in effect a separate range of accommodation. To see how such buildings functioned is a matter of identifying the purpose and status of rooms and their relation to each other: kitchen and chapel usually serving the whole; halls and associated chambers for household units with appropriate heating and access to privies; lastly, service rooms. The household units of the owner and his principal officers may be graded according to positions, size, architectural treatment and the number and quality of associated chambers. There are inevitable uncertainties: for example, whether a large heated room should be classed as a hall, a great chamber or (later in the medieval period) a parlour. The room below a first-floor hall is often considered to be a lower hall, for the lower ranks of the household; that seems accurate when it has a fireplace, as at Wressle Castle (Yorkshire), built c. 1380, but in Richard II's apartments in Portchester Castle, built a few years later, the two service rooms below the hall have no heating and so their use remains uncertain [50].

Throughout the thirteenth century, the houses, royal or baronial, within a great castle remained separate establishments, six or seven of them at Corfe, three placed round the curtain of the lower bailey at Chepstow (1270–1300), a principal and eight others at Caerphilly, begun in 1271. Concentric defences as at Caerphilly and the royal castle of Beaumaris (1295–8) brought the residence closer together and even facilitated a degree of integration, but in the last resort the solution of problems military and domestic remained separate. Even if no royal apartments survive in Welsh castles, the gatehouse at Harlech (1283–9) [51] is complete enough to show how the constable was housed; indeed Master James of St George probably lived in it while he was constable in 1290–3 as well as master of the works.[24]

Castles in the fourteenth and fifteenth centuries

The ancient way of life in which a king or magnate was constantly on the move, keeping a personal eye on dispersed estates and staying long enough to consume their surplus produce, was no longer appropriate to an age when commodities of greater variety could be transported considerable distances. Great men certainly expected higher standards of comfort and convenience in a favourite residence if not in a lodge used for an occasional hunting holiday or for a day's retreat from formality. The size of the household was increasing, as was the elaboration of its

50. Richard II's apartments at PORTCHESTER CASTLE, HAMPSHIRE, built 1396–9 in the inner bailey. The porch led up to the first-floor hall; the kitchen was to the left and the great chamber to the right.

ritual. A potent factor for royalty was the increasing centralization of personal government, which made Westminster more important and residences within easy reach of London more convenient: Eltham [53], a favourite residence in the fourteenth and fifteenth centuries; Gravesend, Kennington, Sheen and especially Windsor. Edward III spent £51,000 on Windsor, the highest recorded expenditure on any medieval building in England[25], but owing to changes in later times it is no longer a clear example of domestic planning for a medieval king.

Portchester is more informative.[26] Richard II in 1396–9 rebuilt the domestic lodgings there at a cost of over £1,700 as the culmination of work designed against French attacks. His palace [50] stands against the south and west walls of the twelfth-century inner bailey. It has a first-floor hall entered by a porch with a chamber over it. The windows to the left of the porch represent a first-floor service room with a chamber above, and beyond it was the kitchen, open to the roof. From the upper end of the hall there was access to the private apartments, with a great chamber larger and more splendid than the hall, and to several other chambers; the private chapel was built against the Norman keep. All the accommodation must have been used when the king was in residence: the Norman keep, although its first-floor hall had no fireplace; the two gatehouses into the outer bailey, both enlarged in the fourteenth century and made more comfortable, and the constable's lodgings in the north-east corner of the bailey. The last had been rebuilt in 1380 with a first-floor hall against the wall and four storeys of chambers in Assheton's Tower. No residential buildings of consequence stood in the outer bailey. After 1399 the castle was virtually abandoned as a royal residence; constables kept the building in order but no further work was done on them, and so the remains of royal apartments are still capable of interpretation.

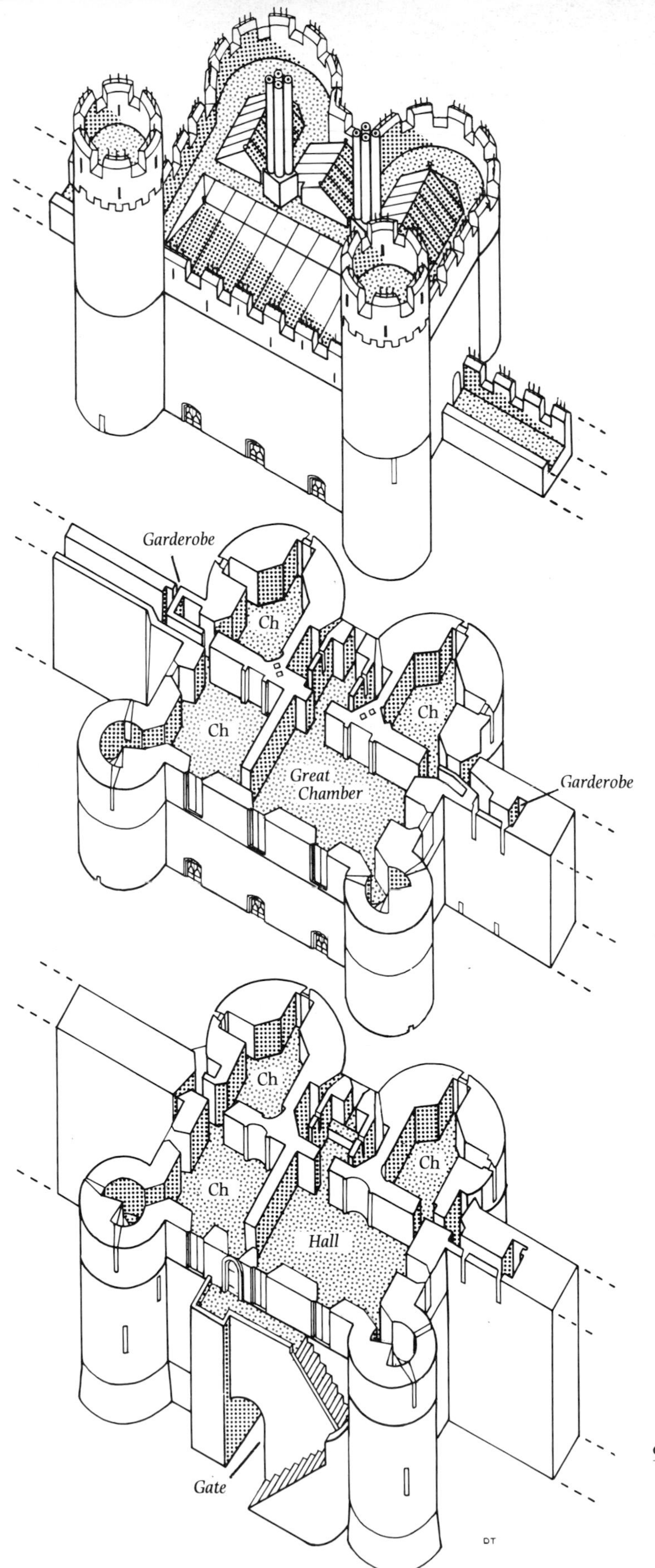

51. The gatehouse of HARLECH CASTLE, MERIONETH, designed by Edward I's master mason, James of St George, and built 1283–9. Exploded drawing to show the accommodation on the first and second floors. Two stacks of round chimneys were the loftiest feature. *After C. R. Peers.*

At Portchester Richard II built within the existing castle with its Roman walls and Norman keep. At Goodrich (Herefordshire), built by the Valence earls of Pembroke, the existing keep was retained in the rebuilding; within the closed square of the bailey the buildings represent a total integration of defensive with residential provision.[27] Here and at Bodiam (Sussex), Bolton (Yorkshire) [52] and Maxstoke (Warwickshire) there are new buildings not subsequently altered and surviving completely enough for analysis. Bodiam (licensed 1385) must have had buildings such as stables outside the wet moat; at Bolton limited stabling was incorporated in the courtyard.

The number of licences to crenellate, greatest in the first half of Edward III's reign (i.e. 1327– c. 1350) can safely be read as a steady increase in the number of new houses and the ambitions they represent.[28] New building by magnates in the middle decades of his reign seems to have been checked more by their being in France at war than by any immediate effects of the Black Death. In the last decades, the profits of war – from pay received, from the ransoms of French prisoners and possibly from handling the great sums dispensed by English kings in the war effort – began to flow back to England. In most cases, licence to crenellate a house meant literally what it said; that the walling, whether of a surrounding curtain or a residential building, might be topped by battlements. Buildings so licensed have not had a high rate of survival. Not all the places and owners named (in the Patent Rolls) can now be identified; we cannot assume that work licensed was actually carried out, though the licence was sometimes obtained *post factum*; in many cases whatever was done disappeared in subsequent rebuilding. The full name of Mereworth Castle (Kent) recalls a licence of 1332 to John de Mereworth to fortify his manor house, though it figures in architectural history as the most distinguished copy in England of a Palladian villa, built in 1723.

The amount of new building in Richard II's reign (1377–99) is, to judge from surviving remains, very impressive.[29] Some new houses such as Dartington Hall, built in 1388–1400 by John Holand, earl of Huntingdon, were not fortified at all. One reason for a low rate of survival of fortified manor houses of this age is that within a walled courtyard, usually with corner towers and a gatehouse, some of the residential buildings against the curtain wall were only timber-framed. That is deduced even of northern castles such as Chillingham (Northumberland, licensed 1344) and Penrith (Cumberland, licensed 1397); Maxstoke (1346) had timber buildings on all four sides except for a hall of stone.[30] Hever (Kent) was entirely of timber within, and its stone buildings, along with the village outside, were created in 1903 onwards by W. W. Astor.

The number of new houses of the grandest character probably lessened in the fifteenth century; there were inevitably limits in practical terms, and the uncertain fate of magnates in unsettled times meant that estates and houses changed hands and tended to concentrate in fewer families; their wealth was proportionately greater and more of it represented by coinage and gold and silver plate, to judge from wills and inventories – portable wealth rather than labour services and crops dispersed over rural manors.

The building activity of fifteenth-century magnates and the ultimate fate of their buildings can be illustrated from the work of two of them. Richard Beauchamp, earl of Warwick (d. 1439), according to William Worcestre writing only a generation later,[31] rebuilt the south side of Warwick Castle with a new tower and various domestic offices; he built a tower and hall block at Cardiff Castle, rebuilt castles at Elmley (Worcestershire), Hanley (Staffordshire) and Hanslope (Buckinghamshire), and also manor houses at Caversham (Oxfordshire) and Drayton Bassett (Staffordshire), all of which have vanished. He restored Baginton Castle (Warwickshire) where earthworks and the base of a tower can still be seen; his manor house at Sutton Coldfield (Warwickshire) may be identified with New Hall, a modern house on a moated site. Worcestre said that he built a 'new lodge' at Claverdon (Warwickshire); a brick tower still stands there but it seems to be of Tudor date. Another great builder was Ralph Lord Cromwell (d. 1456).[32] He rebuilt the castle at Tattershall (as well as the church and a college of canons) and a new fortified house at South Wingfield (Derbyshire), both without a licence; he built a manor house at Collyweston (Northamptonshire) which has vanished, and another timber-framed house at Lambley (Nottinghamshire) on a moated site next to the church which is now a green field (his new parish church there stands unaltered); of his castle at Ampthill (Bedfordshire) there is now no trace. Enough remains at Tattershall and South Wingfield to deduce his style of life, as we shall see (pages 101–2).

Lodgings

In buildings of 1375 and later it is easier to discern additions and modifications than entirely new houses, but those additions reveal a shift in the character of the plan and, in particular, increasing provision of what may be called secondary accommodation. The characteristic plan has two or more courtyards, surrounded by ranges basically one room deep.[33] Eltham can stand as a model at the highest level [53]. The manor house built by Antony Bek, bishop of Durham, came to the crown in 1311 after his death. We first hear of the outer court in Richard III's time; surviving buildings such as the lord chancellor's lodgings were timber-framed in the Kentish style. Edward IV built a new hall in 1475–83, between the inner and outer courts, to serve occupants of both; the distinction between a great and small hall had given way to increasingly formal ranges of private lodgings round the inner court and more lodgings for household round the outer court. The development of lodgings in the fourteenth and fifteenth centuries [54, 55, 56] is in fact one new feature of

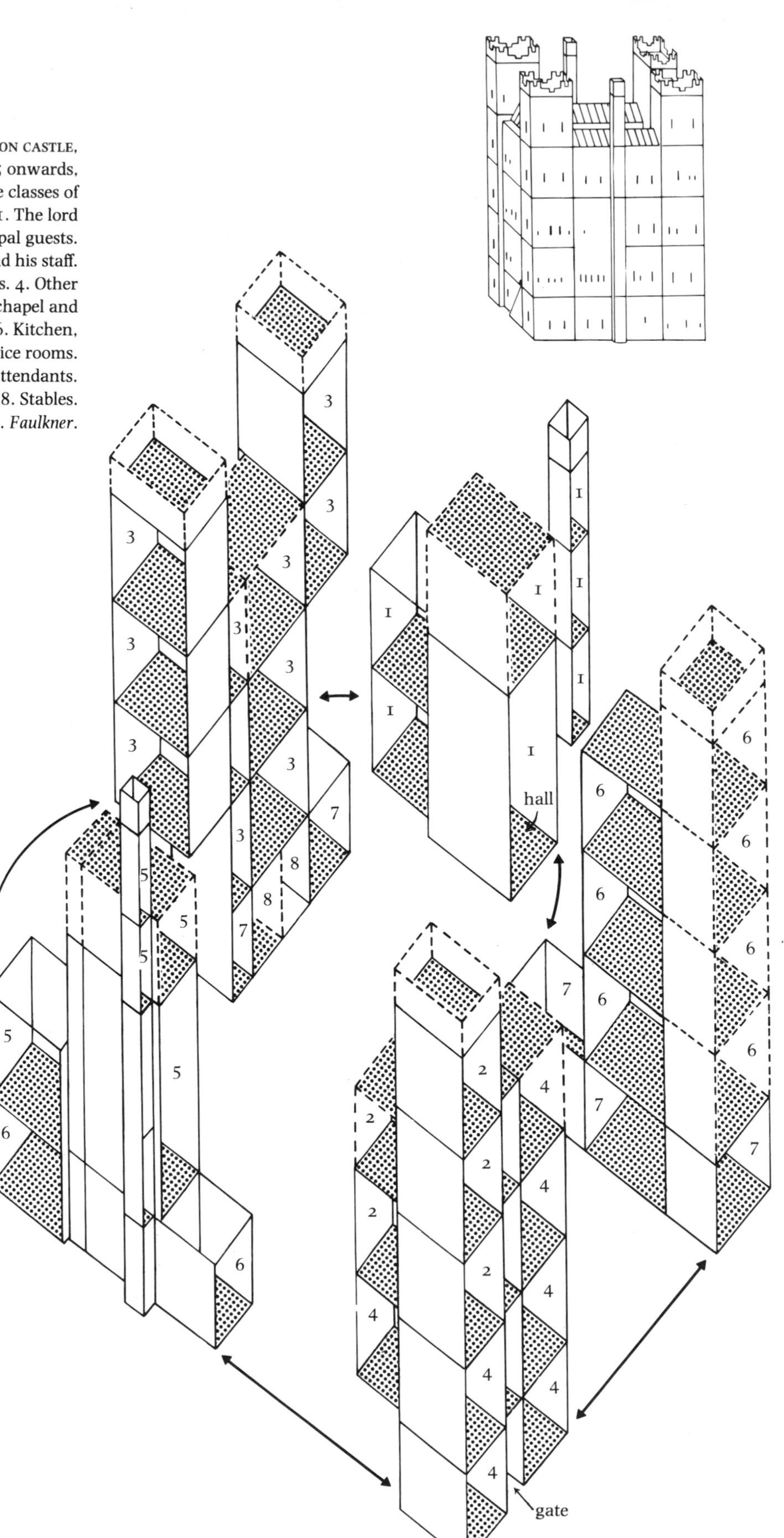

52. Analysis of BOLTON CASTLE, YORKSHIRE, c. 1375 onwards, to show the classes of accommodation. 1. The lord and his principal guests. 2. The steward and his staff. 3. Noble guests. 4. Other lodgings. 5. The chapel and associated lodgings. 6. Kitchen, mill and service rooms. 7. Guards and attendants. 8. Stables. *After P. A. Faulkner.*

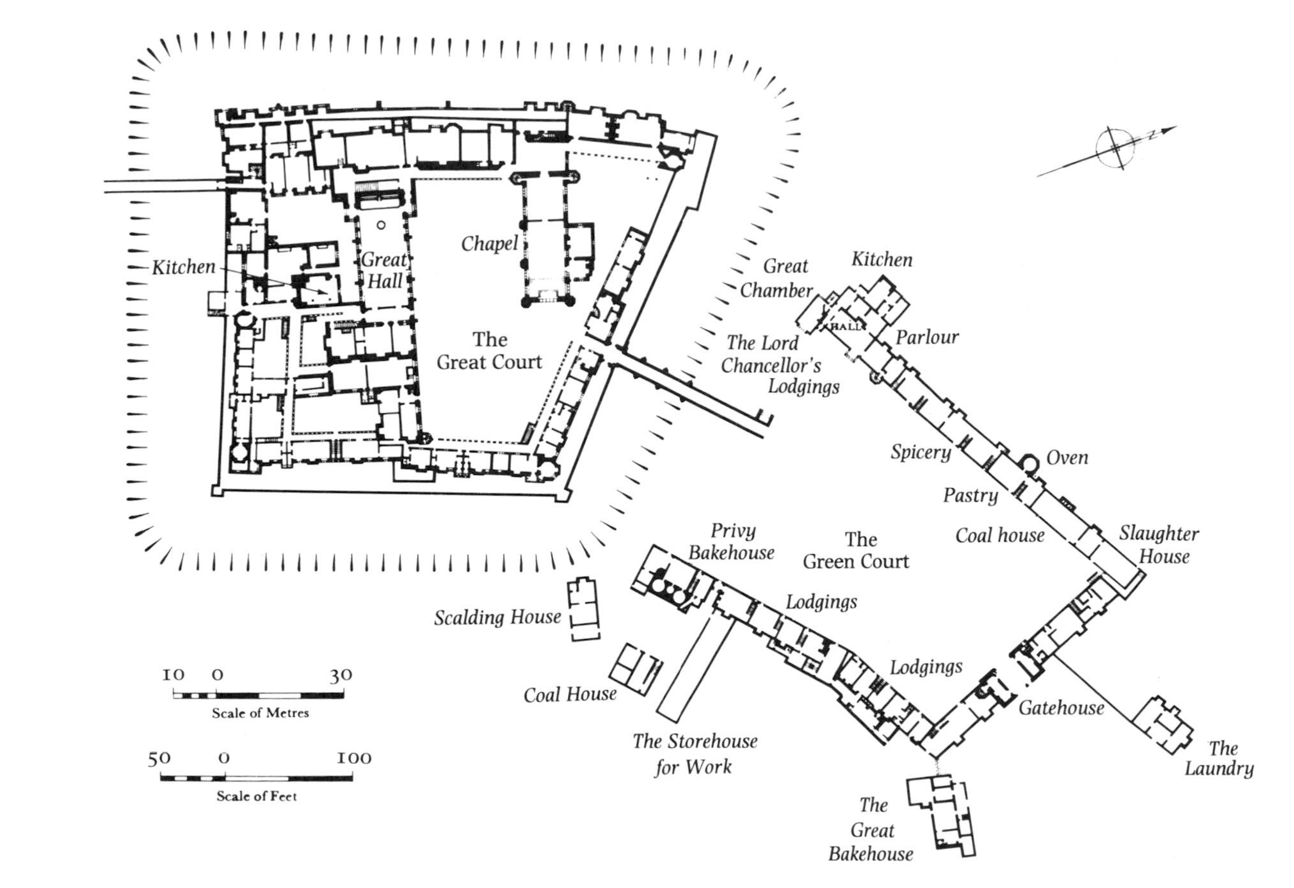

53. Plan of ELTHAM PALACE, KENT, based on survey of c. 1603 and modern excavations. *HMSO.*

domestic planning at the top of society. It goes along with what may be called the first multiple housing: the building of terraces in towns, with the provision for vicars choral and chantry priests serving cathedrals and collegiate churches, for pilgrims at Canterbury (The Bull) and for students in universities. In the rebuilding of the archbishop's palace at Southwell [46], completed by John Kempe (1426–52), the arrangement of the main court can still be deduced although a service court with a kitchen, stables, etc. has disappeared.[34] Interpretation is a matter of observing the size of rooms and the presence of fireplaces and garderobes. A hall with its service rooms filled the west range. The first-floor chamber at the north end of the hall, close to an entrance to the palace from the south transept of the minster (about 9m (10 yd) away), must have served only for the most formal occasions, not for residential use, since it had no garderobe. There were lodgings varying in size on both floors of the north and south ranges. The first floor of the east range contained a second private hall (with its unique garderobe with four seats), and for the archbishop an inner chamber with its own garderobe; beyond was a small room next to the chapel which served as his private pew.

54. Drawing to accompany an Elizabethan survey of MELBOURNE CASTLE, DERBYSHIRE. The gabled louvre of the hall is in the centre, and there are eighteen chimneys. *PRO*.

55. Lodgings range of HOLME PIERREPONT HALL, NOTTINGHAMSHIRE, with four rooms on each floor sharing garderobes in two turrets.

Dartington Hall (Devon), like Eltham, had only the one hall; it provides the clearest picture of a wealthy establishment with retainers.[35] John Holand, earl of Huntingdon, who built it in 1388–1400, took most of his meals in a great chamber at the upper end of the hall, or somewhere else in the inner court west of the hall (and close to the kitchen). In the outer court, all the west and part of the east side were given over to lodgings of essentially standard size, evidently for men of identical status. Each lodging consists of one room with a fireplace and a privy; we can assume from later household regulations that each had a double bed for two men, the important thing being that no man should have to sleep with another of lower social rank than himself. These lodgings were for some of the retainers who figure so largely in fifteenth-century history. A large room on the first floor of the gatehouse range might be considered a second hall but it is far from the kitchen; perhaps it was used as an assembly hall for retainers. Richard Neville, earl of Warwick, the

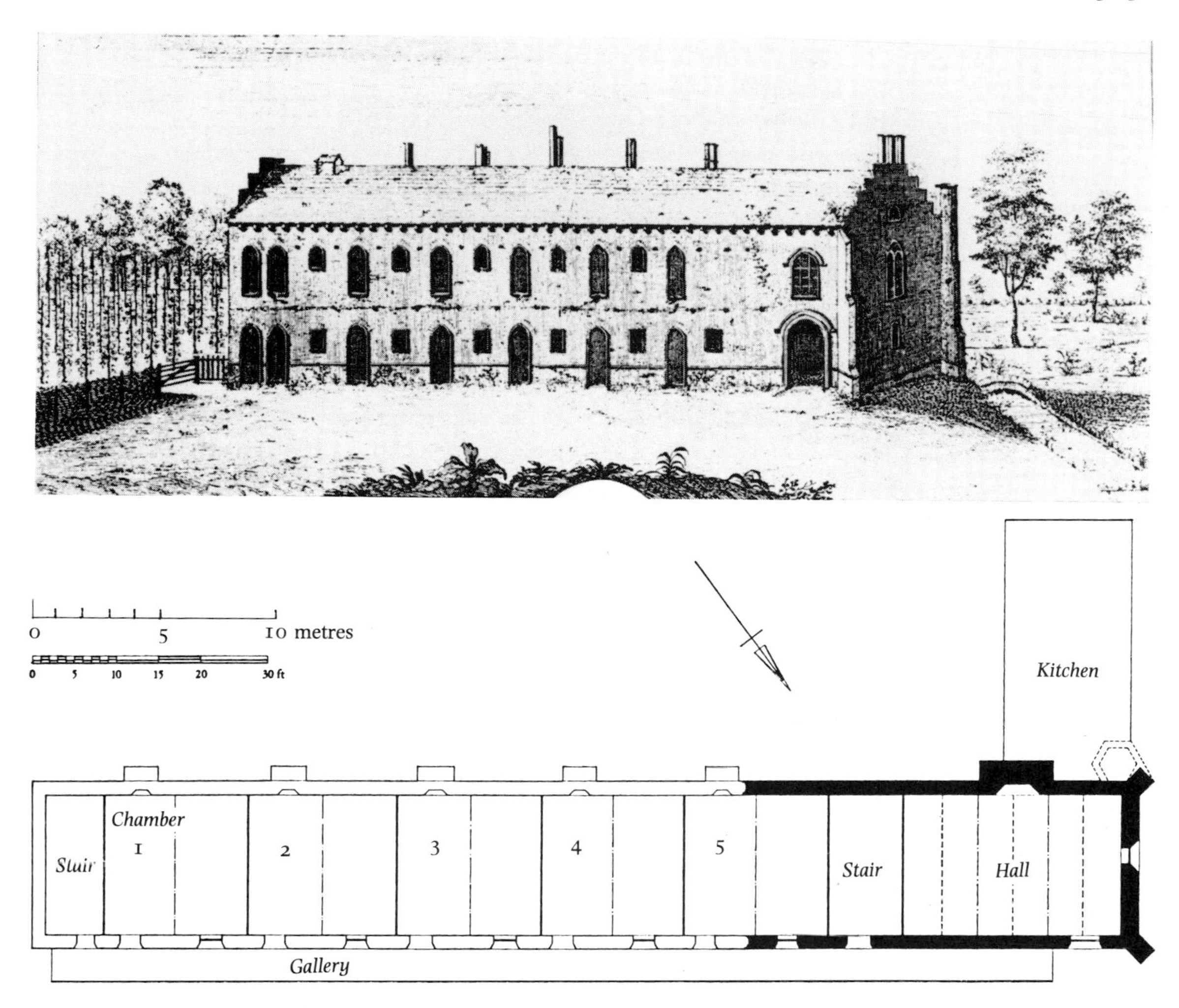

56. Engraving, 1729, and plan of the lodgings of the manor house at EWELME, OXFORDSHIRE, built soon after 1430 by William de la Pole, earl of Suffolk, and his wife Alice, granddaughter of Geoffrey Chaucer, the poet. The lodgings consisted of five rooms on each floor, those upstairs once reached by a covered external gallery. At the right-hand end was a hall on the first floor, reached by a stair-turret. The hall end of the range still stands, much altered. *Engraving S. Buck, plan R. S. Mant.*

kingmaker (1428–71), is said to have been accompanied by some 400 of them, though we do not know what proportion had to be housed and fed as well as provided with a livery or uniform. Whatever lodgings there were for retainers at Warwick disappeared in subsequent rebuilding.

Lodgings for retainers as distinct from household have been identified at Ewelme (Oxfordshire) [56], the residence of Willliam de la Pole, earl of Suffolk.[36] His mother was a Chaucer and his father a Hull merchant; his father's background must be one reason why he chose to build in brick for a new church, almshouses and a school. His house, within a moat, has gone; outside the moat and evidently in an outer court there is a long building with doorways and windows repeated uniformly; it is traditionally known as the manor house but was really a set of lodgings with a hall for retainers at one end of the first floor. A range of similar date has been identified at Burwell (Cambridgeshire).[37] Access to the upper rooms of two-storey lodgings of this standard was either by a series of staircases as in university colleges and at Dartington, where they are external, or else by a passage at first-floor level as at Ewelme.

At Caister (Norfolk) Sir John Fastolf in 1432–5 rebuilt the family manor house with inner and outer courts, each containing lodgings; his unique brick tower, which has provoked comparison with similar lofty buildings in Germany (*Wasserburgen*), had five floors of small heated rooms.[38] Herstmonceux (Sussex, 1441) must have had standardized lodgings in its nine courts and seven towers, though the evidence disappeared with decay and subsequent rebuilding. Similar lodgings were built into the lower courtyard at Haddon Hall (Derbyshire). When Edward duke of Buckingham died in 1521 he left unfinished his castle at Thornbury (Gloucestershire) with extensive provision for retainers.[39] It is not quite the last example of such planning, for there seems no other explanation for the function of the towering gatehouse of Layer Marney (Essex), built in 1523; it contains thirty-nine chambers.

The solar tower

The second new feature in magnates' houses of the fifteenth century is a tower, and its social significance is more complex. Taken simply as a residential building with rooms stacked vertically, the class includes keeps of the Norman period, castles such as Nunney (Somerset, 1373) and Caister (Norfolk); the tower houses of northern counties (see below, page 117); lofty gatehouses of the fifteenth and sixteenth centuries and even a few Elizabethan houses (e.g. Wollaton Hall, Nottinghamshire, and the keep of Bolsover Castle, Derbyshire) which have been likened to keeps and hunting lodges. The desire on the part of landowners to have a residence marked by a lofty feature is evidently deep-seated throughout the Middle Ages. Of the solar towers, Ralph Cromwell's Tattershall is a distinctive example.[40] His rebuilding of a thirteenth-century castle started in 1434–5 as part of a grandiose project which included rebuilding the parish church as a collegiate foundation; the college has gone but its grand scale is known from the gatehouse, which has been excavated. In the castle, Cromwell's tower stands in commanding but misleading isolation on the perimeter of the defences; there must have been lodgings in one or more of the three wards; William Worcestre said that his household at Tattershall numbered one hundred. The hall stood near the tower, which provided him with privacy in a large and busy establishment as well as reflecting the great wealth and status acquired by a man of an old but undistinguished family in difficult and dangerous times. The notion that such men needed to be able to defend themselves against their own retainers by retreating to such a tower no longer convinces historians; there are no known instances in this country.

While Tattershall was going up, in brick, with a labour force led by a German brickmaker, so was South Wingfield, built in the local sandstone.[41] The existing manor house was cleared away and the new one, built in 1439–c. 1450, was planned round two courtyards. The outer court had a barn just inside the gate, lodgings, stables and store-rooms on two sides and on the other a long dormitory with a privy tower for lower servants. The range dividing the courts had lodgings varying in size; one side of the inner court had superior lodgings with oriel windows; buildings on the other side have gone but must have included the chapel. The one hall, at the further end of the inner court and over a vaulted undercroft, had alongside it a great chamber on the first floor and beyond it a complex of rooms round a tiny court which included the kitchen and Lord Cromwell's private apartments. This part had at its west end a tower, tall enough to overlook the whole house.

57. LORD HASTINGS' TOWER, ASHBY-DE-LA-ZOUCH CASTLE, LEICESTERSHIRE, C. 1475, reduced to its present state by Parliament in 1648.

At Ashby-de-la-Zouch [57], William Lord Hastings built a similar tower.[42] Broughton Castle (Oxfordshire) started c. 1330 as a manor house; there was a licence dated 1406 represented now by the curtain wall, but in the 1460s further work included the creation of a tower topping the private end of the house.[43] The Great Tower at Raglan Castle, built in 1461–9 within its own moat and reached only by a drawbridge at first-floor level, was purely military in intent, to protect the new wealth of William Herbert, earl of Pembroke.[44] It was never put to the test and he was beheaded by the earl of Warwick after the battle of Edgecot (1469).

Other houses illustrate the fact that there was a small number of aristocratic families, linked by blood, marriage or friendship and conscious of those links, as indeed are their present-day counterparts; between them they account for dominant strains in building. In 1377 Broughton (Oxfordshire) had been purchased by William of Wykeham, bishop of Winchester, perhaps as a convenient base for overseeing his projected foundation of New College, Oxford. It descended through his nephew to Sir William Fiennes, whose father had been lord treasurer of England (like Ralph Cromwell) and built Herstmonceux. Fiennes preferred it to his manor of Knole which he sold in 1456 to archbishop Bourchier of Canterbury who proceeded to rebuild it and eventually gave it to his diocese. Fiennes bought Hever Castle but sold it again in 1462 (perhaps

58. BISHOP ROTHERHAM'S TOWER, BUCKDEN PALACE, HUNTINGDONSHIRE, C. 1475. Grey bricks were used to form crosses in the red walling (behind the conifer).

to finance work at Broughton) to a prosperous lord mayor of London, great-grandfather of Anne Boleyn.

Even if bishops of this age did not belong by birth to this class – and about one-fifth of them did – their advancement made them part of it and their antecedents sometimes gave them a particular interest in building. Alcock built himself a new palace at Ely c. 1490; his father was a Hull merchant and he went to school at Beverley; his Ely palace has a gatehouse tower like that of Jesus College, Cambridge, which he founded. Thomas Rotherham, bishop of Lincoln, built a great brick tower at Buckden (Huntingdonshire, c. 1475) [58]. William Waynflete, a Lincolnshire man, became bishop of Winchester, was executor of Ralph Cromwell's will and completed the church and college at Tattershall in 1470–5; he added a brick tower containing hall, chamber and kitchen to his castle at Farnham and a brick gatehouse to the manor at Esher; Magdalen College which he founded has the only gatehouse tower in Oxford. 'Of the forty richest sees in the whole of [medieval] Christendom twelve were said to have been in England';[45] this estimate, based on values assessed

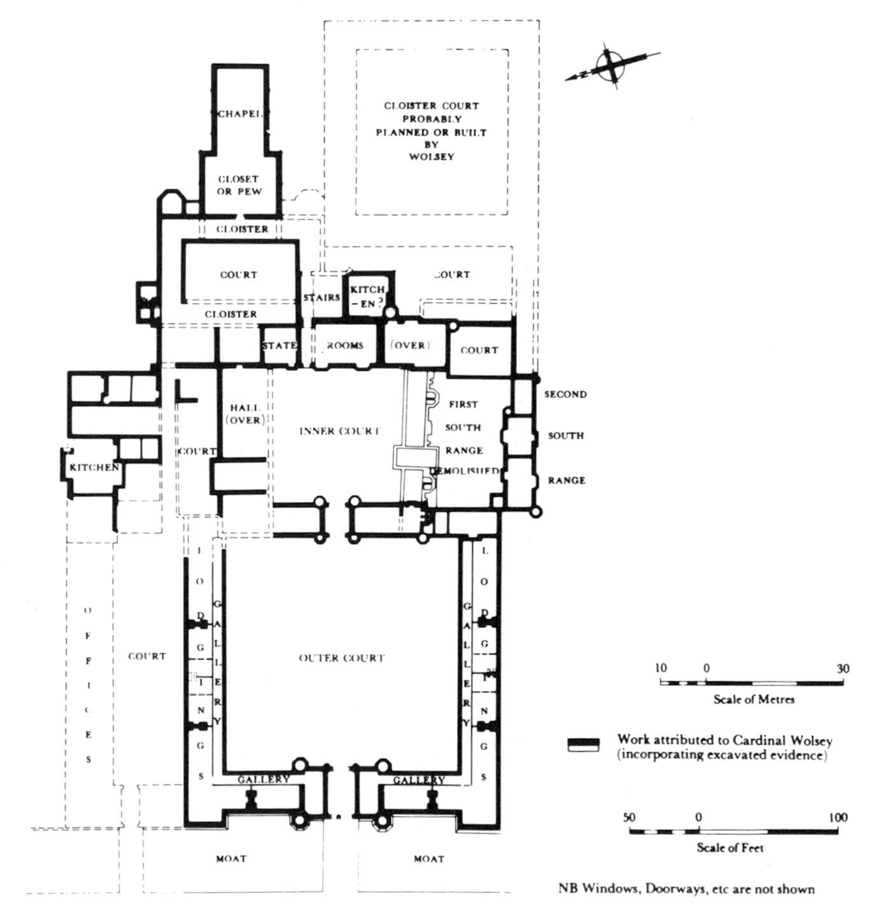

59. Plan of Wolsey's HAMPTON COURT, MIDDLESEX, c. 1525. *HMSO.*

in Henry VIII's time, does not take into account the sinecures – rectories, prebends, wardenships – which bishops collected, or the profits of such high offices as that of lord chancellor which came as a matter of course to ecclesiastics trained in the law. Hence John Morton while bishop of Ely rebuilt in 1478–86 his palace at Hatfield, where his hall survives (page 205); when he was promoted to Canterbury (1500–3) he built or completed the great court at Croydon with its range of lodgings on two sides. His successor Warham, not content with relatively new or newly enlarged palaces (Croydon, Knole) built another at Otford, only three miles from Knole, and spent £33,000 on it.

In this perspective, Thomas Wolsey's Hampton Court is no surprise [59]. He was not the first archbishop of York to mount a display of spendid buildings near London, for George Neville in 1460 had bought the manor of the More (Hertfordshire) and built a courtyard house in brick where Edward IV stayed in 1472; soon after the king seized the house for himself.[46] It evidently attracted ecclesiastical magnates, for a bishop of Durham (Thomas Tuthall), an abbot of St Albans and Wolsey himself each owned it for a time. It had a timber-framed gallery 61 m (200 ft) long in the garden, probably Wolsey's work. The house was demolished c. 1650. Wolsey, who leased the manor at Hampton in 1514, must also have been mindful of new royal palaces – Henry VII's Greenwich (1497–1505) and Henry VIII's principal London residence, Bridewell (1520–3) – when he designed Hampton Court for a household of 500 or more. When he forfeited it in 1529 it was the first of scores of episcopal residences to be acquired by the Tudor crown and nobility.[47]

Notes

1 Volumes I, II.

2 The only distribution map is by P. Hembry, 'Episcopal palaces, 1535–1660', in E. W. Ives (ed.), *Wealth and Power in Tudor England* (1978), 148–9.

3 C. Dyer, *Lords and Peasants in a Changing Society* (1980), 202.

4 For Sonning, see *Bucks. Berks. Oxon. Archaeol. J.*, 22 (1916), 2–21.

5 RCHM, *North East Cambridgeshire*, 58–60; M. Aston, *Thomas Arundel* (1967), chs 6–8.

6 Department of Environment *Guide*.

7 *Calendar of Inquisitions Miscellaneous*, 7, 1399–1422, 150.

8 RCHM, *Beverley, an Archaeological and Architectural study* (1982), 2; N. Summers, *Prospect of Southwell* (1974), 3.

9 C. and P. Woodfield, 'The palace of the bishops of Lincoln at Lyddington', *Trans. Leics. Arch. and Hist. Soc.*, 57 (1981–2), 1–16.

10 M. Aston, *Thomas Arundel* (1967), 236.

11 *Proc. Somerset Archaeol. and N. H. Soc.*, 104 (1960), 91–5.

12 D. Oschinsky, *Walter of Henley ...* (1971), 191–9, 403–7.

13 W. D. Peckham, 'Amberley Castle', *Sussex Archaeol. Coll.*, 62 (1921), 21–63.

14 *Bucks., Berks. and Oxon. Archaeol. J.*, 22 (1916), 2–21.

15 J. West, 'Acton, Burnell Castle, Shropshire: a reinterpretation', in A. Detsicas (ed.), *Collectanea Historica* (1981), 85–92.

16 R. A. Brown, *English Castles* (1970), 54; D. F. Renn, *Norman Castles in Britain* (1968), 16.

17 *King's Works*, I, 369–70.
18 *Archaeol.* J., 118 (1961), 188–9.
19 *King's Works*, I, 121; M. Girouard, *Life in the English Country House* (1978), 65.
20 Corfe: RCHM, *Dorset*, 2, i (1970), 74–7 and R. A. Brown, 88; Wolvesley: M. Biddle 'Excavations at Winchester', *Ant. J.*, 52 (1972), 125–31; 55 (1975), 321–33; Old Sarum: RCHM, *Salisbury* (1980), 8–10. There is no adequate account of Bishop's Waltham in print, but see *Archaeol. J.*, 123 (1966), 217.
21 *King's Works*, II, 864–6.
22 Ibid., 866–88.
23 F. M. Stenton, *First Century of English Feudalism, 1066–1166* (1932), 70–1.
24 C. R. Peers, 'Harlech Castle', *Cymmrodorian Trans.* (1921–2), 63–82.
25 *King's Works*, II, 181–5.
26 Ibid., II, 785–91; B. Cunliffe and J. Munby, *Excavations at Portchester Castle*, 4 (1985), 101–9, figs 91, 94; BE, *Sussex*, 380–1.
27 RCHM, *Hertfordshire*, 1 (1931), 74–8.
28 T.H. Turner and J.H. Parker, *Domestic Architecture in the Middle Ages* (1851–9), 3, ii, 402–22; J. le Patourel 'Fortified and semi-fortified manor houses', in *Château Gaillard*, 9–10 (1982), 187–97.
29 A. Emery, *Dartington Hall* (1970), chs 6, 16.
30 N. W. Alcock *et al.*, 'Maxstoke Castle Warwickshire', *Archaeol. J.*, 135 (1978), 195–233.
31 J. H. Harvey (ed.), *William Worcestre Itineraries* (1969), 219–21.
32 M. W. Thompson, 'Significance of the building of Ralph Lord Cromwell (1394–1456)', in A. Detsicas (ed.), *Coll. Hist.*, 155–62; *King's Works*, IV ii (1982), 67–8; C. Weir, 'The site of the Cromwells' medieval manor house at Lambley, Notts.', in *Trans. Thoroton Soc.*, 85 (1981), 75–7.
33 *King's Works*, II, 930–7; IV, ii, 78–86, fig. 7.
34 P. A. Faulkner, 'Some medieval archiepiscopal palaces', *Archaeol. J.*, 127 (1970), 130–2.
35 Emery, *Dartington Hall*, pt. 2.
36 M. Airs, 'Ewelme', *Archaeol. J.*, 135 (1978), 276–80.
37 RCHM, *North East Cambridgeshire* (1972), 28–9. For lodgings in a manor house at Wooburn D'Eyncourt (Buckinghamshire) see *Records of Bucks*, 23 (1981), 39–50.
38 H. D. Barnes and W. D. Simpson, 'Caister Castle', *Ant. J.*, 32 (1952), 35–51.
39 A. D. K. Hawkyard, 'Thornbury Castle', *Trans. Bristol and Gloucs. Arch. Soc.*, 95 (1977), 51–8.
40 National Trust *Guide*.
41 M. W. Thompson, 'The construction of the manor at S. Wingfield Derbys.', G. de G. Sieveking *et al.* (eds.), *Problems in Economic and Social Archaeology* (1877), 417–38, includes the building accounts.
42 Department of Environment *Guide*.
43 *Archaeol. J.*, 135 (1978), 153–7.
44 A. Emery, 'The development of Raglan Castle and Keeps in later medieval England', *Archaeol. J.*, 172–3.
45 J. R. Lander, *Government and Community in England 1450–1509* (1980), 120.
46 M. Biddle *et al.*, 'Excavation of the manor of the More, Rickmansworth', *Archaeol. J.*, 116 (1959), 136–99; *King's Works*, IV, 164–9.
47 *King's Works*, IV, ii, 127.

6 *Medieval Manor Houses*

The manor house as a residence was the centre for a property, which, even if not confined to one village or parish, could be run from one place. The house accommodated a single family, however extended, with inferior servants rather than social equals or superiors. As the working centre of an estate, the manor had the variety of agricultural buildings making up what would now be called a farm; as a unit of ownership it was supported by the rents and services of tenants, its affairs being managed by a court held by or for the owner.

After that has been said and the history of an individual manor is examined, qualifications and exceptions emerge. It is impossible to quantify the number of manor houses, but the number of manors greatly increased between the eleventh and the fifteenth centuries. William the Conqueror's barons, bishops and abbots were required to put into the field an army of at least 4,000 knights and this obligation was rapidly given a territorial basis.[1] Those knights, originally (as the Anglo-Saxon word *cniht* implies) servants or household retainers, received estates which gave them both social distinction and hereditary properties. We happen to know that at Dover, Bamburgh and Newcastle, knights had houses within the castles there, reflecting a stage before they left residential quarters in castles for the villages and hamlets of the countryside.[2]

By the fifteenth century there were between 10,000 and 11,000 parishes in England, of which perhaps 9,000 were rural parishes, including those chapels-of-ease in large parishes of northern England which were effectively parochial.[3] In Midland counties, parish and manor were coterminous in perhaps as many as 50 per cent of cases, but elsewhere the proportion was lower, and even in the Midlands one parish might contain several manors. Some Domesday manors included many dependent villages, hamlets and farms which became independent manors. They include, for instance, those isolated Devon farmhouses known as bartons with at most a few cottages nearby. In Somerset a parish might contain several nucleated settlements: Charlton Mackrell (Somerset) had six manors in the Middle Ages, and for each there is some documentary reference to a house.[4] One of them survives, Lyte's Cary, rebuilt early in the fourteenth century by the Lyte family in a hamlet on the river Cary. The others have gone, except for a house known (only since 1922) as Charlton Mackrell Court which belonged to the rectory manor; the oldest part of it was built c. 1521. There may have been anything between 25,000 and 50,000 manor houses, a range so wide as to be valueless except as a comparison with the number of castles. Estates were through normal vicissitudes broken down and built up; by the fifteenth century a manor might be a fragment of an earlier estate, owned by a man who could not claim to be a knight, an esquire or even a gentleman. It might then belong to one of those enterprising and ambitious freemen from whom the rising class of gentry was being recruited. By the Tudor period only a small proportion of villages had a resident owner of superior rank.

Names of manor houses

If we seek to identify a medieval manor house by the name it carries, the search is complicated not only by changes of ownership but also by the pretensions of owners in modern times. To the medieval lawyer, a manor house was a capital messuage; that is, a dwelling with special rights attached to it. For general use, two words were taken from Latin into Middle English, first *manerium* (manor) and then, rather later, *mansum* (mansion), the latter probably to find a word with a superior connotation. There is only one instance of the use of the word palace for a private house. Paul Peyvre, a friend of Henry III (d. 1252), built at Toddington (Bedfordshire) a house which a chronicler described as adorned 'with a palace, chapel, bed-chambers and other stone houses ... as to provoke the wonder of all beholders'.[5] This may have been a comment on its splendour, or a solitary instance of the usage prevailing later in Scotland, by which palace meant a first-floor hall. In licences to crenellate, most houses are designated as *manerium* or *mansum*, and since the wording of a licence repeated the petition of an applicant, it reflected his view of the status of his residence. Leland writing in Henry VIII's time referred to Dartington Hall and South Wingfield as manor places.

Ordnance Survey maps show distinct regional variations in nomenclature. Manor house is commonest in the Midlands. In East Anglia and counties north of the Trent, hall is most used: for example Hawkedon (Suffolk) has Hawkedon Hall, Swan Hall and Thurston Hall, all as it happens built before c. 1520; Brampton, near Chesterfield, has four halls. Their precise status in the Middle Ages is unknown. In southern and West Midland counties there is a variety of terms, hall, manor house and court, with court most common in Kent.

Intensive research into manorial history shows how many pitfalls there are in relying on current names. The Treasurer's House at Martock (Somerset) was the parsonage house; the manor house on a moated site next to the church was deserted in 1503 and was later rebuilt; the manor of Milton Fauconberg has disappeared except for its medieval chapel, now converted into a house known as Court Cottage.[6] The many instances of Hall Farm, Manor Farm, Court Farm and the like must indicate a capital messuage leased at some time from a non-resident owner, or a house built by him for the lessee; at any rate, a separation of the business of working a large agricultural unit from the rights and status of a manor.

Moated sites

It is tempting to regard a moat as an indicator of manorial status, but to do so imposes a precision on class distinctions in medieval society that the facts will not bear. Between 3,000 and 4,000 moated sites have been recorded; they seem to range in date from late in the twelfth to the eighteenth century, when some were created as part of landscaping and garden design, and some certainly had no residential buildings.[7] They were naturally most easily made on heavy clay soils. They are commonest in parts of Essex and Suffolk, where more than 1,000 have been recorded, and of Warwickshire and Worcestershire; they are rarest in the south-west, the north of England and in Wales. In the only regional survey so far published, rather more than half the moats were identified as capital messuages of lay or ecclesiastical lords and for a few of these there are licences to crenellate. Of the rest, 15 per cent surrounded granges or other monastic properties and religious institutions such as colleges or hospitals. A small but identifiable proportion (6 per cent) belonged to freemen.[8] Evidently no clear distinction can be made between manorial lords and freemen; the two groups merge. This is in striking contrast with medieval France, where moats are not to be found except round seigneurial properties. In the Forest of Arden (Warwickshire) there seems to be a correlation between the incidence of moats and clearance and colonization of woodland; the density there and in Essex and Suffolk must represent intense activity by a new class of ambitious men, where conditions of tenure particularly favoured them.

Moated enclosures with a wet ditch and more or less rectilinear in plan are distinguished by archaeologists from ring-works enclosing a circular area with a ditch usually dry. Some 200 of these have been identified, and they may be thought of as baileys without moats; they are Norman in date.[9] Any rural residence was surrounded by a fence, a hedge, a ditch or a combination of them – for privacy, for defence, to demarcate property or to contain livestock; the scale and character of the enclosure denoted the status of its owner. It became a fortification and required a royal licence if the ditch was deep ('more than one shovel's throw') and the bank had 'battlements or alures'.[10] Edward I tried to revive the Norman kings' control over such works but without success. A moated site lying away from a village may then be the result of subdividing a manor, clearing land and making a new residence in it or even the addition of a moat to a monastic estate by its lay tenant.

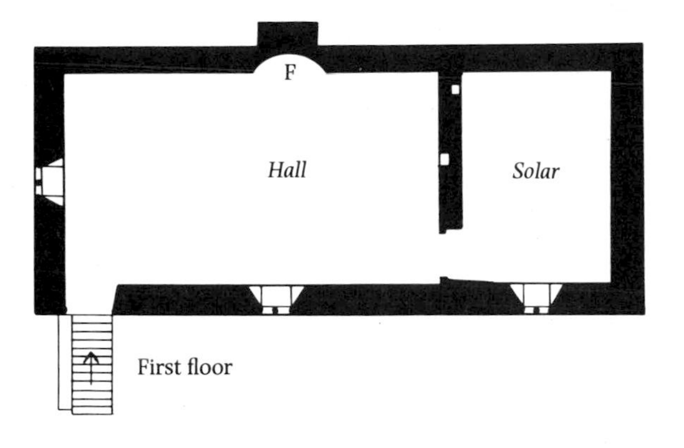

60. Plan of THE MANOR HOUSE, BOOTHBY PAGNELL, LINCOLNSHIRE, built c. 1200. The hall and solar are on the first floor, reached by an outside staircase. Only the hall has a fireplace. The room under the solar has a barrel vault and that under the hall a ribbed vault; the walls are about 1.2 m (4 ft) thick. Minor changes made later are omitted. *Margaret E. Wood.*

61. View of THE MANOR HOUSE, BOOTHBY PAGNELL, LINCOLNSHIRE.

The earliest manor houses

With all these exceptions and variants out of the way, we are left with the ideal manor house, perhaps in a moat with the parish church next to it. Some remains are known of more than thirty stone houses built between the last quarter of the twelfth and the end of the thirteenth century, all of them originally rural manors.[11] A doorway, a window, or a fireplace, and often little more surviving, are nevertheless enough both to date remains and to allow inferences about part at least of the plan: usually a hall, a solar or a chapel. The most complete examples[12] – Boothby Pagnell (Lincolnshire, c. 1200) [60, 61], and Little Wenham (Suffolk, c. 1270) – have naturally been regarded as typical and complete though both assumptions should be questioned. Boothby Pagnell now stands on the edge of the lawn fronting its successor, which has some

62. Reconstruction of the manor house of PENHALLAM, CORNWALL, showing the courtyard within the ring-work. The hall is opposite the entrance. *G. Beresford.*

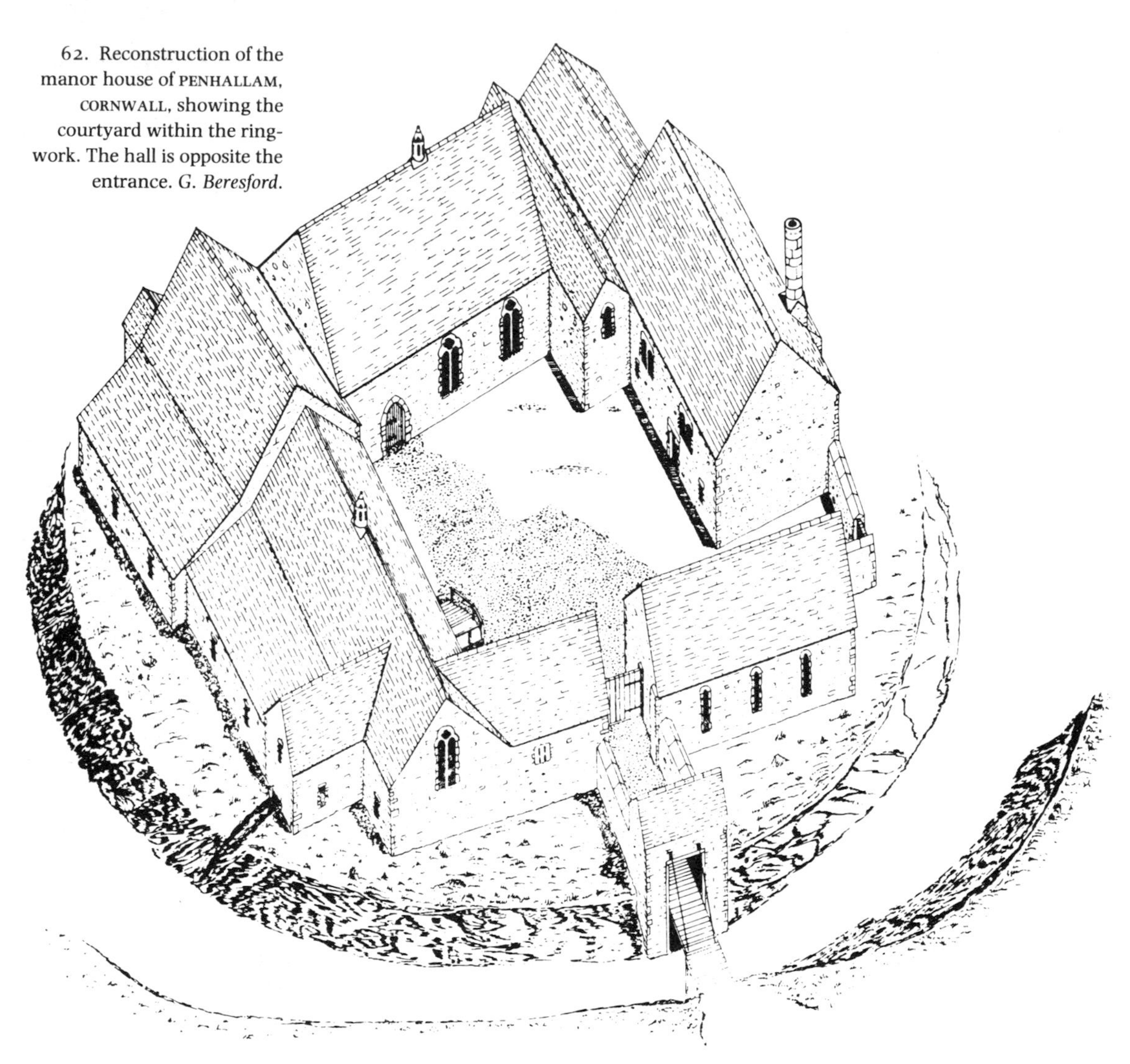

Tudor work; traces of a moat can be seen by the eye of faith, but none of any ancillary buildings, of whatever materials. Little Wenham [14] stands within a moat south-east of the church, again on the lawn of a modern residence. The manor house of Penhallam at Bury Court in the parish of Jacobstow [62] lay near the north coast of Cornwall.[13] It was part of a large feudal estate and by c. 1300 the bank of a Norman ring-work had been levelled to build a house with a completely enclosed courtyard. The house was abandoned later, and when the site was excavated in 1968–73 before the valley was cleared for afforestation, the remains were substantial enough for the rooms to be identified with confidence. The house filled the moated area; the farm buildings presumably

63. NORBURY MANOR, DERBYSHIRE, first-floor hall of c. 1250.

lie under Bury Court, a modern farmhouse standing on the outer edge of the moat.

Stone houses like Boothby Pagnell have long been recognized for what they are, but recent research has added to the known examples of timber-framed manor houses built before c. 1350 [72, 105]. Remains are usually confined to a hall, and particularly to its roof rather than its walls; dating depends on forms of construction rather than decorative detail such as mouldings. Essex has at least nine aisled halls and Kent about thirty; three came to light in an intensive survey of part of Cambridgeshire; Nurstead Court (Kent) has long been known and fragments of the predecessor of Elland Hall (West Yorkshire) have recently been recognized.[14] A major addition to the group came from recognition of manor houses and other residences of similar status (along with barns belonging to monastic houses) which all have a hall cleared of free-standing arcade posts by adopting base-cruck or a related construction.[15] The earliest were built before 1300, the majority in the course of the fourteenth century and the manor houses now number more than fifty; their status extends from Lambeth Palace, Dartington Hall (Devon), Maxstoke Castle (Warwickshire), a fortified manor house licensed in 1345, to modest houses of successful freemen.

First-floor halls

Although the number of recognized manor houses of c. 1180 to c. 1350 is less than one hundred, the remains are homogeneous enough for generalizations about their plan, especially if they are compared with houses of higher status and somewhat different function. Many stone-walled houses had their hall on the first floor over a vaulted undercroft, a design that was rarely built in timber.[16] The first-floor hall [63] marks a higher status, or loftier aspirations, on the part of the owner. It links the rural manor house, and even a few houses of wealthy townsmen, with royal palaces, castles such as Richmond (Yorkshire) and Grosmont (Monmouthshire) and abbots' houses in rich monasteries (Westminster, Chester, etc.). The halls were modest in size, usually between 4.8 m (16 ft) and 7.6 m (25 ft) wide; access by an outside stair segregated the first from the ground floor, and permitted various uses for the space below which was often vaulted. The first floor was usually divided into a heated hall and a small chamber with no heating but very occasionally with a garderobe; it is possible that the ground floor, often divided in the same way, was a servants' hall, though it very rarely had a fireplace [60, 63].

The other form of manor house, with a ground-floor hall and usually built of timber, was an altogether more public affair. It was very rarely more than two bays in length, but aisled or base-cruck construction was adopted as a way of satisfying the first requirement of a working agrarian unit: a large space, usually more than 7.6 m (25 ft) wide and heated by an open hearth in the centre, in which to assemble peasant tenants for formal and informal occasions and to entertain in suitable style. These halls invariably had one end divided off. This structural division has been observed in excavations of Anglo-Saxon houses, and may even be deduced on aerial photographs; what becomes clear only from standing buildings is that the private unit is nearest the doorway, at what is usually called the service end of the house; as early as the thirteenth century it was divided into two rooms, the buttery and pantry of the developed medieval traditions. It is reasonable to imagine tenants queuing at the doors for their allowance of food on days when their labour services were due. The room above was the solar. It was not long before the private chamber was shifted away from the lower or service end of the house to the upper – called the dais-end, though manor houses did not often have a dais or raised platform.

These early halls have survived partly from the quality of their construction, partly because their usefulness might shrink but did not disappear. The easier way to repair a hall roof might be to renew parts rather than rebuild, or to plant a new roof over the old. When open halls went out of fashion, there was enough head-room to insert an upper floor or even two. The rest of the house was changed around the hall; a simple service end might in time be replaced by a cross-wing – a change that can sometimes be deduced from the roof timbers. The supporting buildings of the manorial complex were even more at the mercy of time, and complete evidence of them can come only from excavation and documents. In the Norman phase of Goltho (Lincolnshire) (page 23), a small square building near the hall cannot be other than the kitchen, missing from standing buildings such as Boothby Pagnell. At Canford Manor (Dorset), now a public school, the fourteenth-century kitchen

64. STANTON HARCOURT, OXFORDSHIRE, showing (right) the chapel tower and (beyond) the kitchen; the latter is illustrated by Parker's engraving of the interior.

alone was retained in subsequent rebuilding, perhaps because it was so strongly built; there are two rooms, each with two fireplaces; the smaller room may have been the pantry.[17] Haddon Hall (Derbyshire) best shows the arrangement of c. 1300 with a service end and a great chamber above it; a passage between buttery and pantry led to the kitchen, originally across an open court but now reached under cover. At Stanton Harcourt (Oxfordshire) [64] the early fifteenth-century kitchen was retained – perhaps because it was unusually grand – when in about 1750 whatever then remained of the medieval house (except for the chapel tower) was pulled down.[18] A small square-framed building standing within a moat at Little Braxted (Essex) is thought to have been a kitchen because its timbers are smoke-blackened and the roof has two triangular smoke-exits; it survived because it was converted to a dovecote when c. 1600 a new house incorporating a kitchen was built further south.[19]

The manor complex in documents

Tudor and later estate maps in the Essex Record Offices appear to show a number of such square and detached buildings near manor houses, the only record of a common but vanishing element in the manorial complex. The leases drawn up by the dean and chapter of St Paul's for manors held by individual canons, as their prebends or sources of income, occasionally describe a Norman manor house in such detail that it could be reconstructed, though they are not always precise about the relation of one building to another.[20] A house at Kensworth (Bedfordshire) had in 1152 an *aula* (hall) and a *domus* (?) which led to a *thalamus* (bedchamber), each timber-framed and open to the roof. At Ardleigh (Essex) there was a hall, a chamber attached to it, a passage (*trisanta*), a privy next to the chamber and another in the yard; a good barn, a kitchen and a hayloft perhaps over a stable. No manorial complex of this workaday kind has survived in its entirety, and any sequence of manorial accounts will show that money had to be spent in most years on repairs or improvements.

The accounts for Cuxham (Oxfordshire), a manor given to Merton College in 1271, refer between 1278 and 1358 to work on the wall round the main courtyard and the kitchen garden, the great gate with its solar or chamber above, hall, kitchen, cellar, pantry, dairy; the farm buildings included two barns, a granary and houses for cows, pigs and hens. A new great chamber with a privy was built in 1297–8.[21] The bishop of Winchester's manorial accounts show that in the century and a half from 1232, new halls were built at Adderbury (Oxfordshire), Stoke (?), and Wargrave (Berkshire), but that proportionately much more was spent on chambers and kitchens and even more on farm buildings – sheep and cow houses, barns and granaries. Accounts for nineteen manors belonging to Winchester Cathedral priory exist for the same period; they have few references to new residential buildings, for managing the farms required only a hall, a kitchen, a chapel and chambers for visiting monks and for the bailiff. A new hall was built at Hurstbourne in 1299 and references to a bailiff's hall at Crondal and a servants' kitchen at Silkstead suggest old buildings passed down when new ones were built. Otherwise the accounts speak only of repairs and maintenance, especially to farm buildings, most of them timber-framed. The two barns at Whitchurch needed attention on fifteen occasions over the century, a fact that would not surprise any present-day owner of old property.[22] Attempts at scientific dating by dendrochronology which produce unexpected or inconsistent results, as they have for the monastic barn at Frocester (Gloucestershire) built according to a Gloucester chronicle c. 1300, reflect the necessary renewal, alteration or patching by later generations.

The manor house in border counties

It may seem that a picture of northern counties in the Middle Ages ought to include only castles and other defended houses.[23] There are of course motte and bailey castles, situated mainly along the coastal plains where communications were easiest and agrarian conditions not essentially different from lowland England. The most important of the great baronial castles such as Alnwick were rebuilt in stone during the twelfth century. Relations with Scotland were normally peaceful before about 1300 and many landowners held property on both sides of the border. Recent research has identified, on both sides of the border, remains of thirteenth-century houses with first-floor halls, indistinguishable from those of lowland England. They were originally set in ditched enclosures

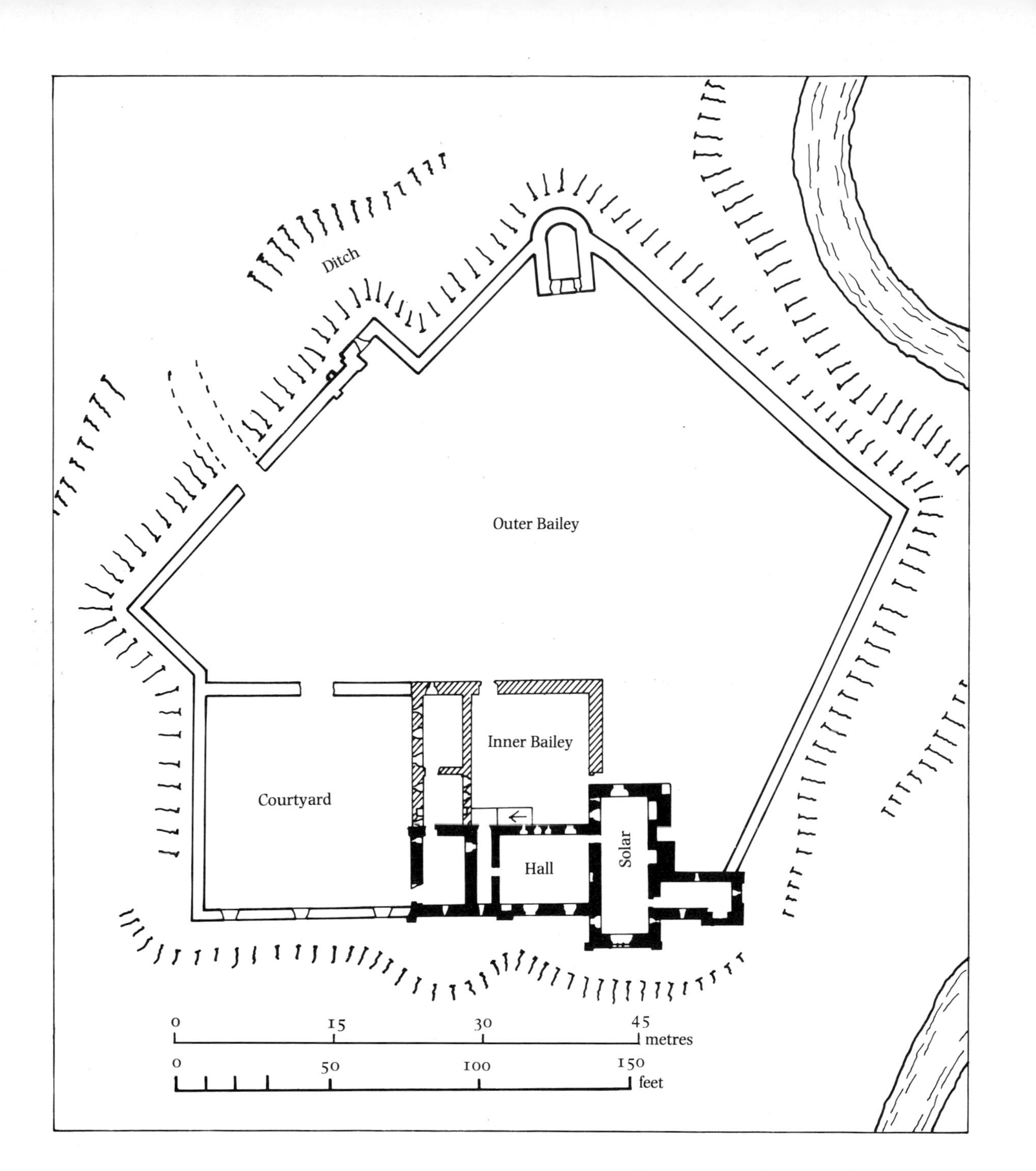

65. Plan of AYDON CASTLE, NORTHUMBERLAND, showing the transformation of a manor house into a 'fortalice'. It was built c. 1280 with a first-floor hall, solar and another chamber with a garderobe. A new owner, licensed in 1305 to crenellate it, built the inner bailey and buildings including a kitchen. Soon afterwards its transformation was completed by adding the outer bailey with its drum tower (modern farm buildings in it are not shown). *After W. H. Knowles.*

– moats in fact – but were topped by a crenellated parapet; they did not anticipate serious attack. The best preserved is Aydon (Northumberland, c. 1296) [65], which had a first-floor hall and a solar cross-wing; it closely resembled Markenfield Hall (Yorkshire, licensed 1310), where the moated enclosure is, and presumably always was, a farmyard;[24] whatever the original setting for Aydon, Robert de Raymes when he received a licence in 1305 built inner and outer baileys with turrets and added battlements to the roof of his hall. This picture of relatively peaceful conditions in the thirteenth century is amplified by the discovery of ground-floor halls such as Drumburgh on the Solway (licensed 1307 but originally built c. 1220) [66] and Featherstone on the South Tyne, built c. 1250.

66. DRUMBURGH CASTLE, CUMBERLAND, showing the blocked doorway of the hall of c. 1220 and entrance of c. 1680 to first-floor hall. There is much stone from Hadrian's Wall in the building. *P. W. Dixon.*

The wars which followed Edward I's intervention in Scotland changed conditions dramatically. Older castles were strengthened as elsewhere in the kingdom; new courtyard castles were built at Naworth (1335), Ford (1338) and elsewhere. The cheapest form of outer defence was a ditch with an earth and timber rampart, and this in the fourteenth century was called a pele. The new form of residence which now emerged was the tower house, a conventional house up-ended for defence.

The tower houses of Cumberland and Northumberland are striking in their uniformity, but they arose out of totally different circumstances. The fact that the archbishop of York built one at Hexham in 1330–50, that the prior of Lanercost built one as his lodging and even the prior of Carlisle within a walled town, shows that the tower house suited both local conditions and the social standards of landowners. In the country-side, about 150 tower houses can still be identified, and some large parishes contain more than one. Owners of scattered estates built several fortified houses and either kept them in their own hands or passed them to cadet lines of the family. The Heron family in 1415 occupied castles and towers at Ford (their principal residence), Chipchase, Crawley, Meldon and Twissell, all in Northumberland. Independent lords of smaller estates no doubt attached themselves to great men, as they did in Scotland, and gave loyalty in return for protection. These houses were not a response to times of greatest danger or major conflicts such as Bannockburn; rather they reflect the fact that landowners were free of royal control and could adapt their way of life to conditions in which raids and counter-raids across the border were annual occurrences. Licences to crenellate are no guide to the date of building; owners did not usually bother to apply for them and the crown was unable or unwilling to enforce control. Most were built in the fourteenth and fifteenth centuries, but the fashion lingered on until the union with Scotland in 1604.

The tower consisted usually of three storeys with a vaulted basement and an internal staircase. Compared with the courtyard castle, the restricted wall-head could be defended by only a few men. The tower is attached to a ground-floor hall. The hall was more susceptible to alteration in later times than the tower, so that it is now impossible to tell whether the latter ever stood alone, though it seems likely. Both tower and hall are plainly built and restrained in their architectural ornament, and so difficult to date; masons long continued to cut doorways with a round head and plain chamfers to the jambs, and windows are scarcely more helpful. Two of the most impressive houses illustrate the problems of analysing their development. Yanwath Hall near Penrith has a tower of c. 1322 and a hall of a century or so later, both dates suggested by documents; the hall may be a rebuilding. Branthwaite Hall, four miles from the Cumberland coast, has a tower of perhaps c. 1525 and the hall is dated 1604. Both were improved later. At Yanwath, the solar in the tower has a plaster frieze and an overmantel with the royal arms (1586); at Branthwaite the hall has on one side a splendid range of pedimented windows inserted c. 1700.

Distinguishing one kind of lofty building from another in terms of function is the most complex aspect of medieval domestic building, and a distinction valid for one age may not apply to another. Height conferred status throughout these times, on an abbey (Bury St Edmunds' Norman gatehouse, the Tudor crossing-tower at Fountains), a cathedral and a parish church as well as a house. A classification of houses must include:

a. The tower house containing all the residential rooms.
b. The solar tower attached to a hall.
c. The hunting lodge, built high to command views of a park.
d. The gatehouse controlling a courtyard house.

67. HALTON TOWER, NORTHUMBERLAND, showing fourteenth-century tower and parlour wing of c. 1675. The medieval hall can be seen only from the rear.

At Halton [67] a tower added c. 1400 to an existing hall ought to be called a solar tower; at Branthwaite Hall (Cumberland) the tower and hall may have been built at the same time, though the hall was later raised in height.

Tall building in lowland England

The rest of England suffered much less from local feuding and raiding so that the tower house proper is virtually unknown; it is also as rare in Wales as it is common in Ireland. At Halloughton (Nottinghamshire) the prebendary of Southwell Minster with an estate there built himself a three-storey tower (basement, hall and chamber) which seems to have been self-sufficient although it may have had a hall alongside;[25] Chesterton Tower was built c. 1350 in the vicarage garden there, after the church had been given to an Italian abbey and to house the abbey's resident agent; since it had only a solar or chamber over the vaulted ground floor, it must be classified as a tower house.[26] In both instances we are left to imagine detached service buildings, including a kitchen. In some circumstances, a tower was appropriate for the head of a monastery, rather than a more spacious lodging. Prior Overton of Repton (Derbyshire), elected in 1437, built himself a brick tower of particularly ornate design, and at Beauvale (Nottinghamshire) the Charterhouse founded in 1343 has a modest tower as lodging for the prior.

Other buildings which have sometimes been called tower houses are really gatehouses, as at Someries (Bedfordshire), Kirby Muxloe (Leicestershire) and Rye House near Hoddesden (Hertfordshire). There are however a few solar towers. The oldest is Longthorpe, Peterborough,[27] built along-

68. ROCHFORD TOWER, near BOSTON, LINCOLNSHIRE, a brick solar tower of c. 1460.

side the hall c. 1300; it has three storeys, the solar on the first floor entered from a gallery or staircase in the hall and the top-floor chamber having a privy. The solar was embellished with a remarkable series of wall-paintings of biblical and secular subjects. Longthorpe is remarkable also for being earlier by more than a century than most comparable buildings, which belong to the middle years of the fifteenth century and imitate, on a more modest scale, the towers of barons and bishops. The will of Sir Thomas Wombwell (1453) of Wombwell near Barnsley includes a bequest of a bed in a chamber called the High Tower; and an Elizabethan survey of the medieval manor house at Wiverton (Nottinghamshire) shows an 'upper tower' with a privy built out at one corner.[28] There are solar towers of similar status in Herefordshire (Kentchurch Court) and in Cornwall (Pengersick, Trerice). On the outskirts of Boston are two neglected buildings inspired by Cromwell's Tattershall.[29] Hussey Tower and Rochford Tower [68] have each lost their halls, and wall-paintings in the latter, exposed to the weather, have virtually disappeared in recent years. Hussey Tower is known to have been built in 1450–60 by a Boston man associated in local affairs with Ralph Cromwell, and both buildings mark the pretensions of new wealth.

Only one hunting lodge deserves mention; the one built by Cromwell four miles north of his castle and now known as Tower on the Moor. Only a fragment of a lofty brick tower still stands, similar in detail to the two Boston houses for which it may have served as a model.

Manorial chapels

Another element in the manorial complex which links it with superior classes and divides it sharply from the lower ranks of rural society is provision for private religious observance. In one sense, the chapel in a manor house was indistinguishable from a parish church, for the lord paid for the building of the latter, endowed it with land (glebe) and a site for a priest's house; hence his right to nominate the incumbent. Bishops assumed control of the parish church, which was the only place for baptisms, marriages and burials; lords, like bishops and barons themselves, incorporated a chapel in their houses for other services and kept a stipendiary priest to perform them. Such a chapel required a licence from the bishop, sometimes limited to the lifetime of the owner or his occupation of the house. At Strelley (Nottinghamshire) the chapel in the manor house was licensed for all services while the parish church was being rebuilt. Bishops' registers from their beginning in the thirteenth century contain licences and accounts of disputes about offerings made in manorial chapels which might reduce the parish priest's income. Registers are thus an important source not only for chapels but also for lost manor houses.

The parish church sometimes continued to be in effect a private chapel, especially in places where the village disappeared during the Middle Ages. At Haddon (Derbyshire) the church was incorporated in the lower court and at Farleigh Hungerford (Somerset) Sir Walter Hungerford, enlarging his father's fortified manor house, built an outer court c. 1425 which enclosed the church. It became the castle chapel and he built another church for the parish. On the other hand, a lord was occasionally content to attend a parish church only just outside his walls. At Dartington

69. BLACKMOOR FARM, CANNINGTON, SOMERSET, 1508, showing (right) the chapel. *NMR*.

70. BENTWORTH HALL, HAMPSHIRE, showing (right) the chapel, its large east window filled in. *A. Howarth*.

(Devon) the parish church stood, until demolished in 1878, just outside the outer court, and so the manor place of John Holand, duke of Exeter, had no chapel. The grand development of Penshurst Place (Kent) from 1338 onwards does not include a chapel. Private chapels were most common in counties such as Devon and Somerset [69, 70] with dispersed settlements.

It remains true, however, that in much of England and especially in nucleated villages, a manor house next to the parish church is the most characteristic arrangement; it may be observed at Burmington (Warwickshire) [71] and Stanton Harcourt (Oxfordshire) [64].

71. BURMINGTON, WARWICKSHIRE, the thirteenth-century manor house (note blocked window) seen from the churchyard.

At its grandest, a free-standing chapel might be intended to be served by a number of priests; a collegiate foundation was proposed in Warkworth Castle (Northumberland) but the building was probably never finished. At Stoke-sub-Hamdon (Somerset) John Beauchamp in 1303 received his bishop's licence to convert his free chapel into a collegiate church and in 1333 royal licence to crenellate his manor house; both manor house and chapel have vanished, though the priests' residence survives, now misnamed the Priory.[30] Such foundations are at the opposite end of the social scale from the chapels at Bury Barton, Lapford (Devon),[31] or Bentworth Hall (Hampshire) [70], which resemble barns but have traceried and moulded east windows; they naturally became farm buildings after the Reformation. In such simple, single-cell buildings, lord and servant presumably sat without anything to separate them. In

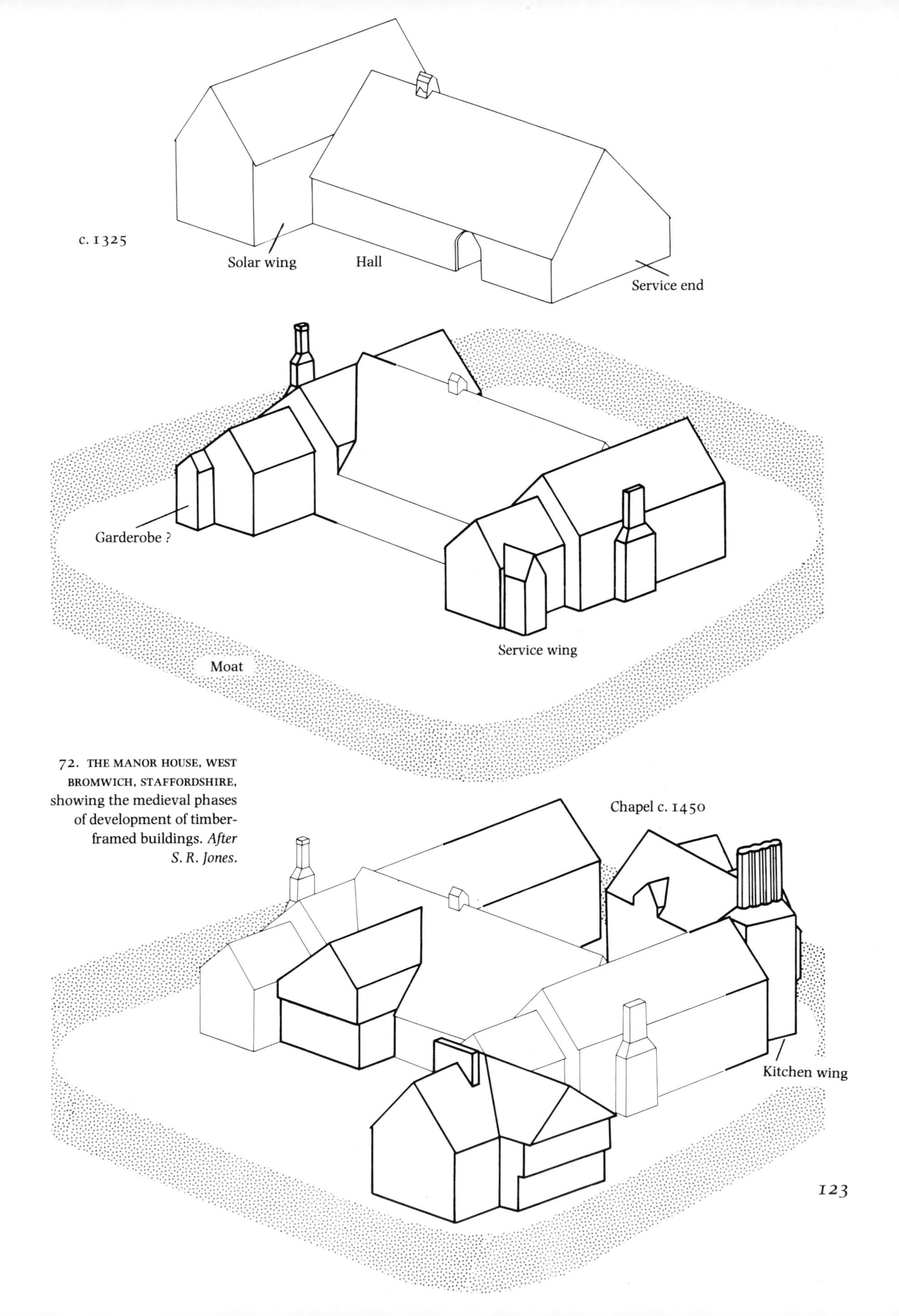

72. THE MANOR HOUSE, WEST BROMWICH, STAFFORDSHIRE, showing the medieval phases of development of timber-framed buildings. *After S. R. Jones*.

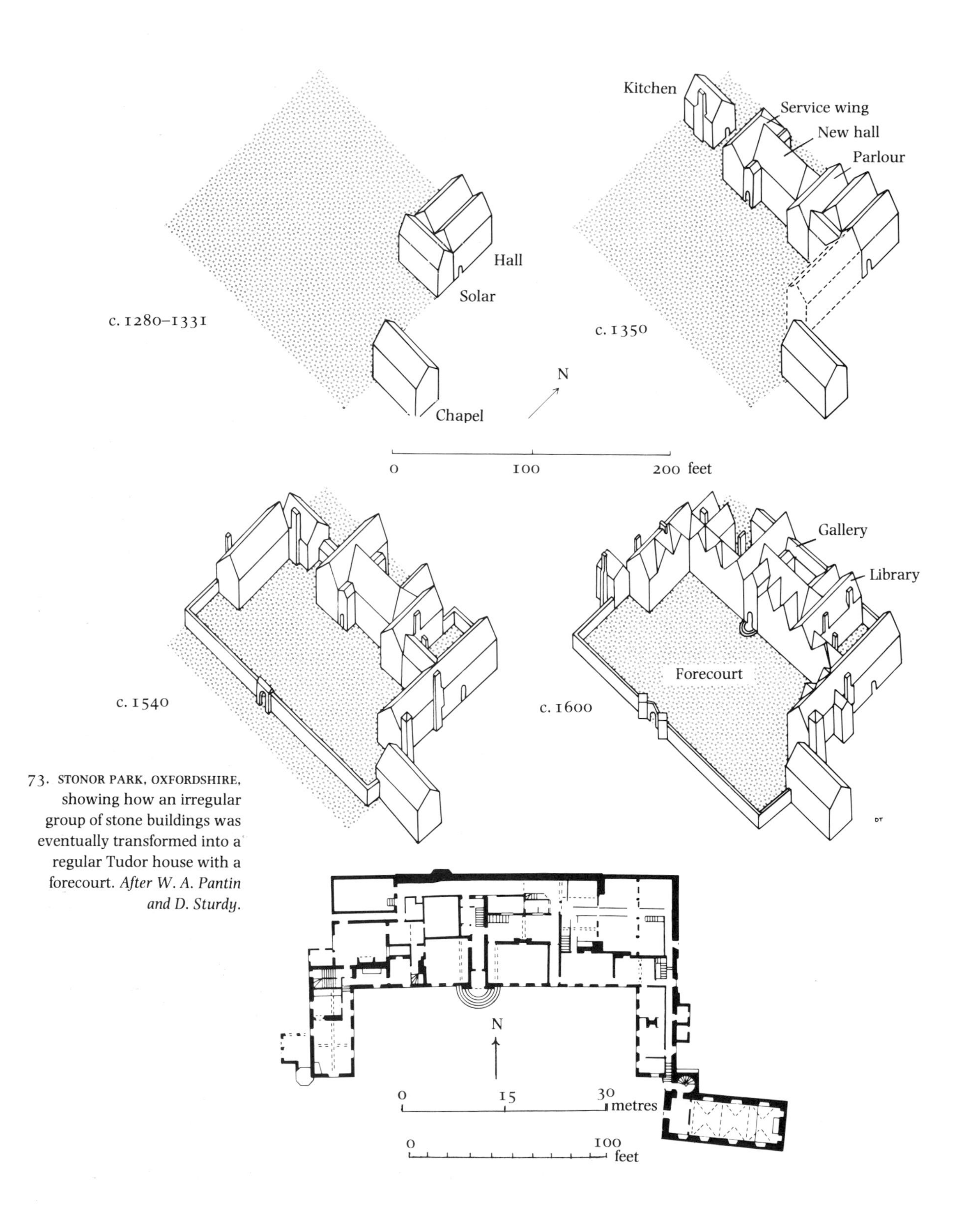

73. STONOR PARK, OXFORDSHIRE, showing how an irregular group of stone buildings was eventually transformed into a regular Tudor house with a forecourt. *After W. A. Pantin and D. Sturdy.*

chapels which were an integral part of the house the rear half, equivalent to the nave, was sometimes divided so that servants and the like sat downstairs, having entered directly from outside, while the family sat upstairs in a private pew. A timber screen allowed all to see through to the altar. Newbury Court (Somerset, c. 1300) and Blackmore Farm, Cannington (Somerset, c. 1500) [69], show the date range, and show the lord of the manor, even in a remote village, adopting a social distinction which runs right through European history, from the age of Charlemagne to that of Philip II of Spain and beyond.

At West Bromwich Manor House (Staffordshire) [72] a timber-framed chapel was added, perhaps c. 1450, to the solar wing,[32] but such chapels are very rare, either because they have had a poorer rate of survival, or because lords felt that a religious building should be of stone. Ockwells at Bray (Berkshire), which has been called the most sophisticated timber-framed manor house in England, once had a stone chapel as well as an outer court with farm buildings and a moat.

Some houses have only a small room or oratory, for private prayers rather than the congregation of the household, but often furnished for mass. It may be part of an otherwise ordinary chamber, occasionally with a fireplace. It may be over a porch and reached from the solar; some of the many references to an oriel indicate such a small room, projecting in some way at first-floor level, serving as an oratory. Only from the fifteenth century was the term oriel reserved for a projecting window.

The manor house plan in the later Middle Ages

Chapels and oratories incorporated in the planning of a manor house are part of the development, evident from the early fourteenth century, of what may be called the double-ended open-hall house: that is, a hall flanked at each end by a two-storey wing roofed at right angles. It was a natural development within a set of conventions, though these were not invariable: a hall should be lofty, lit by side-windows sometimes carried up in a row of gables, as at Stokesay (Shropshire, c. 1290) and with windows in gable ends as well, as at Penshurst (Kent, 1338) and Clevedon Court (Somerset, c. 1320); the wings could be long enough to contain two rooms or more, both accessible from the hall; lastly, the first-floor rooms in the wings might also have lofty windows in their gables, and there the lord and his family might spend their most private hours. This form of house built in stone meant that there was a gutter between hall and wings, usually lined with lead; the same form in timber was more likely to have the hall roof carried through to a wing, so eliminating the hall gable-windows and a problem of maintenance. The convention that the family lived upstairs tended to break down in the fifteenth century, a change marked by the appearance of the parlour: that is, a ground-floor room with an elaborate fireplace, with windows of high quality and with superior treatment, by moulding, of ceiling beams

74. OSTBRIDGE MANOR FARM, OLVESTON, GLOUCESTERSHIRE, built c. 1525, with open kitchen and hall; the south end has a parlour and a solar with its garderobe in a turret.

and joists. There are three contracts for building in London and Alresford (Hampshire) between 1384 and 1418 which provided for a parlour upstairs;[33] perhaps they represent a transitional phase before this new element in the house came generally to be a ground-floor room used to receive visitors, as it was in monasteries where the term was already current. The well-known references by Langland (c. 1362) and Chaucer (c. 1385) to the parlour as a room where the family chose to dine and entertain are earlier than any identifiable parlour in a house. Henry IV in 1399–1407 had a parlour incorporated in new lodgings at Eltham for himself and the queen,[34] but at Haddon Hall the parlour underneath the great chamber is an upgrading of c. 1500 of what had been an ordinary service room, usually called a cellar whether vaulted or not. By that date, many old manor houses must have acquired a parlour by that sort of conversion, and any new house had it as a matter of course.

The kitchen remained to the end of the Middle Ages attached to the house rather than integrated within it. The kitchen at Markenfield Hall (Yorkshire, 1310) was originally alongside the first-floor hall, not below it.[35] A high degree of integration can be observed at South Wingfield (1440) and Gainsborough (c. 1480), each rebuilt in one operation. There the kitchen lay beyond the pantry and buttery, the commonest location, but the plans are advanced in that food was not carried through an open court or under a covered way from a detached building, as was commonly the case. When William Lord Hastings built his solar tower at Ashby-de-la-Zouch in 1474 [57] he had an underground passage dug from the existing kitchen for about 27 m (29 yd), no doubt as much for the sake of warm food as for the safety of those who served it.[36] Supplies in large quantities had to reach the kitchen from some open space and

75. Hall louvre, GAINSBOROUGH OLD HALL, LINCOLNSHIRE, taken down for repair in 1960. The roof has been restored without being replaced.

food then be served into the hall and other rooms; this remained a reason for separating the kitchen somewhat even in a tightly planned house, and makes the location of the South Wingfield kitchen, reached apparently only from the inner court, seem curiously inconvenient. It may be that smaller households, such as that kept up at Manor Farm, Ashbury (Berkshire),[37] which belonged to Glastonbury, provided a reason for making the kitchen a straightforward extension of the main range, beyond the buttery and pantry; that in effect was where the kitchen eventually settled down [74]. The size of a large manorial household had another consequence, namely, the retention of the open hearth in the hall, rather than having a fireplace on a side or end wall. Hence the hearth at Penshurst or Gainsborough, with a louvre in the roof [75], was never superseded; it was the most effective way of warming a large hall full of guests.

It remains to ask what these manor houses, large and small, tell us about medieval society. They are on the whole remarkably uniform; variations are limited, for instance, to the position of the solar or best chamber either over the service rooms or at the other end of the hall, and to the relation of kitchen to hall. Apart from the tower houses in the most unsettled parts of the north and an occasional solar tower elsewhere, there are no marked regional variations in the plans of houses, a striking comment on the coherence of the gentry as a class. The architectural style and features of stone houses are nearly as homogeneous as are the designs of the open roofs of halls and solars. These houses were built by men related by blood or marriage, who met in the castles and halls of the tenants-in-chief or their bishops; who placed their sons to be educated and trained in the households of those greater men; who met in the shire court and served together as justices of the peace or on the various commissions which were the machinery of local government. The class was at the same time open to recruits from trade and commerce: to such men as the builder of Stokesay Castle (c. 1275), the son of a Shrewsbury clothier; of Penshurst Place (1338–9), a leading London merchant-financier. Great Chalfield (Wiltshire) was built in 1467–88 by Thomas Tropenell, a clothier, and Athelhampton Hall (Dorset) by Sir William Martyn (d. 1504) a lord mayor of London, These men evidently knew what sort of houses to build to make their success apparent.

The present distribution probably represents accurately the regions where the most substantial manor houses were built, except for the vicinity of London and industrial towns of the Midlands and Lancashire; West Bromwich nearly in the centre of Birmingham is a remarkable survivor. A dozen or more have been demolished since c. 1960, too small a number to distort the pattern.[38] Nearly all lie south of a line from the Wash to the Severn, in the counties which were by far the richest, at a time when wealth was based essentially on the quality of land and, to an increasing extent in the fifteenth century, on wool and the cloth industry. In a ranking of counties in 1515–35, based on tax assessments,[39] the richest per square mile were Middlesex, Somerset, Essex, Kent and Surrey (an order which may reflect wealth spilling out from London) and the poorest Yorkshire, Lancashire, Staffordshire, Derbyshire, Kesteven, Shropshire (surprisingly) and Cornwall. The correlation between wealth and medieval manor houses is not perfect, but Lincolnshire and Nottinghamshire have perhaps three apiece (including Gainsborough and Holme Pierrepont), East Yorkshire none except for the Norman undercroft in the old Manor House at Burton Agnes. Some counties became markedly richer between 1334 and 1515, among them Somerset, and this may explain why that county has more stone manor houses built before 1500 than any other. What now survives is a measure not only of what was built but also of what was not rebuilt in later centuries. The Somerset houses represent a peak of prosperity or ostentation not surpassed in later times; Northamptonshire's wealth of country houses of the seventeenth and eighteenth centuries conceals remains of even grander manorial halls. At Upton Hall the medieval roof of the hall is hidden by 'some of the finest Georgian plaster work in the country' (Pevsner).[40] At Boughton House, visitors see in the hall the vaulted ceiling inserted by the first duke of Montagu (d. 1709) and painted by Chéron; the fine roof of c. 1475 [76] is totally hidden and is accessible only by ladder through a small trefoil opening in the gable. From its design it was built by Richard Whetehill, who received in 1473 licence to crenellate his manor house. He was the first of three generations of Whetehills who served the crown in Calais and he bought the manor of Boughton for his retirement with the fortune he had made there.[41] When Sir Edward Montagu, another Northamptonshire gentleman, bought the manor in 1528, the buildings round Fish Court were good enough even for a lord chief justice of England; it was left for his eventual successor, the first duke, to disguise them completely in later enlargements.

The survival today of manor houses originally timber-framed has depended on a complex of circumstances. As the largest part of the house, the hall itself was the most substantial construction. Functions in it changed less than that of other parts: the most formal entertainment and the most generous display of hospitality which was the mark of a gentleman; meetings of the manor court, with a jury presenting offences and framing byelaws, old tenants surrendering their holdings and new ones being admitted. The rare instance where the court met in some other room in the house belong to the sixteenth century or later. In Lancashire, where the manorial system was never imposed, there are or were a few halls of massive construction representing the concentration of landed wealth in a few hands: Baguley Hall at Wythenshawe, Ordsall Hall in Salford, Smithill's Hall, Bolton. Stand Old Hall collapsed in 1960 but not

76. This drawing of the hall of BOUGHTON HOUSE, NORTHAMPTONSHIRE, c. 1475, is probably by R. Blomfield, and shows accurately the open roof with its principal and secondary trusses, cusped and carved wind-braces, etc. There was a fireplace in the side wall, but the details are imaginary. *RCHM, by courtesy of His Grace the Duke of Buccleuch.*

before it was recorded; Baguley and Ordsall have survived in spite of gross neglect by the local authorities which acquired them. Tabley Old Hall (Cheshire), of similarly substantial build, was ruined by mining subsidence and a record of sorts was compiled from its fallen timbers.[42]

In these cases urban or industrial development had not only severed the land from the houses but made them unattractive as residences of quality. Where the rural setting has not been destroyed, the medieval manor house is not so large as to be unsuitable for occupation in the reduced circumstances of modern life. Gloom about the occasional demolition, with or without planning consent, ought to be dispelled by the new discoveries made every year behind timber walls renewed in brick or stone.

Notes

1 F.M. Stenton, *First Century of English Feudalism* (1932), ch. 5.
2 *Engl. Hist. Review*, 25 (1910), 712–15.
3 J.H. Harvey (ed.), *William Worcestre Itineraries* (1969), 63, n. 1.
4 VCH, *Somerset*, 3 (1974), 95–108.
5 Matthew Paris, *Chronica Majora* (Rolls Series 1880), 5, 242.
6 VCH, *Somerset*, 4 (1978), 87, 91.
7 J. le Patourel and B.K. Roberts, 'The significance of moated sites', F.A. Aberg (ed.), *Medieval Moated Sites* (CBA Research Report 17, 1978), 46–55.
8 J. le Patourel, *Moated Sites in Yorkshire* (1973), ch. 1.
9 D.J. Cathcart King and L. Alcock, 'Ringworks of England and Wales', in *Château Gaillard*, 3 (1979), 90–127.
10 R.A. Brown, *English Castles* (1970), 49.
11 M.E. Wood, 'Thirteenth Century domestic architecture in England', *Archaeol. J.*, 105 supplement (1950).
12 M.E. Wood, *The English Medieval House* (1965), pl. IVa, 22.
13 G. Beresford in *Med. Archaeol.*, 18 (1974), 90–127.
14 The most recent published list of aisled halls is in *Vernacular Architecture*, 6 (1975), 19–27, but many have come to light since then. A recent example is Annesley Hall, Nottinghamshire; *Trans. Thoroton Soc.*, 87 (1983), 85–6.
15 *Ant. J.* 52 (1972), 132–68.
16 Wood, *The English Medieval House*, ch. 2, with list 32–4. This list too could be considerably augmented.
17 RCHM, *Dorset*, 2, 11 (1970), 210–11, pl. 137.
18 BE, *Oxfordshire*, 781–3.
19 C.A. Hewett in *Med. Archaeol.*, 17 (1973), 132–4.
20 W.H. Hale (ed.), *The Domesday of St. Paul's ...* (Camden Soc. 1858), xcviii–xcix, 129–37; J. le Patourel, in F.A. Aberg, 24–5.
21 P.D.A. Harvey (ed.), *Manorial Records of Cuxham, Oxon* (1976), passim.
22 J.Z. Titow and B.J. Harrison kindly allowed me to use their notes on the records of the bishopric and the priory. Compare also the accounts for the bishop of Exeter's manor of Bishop Clyst in *Trans. Devons. Ass.*, 98 (1966), 132–53.
23 These comments on northern counties are based on the work of P.W. Dixon, especially his Oxford D.Litt. thesis 'Fortified houses on the Anglo-Scottish border' (1976). See also RCHM, *Westmorland* (1936) and BE, *Cumberland and Westmorland* (1967).
24 L. Ambler, *Old Halls and Manor Houses of Yorkshire* (1913), 45.
25 N. Summers, 'Manor Farm, Halloughton', *Trans. Thoroton Soc.*, 69 (1965), 66–76.
26 RCHM, *Cambridge*, ii (1959), 381–2.
27 RCHM, *Peterborough New Town* (1961), 51–2; *Archaeologia*, 96 (1955), 1–58.
28 *Testamenta Eboracensia*, 2 (Surtees Soc. 30, 1855), 164; survey of Wiverton reproduced in *Archit. Hist.*, 5 (1962), 158.
29 T.P. Smith, 'Hussey Tower, Boston ...', *Lincs. Hist. and Archaeol.*, 14 (1979), 31–7.
30 W.A. Pantin, in *Med. Archaeol.*, 3 (1959), 219–24.
31 *Trans. Devons. Ass.*, 98 (1966), 105–31.
32 S.R. Jones, 'West Bromwich (Staffs.) Manor-House', *Trans. S. Staffs. Archaeol. and Hist. Soc.*, 17 (1975–6), 1–37, especially 17–18.
33 L.F. Salzman, *Building in England* (1967), 464, 478, 493.
34 *King's Works*, II, 935–6.
35 *Yorkshire Archaeol. J.* 57 (1985), 101–10.
36 Department of Environment *Guide.*
37 W.A. Pantin, 'Medieval priests' houses ...', *Med. Archaeol.* 1 (1957), 139, fig. 30.
38 Some of these were described in RCHM, *Monuments Threatened or Destroyed* (1963).
39 *Econ. Hist. Review*, 18 (1965), 502–10; W.G. Hoskins, *The Age of Plunder* (1976), 28.
40 BE, *Northants.*, 438–9.
41 *Cal. Patent Rolls*, 1467–77, 392. There is much about the Whitehills (or Whetehills) in M. St C. Byre, *The Lisle Letters* (1981) and there is a 'Whetehill's Bulwark' at Guisnes; *King's Works* III, fig. 16. An account of Boughton will appear in the forthcoming volume on Northamptonshire country houses by RCHM.
42 Tabley: *Monuments Threatened or Destroyed*, 27–8; Stand Old Hall: ibid., 47; Baguley: *Ant. J.*, 40 (1960), 131–51.

7 *Monks and Clergy in the Countryside*

At the end of the Middle Ages between one fifth and one quarter of the land of the kingdom belonged to monasteries; adding the property of secular cathedrals, collegiate churches, and Hospitallers, chantries, minor institutions such as hospitals and the endowments of the parochial clergy (i.e. their glebe) might bring the total to a third. Most of the land took the form of manors ranging from large compact estates given before the Conquest to collections of scattered tenements grouped together for the convenience of administration. Any manor which was an agrarian unit had a building with residential accommodation, if only for a bailiff or lessee farmer.

Monastic granges

A monastic grange cannot safely be identified by the present use of that name for a farm, unless documents show that it belonged to the Cistercians, the Premonstratensians or the Gilbertines. Those which in 1535 were leased to laymen were not included in the *Valor Ecclesiasticus*. A farm which was extra-parochial – that is, exempt from rendering tithes to a parish church – was probably a grange. Such is the case with Grange de Lings, north of Lincoln, which belonged to Barlings Abbey; a house which is apparently Georgian incorporates a vaulted chapel of two bays, its traceried east window visible in the entrance hall and on a landing upstairs.

Where there are now buildings of substantial construction and of broadly secular character on what is known to have been a monastic manor, it is likely that they were used by abbots and priors on their travels about the business of their houses, or for the kind of pleasure which a wealthy head expected to be able to take; hunting or a holiday away from their houses. Newbiggen Hall, four miles from Carlisle, started as a tower house of the prior of Carlisle. The prior of Durham was the richest ecclesiastic in the north after the archbishop and the bishop, and built in the thirteenth century a hunting lodge at Muggleswick, 20 miles from Durham, and a manor house at Bearpark (originally Beaurepair) only 3 miles from Durham; the latter was used as a holiday house, with

A

B

77. PLACE FARM, TISBURY, WILTSHIRE. A. General view. B. Outer gatehouse, looking out.

a park, for himself and favoured monks. Only the remains of a chapel and a dormitory still stand; once there were also a hall and a large kitchen with a lodging for the prior, all except the hall and kitchen on the first floor over vaulted undercrofts.[1] Perhaps Bearpark was used only by the prior and favoured guests, for in 1408 a formal arrangement was made for four Durham monks at a time to spend three weeks at Finchale Priory, 3 miles north of Durham. They seem to have dined with its prior in his lodging, which was converted to a standard manor house with a first-floor hall.[2]

It is reasonable to assume that any substantial house only a few miles from the monastery that owned it was used in the same way. Bodsey House (Huntingdonshire), only 1½ miles north of Ramsey Abbey, has remains of a chapel of the thirteenth century and a dormitory (or first-floor hall) of the fourteenth; other Ramsey manors such as Abbot's Ripton, Houghton, Holywell, Upwood and Warboys all now have houses of post-medieval date. Other examples arc Wykeham (Lincolnshire) near Spalding where the ruin of a large brick chapel still stands; Ince Manor, north of Chester, which the abbot had licence in 1399 to crenellate; Forthampton Court near Tewkesbury. Regulations were laid down for Redbourn, 4 miles north of St Albans, about saying offices and how far monks might go on their walks.[3] The house has gone. At Sutton Courtenay (Berkshire) a house variously known as the Abbey and Abbey Grange was built soon after 1300 by Abingdon Abbey and in too grand a style for merely administrative purposes.[4] The hall had, until recent restoration, a low side-window, the only one in a domestic building, possibly to pass out alms in the form of scraps of food to a queue of poor outside. The prior of Christchurch, Canterbury, had a house at Chartham (Kent) where he and his companions were entertained in 1447 by minstrels in the service of the local nobility; the hall remains though the chapel was demolished in 1572. The demesne was let in the later Middle Ages and the farm buildings lay outside the courtyard, within an earlier moat; there is a fine Wealden house built c. 1500 by or for the farmer.[5] At Salmestone (now part of Margate) St Augustine's Abbey, Canterbury, had an important grange and the medieval buildings are almost complete.[6] They include a first-floor hall built before 1300 and a second hall of a century later, implying much use by the prior and his officers.

The nuns of Shaftesbury had to travel only 5 miles to Place Farm, Tisbury (Wiltshire), where the layout of their grange can still be deduced: an outer court with a gatehouse and a barn of thirteen bays and an inner gatehouse with an opening only for pedestrians, beyond which lay the house [77]. The latter retains part of an open hall with an enormous gable-end fireplace and a stone chimney like a louvre. All the buildings are of the fifteenth century.[7] To round off this impression of the standards of these granges, it is worth mentioning that St Albans had a house at Tyttenhanger (Hertfordshire) good enough for Henry VIII and his then queen to stay there in 1528.[8] No doubt some of his household had to bed down in barns and stables.

Templars' and Hospitallers' manors

The Knights Hospitallers possessed about seventy manorial estates in 1338; the Templars had a similar number when the order was suppressed in 1308 and most of their estates were then tranferred to the Hospitallers. They combined a working manorial establishment with a degree of monastic austerity for the resident brothers. At South Witham (Lincolnshire) [78] – a Templars' manor chosen for total excavation because it was abandoned after 1311 – a large yard was surrounded by three barns and other farm buildings; the residential unit included a hall with a solar, a kitchen, a chapel and a second building which may have had upstairs a

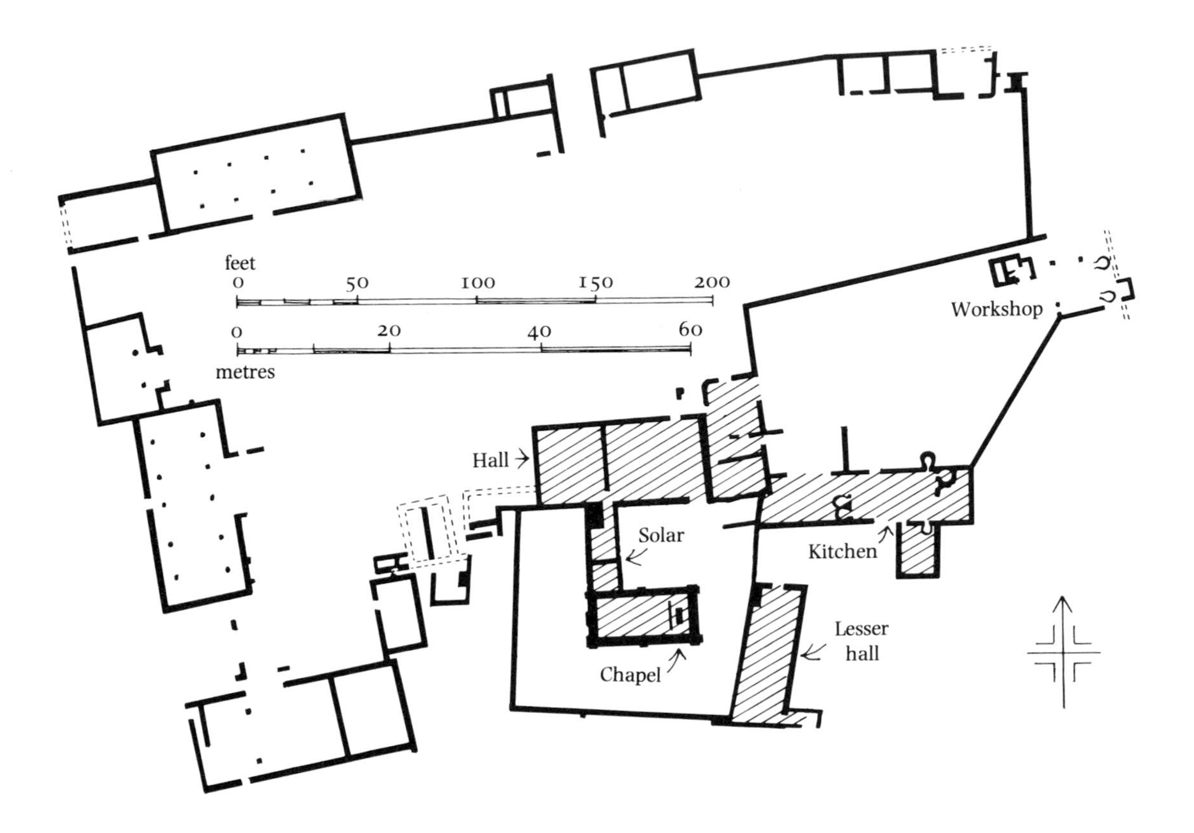

78. Plan of the preceptory of the Knights Templars, SOUTH WITHAM, LINCOLNSHIRE. It was abandoned after the order was dissolved, but excavation has recovered foundations of the manorial establishment. Residential buildings are hatched; they included a first-floor hall and solar and another hall which may have had a dormitory for farm-workers. The farm buildings included three aisled barns. A water-mill and fishponds were outside the complex. *After P. Mayes.*

dormitory for farm workers. At Temple Balsall (Warwickshire) there is another aisled hall, built by the Templars c. 1250. Strood Temple (Kent) and the Hospitallers' manor at Harefield (Middlesex) each had by c. 1250 a stone building with two chambers on the first floor, without a fireplace, for the resident and his guests.[9] The chambers were more substantial and important than the halls, which were used perhaps by the farm-workers; at Strood the hall held four tables, trestles and forms – and one chair for the regular resident. Documents speak of a buttery, kitchen, chapel and barn; of them no trace survives, and the *camera* at Harefield was demolished in 1960. Enough remains at Sutton at Hove and Swingfield (Kent) to show that there too the Hospitallers' establishments consisted of two-storey buildings. By contrast, in Snainton, a parish on the north side of the Vale of Pickering, a farmhouse called Foulbridge [79], apparently Georgian in date, has recently been found to incorporate the remains of the aisled hall of a Hospitallers' manor. An inventory of 1307/8

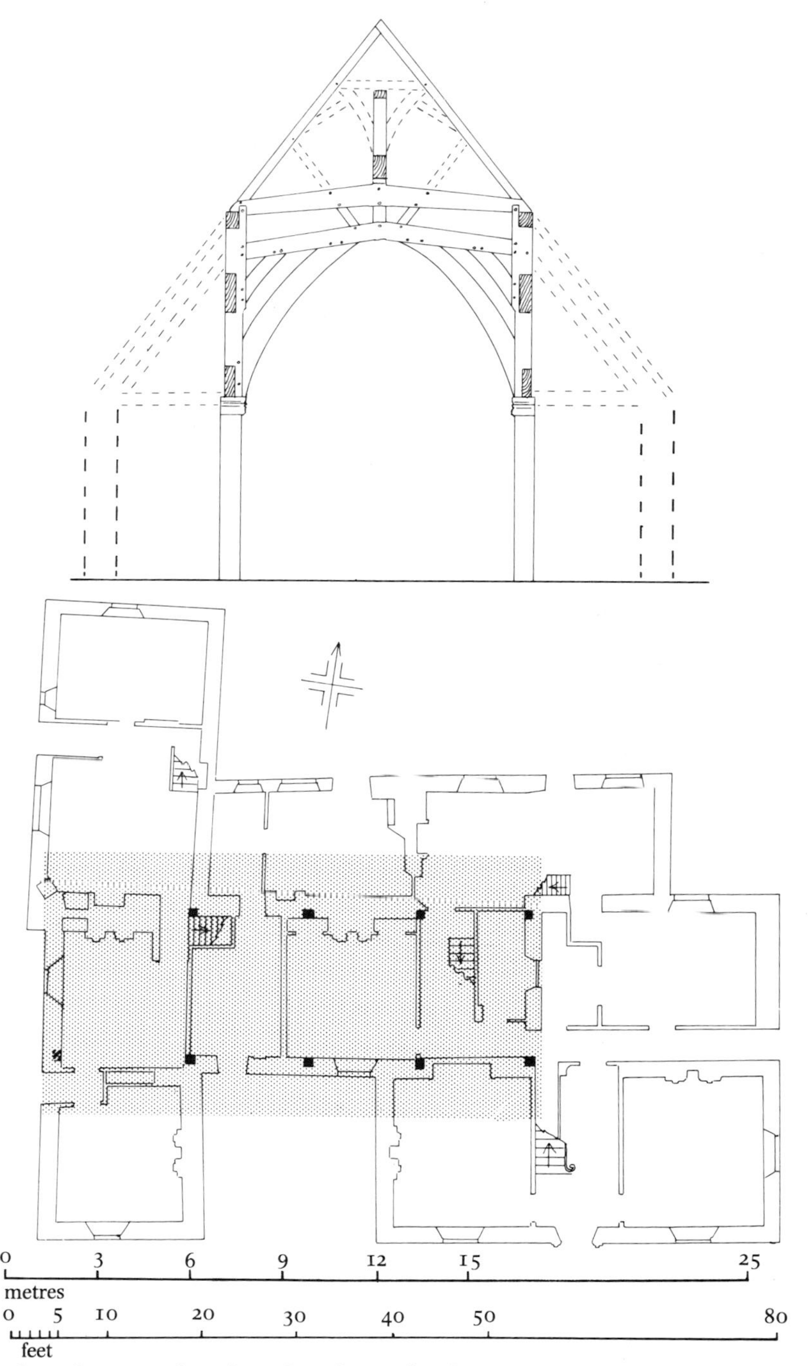

79. FOULBRIDGE, SNAINTON, YORKSHIRE, a large farmhouse apparently modern but incorporating all but the aisles of a hall dated by tree-rings to c. 1295. The area of the hall is stippled on the plan. When an upper floor was inserted in the hall the aisles were demolished. Original rafters were reused when the roof was reduced in pitch so that the original crown-plate now serves as a ridge-piece. The building was much enlarged when it was divided into two houses; it is now in one ownership again and being restored. *After RCHM.*

refers also to a chapel, a chamber, a kitchen and other service buildings, a forge and a barn, all of which have gone.[10] At Duke's Place, West Peckham (Kent), the Hospitallers built a timber-framed open hall. Evidently as with priests' houses there was no standard form.

The parish priest

No visitor to a village church is surprised to find that while the church itself is substantially medieval in date, the parsonage house is modern. It is convenient now to call it the parsonage house, though that term should be used only of the rector's official residence. A list of incumbents, drawn from bishops' registers and displayed in the church, serves to show how often ownership of the priest's house changed hands and there are often gaps which show that the bishop had no record or control of what was happening. The income of a rural benefice could be used to support a man at a university, a clerk in royal service or a chaplain in a noble household; the careers of eminent churchmen show how they collected prebends and rectories as they advanced, leaving their churches to be served by vicars or curates. Wycliffe held three parish churches in succession during the years 1361–82 which he spent at Oxford.

It is easy to find reasons why medieval priests' houses have *not* survived. One of them was the practice of appropriation; a monastery or collegiate church, having been given the right to present the priest to a parish church, then received the bishop's consent to appropriate its income and to divide that income with a vicar who served the church and usually received about a third of the income. Responsibility for providing and maintaining a house usually remained with the rector, with contributions (called dilapidations) from the vicar. Bishops' registers have many records of this process, by which about half the parish churches of England were eventually appropriated. The terms vary considerably. Often in the thirteenth century they merely lay down that the rector was to provide a sufficient house (*competens mansus*). At Bunny (Nottinghamshire) the land on which the parsonage house stood was in 1367 to be divided and part of the rector's barn was to be dismantled to provide for the vicar materials for a hall with a chamber; the vicar was then to enlarge it at his own expense. At Wheatenhurst (Worcestershire) the vicar in 1380 was to have a suitable house not far from the church to be built by the appropriator (the prior and convent of Bruton, Somerset) and kept up by the vicar. Sometimes, as at Sutton-on-Trent (Nottinghamshire) in 1302 and Ebrington (Gloucestershire) in 1385, the parsonage house was to be divided, room by room, but the terms are too vague for the division to be represented on a plan.[11] Such division implies that the monastery retained a parsonage house for the use of its proctor collecting the great tithes. Kentisbeare (Devon) and Kidlington (Oxfordshire) are among the rare cases where both parsonage house or rectory and vicarage house are known to have survived; usually the parsonage house disappears. In one case, it appears that the vicar was to have the whole parsonage house. At Kelvedon (Essex) the abbot and convent of Westminster gave the vicar a hall with a solar, chamber, buttery and cellar, a kitchen with a guest room and bakery, farm buildings and garden, and agreed to build him a barn.[12] It may be that in these later cases the monastery expected to lease out its land and so did not need a residential base for its agent. The common references to a guest room are a reminder that the ecclesiastical superior who saw most of the parish priest was the archdeacon; he was entitled to hospitality when he came on a visitation and no doubt used the guest room.

The priest's house was at the mercy of the impoverishment or incompetence of monasteries before 1540 and after that of lay rectors who acquired monastic property; of pluralism and absentee rectors and vicars; of variations in the value of livings which made poor ones difficult to fill. Surviving medieval houses are thus only a random and tiny sample of those of better quality, though an intensive search, county by county, would certainly reveal many more. As with manor houses and granges, the problem of identifying a medieval house as formerly a priest's should not be overlooked. It was not unknown for the lord of the manor and the parson to exchange houses; at Lamport (Northamptonshire) John Isham took over the parsonage house as his manor house.[13]

It is misleading to imagine the parish priest as a solitary and to contrast him with the married parson of modern times occupying a family home. Certainly the ban on clerical marriages was effective by the thirteenth century, but the priest after all had relatives and must sometimes have been looked after by a mother or other female relatives. The rural parish was served by a priest and his clerk; in all but the smallest parishes there was also a parochial chaplain, who was a priest, and occasionally a deacon or subdeacon as well, in minor orders. In many parishes there were priests serving a dependent chapel or a guild or chantry in the parish church. 'The unbeneficed chaplain, ready to take payment for casual duty, was a familiar figure in medieval society.'[14] No doubt some men of that sort lived in rented houses or lodged with laymen, but we must expect the priest's house to be designed for a number of men and their servants male and female. In some rural parishes, mainly in eastern England, collegiate churches were founded in the fourteenth and fifteenth centuries with endowments for a provost or master and up to twelve priests. They are usually represented now only by a grand chancel, as at Cotterstock (Northamptonshire). The most impressive may have been Ralph Cromwell's at Tattershall; it was systematically demolished after the Reformation but partial excavation has shown that it had buildings round a courtyard and an impressive gatehouse.[15] At Higham Ferrers (Northamptonshire) there are some remains of a gatehouse, hall and chapel. At Cobham (Kent) the courtyard nearer the church was retained when in 1596–7 Sir John de Cobham's college, founded in 1362, was converted into almshouses; the priests' lodgings were rebuilt and the hall retained but the second courtyard containing the kitchen was allowed to fall into ruins.[16]

The parsonage house

The commoner type of parsonage house falls into the main stream of domestic planning and corresponds according to the value of a living with the houses of the lesser gentry, lords of manors and prosperous yeomen. A well-endowed benefice, not appropriated, might be managed like a manor, with a court for its tenants. The Rectory Manor at Guiseley (West Yorkshire) was rebuilt in 1601 round the single-aisled hall of the fourteenth century.[17] At Tankersley the rectory, rebuilt in Victorian times, still stands within a moat next to the church, and there are moated parsonage houses in Suffolk at Bacton and Long Melford. At Bolton Percy the rectory still has a timber-framed gatehouse, jettied on both sides.

80. DEANERY TOWER, HADLEIGH, ESSEX, built c. 1475 by William Pykenham, archdeacon of Suffolk. *NMR*.

Hackney, a rich living and very desirable for being so near London, had in 1530 a house with eighteen or more rooms, a chapel and a gatehouse.[18] Archdeacons had no official residence but bishops naturally preferred them to rich livings. The bishop of Rochester regularly granted Longfield (Kent) to his archdeacon. Longfield Court, demolished in 1962, was a stone house with a hall and a solar wing more important than the hall, reflecting his status and style of life.[19] Hadleigh rectory (Essex) played a similar role; it was held for a time by Thomas Rotherham, later archbishop of York; he was succeeded in 1472 by William Pykenham, archdeacon of Suffolk and a rural dean. He had a house in Northgate Street, Ipswich, whose brick gateway survives; at Hadleigh he intended to build on an even grander scale, but presumably had only built the gatehouse (Deanery Tower)[80] when he died in 1497, for the residence behind is modern.[20] Livings which formed the endowment or prebend of a cathedral sometimes have a substantial house. Horton Court (Gloucestershire), a prebendal house belonging to Salisbury, has thc remains of a Norman hall [82]. The rest of the house was built in 1521 by William Knight, a churchman in the king's service who became bishop of Bath and Wells. He had served on diplomatic missions to Italy and finished his residence with some of the earliest Renaissance style ornament and an arcaded loggia in the garden.[21]

Most parsonage houses conformed to the local idiom. Near the Scottish border at least eighteen priests had tower houses most of which survive to one degree or another [81]. The vicar's pele at Corbridge is the best

81. VICAR'S PELE, ELSDON, NORTHUMBERLAND, a fourteenth-century tower house. *NMR*.

82. HORTON COURT, GLOUCESTERSHIRE, showing (left) the Norman hall close to the church, and the later part of the house including (right) the Renaissance doorway.

83. THE OLD VICARAGE, LINTON, KENT, timber-framed with an open hall and a jettied solar. *NMR.*

84. WEST DEAN RECTORY, SUSSEX, an early example, c. 1270–80, of a rare type: a house originally of two storeys.

known but not the largest. At Houghton-le-Spring, where the vicar embattled his tower in 1483 and was fined by the bishop of Durham for doing so without a licence,[22] the tower is incorporated in a later house now used as council offices. Simonburn (Northumberland), probably the richest parochial benefice in England[23] with a parish which stretched from Hadrian's Wall to the Scottish border, has now a house of 1725, replacing a house of 1666 which in turn replaced a tower house. In south-eastern counties, some parsons built themselves Wealden houses, as at Headcorn (Kent), one of the most superb examples, and at Otham. The Clergy House at Alfriston (Sussex) long owned by the National Trust, is of Wealden design. It is typical in plan, but a recent survey has shown that there was no doorway originally from the hall into the parlour end. It is possible that a female housekeeper was segregated there, but it is also possible that a non-resident vicar expected to let the house and keep the wing for his occasional visits, or that the parlour was intended for the archdeacon or the rural dean when they came for a visitation.[24] In a good many instances, the private end of the house with its first-floor solar is particularly large or well built, underlining the parson's duty of hospitality. At Linton (Kent) [83] the Old Vicarage is an ordinary three-unit timber-framed house but has an end-jetty to the solar, a slight mark of superiority.[25] At the same time it is possible to point to one tiny house, which must have been for a priest, perhaps for occasional use only. At Ichingfield (Sussex) the Priest's House stands in the churchyard;[26] the living was appropriated to Sele Priory which presumably made no other provision for a vicar; it consisted of two small bays with a sleeping loft over one of them.

Houses of wealthy parsons

At the upper end of the scale we find houses in which a grand hall is the dominant feature. The rectory at Kingston (Cambridgeshire) had an aisled hall of c. 1300 to which a cross-wing was soon added, and in 1399–1400 New College, Oxford, built an aisled hall at Hornchurch (Essex) for the chaplain there.[27] The lord of the manor might and often did provide for a younger son willing to enter the priesthood by presenting him to the living of its parish church, and the injection of family money seems to explain two unusually splendid buildings. At Warbleton (Sussex) where a family of that name held the manor, the living was not rich but the hall of the old rectory has a most elaborately moulded arched truss (in timber), and a William de Warbleton was rector in 1315.[28] Coningsby (Lincolnshire) [85] was, on the other hand, a rich living; the rector in 1335–75 was William Hillary, whose father, a midland gentleman with estates in Leicestershire and Staffordshire, had inherited Coningsby and with it the advowson of the church.[29] He presented first one and then another of his sons; the second proceeded to build a larger house and employ a carpenter with midland connections to design an aisled hall with a base-cruck in it and to finish it with decorative carvings. The solar end had its timber walls rebuilt in brick in 1463 by a rector named John Croxby. This is known from notes by a seventeenth-century antiquary, who recorded that the parlour window had heraldic glass with arms of the Lincolnshire gentry and an inscription with Croxby's name and that date. The medieval kitchen and outbuildings have of course disappeared.

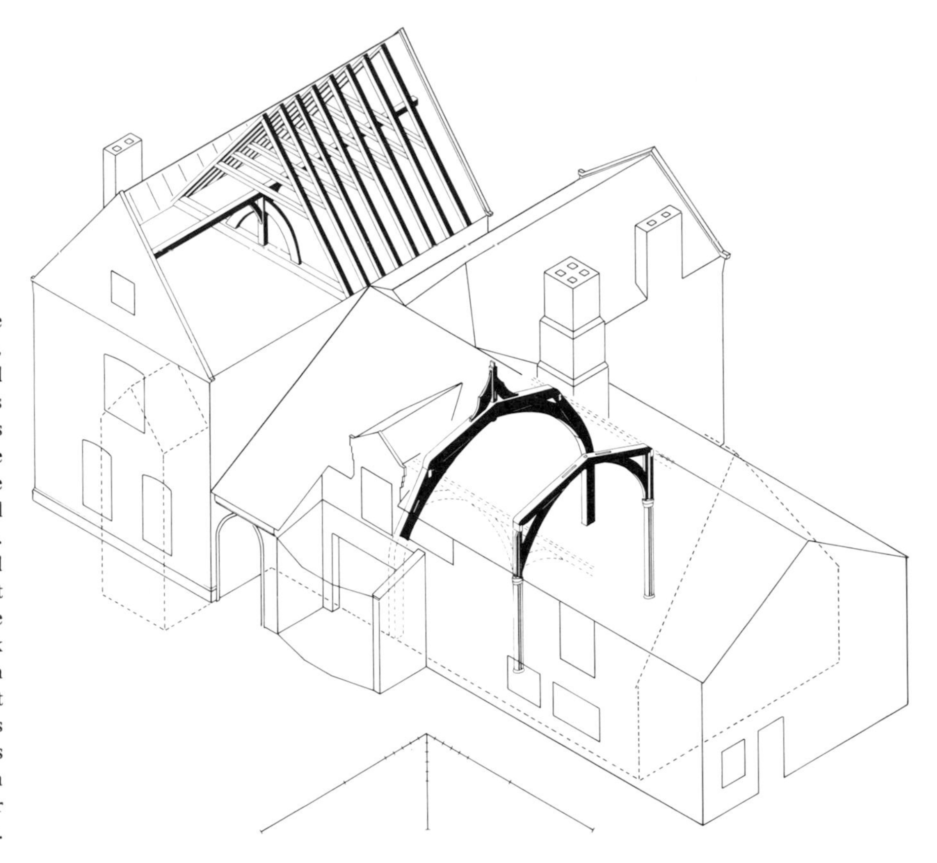

85. Isometric view of the former rectory at CONINGSBY, LINCOLNSHIRE. The original extent of the hall of c. 1345 is shown by broken lines, as is the garderobe-turret of the cross-wing, which can be inferred from a blocked doorway in the great chamber. The main trusses of the hall have survived subsequent alterations, except for the lower part of one base-cruck blade, removed to make a conservatory. The crown-post roof of the cross-wing was retained when the wing was cased in brick; some common rafters have been omitted for clarity.

In such a house the rector could live like a country gentleman, leaving to stipendiary chaplains, of whom there were certainly four in 1526, the routine of church services. The parson of Church Eaton (Staffordshire), another rich living, had in 1380/1 a household of thirteen servants.[30]

The storeyed parsonage house

The rector of Coningsby could entertain in the parlour and offer beds in the great chamber to his guests; whether those stipendiary chaplains lived and slept in the hall we do not know. Another type of parsonage house was more clearly designed for several men of similar standing. The old rectory at West Dean (Sussex) [84], built c. 1280 (according to the style of the openings) of stone, has two virtually identical floors, each subdivided into a larger and a smaller room, with a staircase at each end.[31] There is no garderobe, and the fireplaces in the larger rooms are too small for cooking, so that a detached kitchen and privy must be assumed. Systematic investigation of priests' houses in the south-west shows that this type is represented by rectories and vicarages varying much in the income they provided, and also by houses built for groups

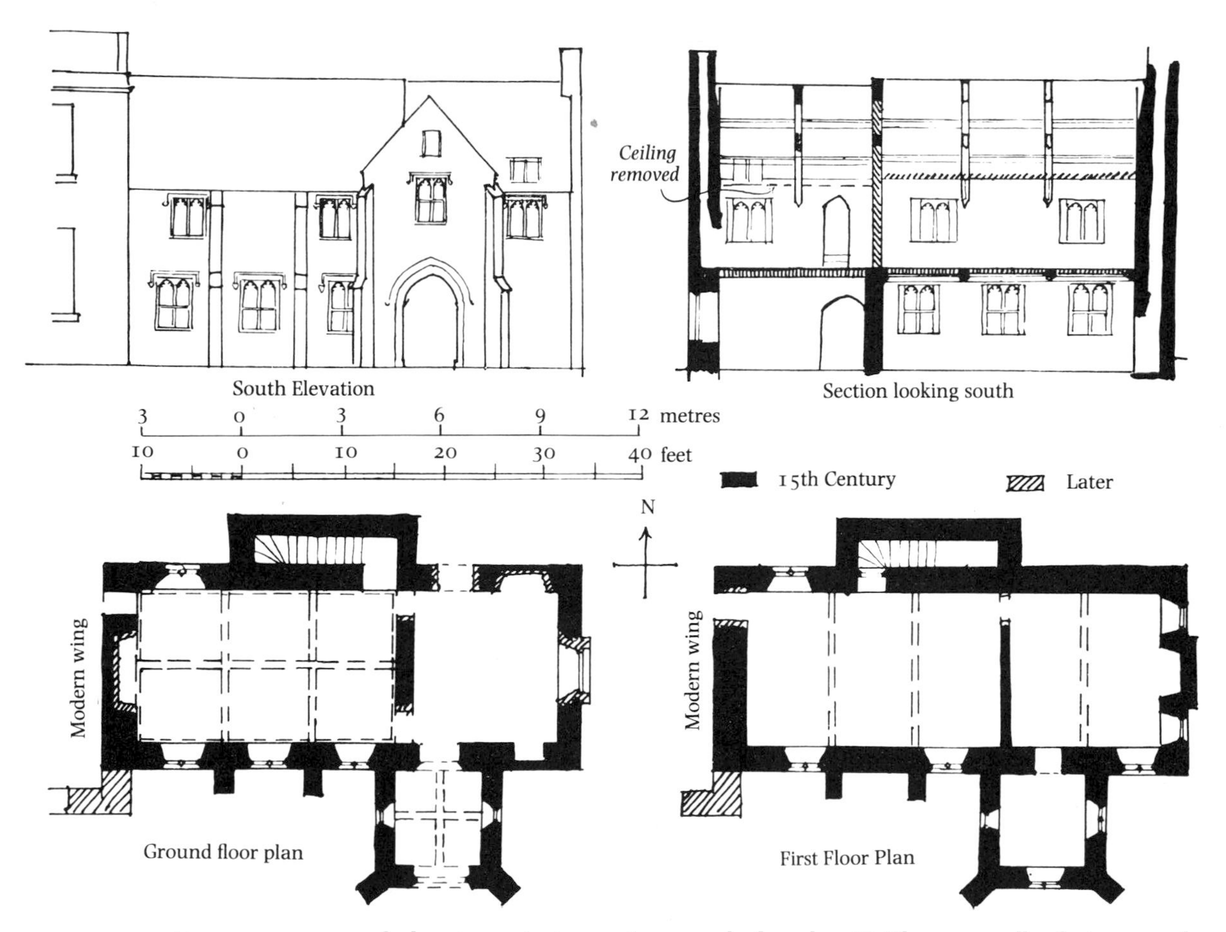

86. THE VICARAGE, CONGRESBURY, SOMERSET, showing the accommodation duplicated on the two floors. *W. A. Pantin.*

of chantry priests serving rural churches.[32] They are all of stone and nearly all of fifteenth-century date [86]; their survival in recognizable form, especially in Somerset, parallels the large number of stone manor houses there. Out of thirteen for parish and chantry priests, ten were of two storeys. Similarly, Glamorgan has remains of six priests' houses of which four had two storeys.[33] The first-floor rooms were not in any way the more important; it seems that the houses were designed for several men leading more or less independent lives and fluctuating in numbers. No other houses of this design, either ecclesiastical or lay, have been noticed, though they may be more likely to have survived in stone than in timber.

In 1535 Henry VIII and Cromwell set in hand a new valuation of all church property, the so-called *Valor Ecclesiasticus*. It is incomplete or sketchy for some parts of the country and may have underestimated monastic income, but it listed 8,838 benefices in England and Wales. We have seen how it is that they are represented by so few houses. Further research will certainly discover more, but it is likely that those of the best quality have already come to notice. Apart from the need to track down further examples and to interpret them, the corpus of late medieval parsonage houses shows the growing stratification of the parochial clergy into a small number of wealthy priests and a large number of poor ones – a problem with which the Church of England has struggled until our own time. Quality of building, whether in timber at Coningsby and Warbleton or in stone at Congresbury, favoured survival. As a consequence, the historian must be content with a picture which is sharp and precise for the rich parson and faded and vague for the poor curate.

Notes

1 *Trans. Durham and Northumberland Archaeol. and Arch. Soc.*, (4) (1896), 289–308; R. Surtees, *Durham* (1820), 2, 372–3.
2 BE, *County Durham* (1983), 275.
3 *Gesta Abbatum S. Albani* (Rolls Series 28, 1867), 2, 203–5.
4 Turner and Parker, 2, 273–4; M. Wood, *The English Medieval House* (1965), pl. 23.
5 *Archaeologia Cantiana*, 53 (1940), 7; 89 (1974), 169–81.
6 BE *North East and East Kent*, 381.
7 *Archaeol. J.* 104 (1974), 168–9.
8 *King's Works*, IV, pt. ii, 282.
9 S. Witham; *Med. Archaeol.*, 11 (1967), 274; Temple Balsall: ibid., 26 (1982), 155–8; S. Rigold, 'Two camerae of the military orders', *Archaeol. J.*, 122 (1965), 86–132.
10 *Yorks. Archaeol. J.*, 29 (1929), 372.
11 A few typical references: *Register of Hugo de Welles* (Lincoln Record Soc.), 1, 60, 74, 189; *Trans. Thoroton Soc.*, 86 (1982), 69–70; *Register of Thomas Corbridge* (Surtees Soc. 138, 1925), 239; *Register of Wakefield* (Worcs. Hist. Soc. 7, 1972), 133.
12 A. Savidge, *Parsonage Houses in England* (1964), 17.
13 M.E. Finch, *The Wealth of Five Northamptonshire Families, 1540–1640* (Northants. Record Soc. 1956), 21.
14 A. Hamilton Thompson, *The English Clergy and their Organisation in the Later Middle Ages* (1947), 143.
15 *Med. Archaeol.*, 12 (1968), 168–9, with plan.
16 P.J. Tester, 'Notes on the medieval chantry college at Cobham', *Archaeol. Cantiana*, 79 (1964), 109–20.
17 *EFC*, 58.
18 N.W. Alcock, *Warwickshire Grazier and London Skinner* (1981), 17.
19 *Archaeol. Cantiana*, 85 (1970), 61.
20 *Proc. Suffolk Inst. Archaeol.*, 3 (1863) 87–9; 7 (1891), 379–80.
21 BE, *Gloucs.*, *The Cotswolds*, 279; *King's Works*, IV, 26n.
22 Turner and Parker, 3, 206.
23 A.H. Thompson, *English Clergy*, 102, n.2.
24 *National Trust Studies 1981* (1980), 103–8.
25 *EVH*, 175 (no. 218).
26 BE, *Sussex*, 251.
27 RCHM, *West Cambridgeshire* (1968), 155; *Med. Archaeol.*, 16 (1972), 197.
28 *Hist. Buildings in E. Sussex* (Rape of Hastings Archit. Survey, 2, 1981), 37–40.
29 M.W. Barley *et. al.*, 'The medieval parsonage house, Coningsby, Lincs.', *Ant. J.*, 49 (1969), 346–66.
30 R. Hilton, *The English Peasantry in the Later Middle Ages* (1975), 34.
31 M.E. Wood, *The English Medieval House* (1965), 90–2.
32 W.A. Pantin, in *Med. Archaeol.*, 1 (1957), 118–40; 3 (1959), 216–58.
33 RCAHM Wales, *Glamorgan*, 3 (1982), ii.

8 *Peasant Houses in the Middle Ages*

All the houses described so far have been placed fairly accurately in their social context from their size and from documentary evidence for them. They belonged to earls, barons, knights or gentlemen and to greater or lesser churchmen. By far the greatest number of medieval houses still standing belonged, from their size and quality of construction, to men lower in rank [87, 88]: to freemen and those who legally were bondsmen (villeins or *villani*). Individual owners cannot be identified, and since documents cannot illuminate the houses, the buildings must be made to throw light on the structure of the society which produced them, the classes of men responsible and the subsequent history of the localities in which they are found. Those small houses that remain are thought to have been built from c. 1350 onwards, with an increasing number allocated to each half-century from then onwards. It may be that taking Britain as a whole the number rises in an exponential curve to the present day.

It is convenient – indeed unavoidable – to call these small rural houses the homes of peasants, but the term is so vague and included men of such varied condition that it would be better not to use it if there was an alternative. In a society which was becoming increasingly diversified, old terms were debased and new ones adopted, by those who were climbing upwards to mark their success. The Anglo-Saxon peasant (*ceorl*) became a churl, 'a rude low-bred fellow' (OED); peasant, rarely used in English but originally the name for a countryman, had by Tudor times become a term of contempt. The first new term for a freeholder under the rank of gentleman was franklin;[1] Chaucer's fourteenth-century franklin travelled to Canterbury in the company of a lawyer, another type of man who flourished in a mobile society. He belonged to that element in the country gentry which did not bother to assume the expense of knighthood; by 1500 he would be designated as esquire or gentleman. The new term for a freeholder under that rank was yeoman, originally an attendant of a knight, armed but not horsed. By 1500 it was in common use and must be our term for a freeholder. The principal problem in putting

87. LE CARILLON, HARWELL, BERKSHIRE, a cruck house built of oaks felled in 1430.

88. THE OLD HOUSE, BLEASBY, NOTTINGHAMSHIRE. Remains of smoke-hood with later brick flue and walling behind it. *NMR*.

small houses into their social context is to know how many to allocate to yeomen, since they were not invariably better off than villeins or husbandmen.[2]

Yet another designation for a peasant appearing by c. 1500 is husbandman, which then became usual for the class below that of yeoman and above that of labourer. This introduces another mode of distinction within the agrarian community: by the way land was held. Estate surveys of the thirteenth century distinguish freemen, villeins and cottagers. The villein, when the term became debased into villain, turned into the husbandman; on the medieval manor he held land of the lord in return for services and payments in kind or cash. It was he who in the fifteenth century might have his house rebuilt or repaired by the lord, or be given some help such as provision of timber to do it for himself. A small fifteenth-century house in a region where manorial control was a reality may well have been occupied by a villein rather than a yeoman; only the documented ownership of a particular house could prove it. Another difficulty in the way of allocating houses to classes is that by the late

Middle Ages it was not uncommon for a man who called himself a yeoman, or even a gentleman, to take land customarily held by a villein, his right being recorded in a copy of an entry in manor court rolls: that is, copyhold land. In all these circumstances it is impossible to discern a peasant class, in the sense of men whose holdings gave their families no more than subsistence, though that is not to deny their existence.

One class certainly not distinguished by surviving houses is that of the cottager who was usually a labourer or craftsman. It is reasonable to assume that he usually had only a one- or two-roomed dwelling, but none is known earlier than c. 1700. Labourers dependent mainly on wages, whether or not they had some land and livestock together with common rights, may by 1400 have numbered up to half the population of the countryside, and the poll-tax of 1380–1 for East Anglia shows that 50–70 per cent of the male population were designated as labourers or servants.

This brings us to the composition of the household. The modern notion of the nuclear family of parents and immature children is quite inappropriate. There were first the old people. Court rolls have many agreements for old people, having given up a holding, to be allocated part of a house such as a cross-wing with a ground-floor chamber or cellar and the solar over it, or else a separate building on the holding, with allowances of food and drink.[3] Sometimes the building had no heating and the old people were then allowed to come into the hall to warm themselves. Personal servants and resident farm-workers do not appear in records of that sort but must have been numerous as a class. Most of them served in gentlemen's households, but the yeoman must also have depended on them. It has been estimated that substantial farmhouses in Kent and Sussex were supported by 60–110 acres of land; such holdings could not have been worked by family labour alone and we must assume servants and labourers whose cottages have disappeared. The peasant with 30 acres or so may have had one or two servants; even labourers, according to the Staffordshire poll-tax returns, occasionally had their own servants.

Distribution of houses

The process of collecting types of house and classifying them cannot directly identify provision for servants and old people though the increase in size of house emerges clearly from it. So does the remarkable variation between regions of England and Wales. The map [89] is an attempt to represent the distribution of surviving houses of less than manorial status built before c. 1550. For those parts where cruck construction was common, the plotting is not much more than an informed guess, since cruck building cannot be dated closely. The map may distort the picture in another way; in alteration or rebuilding, crucks were likely to be retained, in fragmentary but unmistakable form. 'Among lesser buildings, early crucks are overwhelmingly more common than early box-framed

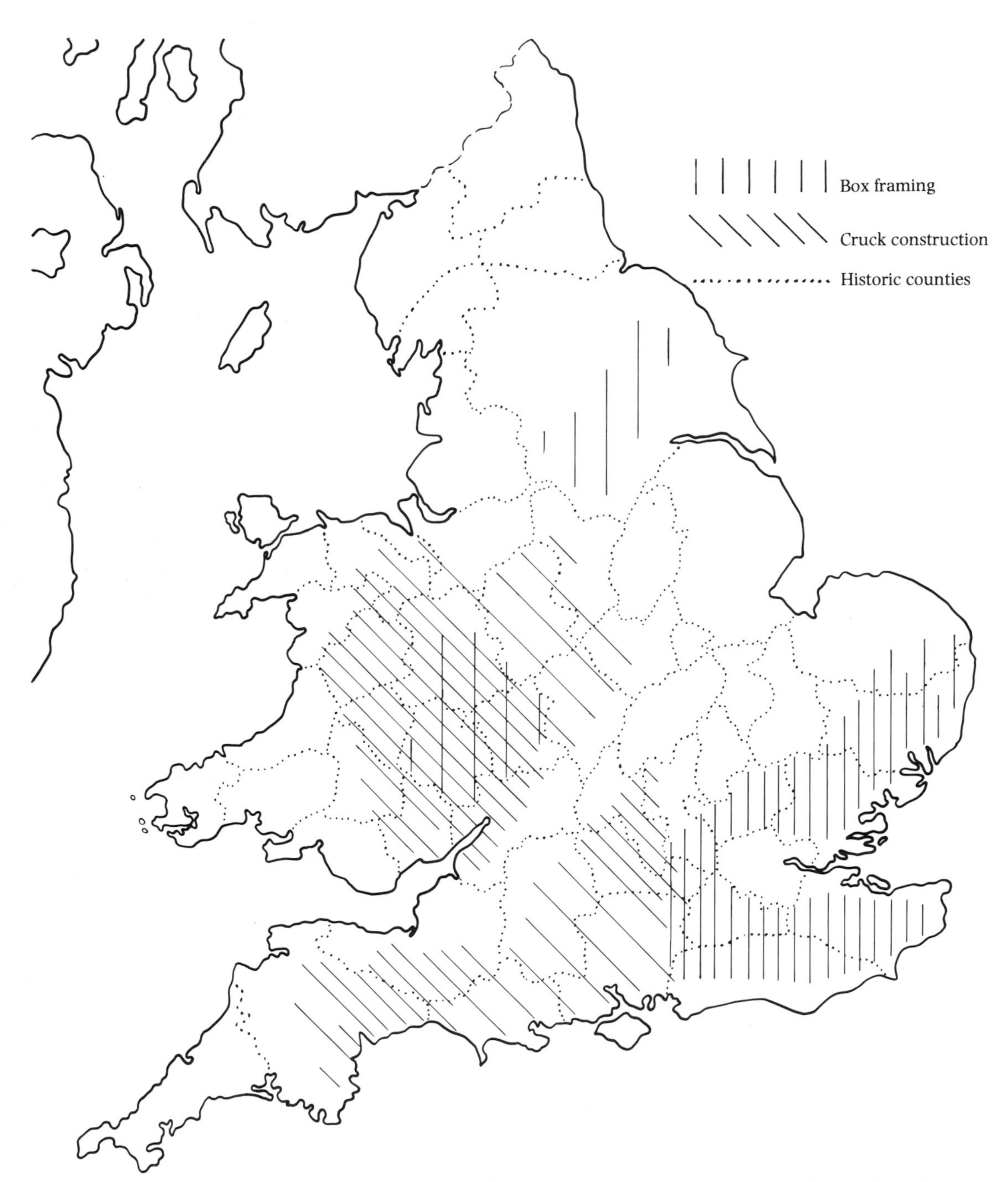

89. A tentative attempt to show where medieval peasant houses, including those of yeomen, survive in England and Wales. Dotted lines represent *historic* counties.

buildings.[4] Cruck construction was abandoned sooner in the south than in the north because lack of headroom made it unsuitable for two-storey building or for inserting an upper floor in an existing house; the tradition of single-storey housing lasted longer in the north and longest in Scotland. The map can only indicate generalizations about historic counties, or large parts of them; present knowledge is too crude to show the wide variations in the social structure of villages in the same county, or varying standards of building, even in the same village, shown by intensive field-work. Equally, it provides no clues to the proportion of houses belonging to peasants in the classic sense of men who, with the help of family labour, could only subsist, with little or no produce to market.

Forms of small house

The diversity of forms of rural house below the level of the manor house may be graded as follows:

A. Houses with an open hall and two storeyed cross-wings.
B. Houses with an open hall and one storeyed cross-wing.
C. Houses with an open hall and two storeyed ends.
D. Houses with an open hall and one storeyed end.
E. Houses open to the roof throughout with two or three units or rooms.

A transect across Britain from the south-east to the north, the north-west or the west would be a progression from the largest houses to the smallest and simplest. It would also be a progression from the wealthiest to the poorest parts of the island. Size is not invariably related to quality of construction, nor presumably to status. Open-hall houses of two units are very rare but a few which survived until recently even in Kent were as well built as larger houses. The carpenter could add distinction to the smallest house by means of mouldings [95], and such distinctions might make later generations reluctant to destroy it.

The open hall

The one universal feature is the open hall. Halls varied remarkably little in width, whether cruck-built or box framed, although greater widths were possible using crucks; barns in both traditions were commonly both wider and more lofty. Halls varied somewhat more in length, two bays with one open truss being the norm. No halls of more than three bays are known, and halls of only one bay are more likely to be found or deduced within the box-frame tradition than in cruck regions.

The aisled hall

The clearest mark of the emergence of a class of prosperous yeomen is that for them the aisled hall of kings and lords was scaled down to suitable dimensions and even built with only one aisle [90–2]. Two groups of them have been found, one in the south-east (Suffolk, Essex, Kent and Sussex) and one in Yorkshire; some were certainly manorial

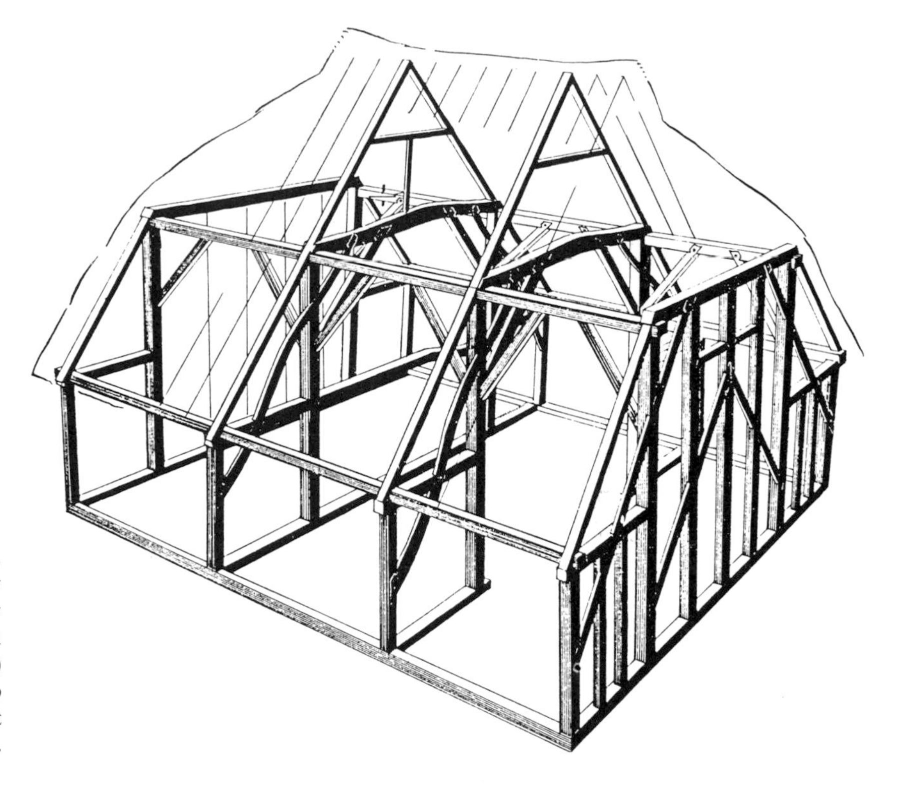

90. SONGER'S, CAGE LANE, BOXTED, ESSEX, with a two-bay hall and a storeyed end bay which measured only 6.7 m (22 ft) across and 7.9 m (26 ft) long. The drawing, designed to show the construction, is not to scale. *C. A. Hewett.*

but most of them not.[5] In every case their original form is incomplete, owing to alterations, but as discoveries have multiplied the local concentrations have been confirmed. A small aisled hall was recorded, while derelict, at Depden Green (Suffolk); it had no embellishment of any kind and its overall width including the aisles was 5.5 m (18 ft); the hall was of two bays with a storeyed bay at each end. Dormer Cottage, Petham (Kent), is an aisled hall of three bays, all originally open to the roof; it is 6 m (20 ft) wide including the aisles. Neither can be dated closely but they may have been built before the end of the fifteenth century.[6] A cottage at Boxted (Essex: Songer's, Cage Lane) [90] may be earlier in date.

Some thirty-three aisled halls have been found in West Yorkshire, most of them in the upper Calder valley and the large parish of Halifax; three are close together in the township of Boothtown.[7] They are heavily disguised by later alterations, especially by casing the framed walls in stone. They had an open hall or housebody, as it was called in Yorkshire, with storeyed ends; the largest had a cross-wing at the superior end of the hall, behind the dais canopy. The lower end beyond the hearth passage was one large room, possibly a workshop; the aisle behind the hall (sometimes the only one) was therefore used for services. The cloth industry was developing rapidly in the Halifax area in the years 1475–1550, and

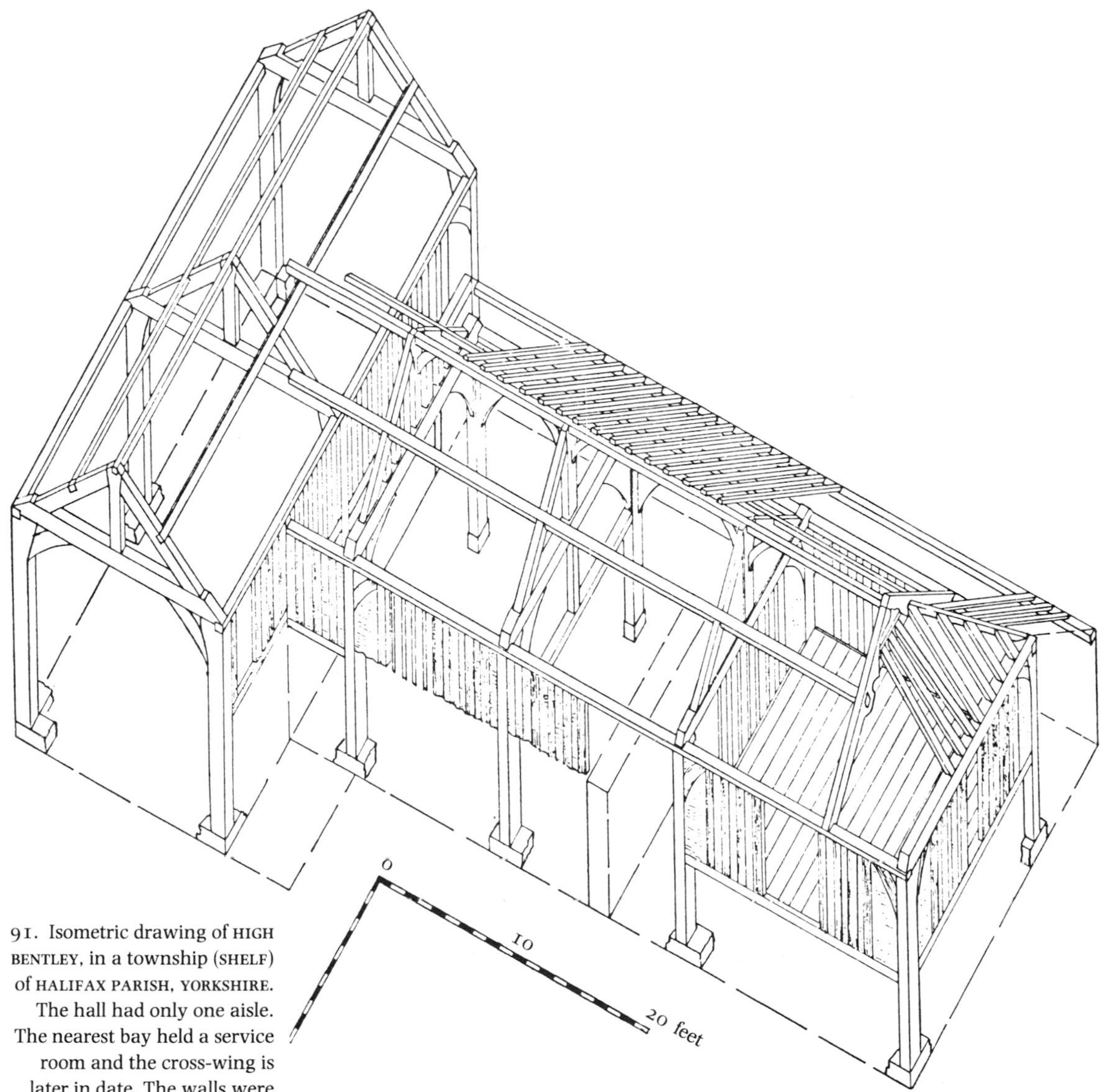

91. Isometric drawing of HIGH BENTLEY, in a township (SHELF) of HALIFAX PARISH, YORKSHIRE. The hall had only one aisle. The nearest bay held a service room and the cross-wing is later in date. The walls were rebuilt in stone in 1661 onwards. *R. W. MacDowall.*

these aisled halls may have belonged to yeomen clothiers. It is also likely that the textile industry contributed directly or indirectly to the building of yeomen's houses in the south-east. On the other hand, small houses in the Vale of York of aisled construction [92] have a simpler and poorer agrarian background. Some of them have been claimed as medieval in date, but it is difficult to distinguish an aisle – and they usually have only one – from the outshot common in the region in later times; it may be impossible to decide whether the extension was originally open to the hall or closed off. These houses form a continuous series beginning

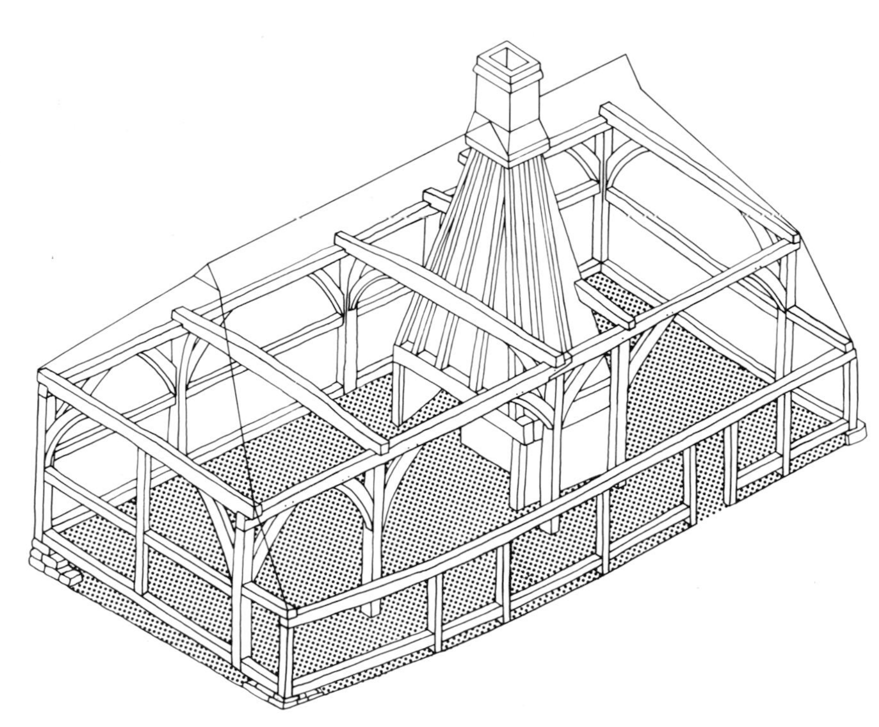

92. THATCHED COTTAGE, CARLTON HUSTHWAITE, YORKSHIRE, if it was built as late as c. 1600, shows the persistence of medieval traditions. It was open to the roof throughout and had one aisle. The framed smoke-hood supported a stone chimney. The house has been restored without its aisle. *After B. J. Harrison.*

c. 1475 and lasting for perhaps two centuries. In Sussex too the aisle became an outshot, sometimes called a cove in inventories.

The base-cruck hall

The southern halls with only one aisle are a special adaptation of the base-cruck hall and were built in the fourteenth and fifteenth centuries. Some, such as the Old Manor House, Keymer (Sussex), were small manor houses and Cayman's Farm, Burstow (Surrey), stands within a moat, but the base-cruck, invented for wealthy lay and ecclesiastical lords, was copied for lesser men; among the sixty to seventy houses (as distinct from barns) of that form are a few which were certainly not manor or parsonage houses.[8] Among them are two Nottinghamshire examples at Bathley and Clifton; in Buckinghamshire, Hertfordshire and south of the Thames are a few with halls a mere 4.5–5.8 m (15–19 ft) in width; they have not retained a name to suggest manorial status and so for want of specific evidence to the contrary may be given to yeomen.

The Wealden house

We have been concerned so far with imitation by wealthy peasants of forms of upper-class house. In Kent and Sussex that same class brought into existence a type of house revolutionary in the high quality of its construction, remarkably standardized in its form and its plan, varying only in size and decorative finishes and without any aristocratic ancestry.

The Wealden house has an open hall and two storeyed ends, all under a hipped roof. The storeyed wings being jettied at the front and the wall-plate carried across from end to end, the hall is recessed at the upper level and the plate usually supported by arched braces from the jettied walls. This integration of hall and ends limited the scope for rebuilding. It was easy to underbuild the jetties if ground-floor walls decayed; if the wall of the hall is rebuilt to give the house a flush front the crown-post of the roof will appear to be off-centre. The Wealden house seems to appear c. 1400 and remained fashionable until the 1530s. The hall is usually of two bays, never of three and occasionally one; if of two, the crown-post of the open truss generally has a moulded base and capital. The upper end of the hall never has a true dais or raised platform, but may be marked by a moulding or cresting to the cross-beam which is sometimes called a dais-beam [95].

In Kent alone more than 350 houses of Wealden design are known and Sussex has a large number, as yet uncounted.[9] Most of them are large with a floor area of 15 by 6 m (50 by 20 ft); some of them ranked as manor houses, or are so called now, including two or three in Benenden; a few were parsonage houses, including the large one at Headcorn and the small Clergy House at Alfriston, but the fact that as many as eight can still be identified in the parish of Marden and seven in the large village of Robertsbridge (Sussex) shows that most of them must have belonged to wealthy yeomen.[10] It is possible in a few cases to demonstrate the relation between a house and its land. Yardhurst at the east end of the Weald (between Ashford and Benenden) had less than 80 acres divided into a dozen small fields; it needed a three-bay barn. Estimates for half-a-dozen Sussex houses of similar quality suggest that they were supported by 60–110 acres. One house at Bridge (Kent) now demolished had a sort of gatehouse; that is, a wagon entrance with a jettied room over it leading to a yard with a barn and a cowshed, but most Wealden houses have not yet been studied in relation to their farm buildings.[11]

It was once suggested that Wealden houses like Yardhurst were supported by mixed farms worked without hired labour; it has been assumed, since they have a hearth only in the hall, that cooking was done there. This seems out of keeping with the quality and size of the house [93, 94]. An Elizabethan survey of Robertsbridge shows that a third of the houses then had a detached kitchen,[12] and a few surviving Sussex examples have been found; no Kentish examples are known but they must have been common and became redundant in the sixteenth century with the installation of brick chimneys. The size of the Wealden house justifies our assuming servants, male and female, living in.[13] It is possible to put together general factors to explain the prosperity on which these houses were built. The church owned more land in Kent than the national

93. A Kentish Wealden house (BAYLEAF), reconstructed in the Weald and Downland Museum, Sussex. A cutaway drawing characteristic of the Welsh Royal Commission. *P. Smith.*

average and most ecclesiastical manors were available for leasing; gentry estates were relatively small; there was no orthodox manorial system and land was arranged in compact farms. London, greedy for produce of all kinds, was near and capital flowed out for investment. The cloth industry developed in the Weald in the fourteenth century and reached its peak in about 1550; the iron industry flourished there on charcoal from woodlands. Instead of the simple distinction between farmer and labourer, we should think of the kinds of by-employment – spinning and weaving, dairying, cheese-making and fattening cattle, burning charcoal and making iron – which along with harvesting and the like made a comfortable living for more families than in midland open-field villages.[14] Some of the Wealden houses must have been built by ironmasters and clothiers.

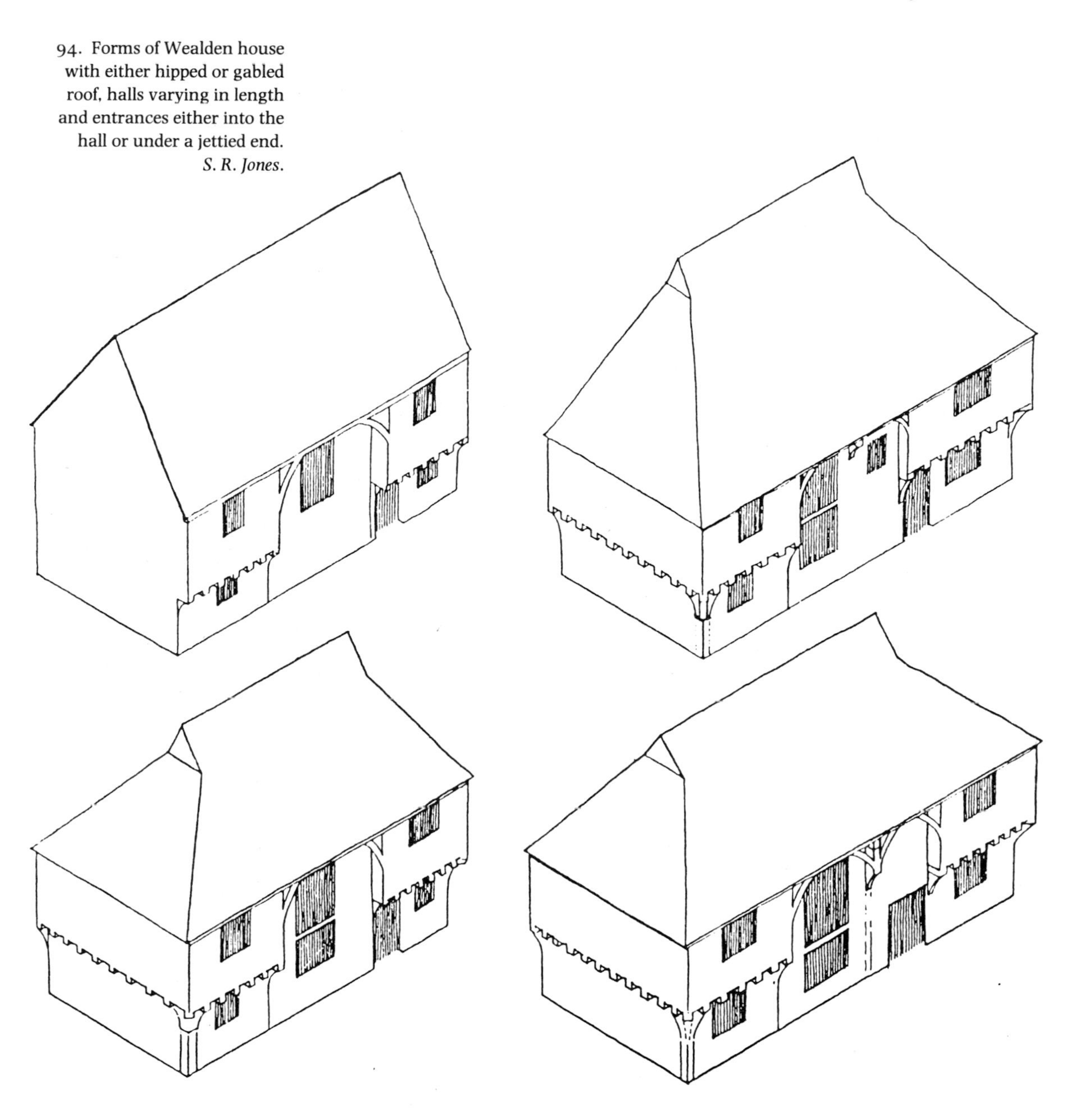

94. Forms of Wealden house with either hipped or gabled roof, halls varying in length and entrances either into the hall or under a jettied end. *S. R. Jones.*

Other houses with storeyed ends

Carpenters, having evolved and standardized the Wealden house, naturally carried it to counties north of the Thames, where it was usually built with a gabled roof rather than hips, and to midland and northern towns (Coventry, Newark, York).[15] Archaeologists have not yet worked out the significance of the distinction between gabled roofs and those with hipped or half-hipped ends. The hipped roof may be an archaic or conservative method, but its carpentry is somewhat more complex. Certainly the yeo-

95. Moulded dais-beam in PICKERSDANE FARM, BROOK, KENT. *A. J. German.*

96. OWL'S COTTAGE, STOCKLAND, DEVON, an internal jetty above the plank and muntin partition. *N. W. Alcock.*

97. I NEW STREET, SALISBURY, WILTSHIRE, joists of internal jetty (dark). The former open hall has a new ceiling (light oak).

98. LITTLE LONDON, ASHFORD, KENT. Victorian drawing of a house with a jettied end. *H. Gaye.*

man's house in Essex and Suffolk has a gabled roof and at its grandest has jettied cross-wings. The quality of a house was marked for the passer-by with curved and moulded corner posts supporting the jetties. It is easier there than in Kent to identify a ground-floor room as a parlour by its moulded ceiling beam and joists and an original fireplace. Whether such slight and tentative distinctions point to a different way of life – and use of rooms by family and servants – is a matter for further study. Houses of Wealden design or with two jettied cross-wings represent the apex of the peasant pyramid. What appears to be a distinct Kentish type of somewhat lower status is a three-unit house with an end jetty [98] to mark the importance of a first-floor room.[16] We can only call that room the solar, though whether the peasants themselves used that aristocratic term we do not know. The clerks who recorded the transactions of manor courts certainly used it. In several cases the service room at the other end of the hall was open to the roof. This Kentish type may well have emerged earlier (say by 1400) than its equivalent north of the Thames, with one storeyed cross-wing containing a parlour and a solar. In the West Midlands a framed cross-wing might be built on to a cruck hall [100]; this certainly occurred before 1500[17] though it is rarely possible to prove that hall and wing are contemporary, since they are separate constructions in most cases, with a space of inches or even feet between them.

It has been estimated that surviving medieval houses in East Sussex, the only area for which a calculation has been attempted, represent between 10 and 20 per cent of those that once existed. All the survivors have been altered in some way and it is sometimes possible only to identify an open hall and therefore by inference a house built before c. 1550. The Wealden parish of Charlwood (Surrey, and large enough to accommodate Gatwick Airport) has been surveyed intensively[18] and still has eighteen houses with smoke-blackened roofs of crown-post form. Most of them are Wealdens and fourteen have a hall of two bays, the others of one bay only. Evidently the heavy clays of the Weald were being exploited well before 1550; soon after that far larger timber-framed houses began to be built by wealthier farmers or industrialists.

Halls with a smoke-bay

The essential change from a medieval to a modern house – from an open hall with a hearth somewhere near the centre to one with a fireplace and a beamed ceiling – was a gradual process, some stages of which can be observed in south-eastern counties. We cannot hope to know the exact position of the hearth in a two-bay hall and the bays commonly differed slightly in length, for reasons connected either with the position of the hearth or the way the hall was used. The carpenter could treat the partition between the hall and one or both of its storeyed ends with the same flexibility. A chamber might be jettied internally to make it larger, overhanging the hall [96, 97], especially at the through-passage end. What archaeologists call an overshot through-passage is common in East Sussex. At the superior end of the hall, an overhang protected anyone sitting there from the draughts sweeping down from the upper part of the hall. A refinement of this sort is not confined to the south-east, nor to yeomen's houses.[19] One bay of a hall might be floored over so that the other became the outlet for smoke: a smoke-bay [175]. This was done in c. 1480 to the manor house at Mancetter (Warwickshire) and in some small Kentish houses before 1550. If the partial flooring ran the length of the hall it provided access at first-floor level, by a sort of gallery, from one storeyed end to the other. This change has been deduced in a few Kent, Surrey and Sussex houses by observing smoke-blackening and differences in parts of the joisting of hall ceilings.

The continuous jetty

An entirely new design embodying this sort of improvement is the house of two storeys throughout with a continuous jetty on the front. There is a contract of 1500 for a house in Cranbrook (Kent) which was to be continuously lofted over and to have a chimney with two fires in it – i.e. with two fireplaces back to back.[20] Houses with a continuous jetty are not uncommon in the south-east, especially in towns; the rural ones are large, with three or four rooms on each floor, and must be the homes of prosperous yeomen [23].

Yet another improvement to the comfort of an open hall was a

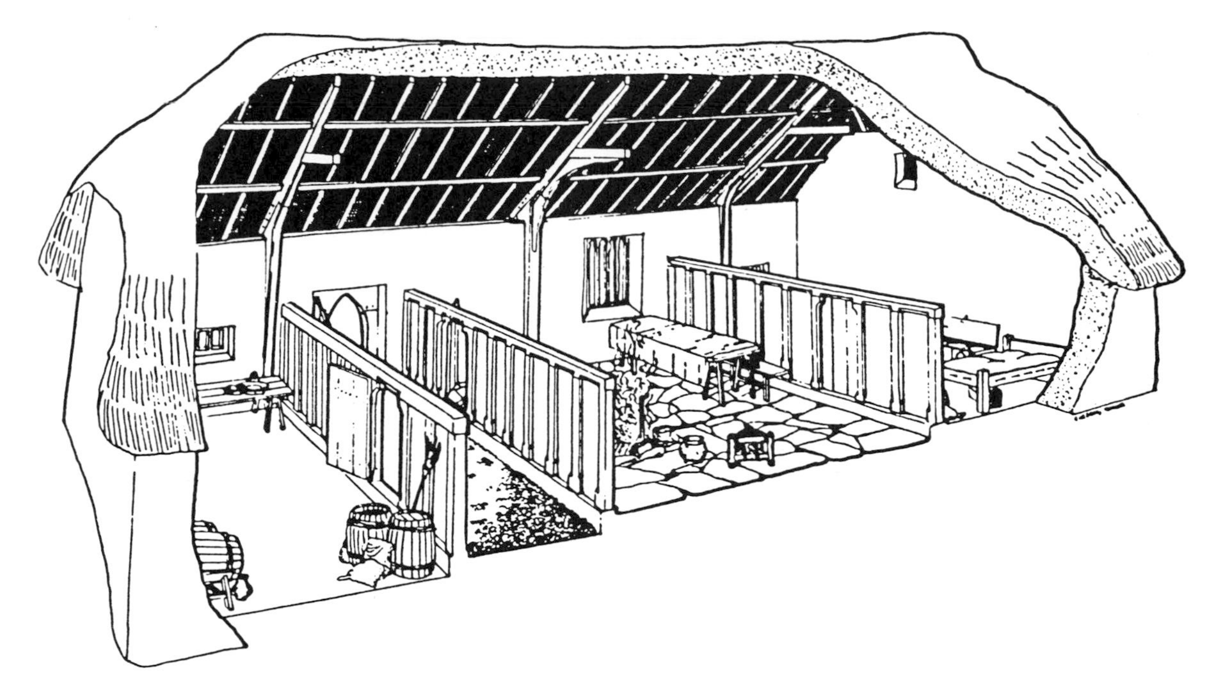

99. Reconstruction of a medieval house in east DEVON, with rooms separated only by screens to head height. *C. Carson.*

smoke-hood of timber and plaster [88]; such hoods have recently been recorded in several parts of England though they were first noticed in the North and the Midlands. There the through passage was separated from the hall by a stone partition, termed a reredos because it reached only to the same height as the walls. The fire burned against it with a hood over the large space around, forming a sort of room within a room. In a two unit house the hood was built against the gable wall; it was usually replaced later by a brick chimney but can often be deduced.

A division between one part of a house and another need not be built as a wall or partition from ground to roof; some well-built houses in the south-west had two or three compartments separated only by screens some 1.8 m (6 ft) high [99]; roof timbers throughout the length of the house are blackened by smoke and the upper parts of partitions are later insertions.[21] In houses with mass walling of stone or cob, roof trusses did not need tie-beams because their feet were secured in the walls and so the top member of a plank partition could be fixed in the walls at any convenient point without being connected to the roof.

The long house

The most enduring feature of houses of all classes was the opposed doorways at one end of the hall. In some small houses, instead of the pair of service rooms (buttery and pantry) or one room serving general purposes, this third room may be as long as the hall, or as the hall and the inner room together. This is the long house of archaeological literature and the question of its antiquity, function and distribution has filled many pages of print. Its ethnic origin has been disposed of; it is not Celtic, in spite of being well known in modern Wales and Ireland; nor was it introduced by Germanic settlers in the migration period, although its suitability for a climate with long hard winters has made it persist on the continent from prehistoric times to this century. The term long house is a literal translation of the Latin *domus longa*, used occasionally in medieval documents simply to mean a long range of building for agricultural but unspecialized use, and it occurs in parsonage terriers of later times in that general sense.[22] It was convenient, both in construction and in use, for a small holding to be run from one range of buildings, whether or not the domestic and agricultural parts communicated internally, and the modern cottage built in one range with a small barn or stable and cowhouse is a commonplace.

The dual-purpose building naturally assumed special forms for which special terms have been coined.[23] In a pioneering book on Welsh houses, the Welsh equivalent of *domus longa*, which was *ty-hir*, was applied to the type which, whatever its length, sheltered the family and livestock under one roof, usually with internal access between the two parts. In a recent book, on Welsh houses, the author preferred to call it a house-and-byre homestead. Byre-house is a simple and satisfactory version of it. The term laithe-house (from the Yorkshire dialect word for a barn) is accepted for a two-storey house built with a hay barn alongside it containing a byre or mistal. Laithe-houses were built on the uplands of west Yorkshire in the seventeenth century and later, and differ from byre-houses in having loftier proportions and a solid wall between house and laithe.

Since the byre-house is the only surviving form of long house it has dominated discussion, but archaeologists working on deserted settlements have served to put it in context. Several houses of the fourteenth and fifteenth centuries at Wharram Percy (Yorkshire) varied in length from 12 to 24 m (40 to 80 ft) in length; they were up to five times longer than wide. In most of them no more than footings for stone walls were found; some had a slight form of framing daubed with mud; only two of them had a stone-lined drainage sump to suggest that animals were housed in them.[24] Wharram Percy is only one of several villages in lowland England to produce evidence of long houses, and it is reasonable to suppose that the low end was used for various purposes such as a stable (after horses came into use in the thirteenth century) keeping pigs, milking sheep or sheltering them at lambing time, or storing farm implements and the miscellaneous gear which any farm accumulates. It has been noticed that on the coast of Brittany fishermen used the low end for storing nets.[25] The village weaver may have had his loom in the hall, near the fire, but the carpenter making ploughs and harrows or turning bowls on a pole-lathe must have had a workshop. The old people disposed of by the manor court in favour of younger tenants (page 148) must sometimes have been allocated the low end. Probate inventories of Tudor times and later sometimes refer, in their lists of names of rooms, to the low house, the nether house, the back end and the back house;[26] it may contain ploughs or hurdles, troughs or coal but has no special or regular purpose and clearly shows the persistence of an old tradition.

Shielings and byre-houses

Long houses survive only in parts of the highland zone where they were used as byre-houses: that is, for wintering cows. Most of them, especially in north-east Yorkshire and Cumbria, were built in c. 1650–c. 1750, and it is curious that they are common in south Wales but unknown in north Wales, to be found on Dartmoor but not certainly in Cornwall. They are evidently a particular response by men of slender means to the circumstances of their time and place, not a general form of dwelling for pastoral farmers in the highland zone.[27] The earliest have come to light in excavations of sites colonized in the twelfth and thirteenth centuries and later deserted:[28] on Dartmoor at a height of 350 m (1150 ft), above sea level [13], and also, more surprisingly, in Wiltshire on the Marlborough Downs. The latter site, on Fyfield Down, may have housed a peasant with sheep rather than cattle. The houses on Houndtor, Dartmoor, probably started as shielings: that is, temporary dwellings of men from the valleys bringing livestock up for the summer grazing on mountain pastures. Another homestead on Dean Moor at a similar altitude had a separate byre but, from the small quantity of pottery found, may only have been used seasonally before it was deserted c. 1350. Transhumance died out only c. 1700 and its latest stages were observed by such writers as Camden (1610) and Pennant (c. 1770). In Wales and the northern counties of England, shieling sites can be located from their names:[29] *hafod, lluest, meifod* or *cynaefdy* in Welsh and *erg* (Old Norse), *scela, sceling* (Old English). The process of converting a shieling into a permanent home started c. 1200 on Houndtor; the byre-houses there eventually had small barns with corn-drying kilns, proving that they were occupied all the year round. In Wales the name *hafod* often belongs now to a substantial farmhouse of the sixteenth or seventeenth century, and no doubt others were renamed when rebuilt; we cannot expect to be able to distinguish seasonal from permanent occupation of a lofty site. Byre-houses of c. 1500 have been identified in Breconshire;[30] the animals were tethered across the byre so that they could be fed from the through-passage, whereas the Dartmoor examples both early (Houndtor and Dean Moor) and late have an axial drain for cows with noses to the side walls. Byre-houses can be identified, at least tentatively, by a few diagnostic features, such as siting down the slope with the byre draining naturally at the lower end; the overall length of the house; the discovery of an axial drain or its exit through an end wall; an opening high in the gable for loading hay; the location of tethering posts; doorways and a through-passage wide enough to admit cattle. The use of the low end as a byre was sometimes abandoned, as can be proved by a drain filled in or doorways reduced in width; the byre then became a service room because the householder's affairs had prospered enough for him to build a separate byre, as happened at Dean Moor within the fairly short life of the homestead there.

The peasant house in the late Middle Ages

A picture of the living conditions in the simplest kind of peasant house in the century before 1550 can only be drawn from the very few houses so substantially built that they have remained more or less unaltered, and that have been carefully examined [12]. They have been found in parts of Devon, especially in Dartmoor, and in Wales and Monmouthshire.[31] The Devon houses have walls of granite or cob and roofs with true or jointed crucks; doorways in massive timber with pointed or shouldered heads may survive alteration or rebuilding. In Wales, cruck construction was equally a factor in favour of survival; cruck trusses or parts of them were retained when framed walls were rebuilt in stone and so provide hints of an original plan.

How many of these simple dwellings were byre-houses it is impossible to know. Certainly 'a great many cruck houses were either long houses originally or represent the complete rebuilding of a long house';[32] in a study of east Devon sixteen small medieval houses were identified of which only two were byre-houses but nearly all were cruck-built. The diversity of social standards within what we can only call the peasantry is just as evident in these remote regions as in the south-eastern counties. The Devon houses are distinctly small, usually only about 5 m (17 ft) wide internally, and the simplest were divided originally into two or three spaces by partitions to head height. The divisions were later rebuilt, in timber or stone, to roof height. The more sophisticated had an inner room, a feature which as we have seen can be traced back to much earlier times. In some houses of later date the inner room is still fitted out as a dairy, and must always, especially in byre-houses, have been used for storage. It is common to find that in later times when a dairy was built elsewhere, the inner room was converted into a parlour by inserting a fireplace, but that leaves unanswered the question whether the inner room was at any stage used for sleeping.

A few houses had a solar over the inner room, jettied out towards the hall, as in Owl's Castle, Stockland (Devon) [96]. The hall remained open until some time later but, surprisingly, was sometimes given a fireplace and a hood before it got a ceiling. These houses are at present impossible to date closely, but it seems certain that some improvements such as making a solar over the inner room were carried out in Devon before 1550. If that is true, it disposes of the notion that the highland zone was backward and that a time-lag must be assumed before improvements invented in the south-east were adopted in the south-west.

The gaps in the map

We are left with the problem of explaining the great rarity of small houses built before 1550, or their total absence, in northern England [89], in much of the Midlands and in parts of the south. The distribution of houses is at odds with that of population. Parts of Somerset and Devon, to judge from the number of taxpayers in the returns for a lay subsidy levied in 1524–5, had a high population and surviving houses are numerous;[33] parts of east Yorkshire and Lincolnshire had as many people but no houses remain. However, the tax returns of 1334 and 1522–5 also reveal the great contrasts in wealth between the richest and the poorest parts of England; the areas blank on the map were by and large the poorest. Henry VIII's so-called loan yielded three times as much (per thousand acres) from Kent as from some midland counties. There are no figures for northern counties in 1522–5, but probate inventories for Elizabeth's time show an equal contrast again between the Midlands and Northumberland.[34] These contrasts reveal profound differences in the social structure of richer and poorer regions. If we think of the farming population as a pyramid, it might be low with a wide base of poor or moderately rich peasants, or have a narrower base and rise to a larger number of rich yeomen. The former model fits the densely populated parishes in the Lincolnshire fens, the latter Kent and other parts of the south and east. Each might, taken country-wide, return the same total yield in taxation; only the latter produced houses of enduring quality.

Behind such contrasts lie differences in the quality of land and the sort of farming it supported. In the Lincolnshire fens a small acreage could support a family, and division of a property between heirs tended to reduce the size of holdings. The same inheritance custom was followed in other regions and did not prevent the emergence of a yeoman class, so that it was not the sole or even the dominant factor.

Environmental conditions and available materials help to explain empty parts of the map. In Cornwall, subject to damp and salt-laden gales, poor in timber but rich in accessible stone, only two small medieval manor houses have been recognized[35] and virtually no peasant houses. There may be yeomen's houses and manor-houses in north Cornwall, suggested by smoke-blackened rafters; they await proper investigation. A close study of the Banbury region produced only three or four small houses built before 1550, with cruck roofs and traceried windows to their halls; they were built by well-to-do tenants of church lands and no lesser houses were found.[36] The area north of Bristol, studied equally intensively, has equally few small houses; one of them was certainly a manor house and may have been leased by a pretentious yeoman,[37] but the average yeoman could not afford to employ a mason and a good carpenter.

100. House at PEMBRIDGE, HEREFORDSHIRE, with cruck hall and box-framed cross-wing either contemporary or not much later in date.

Some rural industries opened up a ladder of advancement as we have noticed in the Halifax area. The Wiltshire cloth industry, using local wool, helps to explain its wealth, second only to Kent in 1522; Essex was third and textiles may have contributed to its position. On the other hand, lead-mining in Derbyshire, which was combined with pastoral farming, has not left small medieval houses behind.

Behind this diversity lie persistent differences in the social structure of regions of England. On the one hand are those with nucleated villages with open fields, managing, through the manorial court and the by-laws it could impose, the economy of the arable and pasture land. The Leicestershire village might have a squire, several yeomen owning upwards of 60 acres of land and more husbandmen with 20–60 acres;[38] the yeomen there might be expected to build lasting houses but few have survived. In lowland Lancashire none of the customary tenants had more than 15 acres. The lighter lands of Norfolk supported a manorialized sheep – corn economy, dominated by large farms which restrict opportunities for upward mobility; hence there are no small medieval houses. The limestone belt from Gloucestershire to Lincolnshire was also dominated by large estates – as it had been in Roman times – and so is blank on the map.

Norfolk has not one medieval aisled hall and few moats. Suffolk has a large number of aisled halls and the greatest concentration of moated sites. These contrasts between adjacent counties are a reminder that characteristics of social structure had begun to emerge by the thirteenth century, if not earlier, and persisted through to modern times. Small houses are to be found in regions of enclosed fields, hamlets and isolated farms. The hotbeds of sedition in the peasant rising of 1381 included

101. A sawpit excavated in a fifteenth-century farmyard in the deserted village of BARTON BLOUNT, DERBYSHIRE, shows that one peasant there could obtain timber requiring the long saw. The pit still had traces of sawdust in the bottom, as well as impressions of posts supporting the balks. *G. Beresford.*

Kent, Essex and Suffolk where free tenure predominated; Jack Cade in 1450 led the Kentish gentry in revolt, not a downtrodden and impoverished peasantry. Both events reflect the advantages already enjoyed by prosperous men and their appetite for more.

The midland yeoman who wished to build a timber-framed house had first to find a suitable carpenter. Surviving small houses, wherever they are, must be the work of specialists – a class of housewrights, brought into existence by plentiful supplies of good timber (mainly oak) and enough well-to-do clients to keep them busy. In the Marcher counties, and even more in Wales, plentiful supplies of oak stimulated carpenters to build halls of good quality [100], with arched braces to the open trusses, for men who, compared with yeomen of Kent or Essex, had poorer land even if they had more acres. In the Midlands, a yeoman wealthy enough to build in a durable fashion probably had to go further afield and find a wright who worked mainly for the gentry; hence the Nottinghamshire base-cruck halls, and there are no other small medieval houses in that county. Otherwise it was a matter of employing the village wright [101]. We can know little of the quality of his carpentry but we can be certain that he used timber sparingly and had to make do with ash, elm or poplar even for cruck blades; his work relied most on the maintenance of its thatched roof and the clay cladding of its walls. All we can surmise about the plan is that it was nearly always open to the roof throughout and usually consisted of two or three bays of building with the simplest sort of division into domestic and other parts.

Notes

1 *Proc. Modern Language Ass.*, 61 (1926), 262–74.
2 R. Hilton, *English Peasantry in the Later Middle Ages* (1975), 23–6, 125.
3 Hilton, 31–6.
4 N.W. Alcock, *Cruck Construction: an Introduction and Catalogue* (CBA Research Report 42, 1981), 1.
5 *Vernacular Architecture*, 6 (1975), 19–27.
6 Ibid., 5 (1974), 14–17; A. Detsicas, *Collectanea Historica* (1981), 225–30.
7 F. Atkinson and R.W. McDowall, 'Aisled houses in the Halifax area', *Ant. J.*, 47 (1967), 77–94.
8 N.W. Alcock and M.W. Barley, 'Medieval roofs with base-crucks and short principals', *Ant. J.*, 52 (1972), 132–68, contains a list with dimensions. See also *EFC*, 25–6.
9 P.C. Drewett (ed.), *Archaeology in Sussex to AD 1500* (CBA Research Report 29, 1978), 93–5.
10 D. and B. Martin, *Historic Buildings in Eastern Sussex*, I (1977-80), and *An Architectural History of Robertsbridge* (Rape of Hastings Archit. Survey, 1974).
11 *Archaeol. J.*, 126 (1969), 267-9; *Archaeol. Cantiana* 79 (1964), 136–42.
12 *Historic Buildings in Eastern Sussex*, I, 18–20; 2 (1980–1), 47–50.
13 P. Clark, *English Provincial Society ... Kent 1550–1640* (1979), 6.
14 *Agr. Hist.* 4, 57–9.
15 S.E. Rigold, 'The distribution of the Wealden House', in I. LL. Foster and L. Alcock, *Culture and Environment* (1963), 351–4.
16 *EVH*, nos. 218, 222, 227; *Traditional Kent Buildings* (Kent County Council 1981), 24–30.
17 F.W.B. Charles, *Medieval Cruck Building and its Derivatives* (1967), 24–30.
18 P. Gray, *Charlwood Houses* (privately published 1978).
19 N.W. Alcock and M. Laithwaite 'Medieval houses in Devon and modernization', *Med. Archaeol.*, 17 (1973), 11–21; VCH, *Warwickshire*, 4 (1947), 117–9; *EVH* 20, nos. 162, 230; E.R. Swain, 'Divided and galleried hall-houses', *Med Archaeol.*, 12 (1968), 127–45.
20 *EVH*, 28.
21 *Med. Archaeol.*, 17 (1973), 100–4; L.J. Hall, *The Rural Houses of North Avon and South Gloucestershire* (1983), 8.
22 *Vernacular Architecture*, 3 (1972), 9–10.
23 I.C. Peate, *The Welsh House* (1946), ch. 4, and in *Culture and Environment*, 439–44; P. Smith, *Houses of the Welsh Countryside* (1975), 144 and in *Culture and Environment*, 415–37; *EVH*, 46.
24 J.G. Hurst (ed.), *Wharram: a Study of Settlement on the Yorkshire Wolds*, 1 (1979), 68–9.
25 G.I. Meirion-Jones, *The Vernacular Architecture of Brittany* (1982), 192.
26 *EFC*, 75–6, 119–20, etc.
27 *EVH*, 46–9.
28 *Med. Archaeol.*, 2 (1958), 141–57; 5 (1961), 330–1; 23 (1979), 98–158.
29 P. Smith, 142–4; H.G. Ramm *et al.*, *Shielings and Bastles* (1970), 1–8.
30 J.T. Smith, 'The evolution of the English peasant house to the late seventeenth century; the evidence of buildings', *J. Brit. Archaeol. Ass.*, 33 (1970), 128, fig. 3a.
31 *Med. Archaeol.* (1973), 100–25; *Trans. Devonshire Ass.*, 101 (1969) 83–93; 112 (1980) 127–69; *Proc. Devonshire Archaeol. Ass.*, 30 (1972), 227–32.
32 J.T. Smith, loc. cit., 132.
33 W.G. Hoskins, *The Age of Plunder* (1976), 19–20.
34 P. Dixon, 'Towerhouses, pelehouses and Border Society', *Archaeol. J.*, 136 (1979), 240–52.
35 V.M. and F.J. Chesher, *The Cornishman's House* (1968), 27–33; *EVH*, 18.
36 R.B. Wood-Jones, *Traditional Domestic Architecture in the Banbury Region* (1963), ch. 3.
37 L.J. Hall, 177, 197.
38 W.G. Hoskins, *The Midland Peasant* (1957), chs. 6, 7.

II THE MODERN HOUSE 1550–1900

9 *Building and Materials*

There is no doubt about the vast increase in the amount of new building which characterized the later Tudor period. The first new factor after 1536 was what Hoskins chose to call the Great Plunder; 'the greatest transference of land in English history since the Norman Conquest', in which more than half the estates of the church passed via the crown to the nobility and gentry, mostly the latter.[1] At the same time a steady rise in the prices of agricultural products, greater than those of other products and especially after 1550,[2] enabled their producers to adopt better standards of home life, in terms of materials and of the design of the house. These familiar generalizations conceal significant regional variations when it comes to the distribution, chronology, design, and the materials of houses. Essex had in 1594 no less than 354 houses of the nobility and gentry, most of them substantially of Tudor date, and well over a hundred of them still survive; poorer and more remote counties such as Cornwall and Lincolnshire never had a tenth of that number, and in both the climax of country-house building was in the Victorian age. Although English bishops were despoiled of a large part of their temporalities, no bishop had owned a single manor in Lancashire, so that it was totally unaffected by that particular act of plunder.[3] These contrasts between the wealthier and the poorer parts go right down the social scale, as we shall see.

Henry VII, as soon as his prudence allowed, built at half-a-dozen places but his son started sooner after his accession and acquired by purchase, exchange, by politic gift or by surrender; by the end of his reign he owned over fifty houses – more than any other king of England before or since.[4] They were concentrated in south-eastern counties; the few in the north and west were used only for administrative purposes – at Newcastle-upon-Tyne and York (King's Manor) for the Council of the North and Tickenhill manor house (Worcestershire) for the Council of the Marches – and though designs were prepared for improving the manor house at Hull there is no evidence that they were carried out; the house was disposed of in 1550.[5]

Edward VI and Mary had neither their father's acquisitiveness nor strength to resist courtiers such as Robert Dudley; Elizabeth, James I and Charles I disposed of yet more houses so that by the 1640s Henry's fifty had been reduced to eight, called standing palaces because their complement of furniture was never moved from one house to another.[6] No royal residence of capital importance was built between 1547 and 1661. The concept of a new palace emerged again near the end of Charles I's reign, but Wren's design for an English Versailles at Winchester was halted in 1685 and never resumed; henceforward the story of new royal houses is a matter of modest undertakings such as Kensington Palace and Buckingham House.

Bishops' residences

After Henry VIII appropriated Wolsey's Hampton Court in 1525 and his York Place (Whitehall Palace) in 1529, no bishop henceforward built a new palace. By the 1530s the king's acute need for money, allied to the envy of courtiers and supported by a moral conviction that the income of bishops ought to be related to their social responsibility, produced the startling proposal that instead of widely varying incomes from estates they should have a standard salary of 1000 marks (£666), with more for Canterbury and York. That was about the income of the poorest bishop, while the richest had six times as much. The proposal never reached Parliament but it indicates the climate in which bishops were by 1549 deprived of many manors.[7] Their incomes were not proportionately reduced since they received spiritualities (rectories and similar dues) instead, but some were seriously impoverished, at least for a time.

Their peripatetic life of conspicuous consumption was no longer seemly or practicable. There is little evidence of work on their remaining houses, except for what Williams of Lincoln did at Buckden (Huntingdonshire),[8] his principal residence. Bishops of Henry VIII's new dioceses were suitably housed in the lodgings of former abbots at Bristol, Chester, Gloucester and Peterborough; all were subsequently rebuilt or demolished. Bishops' residences were sold during the Commonwealth; after the Restoration each bishop put at least one in suitable order again, though not necessarily that in the cathedral city. Their work might be sumptuous in design like that of Cosins at Bishop Auckland and Durham, but was modest in scale by medieval precedents. A new palace was built at Lichfield [187], but at York an Elizabethan archbishop began the demolition of his palace there; the remains of the great hall, after use as a riding school, were pulled down in 1814–16.[9]

Houses of the landed classes

No other country offers the same chances to see the houses of the landed classes – what have been called the power bases from which they ruled until 1850; they exercised a rule which they no longer had to share with the dignitaries of the church. The greatest difficulty in the way of discovering what an old mansion was originally like – of unpicking its development, so to speak – is the fact that it has been continuously occupied. It is impossible to discover one completely unaltered and every kind of change can be observed: enlargement, reduction, remodelling. The largest houses have been the most susceptible because of their scale.

Rich as this country may be, many great houses have vanished. When the earl of Kingston died in 1726, he owned seven houses, none containing less than thirty rooms and most of them more than fifty.[10] All have vanished except for about half of Holme Pierrepont Hall (Nottinghamshire) [55], and most of them without trace. Only monuments in churches at West Dean, Wiltshire (Robert Pierrepont 1669), and Tong, Shropshire (Elizabeth Pierrepont 1696), show that the family once had a 'mansion house' at West Dean and a castle at Tong. We can see nothing and know very little of his town house in Arlington Street, St James's, and his houses at Acton (Middlesex), Hanslope (Buckinghamshire) or Thoresby (Nottinghamshire). By a recent estimate, out of a total of about 5,000 country houses in 1675, about a thousand remain in private hands and another hundred or so belong to the National Trust.[11] More than 250 have been demolished since 1945, most of them of nineteenth-century date and representing the last fling of old landed gentry or of new magnates of commerce and industry. So the body of evidence of historic country houses is shrinking and is only to a degree offset by revelations when houses are properly examined. To say so is not to adopt a catastrophic view of our present age; a more extended quantitative assessment would probably show that, of thousands of houses built by the nobility and gentry in the sixteenth century, some were rebuilt in the seventeenth century, many more in the Georgian period and in Victorian times.[12] Certainly in Hertfordshire, for which a quantitative assessment has been attempted, the eighteenth century figures as an age of demolition and rebuilding. A graph would show peaks of new building in 1560–1620, 1660–80 and 1780–1820.[13] Other graphs, of comparable significance, might be constructed to show the size of great houses and of the households for which they were designed. They would show peaks early in the periods in question, and especially if royal palaces were included in the first, but the great Palladian mansions such as Blenheim, Horseheath and Eastbury were not matched later. As households diminished, the proportion of women servants increased. The largest Victorian houses such as Eaton or Thoresby had an indoor staff of forty or more.[14]

Building operations

The study of building by classes below the level of the gentry has naturally concentrated on houses in the countryside since until the nineteenth century England was a predominantly agricultural society. Hoskins's concept of a Great Rebuilding in the period 1570–1680[15] caught the imagination, but it has had the effect of attaching too much importance to changes during that time and away from what happened before and after it. The concept was nourished by use of a class of document which had not hitherto been used. Probate inventories, rare before 1550 and prepared only for the rich, survive in enormous quantities after 1560 for yeoman, husbandmen, village craftsmen and even, in smaller numbers, for labourers. They became accessible to students for the first time when they were transferred to newly-opened county record offices and served to concentrate interest in the period down to about 1750, after which they are less numerous and informative. It was fashionable from Elizabeth's time onwards to mount a date on a house and collecting evidence of that sort has shown that, taking England as a whole, new building reached a peak in c. 1700 and went on well into the eighteenth century. Any great rebuilding in Lincolnshire and East Yorkshire would have to be put into the century following 1775. It is significant that these two counties have fewer country houses of size than any others, and that their most pretentious, such as Harlaxton Manor, are products of the Victorian peak of prosperity for the landed classes.

Building accounts are naturally more plentiful for the modern period and indicate both the scale of operations and the character of the labour force. Henry VIII's palaces required larger bodies of men than had ever been got together before;[16] although building was all near London, whose population was growing, the king had to use the royal right of impressment both for tradesmen and to a lesser extent for materials. For Hampton Court in 1534–5 bricklayers were recruited from Berkshire, Buckinghamshire, Essex and Suffolk, and masons from Dorset, Gloucestershire, Somerset and Wiltshire. At Whitehall in 1531, by those means, it was possible to have more than nine hundred men on site, nearly half of them labourers. The king was so impatient that at Whitehall overtime was paid and lights were provided so that painters could work after dark; canvas awnings over the new gate enabled workmen to ignore the weather. In Elizabeth's time and later, landowners competed with each other for craftsmen such as plasterers with special skills.[17] The staff of the king's works were free, as civil servants are not today, to engage in private practice, at the design level and as administrators on behalf of grandees; they too could help to recruit craftsmen.

The most skilled craftsmen could find continuous employment, moving from one great house to another, rarely more than 20 to 30 miles from home but beyond the range of daily travel. Most workmen were not continuously employed as they would be today; many had agricultural holdings and could return to them as the season required. During the years 1700–24 when, as Vanbrugh remarked, 'All the world are running mad after Building', he himself had nearly 200 men at work on the site

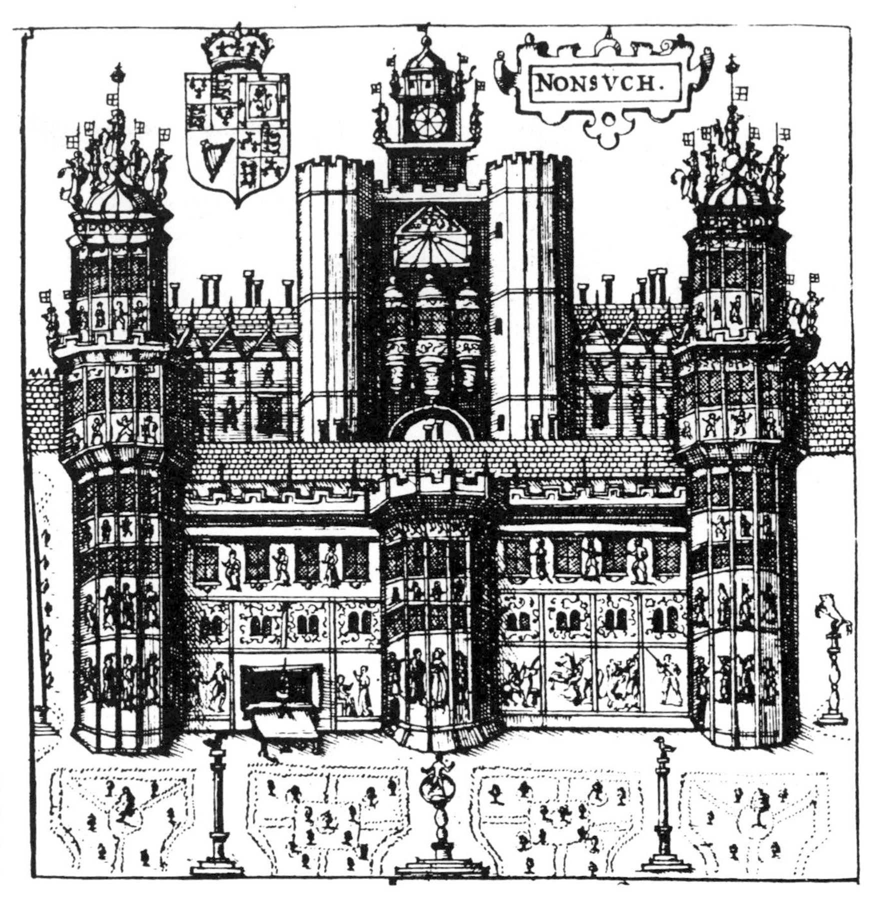

102. The south front of NONSUCH PALACE, SURREY, built of timber for Henry VIII.
John Speed.

of Castle Howard.[18] The village houses of Hinderskelfe were demolished, the main street becoming a terrace walk with a temple at the end of it; where the men lodged we do not know. At Blenheim Vanbrugh had 1,500 men employed at one time in preparing the site of the house and its gardens;[19] they must have filled the houses, inns, stables and barns in the little town of Woodstock. One solution was to allow workers to live in the house as soon as parts of it were habitable. In 1721 when Sir Robert Walpole was building Houghton Hall (Norfolk) he was giving employment to twenty-nine men and fifty women in laying out and planting the park and gardens; how many craftsmen and labourers were working on the house we do not know. Concentrating such forces in and round a village must have been as disturbing as the navvies' camps of the railway age. At Houghton the village publican had to be threatened with eviction unless he closed his house at 10 p.m.[20]

Materials: timber

To demonstrate how building houses of timber gradually ceased is a matter of identifying a balance of considerations at a given time, in a given region and among persons of a particular class. Choosing the most durable walling material providing the best insulation was the most influential factor. Another was speed of construction and readiness for

103. RUSHBURY MANOR (so-called), SHROPSHIRE, built c. 1650 with three gables at the front and two at the rear. The masonry walling is recent.

comfortable occupation. The price and growing scarcity of good timber eventually influenced choice but was certainly not the dominant factor; in regions with a powerful tradition of framed building, houses of the seventeenth and eighteenth centuries with stone or brick walls often have internal partition walls and roofs of very substantial timber construction, and inferior oak or softwood for walling could be protected and insulated with plaster or hung tiles.

Henry VIII's palace of Nonsuch [102] was the largest framed building ever erected in England.[21] Most of the timber came from the Weald; external members were covered with carved and gilded sheets of slate and the panels filled with plaster-stucco bearing pictorial, floral and other designs, and the building was substantially completed in three years. Building in timber for Tudor and Stuart monarchs was otherwise confined to modest additions, temporary structures and buildings not for regular use. Lodgings of timber were built at Kenilworth for Henry VIII and at Havering (Essex) for Elizabeth; the latter were of two storeys, 55 m (180 ft) long and provided twenty-six rooms. Banqueting houses were put up at Collyweston (Northamptonshire) and Clarendon (Wiltshire) for visits of Elizabeth.[22]

New houses for the nobility and gentry in south-eastern counties had as a matter of course walls of brick or stone, even if as in the cases of Hatfield (Hertfordshire) and Blickling (Norfolk) they were designed by a carpenter, Robert Lemynge.[23] The men responsible for the spectacular black and white buildings of the Welsh Marches and of Cheshire and Lancashire such as Bramhall Hall, Little Moreton Hall and Speke Hall have not been identified. They worked mostly for the lesser gentry [103]. Wales had some large framed houses such as Lymore, built c. 1675 near Montgomery to replace the castle there, destroyed in 1649. Lymore was

104. One end of a row of almshouses at PEMBRIDGE, HEREFORDSHIRE, built 1686 by Thomas Powle, carpenter.

demolished c. 1930. Some of the houses of the gentry in the north-west have a medieval core, but alterations in Tudor and Stuart times gave them their most distinctive quality. Chorley Hall (Cheshire) illustrates the process; a fourteenth-century stone open hall was modernized c. 1560 by being converted into two storeys and a timber-framed wing was added, its walls richly decorated with diaper pattern.[24] The diversity of regional fashions is shown by what happened to a Rutland manor house (Quaintree House, Braunston) at about the same time; the timber walls of the hall were rebuilt in stone and an upper storey inserted but without destroying the fine medieval roof [105].

The first name in Colvin's *Dictionary of British Architects 1600–1840* happens to be that of a carpenter known to be responsible for particular timber buildings: John Abel whose tomb in Sarnesfield churchyard (Herefordshire), dated 1674, named him 'architector'. A contemporary credited him with several market halls, of which Leominster survives (moved to another site in 1861), and he worked on Abbey Dore church; he must have built houses but none can be identified. His appearance in the dictionary among masons, bricklayers, land surveyors and amateur architects underlines the persistent status of carpenters as members of a traditional, unlettered craft, patronized by landowners for their tenants' houses and farm buildings rather than their own residences, by freeholders and by innkeepers, merchants and shopkeepers in market towns: classes whose private accounts and personal papers even if they kept them have not survived. A rare if not unique instance of a carpenter inscribing his building is a row of almshouses at Pembridge (Herefordshire) [104] 'builded by me, Thomas Powle, carpenter, according to the donor's will in 1686'. When Richard Neve compiled his *City and Country Purchaser*, published in 1703 and again in 1726 as a guide for builders,[25]

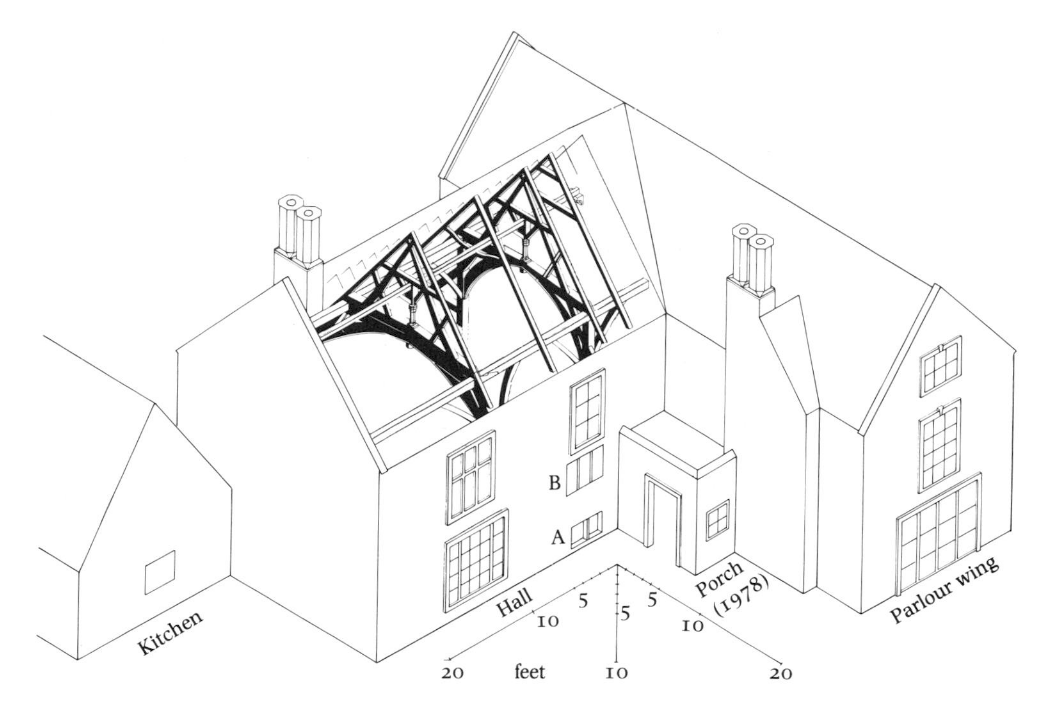

105. Isometric view of QUAINTREE HOUSE, BRAUNSTON, RUTLAND. In a Tudor modernization, the timber walls of the hall were replaced in stone but the roof of the 1290s was retained. An upper floor was inserted, with a staircase lighted by a landing window (B, now blocked) with a small buttery (A) underneath. The kitchen has no datable features but may be medieval in origin; the parlour wing has Tudor fireplaces; most windows were renewed in the nineteenth century.

he wrote under 'Framing' that he knew 'some workmen in Sussex that do all the framing in a house, viz, the carcase, flooring partitioning, roofing, ceiling beams, ashtoring [?ashlaring] etc. all together and make the windows and lantherns [?dormers] and hew and saw the timber for 12s. per square [foot]'. Men with that simple approach were responsible for the vernacular building in well-wooded regions; standardized with panelled framing, roofs with side-purlins clasped between rafters and collars, and ornament confined to a stopped chamfer on ceiling beams and fireplace bressumers. As prices rose it was realized that smaller and fewer timbers made equally durable houses. In the south and east, imported softwood came into common use and walling was covered with plaster, weatherboarding or tiles.[26] Timber-framed houses of this meagre construction were built in the nineteenth century.

Many market towns were devastated by fires in the seventeenth century (page 280); no doubt thatched roofs were the principal source of danger. In some western towns (e.g. Corfe Castle, Bristol, Totnes and Plymouth) the risk of fire spreading was reduced by building side-walls of stone and front and rear walls of timber [106]. Evidently a close-studded front to a town house, or framing in classical style, remained a mark of fashion until c. 1700.

In the East Midlands, small houses, if not built with load-bearing mud walls, were built of 'mud and stud', a local designation that goes back to Elizabethan times [107]; none of the few surviving examples is certainly earlier than that and the method was still used for labourers' cottages until c. 1850.[27] It used a minimum of timber: sills, widely-spaced posts braced to the wall-plate and mid-wall rails; laths nailed to the horizontals as a base for a thick casing of mud. Arthur Young writing in 1799 quoted comparative costs of cottages at Frieston: £30 for a detached cottage or £40 for a semi-detached pair, compared with £60 for the latter in brick.[28] A similar method was used in the north Lancashire plain; timber uprights were set in the cobblestone plinth and clay was then daubed on to both sides of this frame. This technique was traditionally known as 'clam staff and daub'; if the uprights were slighter, as they might be for an internal partition, withies of willow or hazel could be woven through them and then daubed. This was called 'clat and clay'.[29] These survivals into the twentieth century in the poorest parts of England provide the only evidence to fill the empty parts of the map (page 149) of medieval peasant building.

106. THE MERCHANT'S HOUSE, PLYMOUTH, DEVON, with stone side-walls and framed front. *Plymouth Museum.*

Mass walling: brick

The key to understanding the variety of materials used for mass walling in modern times, far greater than in the Middle Ages, is the distance between source and building site and the cost of transport between them.

The variety cannot be presented on maps. Geological terms such as Tertiary for deposits in the Thames Basin and East Anglia conceal the possibility of using flint or making bricks. Norman Davey has prepared maps of the 'principal quarries' in England and Wales for limestone, sandstone, slate and granite; they omit, for instance, Leicestershire quarries for slate at Swithland and for granite at Mountsorrel; the maps could not show, as building material, the conglomerates used in Devon or Hertfordshire, or the clunch (hard chalk) of Cambridgeshire, where it was quarried until 1962.[30] Bricks could be made almost anywhere.

107. Mud and stud at THIMBLEBY, LINCOLNSHIRE, later faced with brick up to sill level.

It is not uncommon today to see one house in a brick terrace which has recently been given a thin skin of synthetic stone, a technique once possible only for the wealthy but now within anyone's reach. Inigo Jones' Banqueting House in Whitehall, finished in 1621, had some internal parts of brick with three different facing stones; it was intentionally polychrome.[31] To suit changing tastes, it was refaced with white Purbeck stone in 1829. Chevening Park (Kent), now an official minister's residence, was built in red brick c. 1630; late in the eighteenth century it was clad in 'singularly unattractive' mathematical tiles which were removed in 1970.[32]

The extent to which brick was used for walling and then disguised by stone cladding has hardly figured in histories of architecture. Henry VIII, for the sake of economy or speed, built Richmond Palace in 1498–1501 of brick with stone facing for the main buildings, and this practice was adopted increasingly by the great; since the bricks were concealed their use has not always been recognized. Bricklayers finished several of Henry VIII's palaces by painting brick walls with red ochre, picking out the joints with Spanish black.[33] They presumably followed the brick courses exactly, rather than imitating masonry with deeper courses, but there is at least one instance of brick walling painted to look like coursed stone: Thurton Hall (Norfolk), built late in the seventeenth century. In East

Anglia and Essex, window openings with moulded brick mullions, jambs and pediments were often, even in small houses, plastered to look like stone but overall treatment is unusual.[34]

108. MORETON CORBET CASTLE, SHROPSHIRE, had a new range built, in 1579, of brick faced with local sandstone.

Instances of aristocratic houses built in brick and then cased in stone show how widely it was practised. Most of Cowdray House (Sussex) was built like that, by Sir William Fitzwilliam and his half-brother; they were favourites of Henry VIII. The tower of Canons Ashby (Northamptonshire), which may be before 1551, and another at the corner of Deene Park, built soon after 1600, are each of brick faced with stone, here perhaps because of the ease of lifting bricks to the top of a lofty structure. The combination is easiest to observe in ruined buildings, such as the Elizabethan range of Moreton Corbet Castle (Shropshire) [108]. Lulworth Castle (Dorset) was built in 1608–9 as a lodge for occasional use by Lord Bindon, whose home, Bindon Abbey, was only a few miles away. The east front was faced with Purbeck stone and the others with coursed rubble; the construction must represent calculations about the relative cost or convenience of bricks made on site, of rubble stone from nearby quarries and of Purbeck stone carried about 14 miles by water.[35] Wollaton Hall (Nottinghamshire) was built in 1588 by Francis Willoughby, apparently with stone from Ancaster (Lincolnshire). The fragmentary building accounts happen to preserve a contract of 1585 for making 189,000 bricks. They were certainly used to line underground passages to the water supply; only recently has repair and maintenance work begun to show that some of the main walls at least have a brick core.[36] While Dingley Hall (Northamptonshire) was being restored in 1980 and converted into a number of smaller units, the brick walling of the 1680s was for a time exposed; it is now hidden again.

The most precise explanation of this practice comes from Burley-on-the-Hill (Rutland), built in 1696–1708 for Daniel Finch, earl of Nottingham. He may have designed it himself, and he was certainly responsible for the decision to build the carcase of brick, so that it would be habitable more quickly and not 'green, moist, cold and unfit to dwell in'.[37]

The problems of cost and timetable in using stone are illustrated in the building of Blenheim (Oxfordshire) for the duke of Marlborough. Vanbrugh had to bring stone from as far away as 25 miles, and could hire wagons only when roads were passable enough and harvesting was not more urgent for the farmers who owned them. The last manorial right to disappear was that of obliging tenants – with payment – to carry stone, and it was sometimes enforced in the eighteenth century.

If a landowner could not open a quarry on his own land, buy or rent one within a short distance or bring stone from further afield by water – even to bring it from north-east Yorkshire for Houghton Hall (Norfolk) – the alternative was to have bricks made on site. There is ample evidence of the practice, from Henry VIII's activities at Hampton Court and Charles II's at Winchester[38] to remote farmhouses in the nineteenth century. Builders in and near coastal ports had long had opportunities to use small quantities of bricks and tiles carried as ballast by vessels in coastal and maritime trade, and this must have stimulated local enterprise. Pantiles as well as bricks were being made in Liverpool as early as 1701. At Barnstaple the existence of a local pottery industry meant familiarity with a related technology. Celia Fiennes noticed how much brick building there was in Newcastle-upon-Tyne, reflecting no doubt the ballast carried by colliers returning from London or Hull.[39]

The spread of brick-making

The influence of royal and aristocratic brick building in training artisans cannot be overestimated [109, 110]. Henry VIII employed seventy to eighty bricklayers at Hampton Court in 1535, at Oatlands in 1538 and at Dartford in 1541; for the walls of Hull it was estimated in 1542 that 120 would be needed. Contracts for Charles II's palace at Winchester provided for nearly 7 million bricks; an ordinary modern house uses about 30,000. The influence of south-eastern brick-makers can be traced in phased distribution maps of brick bonds; they show how Flemish bonds [113], first used regularly in the Dutch House, Kew, in 1631, spread west, north-west and north through the next two centuries.[40] A bricklayer who could build in Flemish bond might be employed on the front of a building while those with experience only of English bond or its variants built the other walls. The individuals responsible for the spread of brick-making can sometimes be identified. The earl of Nottingham, moving from Kensington to Rutland, engaged bricklayers from London

109

111

110

109. Elaborately moulded bricks in fireplace and chimney of TUDOR HOUSE, NEWPORT, ESSEX.

110. Pilasters and pediment, WHARLEY HALL, BARSTON, WARWICKSHIRE, 1669. *NMR*.

111. Inferior bricks in barn, SPRINGFIELD FARM, PREESALL, LANCASHIRE, 1758.

as well as Nottingham at Burley-on-the-Hill in the 1690s, and at about the same time the duke of Montagu, enlarging and modernizing Boughton House (Northamptonshire) employed Thomas Hues to build the beautiful brick stable block. Hues had worked on Kensington Palace in 1689 and was later master bricklayer to the Office of Works. The block is faced with stone towards the house, and according to the estate mason repairing it in 1980, the stone is not tied to the brickwork.[41] An early brick house in a stone or timber region may be the work of a London merchant turning country gentleman: Woolmore House, Melksham (Wiltshire) was built in 1631 by George Herbert, citizen and vintner of London.[42]

Otherwise a landowner might turn east or south-east for a brick-maker. In 1599 Sir George Cary at Feniton (Devon) contracted with a brick-maker from Netherbury in West Dorset for 52,000 bricks.[43] In c. 1611 Richard Cholmeley of Brandsby contracted with:

> Thomas Horsham, his sons or sons-in-law and friends, brickmakers of Wystow, that they should come to Brafferton ... and if they found any of my earth there good to make bricks they should then ... work the earth and make me 300,000 bricks good and sufficient to be put in work in building ... for 3s 6d a thousand but I am to find and lay by them elden [rye] straw, sand, moulds, tables or boards to work upon.[44]

The men came from Wystow near Cawood, down the Ouse from York, where bricks had been made in the fifteenth century for the archbishop of York's manor house there, and had no doubt continued to be made; Brafferton is 14 miles north-west of York. No other contract illustrates in such personal terms the way the new industry spread from the river basins of the Thames, the Severn, the Wash and the Humber.

For the needs of someone like Richard Cholmeley bricks were fired in a clamp: that is, a stack of raw bricks packed with fuel, covered to retain heat and then fired. Wood was used as fuel, both for kilns and clamps, until the eighteenth century when coal began to take its place. The use of clamps lasted longest in Kent, Essex and Sussex for producing stock bricks; they might hold as many as 100,000 bricks, but produced a proportion of over-fired and under-fired bricks; the former could be used for foundations and the latter (sometimes called samwells), if not given a second firing, for internal walls to be plastered.[45] In the Fylde of Lancashire, where unsuitable materials or inadequate technology produced poor results, soft bricks may be seen in barns of the eighteenth century [111].

For larger and especially for more lasting operations, brick-built kilns were preferred, of the type used in the Middle Ages and of which the last examples ceased to be used only in 1968. They would now be classed as intermittent kilns, as against the continuous firing now practised, and are described as open updraught or Scottish kilns. Observations in 1968 of the operation of such kilns in the brickyard of the Ashburnham estate (Sussex) placed on record the combination of simple technology with the experienced skill of the brick-makers which produced the attractive and high-quality bricks [112] characteristic of south-eastern counties.[46] Normally 75 per cent of the Ashburnham bricks were first class. Each kiln produced 20,000 bricks at a firing. There is plenty of evidence from estate accounts of the quantities of brick produced for great houses. For Hatfield, started in 1607, 1–3 million bricks were made each year for at least four years.[47] George Vernon started building Sudbury Hall (Derbyshire) in

112. House in THE SQUARE, WICKHAM, HAMPSHIRE, with grey-blue brick walling and red details.

113. House in LOW STREET, COLLINGHAM, NOTTINGHAMSHIRE, with yellow headers in the gable-end.

1661; by 1690 he had noted the manufacture of 1,377,000 bricks and appropriate quantities of tiles, made in the park and elsewhere nearby; each firing produced 16,000 to 20,000 bricks.[48] Most went into the house, but he was rebuilding the village, including an inn, at the same time.

Estate brick-making

Some estate owners also had in mind, when they started to have bricks made, the needs of their tenants. Roger North, who rebuilt Rougham Hall (Norfolk) in 1693, wrote in January 1692 to a friend:[49]

> I have contracted for 100,000 bricks to be made next summer, and of all one 10,000 will not come to my share, for I do but contrive, for the benefit of mankind, to convert rascally clay walls that the wind blows through and through, to bricks that will keep folks warm and alive.

An equally vivid comment comes from the notebook of Drayner Massingberd of Bratoft (Lincolnshire) who was having bricks made in 1652 onwards; his house was demolished in 1698 when the family moved to Gunby. His brick-makers produced 33–48,000 bricks at a 'kilning'. His memorandum book includes such items as: 'Will Wikam is to have all the pasture and arable and other things which he had in his former lease ... And he is to have a brick chimney built for him this spring' – no doubt in a mud and stud house. It took 5000 bricks and eleven seam of lime mixed with three parts sand and was finished on 11 June 1657 'by Pedigreene Witton and John Pape of Partney with two little boys'.[50] Nicholas Blundell, the Catholic landowner of Little Crosby (Lancashire), had bricks made in 1712–19 for his house and farm buildings and for a Catholic chapel.[51] Sir Robert Walpole's brickyard at Houghton (Norfolk) when his house was finished produced the bricks for the new village outside the park gates in 1729–30 [181] and continued to produce for the estate.[52] Viscount Howe had a brickyard in the park at Langar (Nottinghamshire) and the village inn, the Unicorn Head dated 1717, and a farmhouse in the village were almost certainly designed and built by his employees. Some of these estate brickyards, such as Holkham (Norfolk), Hinton St George (Somerset), Stoneleigh (Warwickshire) and Ashburnham (Sussex) were kept going until c. 1900 or longer, producing bricks for estate needs and a surplus for sale.

By 1700 or so, tenants in many parts might feel aggrieved if they were unable to get bricks cheaply for repairs or improvements. The prices given in contracts vary so much that no table would be worth compiling or an average calculated; a landowner often provided fuel and such transport as was required. Bricks bought in cost as much as twice those made on site; whether a tenant did his own improvements and repairs or expected help from a landlord seems to have depended on their relations. A Cheshire land agent wrote in 1727:[53]

> Many of the tenants are not able to make bricks and build their buildings and they think it very hard to be at the cost, for Sir Robert Cotton allows his tenants brick and timber and they have put their buildings in extraordinary repair and now I am told Lord Cholmondely is making bricks at half price for his tenants. If your Lordship would do the same the buildings in 2 or 3 years' time would be put in good order. It is best to cart clay at Michaelmas and make the bricks next spring.

Small-scale brick-making

The reference to tenants making bricks introduces another aspect of the transformation of houses in the sixteenth and later centuries. Field names such as Brick Clamps in Childerley (Cambridgeshire) in 1686 or Brickkiln Close at Gainsborough (Lincolnshire) in c. 1690 are a commonplace. Manorial records contain many references to brick-making. At Crowle (Lincolnshire) the jury in 1649 presented William Occorbie for making bricks on the common and selling them out of the manor. The Nottingham Corporation in 1683 ordered that persons who dug clay on the Plains should be discharged and their kilns and hovels [for drying bricks] should be pulled down forthwith. At Wakefield in 1709 'there were formerly Brick Kilnes formed of the Lord of the Manor on the East Moor of Wakefield; now the Inhabitants make for their own use and pay 4d per 1000 to the Lord of the Manor'.[54] Since making bricks was a seasonal occupation it naturally became one of the forms of employment characteristic of rural England. It must have flourished in wooded districts such as the West Midlands, and perhaps particularly in royal forests such as Malvern Chase where the standard of management had declined, but it must have been easy enough in open-field England; furze, the essential fuel, was plentiful on commons before enclosure. Two probate inventories must suffice to illustrate how a small-holder eventually became owner of a village brickyard.[55] Henry Wiseman of Ipswich, 'brick-striker' when he died in 1589, had bricks ready burnt and unburnt, four loads of blocks, fuel for his kiln consisting of loads of brush [wood] whins and long logs, burnt pavements [tiles] and livestock – eleven cows with some calves, fifteen sheep with some lambs and two sows with five suckling pigs. Richard Harrison of Babworth (Nottinghamshire), tile- and brick-maker, died in 1742 owner of four kilns in different places with their hovels and a stock of 106,000 bricks, 5,000 pantiles and 2,500 flat tiles. For an isolated house or one with poor access, such a man might fire in a clamp in the client's orchard or garden, and in the Fylde some such workings can still be seen. Alternatively the brick-maker had to rent a brick close as near as possible to his job.[56]

How and when small towns as well as villages were transformed is illustrated by a comment of Abraham de la Pryme, a Yorkshire parson writing c. 1690. Hatfield had been transformed from a little town 'all of wood clay and plaster' because 'everyone now, from the richest to the poorest, will not build except with brick', and it had become 'a very handsome and neat little place'.[57]

The ingenuity displayed in Tudor, Stuart and Georgian times in exploiting the range of shape, colour and texture which the brick-maker could produce can only be read as a happy agreement between all those involved. By c. 1730 the taste for red brick was diminishing. In eastern counties clays were suitable for making a grey brick; brick-makers had long known how to do so – witness Little Wenham Hall (c. 1280) [14] and Bishop Alcock's gateway (1496) for Jesus College, Cambridge. Gunton Hall (Norfolk), built c. 1742 by Matthew Brettingham, a bricklayer of Norwich and son of a bricklayer, has grey brick walls with details in a yellowish terracotta. South of the Thames, bricks with a blue-grey side or end were produced in quantities, probably by sprinkling powdered flint on them; they were used with red brick to achieve a polychrome effect [112]. An artisan brick-maker such as Brettingham thus had a chance, which he took, to challenge the monopoly of the mason in designing as well as building. London has been identified as the source of what architectural historians call the Mannerist style and which bricklayers developed; there is no better designation for their virtuosity or extravagance in decorative detail. The earliest rural example is Brooms Park (Kent, 1635–8); after 1660, Artisan Mannerism is largely confined to manor houses and others of similar status built between then and c. 1700. The bricklayer was still an itinerant worker; how else to explain a Northumberland house, Higham Dykes, with the shaped gables characteristic of eastern England from York to Kent? Houses of more subdued design but remarkably similar are to be found in the Soar valley between Nottingham and Leicester and in the hinterland of Bridgwater (Somerset).

Mass walling: stone

The emphasis on brick must not suggest that stone masons were less busy than before. A brick mansion to achieve the height of fashion required ashlar for quoins and openings and a moulded cornice or parapet. The status conferred by stone quoins can be gauged by the very occasional use of wooden quoins nailed on to modest houses. The work of country masons, as at Higham Court (Gloucestershire, c. 1658), Leadenham Old Hall (Lincolnshire, c. 1680–90), or Capheaton Hall (1668) and Bockenfield (c. 1690, both in Northumberland), has the exuberance of men working in a new style if not a new material, but masons on the whole had less scope for innovation than bricklayers. In the Cotswolds the mullioned window could be given a decorative terminal to the traditional hood-mould; without that it is difficult there to distinguish Tudor from Stuart doorways. In the Jurassic zone there was in 1660–1700 a vogue for a canted bay-window with mullioned openings, two storeys high and finished with a gable; they were clearly made in such quarries as Ham Hill (Somerset) and Ketton (Northamptonshire). In the northern half of England masons responded more readily to new demands, particularly from a market hitherto closed to them [116, 117]. Window openings with a raised and moulded surround were in fashion after 1660 and can be seen in both superior and modest houses. In the West Riding and especially round Halifax, farmers, clothiers and lesser gentry built, especially between 1630 and 1650, houses characterized by storeyed porches with elaborate doorways and sometimes a rose window for the room over the entrance. A mason who had worked with Robert Smythson at Wollaton Hall (Nottinghamshire) in the 1580s may have had a hand in starting the fashion; the earliest Yorkshire example, Bradley Hall, Stainfield (demolished), had resemblances to Wollaton and to a Smythson drawing.[58] Certainly some later examples were copied from Bradley Hall by a local group of masons. As in the Cotswolds, northern masons enjoyed cutting elaborate terminals for hood-moulds [114] over windows and produced a variety of bay-window designs.[59] On both flanks of the Pennines there are hundreds of small houses whose only decorative feature is the doorhead [115]. They often bear a date within the century 1630–1730, the majority late in the seventeenth century. They show

114. Doorway of THE OLD SCHOOL, ASTON-SUB-EDGE, GLOUCESTERSHIRE, 1663.

115. Doorway on the Lancashire side of the Pennines at WHITTINGTON, LANCASHIRE, 1681.

116. More classical doorway of ELYHAUGH FARMHOUSE, LONGFRAMLINGTON, NORTHUMBERLAND, 1732.

117. Window of SWARLAND OLD HALL, NORTHUMBERLAND, 1690–1700.

how Artisan Mannerism worked its way through the classes of society, from the capital to northern counties, from the gentleman to the yeoman.

The use of stone for decorative features is only a small part of the story. Wherever it could be got, however inferior and however intractable, stone was used to lengthen the life and improve the insulation of houses in the countryside. Most inferior stones had already been used in medieval churches and their use by improving landlords and by freehold and tenant farmers came to a peak in the eighteenth century, for rural society could afford by then to exploit the knowledge which every generation of countrymen renewed for itself of what lay beneath the soil. Such stone could be used for walling only because bricks were available for quoins and openings, and eventually it retreated to the side and back walls of brick houses. This exploitation of stone went along with improved and extended arable farming which cleared fields of sarsens, moorstones and glacial boulders; with quarrying material for turnpike roads; with digging canals and eventually with constructing railways. In Leicestershire, Mountsorrel granite, rarely if ever quarried in the Middle Ages, was used to a very limited extent for random rubble walling in houses near the quarries which were beginning in the eighteenth century to produce road material. In and near Swithland, the houses and garden walls built of thin and irregular slate are a by-product of the revived use of the slate for roofing, of the new fashion for headstones in churchyards and new demands for slate gate-posts, cheese-presses, paving for yards and the like.

Mud walling Mass walling of mud was the cheapest method of building since, apart from timber for floors, roof and fittings, the only cost was labour – if it was paid. A county historian writing in 1794 said that mud-walled houses in Cumberland could be expected to last for 150 or 200 years. His estimate is confirmed by the fact that those recorded there and elsewhere prove to have been built from the late seventeenth century onwards. Only in Cumberland and Northamptonshire have they been systematically examined and the results published;[60] in several counties where they were once known, survivals are very rare or unknown. If, as was common, they were later cased in brick, clay walls can only be deduced from their thickness (usually more than two feet). No doubt more examples will come to light in the course of demolition [120].

The essential ingredients of mud walling were the aggregate (ranging from small stones to sand), a binder (clay, chalk, lime and fibre) and water. A recent survey has shown that the particular mechanical and chemical qualities of aggregate and binder affected the speed with which walling could rise and its durability once built.[61] They therefore go far to explain the persistence of mud building in some regions. It had to compete with brick and so was almost unknown in towns. In Cockermouth, to judge from recent excavations, mud-walled houses were being built down to about 1680 and the same may have been true elsewhere. In Devonshire, town houses and even industrial buildings were erected in cob in the nineteenth century and in the countryside there the tradition never died. Elsewhere, mud was used for cottages, barns, dovecotes and boundary walls. Where stone was available, footings were laid and the mud piled to a height of no more than about two feet and a similar thickness before being left to dry out; its sides were then pared down to a near vertical and another layer piled on top. When such walling is

118. Flint walling with brick details, METTON, NORFOLK, early seventeenth century.

119. Carstone in the DUKE'S HEAD, WEST RUDHAM, NORFOLK, 1663; the date is done in bricks.

120. Cottages with mud walls, largely faced with brick, SOUTH KILWORTH, LEICESTERSHIRE, eighteenth century (?).

121. Clay lump at HINXTON, CAMBRIDGESHIRE, with brick quoining. *P. M. G. Eden.*

stripped of its protective rendering of plaster or limewash the separate lifts can be seen. In Northamptonshire, where coal and wood were expensive, the cow-dung intended for fuel was spread on walls to dry and served also to protect them. Building with mud was usually a slow method; earth rammed between shuttering (*pisé de terre*) would have been quicker and though architects working for wealthy landowners introduced it in the 1790s it was not widely adopted.[62]

East of the limestone belt, the brick industry produced a cheap alternative: an unfired brick known as clay bat or clay lump. A fired brick weighs 200–226 g (7–8 lb); the clay bat, measuring about 45 × 23 × 12.7 cm (18 × 9 × 5 in), weighed at least twice as much and cannot have been made far from a building site. This technique which had originated in East Anglia in the later Middle Ages was most popular in Cambridgeshire in the eighteenth and nineteenth centuries [121].

Mud and stud building in the East Midlands and the clam-staff and daub of the Lancashire plain are derived from box-frame construction. In the Solway plain of Cumberland and possibly in the East Riding of Yorkshire, the other mode of mud walling is related to cruck building.[63] Crucks resting on bay stones made the roof independent of the walls. Starting with cobble footings, the mud was then laid in thin courses separated by straw. Such walling dried quickly and building was a matter of days rather than weeks; thatching could go on before the walls were finished.

Some cob houses in Devon and clay-lump houses in East Anglia were, to judge from their size and such details as elaborate plaster ceilings, built by well-to-do yeomen;[64] some of the Northamptonshire houses had two storeys with upper cruck roofs. They were built with paid labour. Most mud-walled houses were built by the poorest members of the rural community for themselves; labourers building on the common or on waste ground with the help no doubt of family and friends. Such men rarely attempted a second storey. In the Lake District, which was by 1800 the most popular part of Britain among tourists, guide books, local histories and the like describe clay houses as well as the society which built them. Building might be a communal venture, neighbours turning out with their tools to get the walls up in a day, finishing with eating, drinking and dancing in the house as guests of the lucky householder. This is the last trace of a common medieval practice.

Notes

1 W. G. Hoskins, *The Age of Plunder* (1976), ch. 6.
2 J. Thirsk, *Agr. Hist.*, 4, 594–5.
3 F. Heal, *Of Prelates and Princes* (1980), 22–3.
4 *King's Works*, IV, ii, 1–2.
5 L. R. Shelby, *John Rogers* (1967), pls 10–13.
6 *King's Works*, ibid., 28.
7 Heal, ch. 3.
8 RCHM, *Huntingdonshire* (1926), 34.
9 RCHM, *York*, 5, 69, 129.
10 Nottingham University Archives, Manvers Coll., 4883.
11 R. Strong, *The Destruction of the Country House 1875–1945* (1974).
12 M. Airs, *The Making of the English Country House* (1975), ch. 1.
13 L. and J. Stone in W. O. Aydelotte (ed.), *Dimensions of Quantitative Research in History* (1972), 116.
14 M. Girouard, *The Victorian Country House* (1979), 28.
15 *Past and Present*, no. 4 (1953), 44–59; no. 77 (1977), 33–45; *Vernacular Architecture*, 14 (1983), 45–7.
16 *King's Works*, IV, ii, 129, 307.
17 Airs, 60–4.
18 G. Webb (ed.), *Complete Works of Sir John Vanbrugh*, 4 (1928), 25; *Ant. J.*, 58 (1978), 350–60.
19 D. Green, *Blenheim Palace* (1950), 56–9.
20 J. H. Plumb, *Sir Robert Walpole* (1956), 1, 359–61.
21 *King's Works*, IV, ii, 193–4.
22 Ibid., III, 259; IV, ii, 150–3.
23 H. M. Colvin, *Biographical Dictionary of British Architects* (1978).
24 R. A. Cordingley and R. B. Wood-Jones, 'Chorley Hall, Cheshire', *Trans. Anc. Mon. Soc.*, 7 (1959), 61–86.
25 Reprinted 1969, 138.
26 *EVH*, 125–6.
27 *EVH*, 23–4; *EFC*, 80–2.
28 *General View of the Agriculture of Lincolnshire* (1799), 35–6.
29 R. C. Watson and M. E. McClintock, *Traditional Houses of the Fylde* (1979), 15.
30 Norman Davey, *Building Stones of England and Wales* (1976); A. Clifton-Taylor, *Pattern of English Building* (1972), 62.
31 *King's Works*, IV, ii, 37, 330–1.
32 Clifton-Taylor, 238, 282, 285.
33 *King's Works*, IV, ii, *passim*.
34 BE, *North-West and South Norfolk*, 352; Airs, 96.
35 RCHM, *Dorset*, 2, i, 146.
36 *Nottingham University Archives*, Mi A 60/4.
37 H. J. Habbakuk, in J. H. Plumb (ed.), *Studies in Social History* (1955), 147–57.
38 *Wren Society*, 7 (1930), 22–67.
39 VCH, *Lancashire*, 2 (1908), 403; C. Morris (ed.), *The Journeys of Celia Fiennes* (1947), 209.
40 *Vernacular Architecture*, 13 (1982), 31.
41 I am indebted to Major E. M. Warrick for passing on this information.
42 VCH, *Wiltshire*, 7 (1953), 103 and facing plate.

43 Somerset Record Office, DD/WO 55/5.
44 N. Yorkshire Record Office, 2 QG.
45 A. Rees, *Cyclopaedia* or *Universal Dictionary of Arts, Sciences and Literature* (1819), articles Brick, Clamp.
46 *Sussex Industrial History*, 1 (1970–1), 1–17.
47 *Archaeol. J.*, 112 (1955), 107.
48 I am indebted to Adrian Tinniswood for notes on the Sudbury household accounts, *penes* Lord Vernon.
49 R. North, *Lives of the Norths* (1890), 3, 230.
50 Lincolnshire Record Office, MM VI/1/5. His brother Sir Henry Massingberd kept an equally interesting notebook for the years 1649–80.
51 J. G. Bagley (ed.), *Nicholas Blundell's Diary 1720–29* (Lancashire and Cheshire Record Society, 114, 1972), *passim*.
52 Cambridge University Library, Cholmondeley Account Books 40/1.
53 Cheshire Record Office DCH/6/34.
54 Lincolnshire Record Office, CM 4/4/7; *Records of the Borough of Nottingham*, 5, *1625–1702* (1900), 323; J. Charlesworth (ed.), *Wakefield Manor Book* (Yorks. Archaeol. Soc. Record Series, 101, 1939), 184.
55 M. Reed (ed.), *Ipswich Probate Inventories 1583–1631* (Suffolk Record Soc. 22, 1981), 25; Nottinghamshire Record Office.
56 Watson and McClintock, 18.
57 C. Jackson (ed.), *The Diary of Abraham de la Pryme* (Surtees Soc. 54, 1870), 114.
58 A. J. Pacey, 'Ornamental porches of ... Halifax', *Yorks. Archaeol. J.*, 41 (1965), 455–64.
59 L. Ambler, *Old Halls and Manor Houses of Yorkshire* (1913), 26–7.
60 *Trans. Anc. Mon. Soc.*, 10 (1962), 57–80; *Northants. Past and Present*, 3 (1960–6), 215–28.
61 Extensive research is summarized in J. R. Harrison, 'The mud wall in England ...', *Trans. Anc. Mon. Soc.*, 28 (1984), 154–74. I am grateful to Mr Harrison for a sight of his article at proof stage.
62 Clifton-Taylor, 291–2.
63 K. S. Hodgson *et al.*, 'Lamonby Farm ...', *Trans. Cumb. and Western Archaeol. Soc.*, 53 (1954), 149–59.
64 *EVH*, 135.

10 *Country Seats*

The great houses of Tudor England belong to a new age, for they were built by laymen holding the offices of state formerly held by ecclesiastics. Their lives as officers and members of the court circle required a house in London, and so Sir Christopher Hatton, lord chancellor, persuaded Elizabeth to grant him Ely Place, Holborn, formerly the town house of the bishops of Ely. All the episcopal residences in London came into the hands of similar men. Somerset House in the Strand, built by Protector Somerset in 1548–51, was the first house in England of entirely classical design. Several other courtiers built between the City and Westminster.

Such men also needed a large house within a day's journey of Westminster. William Cecil's Wimbledon House was 7 miles away; a nunnery at Isleworth (now Syon House) was converted to a residence by Somerset, at a cost of over £5,000. From 1559 onwards it belonged to the Percy earls of Northumberland, whose town house was where Charing Cross Station now stands. William Cecil built Theobalds (Hertfordshire), 13 miles north of London, in 1564–85; his son Robert offered it to James I in exchange for the former palace of the bishops of Ely at Hatfield, where Robert proceeded to build a new house at a cost of nearly £40,000.[1] These houses near London served as a stage on the journey to London from the principal country seats. William Cecil's Burghley House near Stamford (built 1561–87) descended to his elder son Thomas; Robert Cecil's Cranborne Manor (Dorset) was a remodelling in 1608–20 of a semi-derelict royal hunting lodge.[2] Hatton built two houses in Northamptonshire, at Holdenby [122] and Kirby; Cowdray House (Sussex) was begun by William Fitzwilliam who succeeded Sir Thomas More in 1529 as chancellor of the duchy of Lancaster and became in 1539 lord keeper of the privy seal. One example must suffice of how this pattern of life persisted in later times. Sir Robert Walpole (1676–1745) during his twenty-one years as first lord of the treasury and chancellor of the exchequer had a house in Arlington Street, St James's, which, he used principally as an office, and also Orford House, Chelsea; his weekends at Ranger's Lodge, Richmond (on which he spent £14,000), were passed in

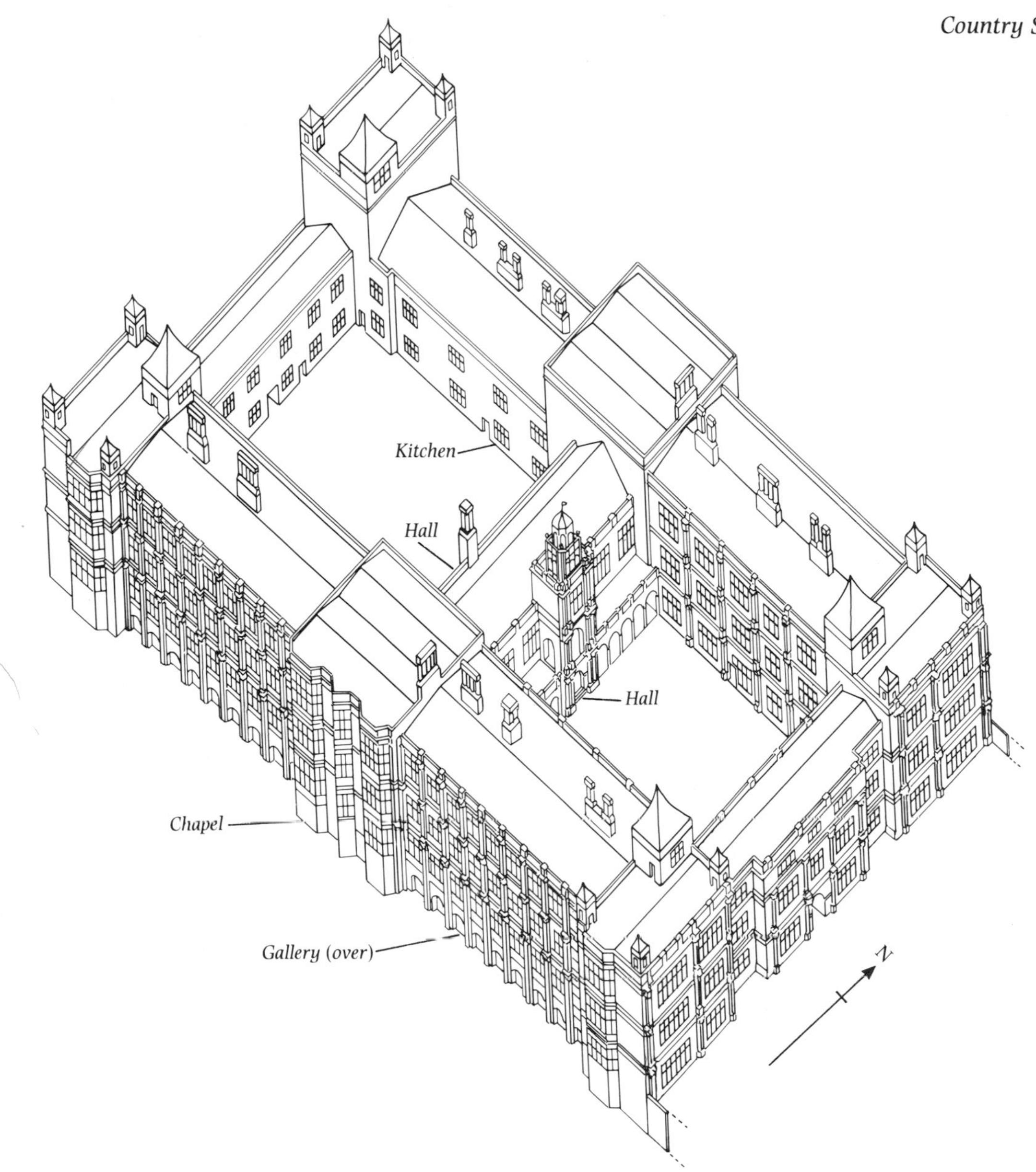

122. Reconstruction of HOLDENBY HOUSE, NORTHAMPTONSHIRE, built 1578–83 by Sir Christopher Hatton, the largest and most magnificent Elizabethan house, demolished (except for the kitchen range) in the seventeenth century. *After M. Girouard.*

a mixture of working and hunting; his country seat was Houghton Hall (Norfolk) built in 1721 onwards, but his busy life allowed him to use it only for house-parties during the summer recess.[3]

While such great men built new houses or rebuilt old ones to suit a way of life indistinguishable from that of medieval nobles, there was a second rank of men equally anxious to mark their success and status: lesser courtiers and officials; stewards of great men such as Somerset. Ightham Mote (Kent), a fourteenth-century house, was remodelled by a minor courtier of Henry VIII's, Sir Richard Clement, so that the older parts of the house and especially his new chapel display wherever possible the badges of Henry VIII and Catherine of Aragon.[4] Ightham is a remarkable survival; other Tudor houses, continuously occupied by families of great wealth and changing taste, have been so altered that often their original plan and interior decoration are unknown. Sir Thomas Kytson, a London merchant, built Hengrave Hall (Suffolk) in 1525–38 and 'some significant Renaissance detail' can still be seen but it has been partially rebuilt and the kitchen court demolished. Sutton Place (Surrey), built c. 1530 by a courtier named Sir Richard Weston, in Tudor Gothic with terracotta panels ornamenting its symmetrical elevation, is no longer a courtyard house because its front range with a lofty gatehouse was demolished in 1786. Sir John Thynne (d. 1580), who had been Somerset's steward, bought in 1541 a small monastic house at Longleat in Wiltshire; by the end of his life, through a succession of changes of design, it became the first of what have been called the Elizabethan prodigy houses. It was built round two courtyards, the novelty being the uniform and symmetrical elevations looking outwards.[5] None of Thynne's rooms survives; Hatfield House (Hertfordshire) has been remodelled inside and so has Wollaton Hall (Nottinghamshire).

The great household

Within the walls of the new mansions of Tudor and later England, the life of the household was governed by standards and conventions inherited from the Middle Ages. Although no nobleman ever maintained as large an establishment as Wolsey's, the size of the greatest households diminished little and slowly before the eighteenth century, and self-made men like William Cecil, Lord Burghley, kept up a grand, old-fashioned state. The earl of Derby's household in the 1580s varied between 115 and 140 people, exclusive of family; in 1677 the duke of Grafton had a hundred staff at Euston and when Roger North visited Badminton he noted that the duke of Beaufort's household numbered about 200 persons. When Sir Dudley North travelled in Italy c. 1660 he commented that it was not usual there, as it was in England, 'for a gentleman to keep many servants, but as for their gardens and waterworks, they are very sumptuous'.[6] On the move from a country seat to London or on other special occasions, great men might still be accompanied by retainers to a number licensed by Elizabeth. Household regulations, of the sort compiled by bishop Grosseteste in the thirteenth century and defining the duties of the staff,[7] are most common in the sixteenth and seventeenth centuries; this may partly be due to the better survival of later documents, but they show that service in a nobleman's household was still held to be a suitable upbringing for sons of the local gentry. In the earl of Northumberland's household book drawn up in 1502 for Wressle and Leconfield castles, some of the young gentlemen were 'at their friends' finding' – that is, not paid by the earl – but at Woburn Abbey in Charles

II's time the gentlemen were salaried like everyone else. The principal officer, usually called steward (or receiver-general at Woburn) was a gentleman; others of that class at Ashby-de-la-Zouch in 1609 were the gentleman usher and the gentleman of the horse, each with his staff of gentlemen, yeomen and grooms.[8]

No great new palaces were built c. 1625–c. 1700 and the size of the aristocratic household declined. The building of the great Baroque houses such as Blenheim must indicate larger households again. The duke of Chandos at Canons (Middlesex) in 1718 had a household of eighty-three persons but it included the duke's private orchestra of two dozen performers and the half dozen Chelsea pensioners living in lodges by the great gate. When guests had servants to be accommodated the musicians had to sleep over the stables. The duke no longer expected to be served by gentlemen and was disconcerted when an applicant concealed his superior birth.[9]

The cost of building

The earl of Suffolk who in 1603 began to build Audley End (Essex) [123], the last of the great palaces of the Tudor and early Jacobean age, is said to have told James I that the house cost £200,000. Suffolk became lord treasurer in 1604 and no doubt the profits of office contributed, but like several aristocrats of his age he left an estate deep in debt when he died in 1626.[10] Nevertheless, if the figure is impossible to believe, the assertion illustrates the difficulty of discovering precisely what such buildings cost and the source of the money. Some other high figures are a matter of gossip in aristocratic circles. Wanstead House (Essex, begun 1715, demolished 1822) cost £100,000 and the gardens as much again, according to Horace Walpole; Eastbury (Dorset, completed 1738, demolished 1782) was said to have cost £140,000 and Moor Park (Hertfordshire, c. 1725) £130,000. They were among the grandest houses of their age, built out of City fortunes, but Castle Howard (Yorkshire, 1699–1737) cost £78,240, including the works in the park. At the top of the scale comes Blenheim Palace (Oxfordshire, begun 1705), which by the end of the duchess of Marlborough's life had cost about £300,000. Once the fashion for these leviathans of the Baroque period had subsided, the next generation of builders was less extravagant. Edgecoat House (Northamptonshire), a house of moderate size built in 1747–52, cost £17,288 16s 8d.

Figures based on surviving accounts seem remarkably modest but it is rarely possible to be certain how much they included. Sir Thomas Kytson spent more than £3,500 on Hengrave Hall in 1525–39; Sir William More's Loseley House (Surrey) cost him less than £1,700 in the 1560s, probably for the north wing only, which is all that still stands. Sir Roger Townshend spent £3,500 on Raynham Hall (Norfolk) in 1619–22 but it was certainly not completed by then. Broome Park (Kent), the most splendid example of Mannerist design in brick, cost £8,000 in 1635–8. More

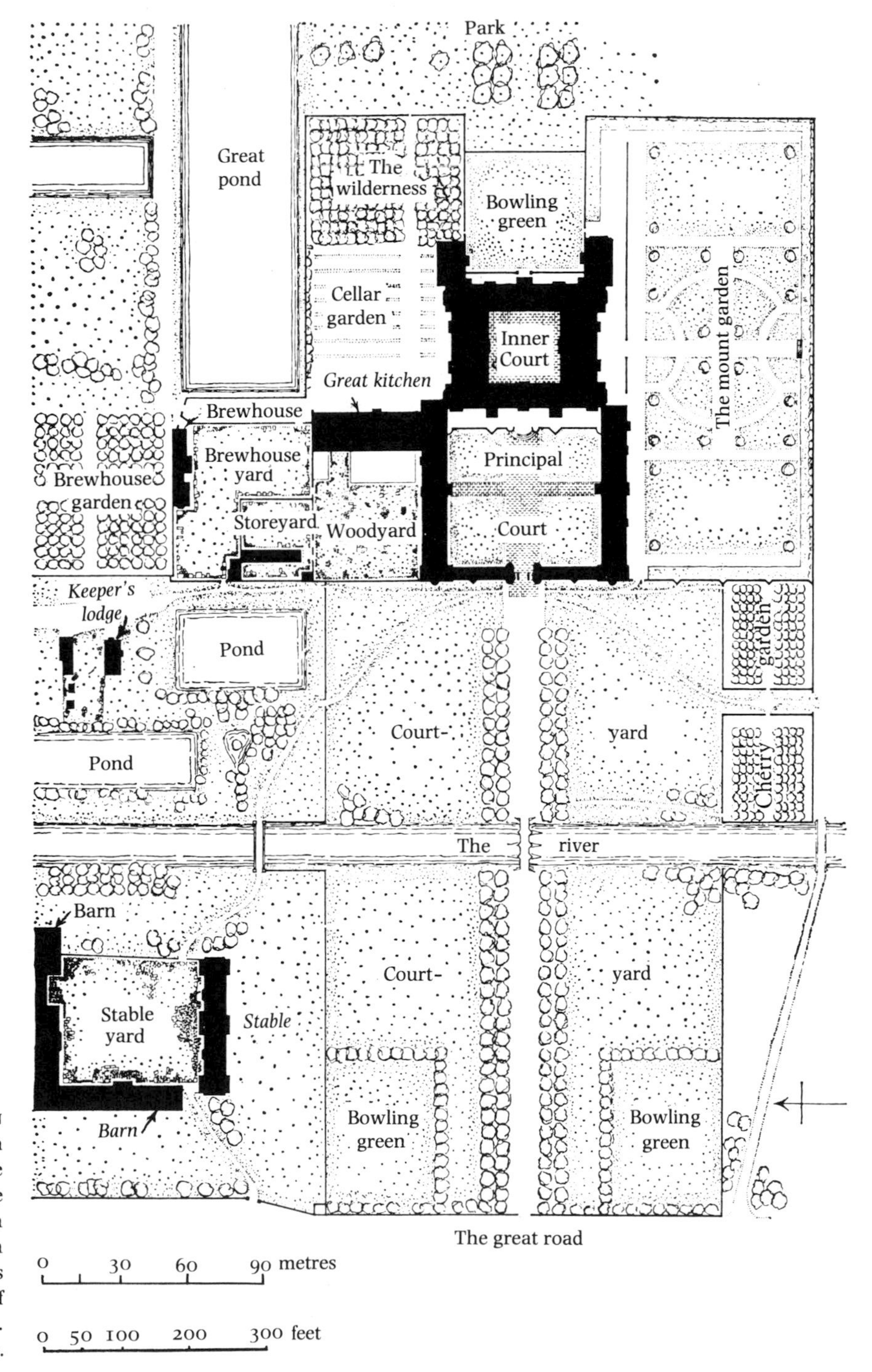

123. AUDLEY END, SAFFRON WALDEN, ESSEX, based on a survey of 1688 and before Vanbrugh demolished the principal court. It was built in 1603 on thc site of Maldon Priory and the inner court was laid out exactly over the site of the cloister garth of the priory. *Agr. Hist.*

precise figures can be found for houses built after 1660, modest in size, and their cost not swollen by elaborate interior finishes and decoration. Sir Roger Pratt designed and built Ryston Hall (Norfolk) for himself in 1669–72 and spent £2,800; his papers show a careful control over operations. It was similar in size to the new palace for the bishop of Lichfield [187] in his cathedral city, which cost £3,972 in 1685–9. William Stanton, a master mason, was paid £5,000 in 1685 for Belton House (Lincolnshire), possibly only for the carcase. The duke of Newcastle in 1674–9 demolished the remains of Nottingham Castle and built a Baroque mansion on the site [124] and according to his widow it cost £14,000; the earl of Rutland had in 1655–68 built a mansion on the site of Belvoir castle, at a total cost of £11,730 in identical circumstances. In both cases the medieval castle must have been a useful quarry. Burley-on-the-Hill (Rutland) cost the earl of Nottingham £30,657 in 1694 and onwards.[11] The house had been estimated at £15,000 before work started and it probably cost about £19,000 eventually, the balance being spent on decoration, erecting stables and other ancillary buildings, laying out gardens and forming a park. It is a pity that there are no accounts for Sutton Scarsdale, remodelled by Francis Smith in 1724 for the earl and a roofless shell since 1920.[12] It once carried an inscription listing the team responsible, all of whom were described as gentlemen: a carver, a joiner and a carpenter; two Italians for the stucco work; a plasterer, a plumber, an upholsterer, a locksmith and the earl's steward, gardener and keeper.

124. Model of NOTTINGHAM CASTLE, possibly made in connection with the trial after the fire of 1831. *Nottingham Castle Museum.*

This expenditure of the aristocracy and wealthy gentry is worth quoting mainly for comparison with the costs of manor houses, farmhouses and cottages; of the mansions named, few survive and later changes in them have destroyed the original plan and internal design. Where a proposed plan is known there is no certainty that the design was actually carried out. The most exact evidence comes from later surveys and the nearer they are to the date of the original building the more reliable they are [123, 128].

125. The Stables at CALKE ABBEY, DERBYSHIRE, built in 1712–16 by a mason-builder from Burton-on-Trent who had also worked at Burley-on-the-Hill. This shows the elevation of the outer courtyard, built in brick with stone details.

The courtyard plan

The traditional courtyard plan, with either one or two courts, is represented by monastic buildings converted, by piecemeal rebuilding of old houses and by new houses on clear sites. Sir John Byron acquired Newstead Priory (Nottinghamshire) in 1539; he took off the church roof but used the prior's hall in the west range as his own and the refectory became his great chamber.[13] Longleat (Wiltshire) throughout Sir John Thynne's alterations retained two courtyards, one of which almost certainly represents the cloister garth of the house of Augustinian canons which had occupied this site.[14] One of the most spectacular conversions was at Leez Priory (Essex), by Richard, Baron Rich, the most powerful and obnoxious of Henry VIII's ministers after Cromwell.[15] At Leez, as at St Bartholomew's in Smithfield, he must positively have rejoiced to put religious buildings to a secular use; the nave of the priory church became his great hall. How he converted the claustral buildings we do not know, since they were demolished in 1753, leaving only his towering brick gatehouse and part of his new outer courtyard with another smaller gatehouse.

Partial rebuilding

In some medieval and Tudor houses the stages of rebuilding can be observed in the fabric, though such traces may tell nothing about changes of plan. At Kimbolton (Huntingdonshire) the medieval castle had been rebuilt in 1525 (according to Leland) and again in 1617–20 and 1690; traces of each phase can be seen, especially of the refacing in brick of the inner walls of the courtyard in 1690. Vanbrugh was called there in 1707 by its owner, the earl of Manchester, because a corner had collapsed and he was allowed to rebuild or reface the whole exterior. He wished to do the same at Grimsthorpe Castle (Lincolnshire), the home of the first earl of Ancaster, but was only allowed to build a new north front [126] to a courtyard house which still retains one thirteenth-century corner tower.[16]

126. GRIMSTHORPE CASTLE, LINCOLNSHIRE, Vanbrugh's front.

At Wallington (Northumberland) a medieval castle was replaced in 1688 by a courtyard house apparently new above ground; all four ranges have cellars which may be medieval in origin though there is nothing visible to demonstrate it. Happily the plan of William Blackett's house of 1688 [127] is known from a survey of 1736, prior to alterations which were the first stage of filling in the courtyard.[17] Short of a calamity such as the reduction of Chatsworth to a shell of brick and stone, stripped of all fittings and finishes, it is impossible to say whether anything remains of Bess of Hardwick's house begun in 1552; as it stands the house represents a rebuilding by the earl of Devonshire in 1687–1707 in the original form, with an enormous wing added in 1827 by the sixth duke.

Walls may be rebuilt or refaced and new openings made without necessarily renewing roofs, and recent examination of Boughton House (Northamptonshire) has shown that buildings round all four sides of a small courtyard there, now called Fish Court, still have medieval roofs [76]. The ordinary visitor sees Elizabethan doorways and fireplaces and especially the work of the first duke of Montagu who inherited in 1683; he added the range of rooms and wings north of the medieval hall, creating what Pevsner called the most French-looking seventeenth-century house in England. Boughton is only one of nine courtyard houses in Northamptonshire; proper examination of them might well show that more of them have a medieval nucleus than is obvious.

A major innovation in the houses of Tudor courtiers was to have ranges of building two rooms deep. A courtyard could provide light for the inner row of rooms, as it did at Sir Christopher Hatton's Holdenby.[18]

127. WALLINGTON, NORTHUMBERLAND. A. Plan of the ground floor of the courtyard house built in 1688. B. Proposed alterations of 1736, reducing the courtyard and fitting new staircases into it to eliminate passage rooms. *Agr. Hist.*

This advantage seems to explain why James Brydges, first duke of Chandos, retained the courtyard plan of an older house when he built Canons (Stanmore, Middlesex) in 1713–25. He also rebuilt the parish church 'very much in the style of a private chapel' (Pevsner) and it still stands, but his house was demolished soon after his death in 1744; it and its predecessor are known only from plans.[19] He had made a fortune as Marlborough's paymaster-general, and Daniel Defoe's *Tour through England and Wales* has pages of fulsome praise of his ostentatious style of living.

The base-court and the forecourt

Many a great house of the sixteenth and seventeenth centuries is now to be viewed across an expanse of lawn, but this was rarely its original setting. The stages by which the double courtyard house of the Middle Ages was opened to the visitor reflect changes within the house and in relations between an owner and his household staff. South Wingfield was entered by an outer court used mainly by servants, and the term base-court for it is first recorded in 1491 (OED). The Elizabethan Hawstead Place (Suffolk) had, round three sides of its base-court, barns, stables, a mill-house, slaughter-house, blacksmith's shop and various other offices and there were chambers for carters over the gatehouse. Several such base-courts in front of the hall have been demolished, as at Compton Wynyates. When Chaloner Chute, speaker of the Commons, bought the Vyne (Hampshire) in 1653, he demolished both the courtyards of the early Tudor house, and on the north side, where the base-court had included dormitories for yeomen, he got a fashionable architect, John Webb, to design a new portico.[20]

The term forecourt, also of Tudor origin, was more appropriate when it was surrounded only by lodgings for superior persons, as at Sir Christopher Hatton's Kirby Hall (Northamptonshire, 1583) and the earl of Suffolk's Audley End (Essex, 1616). The forecourt at the latter house was demolished by Vanbrugh in the 1720s, presumably because lodgings on that scale were redundant and not worth the cost of maintenance. Fortunately the original plan and the ancillary buildings are known from a survey of 1688 [123]. Wren's design for a royal palace at Winchester, half built when Charles II died in 1685 and never completed, was the last example of a new forecourt with lodgings. Henceforward in new aristocratic houses most of the household staff, with a dwindling number of gentlemen in it, was accommodated on upper floors, as they must have been at Holdenby, Hatton's other Northamptonshire house. Although the outer court there was still called the base-court [122], it certainly had no stables or the like in it.

These changes are also reflected in the treatment of the entrance and the corners of the outer court; any defensive quality gradually disappears. Battlements become an openwork parapet; the gatehouse is reduced in size (four storeys at Burghley, three at Audley End); turrets are topped by leaded cupolas of the sort which first appeared at Henry VII's palace at Richmond, and the architectural historian prefers to call them pavilions.

The total enclosure of the base-court was eventually reduced to a walled forecourt with at most a gatehouse. Hatfield House (Hertfordshire, 1607–12) which like so many mansions and manor houses of this time faced north, has a shallow walled space flanking the entrance steps. Wimbledon House had an elaborate double forecourt with access by coach only to the outer part.[21] Doddington Hall (Lincolnshire) built in 1593–1600 by a legal officer of the diocese of Lincoln, still has its leaded cupolas and a gatehouse. In several cases an architect's design was not carried out. Robert Smythson's Wollaton Hall, which also faces north, was intended to have a large gatehouse incorporating a flight of steps leading to covered walks or loggias.[22] Vanbrugh's designs for Castle Howard and Blenheim also incorporated gatehouses leading to great courts, as they were termed in the published designs. In none of these cases was the great court actually built.[23]

Stables The flight of steps up to the forecourt of Wimbledon House and within the proposed gatehouse at Wollaton Hall are a reminder that visitors walked across the forecourt while their coaches were driven or their horses led away to the stables. In the eighteenth century the porch of a mansion was often designed with open sides so that a coach could draw up under cover; the French term *porte-cochère* occurs first in 1698. For a century before that, location and design of stables had reflected the popularity of hunting, racing and equestrian skills. The stables at Audley End may have been adapted from the guesthouse of the Benedictine priory acquired in 1544 by Lord Audley and at Hatfield House the earl of Salisbury converted the bishop of Ely's medieval hall, but by Charles I's time new stables were being built whose character remained unchanged to the end of the Victorian age. In 1620–30 the first duke of Buckingham, George Villiers, built at Burley-on-the-Hill (Rutland) a stable block described in 1684 (by a proud local historian) as 'the noblest building of this kind in England'.[24] It looked quite like a house, with central entrance and wings, symmetrically treated. The stalls had vaulted ceilings, an unusual precaution to reduce fire risk; the block was typical in having lodgings or dormitories for grooms on the first floor and in the garrets. The views in Kip's *Britannia Illustrata*, published in 1714 and 1715, show stables invariably of either one and a half storeys, with dormers, or of two full storeys. If they were not built round one or two closed courtyards as at Wollaton Hall and Calke Abbey (Derbyshire) [125], they were often placed on one side of a forecourt, and this concept reached its most monumental expression in Vanbrugh's designs for Castle Howard, Blenheim, Seaton Delaval (Northumberland) and Eastbury (Dorset). None of his stables can now be seen, except in a reduced form at Eastbury; the other designs were not realized. Massive stable blocks are a particular feature of eighteenth-century mansions; the new stables built at Chatsworth in 1758–63 had eighty stalls. They recall Osbert Sitwell's phrase about Blankney Hall (Lincolnshire) in the time of his grandfather, Lord Londesborough; there 'horses were enthroned in a state which even Caligula never dreamt of for his favourite'.[25] The stables at Stapleford Park (Leicestershire) built in 1899 mark the end of an era. They still have, unaltered, six coach-houses, a blacksmith's shop and a horse-hospital; stalls and tack rooms; rooms for washing and drying horse blankets; bedrooms for grooms and a feed-loft. The building is certainly the finest and best preserved in the hunting shires, though there is not now one horse to be seen.

Baroque and Palladian houses The building of country houses reached its climax, in terms of their scale, in 1700–60, first in Vanbrugh's Baroque mansions such as Castle Howard and Blenheim, followed by 'vast and emphatic piles' (Pevsner's phrase) in Palladian style, such as Wanstead (Essex), begun in 1715 and

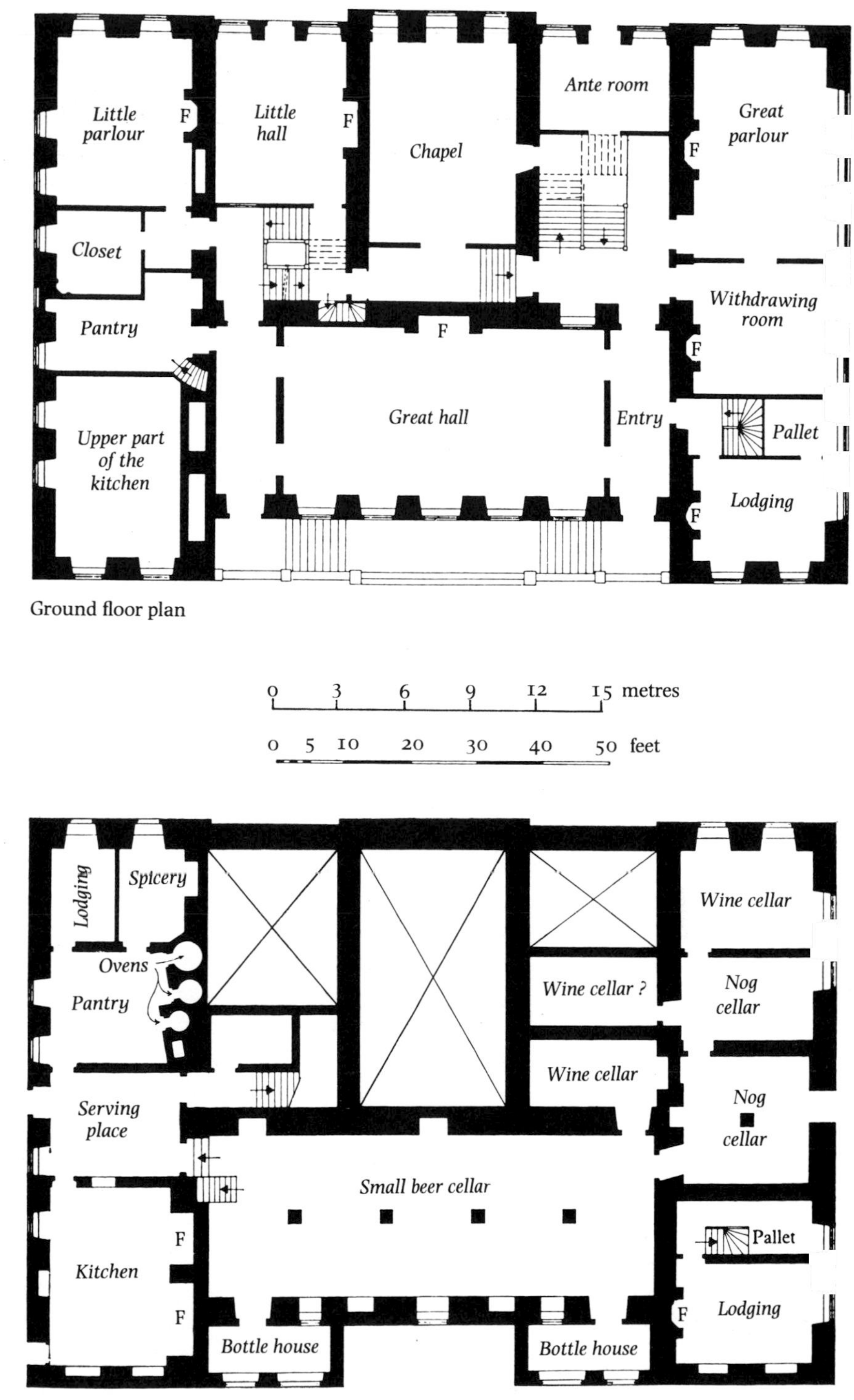

128. Plans of the ground floor and basement of RAYNHAM HALL, NORFOLK, designed in the 1620s; the names of rooms taken from a survey of 1671 show how the basement was used. *Agr. Hist.*

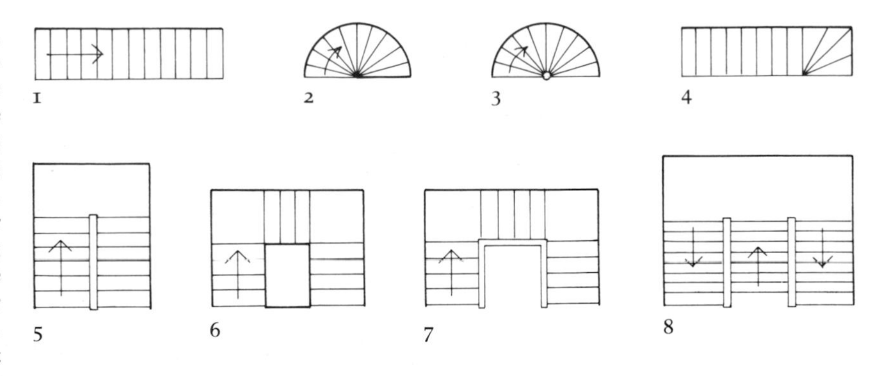

129. Forms of staircase, showing the sorts of space into which they fitted. The average flight needed nine to twelve stairs with treads 22.8 cm (9 in) deep and risers 19 cm (7½ in) high, for a single storey. 1. Straight flight. 2. Winder stair, each tread supporting the next. 3. Newel staircase with a newel post, suitable for two or more storeys. 4. Straight flight with winders at top or bottom. 5. Dog-leg staircase with a half-landing. 6. Well type with a solid well (needing less timber) and quarter-landings. 7. Open well type. 8. Imperial type, rising to a spacious landing and dividing. Medieval forms 1–3 persisted for small houses; forms 5–7 emerged in the Tudor period; type 8 is only one example of the grandiose forms appearing in Baroque houses.

Walpole's Houghton (Norfolk) begun in 1721. Some of them have gone, including Wanstead; some were never completed as designed. The architectural historian judges them by designs published for instance in Colen Campbell's *Vitruvius Britannicus*, which appeared in three folio volumes in 1715, 1717 and 1725. The houses appear to rise out of the ground with a basement, often rusticated, containing service rooms taken for granted by the architectural historian, very rarely shown on his plans but essential to understanding how a house worked. In medium-sized houses of the seventeenth century such as Raynham Hall (Norfolk, c. 1630) [128] all services were in the basement.[26] The Palladian house had a central range, nearly always a double pile, with balancing wings or pavilions for services and the like, so that the visitor could be impressed by seeing a front extending 90 to 150 m (300 to 500 ft) or more. In the central block, the principal rooms were on a 'piano nobile' over a 'rustic' ground floor. In such a spread of building there was no question of three storeys, as at Tudor Holdenby or Carolean Bramshill; the norm was two storeys excluding the basement and any rooms in the roof space lighted by dormers; at Blenheim only part of the house had two full storeys, and Holkham (Norfolk) was entirely on one principal floor. A few provincial architects such as Francis Smith of Warwick, with less ambitious clients, built three storeys, as at Stoneleigh Abbey (Warwickshire 1714–26).

The first-floor rooms

With so many rooms, no two generations can be assumed to have used a house in the same way. The duchess of Devonshire, describing Chatsworth, remarks that scarcely a room has not at some time been a billiard room.[27] Walpole's twice-yearly house parties used only the rustic ground floor; Lord Hervey commented that 'there is a room for breakfast, another for supper, another for dinner, another for afternooning and the great arcade [linking the wings] for walking and quid-nuncing'. He went on to say that the next floor was 'the floor of taste, expense, state and parade', and the staircase to it was the first thing to impress the visitor.[28]

130. Staircase of c. 1660 in HOLME PIERREPONT HALL, NOTTINGHAMSHIRE, recently restored and awaiting repainting. *Country Life*.

Staircases and state rooms

In the Tudor period, the task of constructing a suitable staircase to the upper floors was (with rare exceptions such as Burghley and Hardwick) taken over from the mason by the carpenter and the turner; the framed staircase [129] distinguishes English from continental houses of the same class, while the stone staircases of Scottish tower houses of the seventeenth century demonstrate Scotland's French connections. A framed staircase could be fitted into a smaller space and was potentially more flexible in design;[29] with boards for treads and risers instead of stone or solid blocks of wood, it could be supported on posts rather than parallel walls, or even cantilevered out from the walls of the hall as at Coleshill House (Berkshire, c. 1650–62) and Belton House (Lincolnshire, 1685–8). For the grandest staircases, panels of strapwork or balusters turned or moulded gave way after c. 1650 to panels of carved foliage as in Durham Castle (1665) and Holme Pierrepont Hall [130], and those in their turn to wrought iron panels of the sort introduced in Hampton Court c. 1700.

Henry VIII's palaces with their apartments on the first floor were the first houses with staircases of ingenious form and ceremonial importance.[30] They naturally became a feature of such Elizabethan houses as Hatfield, designed for entertaining the monarch, in which the first floor had a suite of rooms like those in a royal palace. In later changes at such houses framed staircases may have been renewed but usually occupy the same space while the rooms round them have been altered or changed their use. For that reason, guide books to country houses do not describe the original planning, which can only be deduced from contemporary records and plans. The elaborate suite of a palace was somewhat reduced, to a withdrawing or antechamber, a bedchamber and an inner room (closet, cabinet or dressing room); such a suite, leading off the saloon, might be repeated for several favoured guests. This formality of planning for entertainment became most explicit after 1660, when the word 'state' came into use for it.[31] The medieval great chamber became the saloon. John Evelyn, writing a diary in Charles II's time, did not use the word 'state'; Celia Fiennes, arriving at Stoke Edith (Herefordshire) in 1698 noted that a new wing was then being built, 'all for state'. Roger North reported at Badminton that 'all the beds of state were made and finished in the house', for the ordinary pastime of the ladies of the house, led by the duchess, was embroidery and fringe-making. Such must have been common practice. Loose covers, now the pride of the 'lounge', were invented at this time to protect elaborate furnishings while a house was closed up.[32]

Visitors to country houses today find that state rooms have been named after their associations or their furnishings and the formal sequence of rooms in the state apartment has been broken by later alterations. At Hatfield, for instance, a library was made by turning a great chamber and its withdrawing chamber into one room.[33] As in medieval palaces and castles, the provision for exalted guests can only be deduced.

The one unaltered room in a Tudor or Jacobean mansion is the gallery, peculiarly English in its length, its bay windows and the quality of its fittings [131], though it was not originally intended for hanging paintings. It was no part of a Palladian house such as Houghton. Libraries came into fashion only after c. 1700, when the private cabinet was no longer large enough for gentlemen who collected books as well as paintings and sculpture. Rooms for the family might be on the principal floor and the floor above. The hall became a grand reception room for visitors,

131. Long gallery in CHASTLETON HOUSE, OXFORDSHIRE, built soon after 1602 by Walter Jones, a Witney wool merchant. The sparse furnishing reflects its original character.

132. The basement kitchen of WOLLATON HALL, NOTTINGHAMSHIRE, 1580–8. The published plans of the house are wrong in showing it on the main floor.

a place where servants waited, used occasionally for the most formal dinners but not for regular household meals; a servants' hall appears for the first time at Coleshill (Berkshire, c. 1650) and Wallington Hall (Northumberland, 1688). Back staircases provided discreet access to state rooms, but were essentially for servants carrying water and fuel to bedrooms and the chamber pots from close stools. Their work upstairs was very gradually made easier, after c. 1660, by installing piped water fed by a household cistern, and later by the provision of water closets.[34]

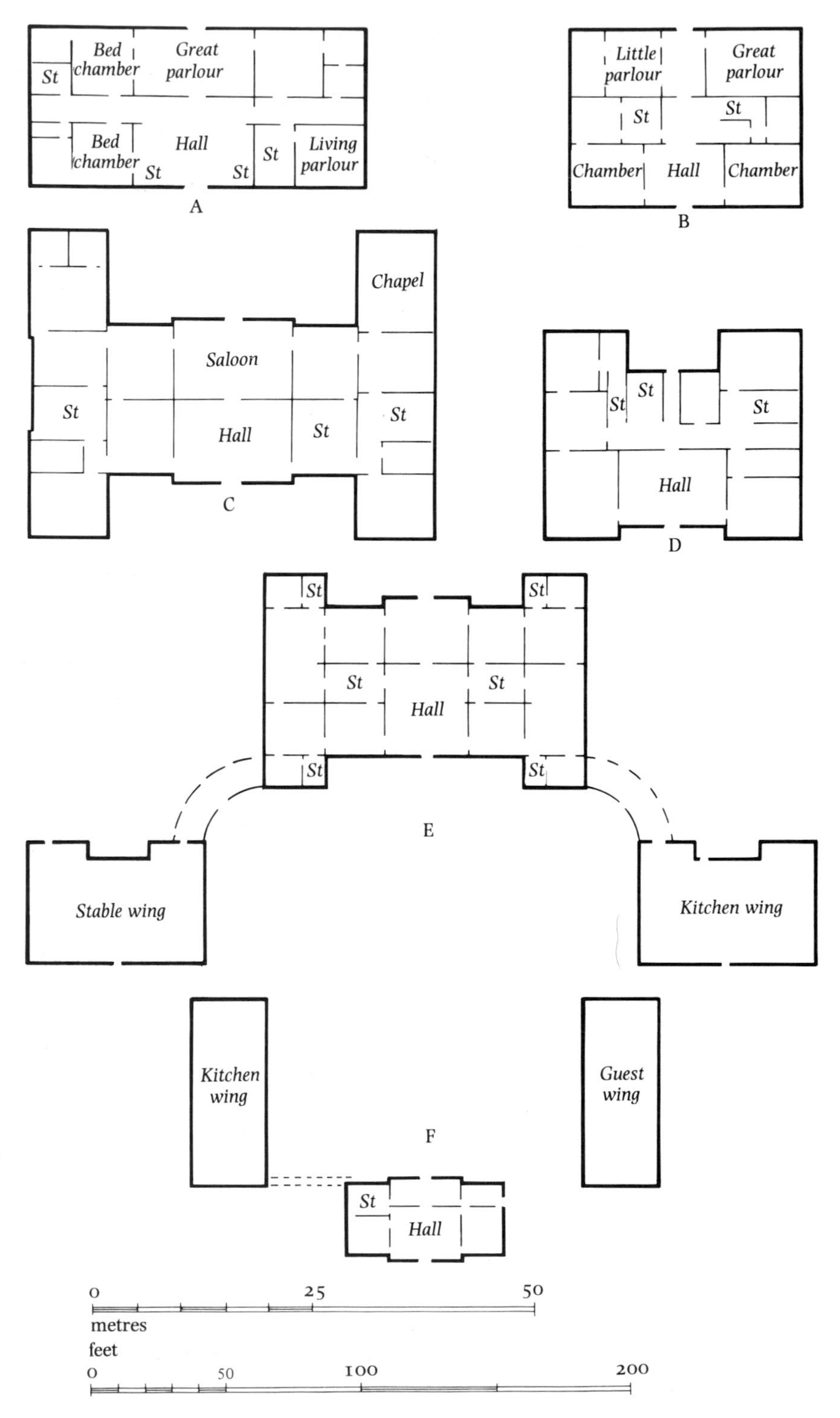

133. Comparative plans of houses of the gentry: *Agr. Hist.* A. COLESHILL, BERKSHIRE; B. ELTHAM LODGE, KENT; C. BELTON HOUSE, LINCOLNSHIRE; D. STANFORD HALL, LEICESTERSHIRE; E. DITCHLEY PARK, OXFORDSHIRE; F. AVERHAM PARK LODGE, NOTTINGHAMSHIRE.

The compact plan

So far we have pursued traces of continuity from medieval to modern times in the design of the largest houses. From c. 1575 onwards a revolutionary feature appears: for the sake of a more compact plan, the kitchen and its associated rooms were placed in a semi-basement, separated by a flight of stairs from the hall [132]. The arrangement was specifically French in origin. Elizabethan patrons and their masons shared a strong interest in French architecture; Robert Smythson, who designed several houses with this feature, may have picked up the idea at Longleat, where he worked alongside French masons.[35] It found favour in town and country. It was particularly suitable for a sloping site, such as Wimbledon House and Fountains Hall (Yorkshire, 1610), and was convenient on a restricted urban site; from grand residences such as Nottingham House, Kensington, built c. 1605 with 'All Offices and Cellars underground', it passed down the social scale to terrace housing in London and some provincial towns.

Compactness of design appears in the most explicit form in the later seventeenth century, in the form called then the double pile, combining a plan two rooms in depth with basement services [133]. It was established in fashionable esteem by Sir Roger Pratt (1620–84) a gentleman architect; he only designed four houses, only one of which, Kingston Lacy (Dorset), survives though altered in appearance and plan; the best known, Coleshill (Berkshire), was demolished after a fire in 1952.[36] The house he built in Piccadilly for Lord Clarendon must have made a great mark and in notes for a book he never completed his arguments about its economy of construction and technical advantages must have expressed widely held views. His double pile was the model for new country seats in later Stuart times; without the basement services it was equally fashionable for new manor houses and new homes for wealthy clergy.

The passion for building, and for displaying both to compeers and to the growing number of visitors to country houses the taste and wealth of an owner, was not easily exhausted. For some it took the form of building a lodge in a park. This descendant of the medieval hunting lodge ranged in size and comfort from a mere covered and heated grandstand architect-designed, like that at Swarkeston (Derbyshire, c. 1625) or Lodge Park, Sherborne (Gloucestershire, c. 1650) to a small but lofty house on a hilltop such as Ashdown House (Berkshire, c. 1660) and Averham Park Lodge (Nottinghamshire, c. 1725), with pavilions for guests and services. Ashdown went with the great courtyard house of the earl of Craven at Hampstead Marshall, 17 miles away; Averham with the Sutton's manor house at Kelham, only 3 miles away. Robert Cecil built Wothorpe Lodge [134], just across the north road from Burghley Park, 'to retire to out of the dust while his great house was a sweeping'.[37] These lodges were fashionable retreats. In the genuine hunting lodge, small and simple, the great man and his friends might picnic for a day or two.

134. WOTHORPE LODGE, NORTHAMPTONSHIRE, built c. 1610–20 by Thomas the second earl of Exeter, across the road (A1) as it were from Burghley House, his principal residence.

In the eighteenth century, the villa took the place of the lodge as a retreat for noblemen and courtiers and for the prospering London merchant. The spas at Epsom and Tunbridge were an attraction, but the Thames valley offered a landscape of unsurpassed beauty, accessible by boat from London and on the axis between the capital and the court at Richmond. According to Defoe, writing in 1724, the 'distant glory' of the villas along the valley such as the earl of Burlington's at Chiswick could not be matched in the valleys of the Seine, the Danube or the Po [135]. The word villa originally meant a country estate but came by c. 1750 to mean a miniature house. Some early villas copied exactly Palladio's small country houses; they had two storeys over a rusticated basement, but their fronts were only five bays in length even if they had a pediment and a dome. Burlington's villa at Chiswick (1724), based like Mereworth (Kent) on Palladio's Villa Rotonda at Vicenza, has a square plan of only 20.7 m (68 ft).

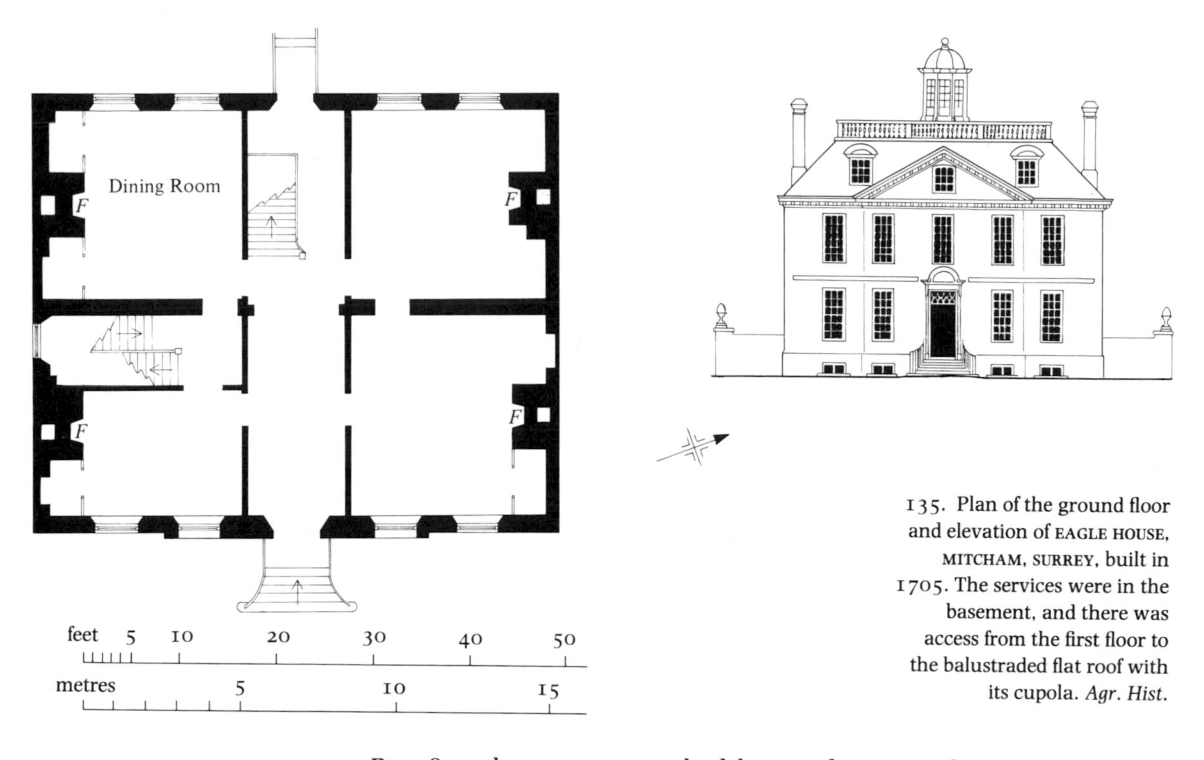

135. Plan of the ground floor and elevation of EAGLE HOUSE, MITCHAM, SURREY, built in 1705. The services were in the basement, and there was access from the first floor to the balustraded flat roof with its cupola. *Agr. Hist.*

By 1800 the country seat had lost its distinctive features of size and plan. Its scale was smaller; formal provision for state and parade had been abandoned; instead of a rustic ground floor or semi-basement the house was planted on the ground and the principal rooms, with French doors or windows with low sills, opened directly on to gardens and a 'natural' landscape created by Capability Brown or Repton. To achieve that sort of effect, an outer courtyard was demolished at Compton Wynyates (Warwickshire) and the moat filled in; the romantic quality of the house and its setting which appeals so strongly today was created by destroying its medieval character.

More profound than such changes in taste were changes in the compositions of the gentry. In an open and mobile society such as England was from the later Middle Ages onward, the country seat, originally dependent largely on income from land, was increasingly the product of profits of office, of war and of success in business. The number of country seats grew steadily from 1540 to 1800 in every county, but most in Hertfordshire and Surrey, favourite counties for London merchants turning country gentlemen. A graph of Hertfordshire country houses built has peaks in 1540–70, 1670–1710, 1770–1810 and 1840–80; the same is probably true in other counties but numbers diminish as the distance from London increases.[38] The latest peak in the Hertfordshire figures represents gentlemen of modest means, with incomes derived from rising rents from a few hundred acres of land at a time of agricultural expansion but more from investments in business companies and in the Funds. Only intensive surveys, analytical rather than descriptive and county by county, of the rise and fall of the country house would show how far the Hertfordshire pattern differed from other regions.

Notes

1 BE *Surrey* (1971), 521; J. Summerson, *Architecture in Britain 1530–1830* (1953), pl. 22a; *Archaeol. J.*, 97 (1959), 107–26; ibid., (1955), 100–28.
2 RCHM, *Dorset*, 5 (1975), 7–12.
3 *Agr. Hist.*, 5 (1984), 615.
4 D. Starkey, 'Ightham Mote ...', *Archaeologia*, 107 (1982), 153–63.
5 M. Girouard, *Robert Smythson and the Architecture of the Elizabethan Age* (1966), ch. 1.
6 R. North, *Lives of the Norths* (1890), 2, 99.
7 List in M. Girouard, *Life in the English Country House* (1978), 319–20.
8 G. Scott Thompson, *Life in a Noble Household 1641–1700* (1937), ch. 6; J. Nichols, *Hist. and Ant. of ... Leicestershire* (1804), 3, ii, 594–7.
9 *Agr. Hist.*, 5, 611.
10 M. Airs, *The Making of the English Country House* (1975), ch. 8.
11 Some of these figures, collected from various sources, will be found in *Country Life* volumes on *English Country Houses* by J. Cornforth, C. Hussey and J. Lees-Milne. I am indebted to Mr H. M. Colvin for figures found by him in manuscript sources. See also L. and J. C. F. Stone, *An Open Elite? England 1540–1880* (1984), part III, and especially pp. 353–8.
12 H. M. Colvin, *Biog. Dictionary of British Architects* (1978), 751.
13 *Trans. Thoroton Soc.*, 83 (1979), 52–3.
14 Girouard, *Robert Smythson*, 52–3.
15 W. G. Hoskins, *Age of Plunder* (1976), 107, 132–3; RCHM, *Essex*, 2 (1921), 158–61; BE, *Essex*, 263–4.
16 RCHM, *Huntingdonshire* (1926), 170–1; L. Whistler, *Sir John Vanbrugh* (1938), 275–9.
17 *Agr. Hist.*, 5, 610.
18 M. Girouard in *Country Life*, 19 October 1979, 1286–8. I am indebted to him for permission to reproduce his reconstruction [122].
19 Plans in Nikolaus Pevsner, *The Planning of the Elizabethan Country House* (inaugural lecture, Birkbeck College 1960), fig. 14; C. H. C. and M. I. Baker, *The Life and Circumstances of James Brydges, First Duke of Chandos* (1949), 116, 129, 144; *Tour through England and Wales* (Everyman), 2, 5–8.
20 J. Gage, *History of Suffolk* (1838), 439–40; T. G. Jackson, *The Renaissance of Roman Architecture* (1922), 2, 48.
21 Summerson, pls 229, 23a.
22 *Architectural History*, 5 (1962), 89.
23 Summerson, 171, 173.
24 *Agr. Hist.*, 4, 704.
25 *Left Hand, Right Hand* (1945), 103.
26 *Agr. Hist.*, 4, fig. 19.
27 *The House: a portrait of Chatsworth* (1982), 154.
28 Earl of Ilchester (ed.), *Lord Harvey and his Friends* (1950), 71.
29 W. E. Godfrey, *English Staircases* (1911).
30 *King's Works*, IV, ii, 58, 477.
31 Girouard, *Life in the English Country House*, ch. 4; *Agr. Hist.*, 5, 612.
32 J. Fowler and J. Cornforth, *English Decoration in the Eighteenth Century* (1974), 160–2.
33 Compare the plans of Hatfield House in BE, *Hertfordshire*, 166 and Girouard, *Life* ..., 115.
34 *Agr. Hist.*, 5, 612–4.
35 Girouard, *Smythson*, ch. 1.
36 RCHM, *Dorset*, 5, 46–7, pls 67–9; *Agr. Hist.*, 5, 603.
37 T. Fuller, *Worthies* (1662), 280.
38 L. and J. C. F. Stone, 'Country houses and their owners in Hertfordshire 1540–1879', in W. O. Aydelotte *et al.* (eds), *Dimensions of Quantitative Research in History* (1972), 56–123. The authors have now completed comparative studies of Northamptonshire and Northumberland, in *An Open Elite? England 1540–1880* (1984).

11 *Manor Houses*

As what was left of the manorial system dissolved in the two centuries or more after 1550, manor houses took on a more varied economic and social status. The system lasted longest in the nucleated villages of lowland England, except where an absentee or incompetent landlord allowed it to lapse. As we have seen, it had never been strong in pastoral districts or in south-eastern counties where manors had little or no demesne, few customary tenants and a high proportion of freeholders whose fixed rents and token payments ceased to be worth collecting. The problems of identifying the manor house in any part of England are the results of changes in these post-medieval centuries. Nevertheless, it seems better to cling to the concept of the manor house, however tenuous, as the largest rural house occupied by a family with no other residence. The greatest area of uncertainty is whether the house was a working farm, because students of houses have often failed to pay more than passing attention to farm buildings, and in a great many cases these have been demolished. Boughton Monchelsea Place (Kent) now consists of one range of a manor house c. 1567–75 by Robert Rudstone, with another range rebuilt c. 1819; the other half of the courtyard has gone. One large timber barn remains, but there was originally more than one, with a milk-house, stilling-house, wheat-loft, brewhouse, fish-house, bakehouse, work-house and stables – all round one or more other courtyards.[1] The systematic study of farm buildings, much talked of at present, would among other benefits throw light on the status and function of such houses.

Social mobility took two principal forms: the lateral mobility of the merchant or lawyer who acquired a country estate and the vertical mobility of the yeoman farmer successful enough to become a gentleman or even a peer. The former was not unknown in medieval times, but Tudor and later examples are more numerous and better documented. Whitehall, on the outskirts of Shrewsbury was built in 1578–82 by a lawyer; a barn and a dovecote remain, and it may have been a farm. Another lawyer in 1680 built Bell Hall, Naburn [137], a few miles from York which he represented in Parliament; it was never a farm. London

136

137

136. Gatehouse, 1580, UPTON CRESSETT HALL, SHROPSHIRE, well enough finished inside to be intended for guests.

137. BELL HALL, NABURN, YORKSHIRE, 1650. The roof has lost its balustrading and cupola.

138. BRINKHEUGH, NORTHUMBERLAND, built c. 1720 with rusticated piers to its forecourt gateway.

merchants built Franks, Horton Kirby (Kent) in 1591 and Honington Hall (Warwickshire) in 1682; neither was a farmhouse and each has a mark of its time; Franks is a tiny courtyard house and Honington had a park with such fashionable features as a temple as well as stables and a dovecote. A fortune in tin and wool built Lanhydrock, one of the grandest houses in Cornwall (c. 1620–58) in courtyard form; Shaw House, the largest Elizabethan House in Berkshire was built in 1581 for a clothier. Pitchford Hall (Shropshire, 1560–70) and Chastleton House (Oxfordshire, 1602) were built by wool merchants and they are particularly important since they are virtually unaltered, the former timber-framed, the latter of stone [131]. By 1638, Thomas Tolson, tobacco merchant (perhaps in Liverpool), had made enough money to retire to his place of origin, Strickland Ketel in Westmorland, and build Tolson Hall; the windows have painted glass with pipes and plugs of tobacco, together with pious inscriptions thanking God for his success.[2] Sir William Blackett's Wallington Hall (Northumberland) was built out of a fortune made in coal and lead-mining and shipping in Newcastle-upon-Tyne [127].

These houses are only the most easily named examples of a class which grew in numbers steadily through modern times, of houses of quality built or occupied by men who if they owned land rented it to others.

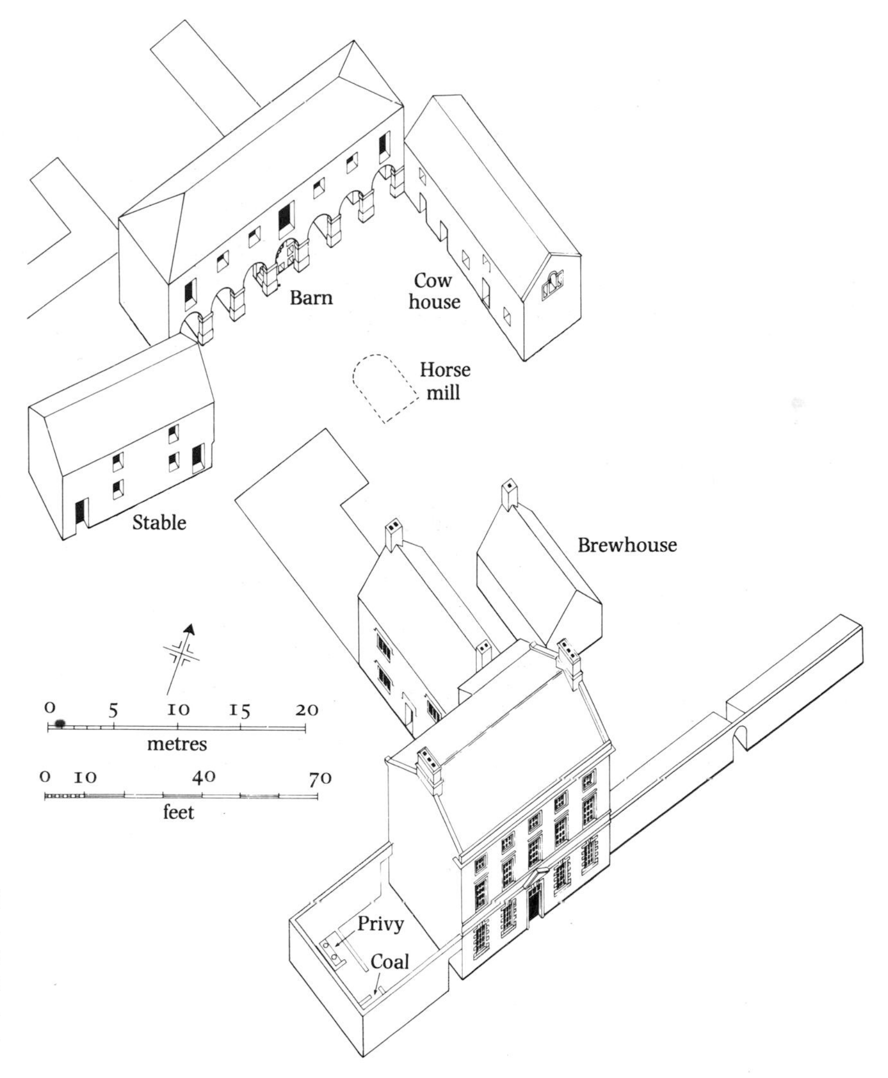

139. Isometric view of HUTHWAITE HALL, THURGOLAND, YORKSHIRE, showing John Carr's new house built in front of an older one and his farm buildings. *Agr. Hist.*

They are likely to stand away from the nucleated village if there was one and in a park, however modest in size – a pleasure ground rather than a hunting park; they are also likely to have what has been called 'a certain amplitude of public rooms for entertainment'.[3] The process of converting farmhouses into country houses and villas grew in pace after c. 1750 and so the number of manor houses in the medieval sense diminished. In Hertfordshire, eminently accessible to Londoners, the number of parks doubled from twenty in 1596 to forty or so in 1725, to eighty in 1800 and still more in 1880. 'Those who inherited ancient manor houses in villages tended to abandon them to the little parish gentry and to move elsewhere', and the old manor house became Manor Farm. With the largest of these – say houses with a front of more than

140. MANOR HOUSE, ELMSWELL, YORKSHIRE, built c. 1630 by Henry Best, author of a well-known treatise on farming practices. The remains of the large dovecote have now disappeared. *D. Neave.*

seven bays in the idiom of Classical architecture – we shall not be concerned. In counties further from London, the small country seat of the *rentier* is less common but there are instances of the industrialist apparently taking seriously to farming when he bought an estate. In 1748 John Cockshutt, owner of the Wortley ironworks north of Sheffield, employed the young architect, John Carr, to design Huthwaite Hall, Thurgoland [139], which was in effect built in front of an existing house which became the kitchen and services; Carr also built new farm buildings around a yard.[4]

To give a manor house a forecourt was an easy way for an owner to make it look fashionable. At Upton Cressett (Shropshire) a medieval timber-framed house was cased in brick in c. 1600 and a new detached gatehouse built [136] with well-finished rooms, possibly intended for guests to judge from fireplaces, a plaster overmantel and ceilings. The larger gate house at Burton Agnes (East Yorkshire) was built in 1610, with a plastered interior. The latest gatehouses are those miniature and timber-framed examples in the west of England, such as King's Pyon (Herefordshire, 1632) and Stokesay Castle (Shropshire). A gateway, as distinct from a gatehouse, interfered less with a view of the house and its more or less symmetrical elevation, and belongs to the years after 1660. It is no surprise to see that the Manor House at Offham (Kent), built c. 1725, has a forecourt with a low brick wall topped by wrought ironwork, but a forecourt can also be seen in remote houses in the north. Brinkheugh in Coquetdale (Northumberland) has a low wall and rusticated gate piers dividing its front garden from a field [138]. An equally remote house in upland Staffordshire, Whiteclough, Ipstones, with building of 1620 and 1724 has a gateway leading to a steep hillside, and a gazebo in the corner of the garden, both belonging to the second phase. A gazebo or summer house, however little used, was not uncommon, but a dovecote could be both decorative and useful [140]. Pigeons were collected in great quantities both for the table and for the market, especially in the century following 1660. Roger North, a gentleman lawyer who mixed with architects and himself produced competent designs for houses, wrote about the one he designed at Rougham (Norfolk) and which still stands: octagonal with brick walls and a thatched roof.[5] In Nottinghamshire, where dovecotes were particularly numerous, some of them have the nesting boxes plastered, a by-product of the gypsum-plaster industry; the octagonal brick dovecote at Manor Farm, Barton-in-Fabis, has 1,200 nesting boxes and (inside) the crest in plaster of William Sacheverell, lord of the manor and MP for the shire, who built it in 1677.[6]

Lodges The lodge as a form of rural building contributes to the variety of houses of superior quality or unusual design in the sixteenth to eighteenth centuries. The contribution has yet to be measured exactly. Some of the grandest are now ruins, as is Lulworth Castle (Dorset) begun in 1608 by Thomas Howard, Viscount Bindon, who lived at Bindon Abbey a few miles away. It was gutted in 1929. Thomas Cecil's Wothorpe (Northamptonshire c. 1620) has been a ruin since the eighteenth century [134]. Lodge Park, Sherborne (Gloucestershire, c. 1650), was built as a grandstand from which to view greyhounds coursing deer; it was converted into a residence, by dividing its two large rooms, only in 1898.[7] Standings built as very tall towers, like Freston Tower (Suffolk, c. 1550) were unsuitable for conversion.[8] There are brick houses in Suffolk apparently designed as lodges or standings: tall rectangular blocks with no cross-wings such as Thorpe Hall, Horham (c. 1560), and Ross Hall, Beccles (1593). Yet others were built as hunting lodges and became farmhouses when they changed hands, their parks given over to the plough. They include New Parks, Huby (Yorkshire), built in the 1640s by Sir Arthur Ingram of Temple Newsam near Leeds, and Averham Park Lodge (Nottinghamshire, c. 1720) [141], built by the Suttons of nearby Kelham.[9] One of the grandest is Gaythorn Hall, Asby (Westmorland), built c. 1625 by an owner familiar with ideas current in court circles;[10] it became a farmhouse in 1702. Its distinctive feature is the two turrets attached to the sides of a square plan and containing well-type staircases. It is virtually identical (though it has one more storey) with Kiplin Hall (Yorkshire), built by Sir George Calvert (1579–1632), who had risen from a place in Sir Robert Cecil's household to be principal secretary to James I.[11] The lodge as a form of residence evidently attracted ambitious men not dependent on an income from land. Frodesley Lodge (Shropshire) is

141. AVERHAM PARK LODGE, NOTTINGHAMSHIRE. William Stukeley, the antiquary, rarely drew country houses and his two drawings made in 1728, of which one is here reproduced, show that the lodge built by the Sutton family, on the highest point near their manor house, must have been a notable building. There were two large oil paintings in the house, of which the one corresponding to this drawing showed that open-field farming was being carried on in the foreground (see frontispiece to C. S. Orwin, *The Open Fields*, 1967). *Curators of the Bodleian Library, Oxford.*

a tall Elizabethan building with a staircase turret as its loftiest feature and built in commanding isolation; it must have become a gentleman's home to have survived. These comments about status and changes of function can only be tentative without more information about owners and their sources of income.

If what we are calling manor houses are often difficult to fit into their social context, they are certainly easier to date than their medieval predecessors. Documentary evidence of ownership and sometimes for building is naturally more plentiful. Distinctive features of construction or decoration are more common and may be fitted into a chronology, although some features may last for as long as a century and differ in date from one region to another. The greatest help comes from the fashion for inscribing a date, often accompanied by initials, on the outside of a house, incorporated in doorway design or as a panel set in walling, or else in a fitting inside the house. There are plenty of pitfalls in judging whether a date applies to a whole house or to a particular part of it, whether it merely means a change of ownership or whether it has been saved and reset in a rebuilding, but date stones are a measure of the amount of new building from c. 1550 for about two centuries, after which the fashion declined. Their most important contribution to the history of the house is in indicating what classes were engaged in building and regional variations in the timing and extent of it.

Carpenters' staircases

The new manor house was essentially more compact than its medieval counterpart. It was of two storeys throughout; the kitchen was incorporated in the plan and it was intended that the roof-space should be capable of use [142]. For that reason a framed staircase rises not only to the first floor but also, sometimes in a slightly cheaper form, to the level of the garrets in one construction. 'The skill of master carpenters, lavished in the Middle Ages on the roof, was transferred to the staircase.'[12] They also put up and carved splendid ceilings for halls and parlours, but the framed staircase in the manor house, with moulded posts, finials, pendants and turned or twisted balusters, is an essentially English development in the sixteenth century, Welsh in the seventeenth century but not Scottish at all, since oak was not plentiful enough in Scotland for carpenters to take over from masons in the task of building it. The framed staircase is simply not found in French manor houses or the homes of the Dutch bourgeoisie.

In the grander manor houses the staircase led to the long gallery, as it does at Sawston Hall (Cambridgeshire, 1557–84), Chastleton (Oxfordshire, c. 1610) [131], or Sudbury Hall (Derbyshire, 1675–6) and those dates span the century in which it was most fashionable. At Little Moreton Hall (Cheshire) the long gallery was planted on top of the hall range, on the second floor, and this as early as c. 1560. In smaller houses it was formed in the roof space; at Mere Hall, Hanbury (Worcestershire, c. 1560), a row of windows topped by timber-framed gables looks like a long gallery. In an inventory of 1633 for Red Hall, Bourne (Lincolnshire), the high gallery in the roof contained spare beds, cheese and butter, and the Saviles of Rufford Hall (Nottinghamshire), a much larger house, used it simply as a store for surplus bedding.[13] The inventories of Lancashire gentry give the impression that the gallery served as a general store place, not to say junk room.

Plaster decoration and insulation

In the century or so from 1550 the plasterer made as distinctive a contribution as the carpenter to the interior of the manor house. Ceilings had in any case to be plastered between joists, but wealthier and more pretentious clients had the timber covered to one degree or another with moulded plaster work and decorated friezes above the wainscotted walls [131, 152]; plaster was somewhat cheaper than stone for the overmantel to the fireplace of a hall or best chamber, but could be equally elaborate. The practice of making plaster floors as an alternative to boarding developed at the same time, especially where gypsum was available locally. There are plaster floors at Hardwick Hall (Derbyshire, 1597) and at Bolsover Castle in the keep (1612–21). In East Anglia the plasterer was called on to make brick mullions look like stone, or to parget a timber-

142. The loft in CANONTEIGH BARTON, CHRISTOW, DEVON, designed for storage. *NMR*.

framed house; in the western half of England (and in Wales) where stone-walled houses did not need that disguise, the plasterer's contribution was confined to the interior. While the carpenter's staircase made access to upper rooms more convenient and dignified, the plasterer provided better insulated living rooms at a time when winters tended to be colder.

Gabled roofs

Rows of gables on every elevation are the external mark of roof-space lighted and intended to be used, either as servants' bedrooms or for storage of produce. Timber-framed houses in the West Midlands had gables as long as timber was so used. Building in brick in southern and eastern England gave a long life to gables of one shape or another – crow-stepped from c. 1530 and curved, with or without a pedimented top, from c. 1575 until well past 1700. The pedimented form, the only one to be properly called Dutch, appeared c. 1635 (for instance at Broome Park, Kent); shaped gables with straight-sided pediments over windows in East Anglia and curved pediments like eyebrows in the Humber basin and the Severn Valley were the most lasting expression of Mannerism in brick. The hipped roof replaced the gable earliest in the south-east; the carpenter reverted readily to his traditional type.

The mason's rows of gables might be elaborately shaped, as they are in the Elizabethan wing of Trerice (Cornwall), said to be c. 1572.[14] His special form was what has been called the Holborn gable, with ogee sides coming down to a volute. The gable of that shape over the porch at

143. NEW DEANHAM HALL, NORTHUMBERLAND, with small windows under the eaves, 1670.

Cotterstock Manor House (Northamptonshire) is dated 1658, and the manor house at Allington (Lincolnshire) with the same feature must be of similar date. Repeated stone gables were most common in 1600–50; after that they were confined to yeomen's houses, but dormers, rising from the wall head rather than planted some way up the roof slope, were an alternative (whether in brick or stone) until c. 1675.

Builders in both timber and stone then began to provide light for the roof space in a simpler and cheaper way which was also more convenient for the householder, by raising the side walls so that there was room for small windows under the eaves. Lee Farm, Fittleworth (Sussex, c. 1600), has a lofty roof space but lighted only at the gable ends. Canonteigh Barton, Christow (Devon) [142], shows the potential of this clearance of the roof space. New Deanham Hall (Northumberland) [143] was built in 1670 with small windows under the eaves.[15] There are other examples in Derbyshire (Bothe Hall, Sawley) and in Herefordshire (New House Farm, Lucton). It was most convenient in northern houses with heavy slates on the roof and therefore a shallow pitch. There are examples in Cumberland, and so the innovation is best regarded as northern in origin. It evolves into the common midland type of Georgian farmhouse with three storeys. In the south-east, dormers framed into the roof were thought more elegant and were no problem for carpenters used to hipped roofs.

In the villages between Bristol and Stroud, builders of small manor houses contrived to clear the roof space of their gabled houses in a way not found elsewhere; since some roof trusses had to be placed within the gabled bays, an extended collar, supporting short principal rafters, was lodged in the wall over the window of the gable.[16] This device is a reminder that builders of this age never hesitated to lodge a main beam over a fireplace or window opening [160]. Gloucestershire builders also

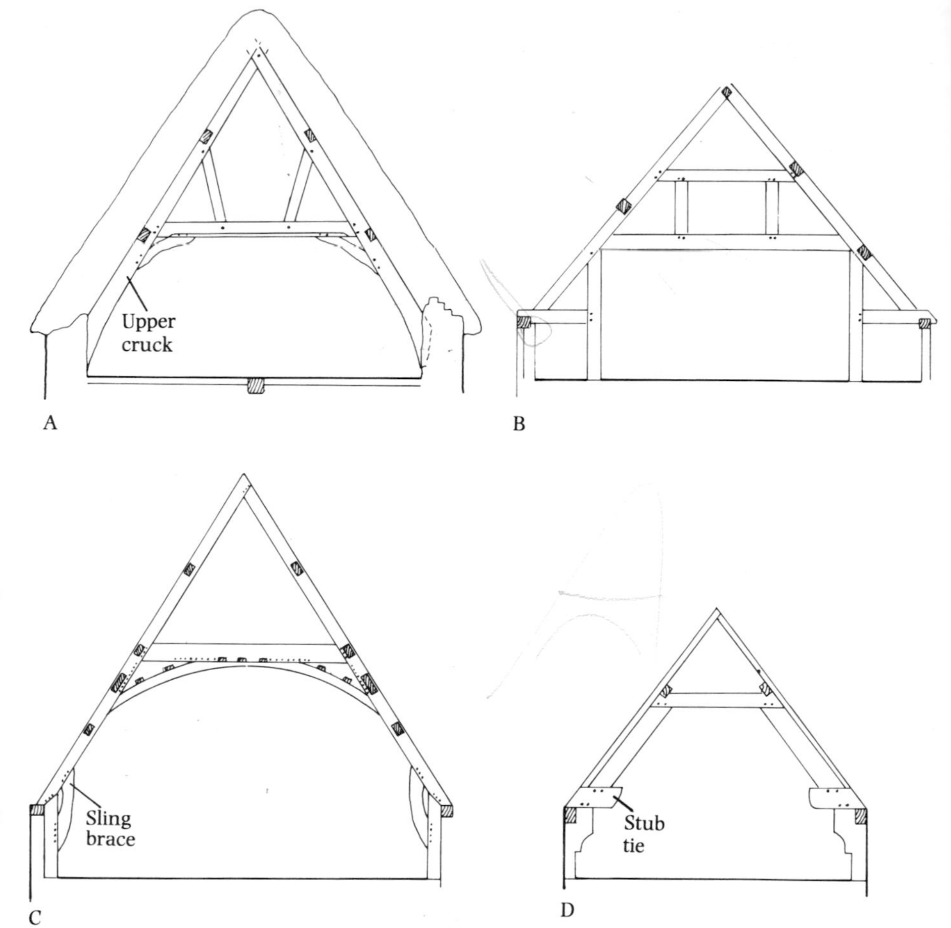

144. Forms of roof evolved after c. 1550 to clear roof-space of cross-members. A. Upper crucks, the feet lodged in stone walls, in a cottage at BLOXHAM, OXFORDSHIRE. The other examples all have tie-beams well below the level of the wall-head. B. 1–2 THE SHAMBLES, WORCESTER. This form, evolved for framed buildings, was also used with mass walling. C. With sling-braces, in the RED HALL, BOURNE, LINCOLNSHIRE. D. With stub-ties supporting short principals, in 111 MICKLEGATE, YORK. *After R. B. Wood-Jones (A), NMR (C), RCHM (B, D).*

provided more light for the garrets by a tiny opening, often round or oval, near the top of the gable. These garrets were used for ripening cheeses, or perhaps for weaving or storing cloth or wool.

The pace of building and costs

Without claiming that the view has a statistical basis, it may be said that the lesser gentry did not start building as early in Elizabeth's reign as did the courtiers and that the pace slackened after c. 1625. A list of houses built during the Commonwealth would be a long one; how much was due to the special circumstances of the time – houses damaged or destroyed during the Civil War, houses which deteriorated during the absence of an owner, houses built by new landowners – it is impossible to say. The pace of building increased steadily after 1660 to a peak early in the eighteenth century. It was then checked by a slump in prices and profits from land but the impression of a slackening after 1725 for fifty years or so may be exaggerated by the reaction to plainer styles after the exuberance of Mannerism and Baroque fashions.

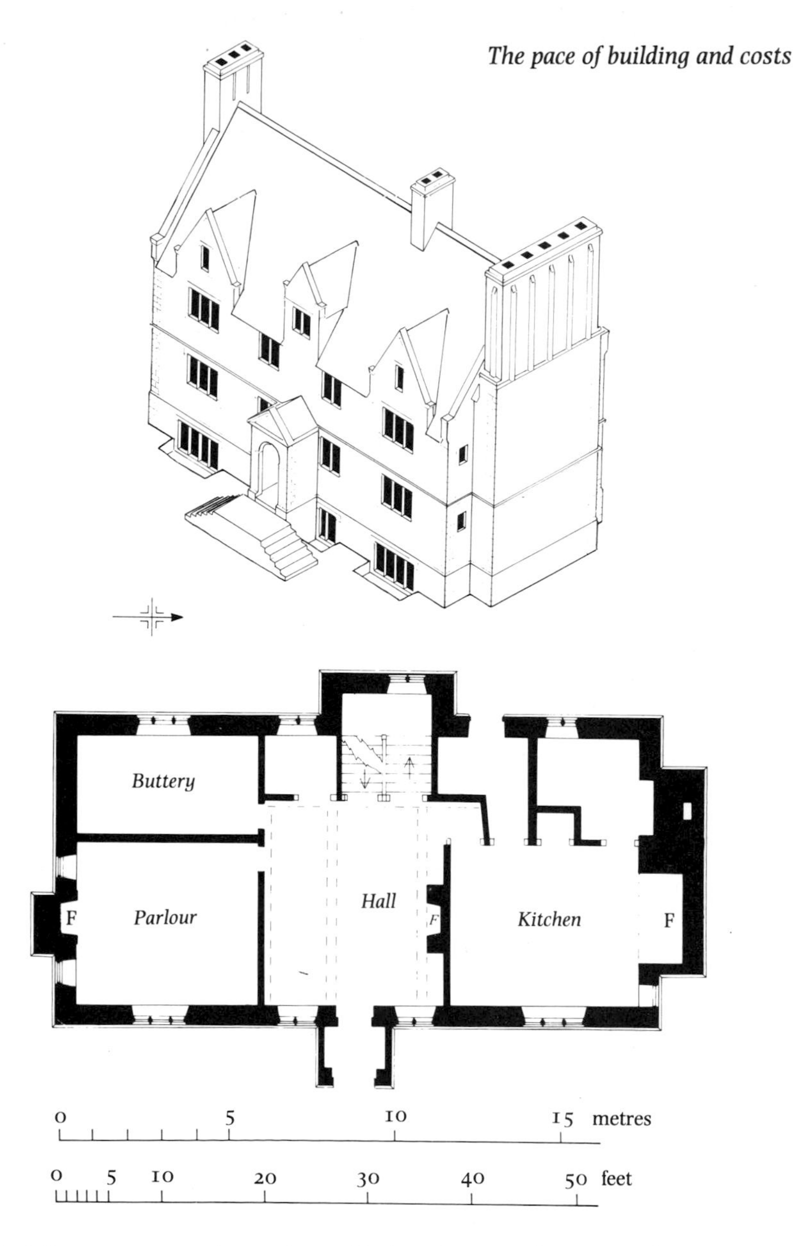

145. Plan of the ground floor and isometric view of the OLD HALL, FORTON, STAFFORDSHIRE, showing the staircase wing at the rear. Under the kitchen there was a brewhouse in the basement. *Agr. Hist.*

Building costs must be reckoned in hundreds rather than thousands of pounds.[17] Forton Hall (Staffordshire) [145], built in 1665 of brick on a stone basement, cost £100 exclusive of the carriage of materials, all of local origin. It was slightly larger than New Deanham Hall (Northumberland) [143] for which the owner contracted to pay £250 in 1669; he was to lead all the hewn stone from a quarry at Bolam, about four miles away, and lead timber no more than twelve miles. Morton Hall near Bridlington, a five-bay brick house, cost £52 4s 3d for materials and £98 8s 3d for labour. We rarely know the cost of interior finishes such as panelling and plasterwork, often lavish. Lyndon Hall (Rutland), a

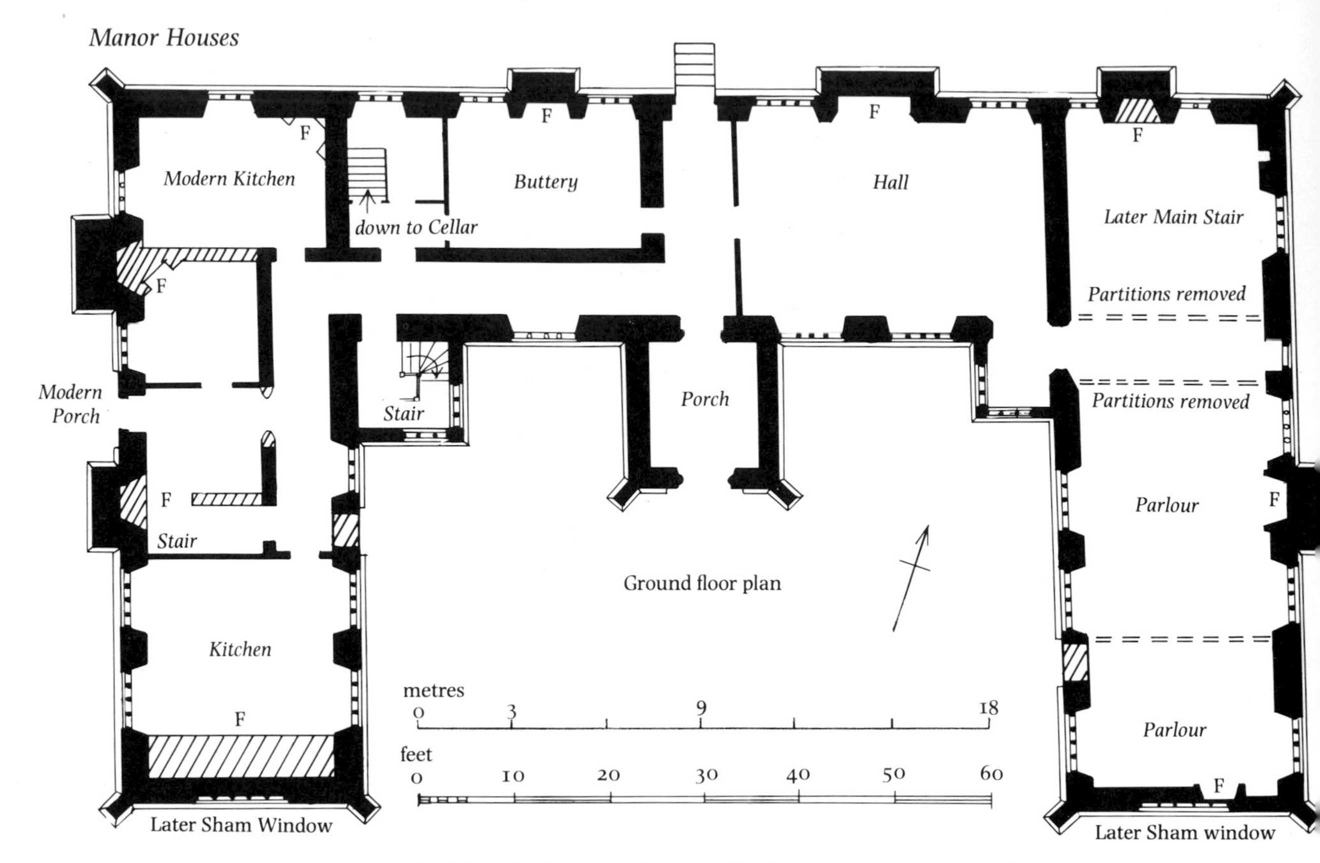

146. BARRINGTON COURT, SOMERSET, as built, with an E plan. The appearance of the house was 'improved' c. 1900 by having sham windows inserted in the fronts of the wings. E. Mercer, *English Art, 1553–1625*, Oxford 1962.

double-pile house of stone built in 1672–7, cost £1,690 exclusive of interior painting. It is unchanged outside, but the inside has been completely altered.

Plans

At this social level, a new house such as Boughton Monchelsea (page 216), built round a courtyard, was a rarity. Hanford House (Dorset), finished in 1613, is the sole instance with the hall on the further side of the courtyard from the passage entrance. Littlecote (Wiltshire) is a medieval house remodelled c. 1590 for a lawyer who later became lord chief justice; it may like Wallington (Northumberland) have been built on old foundations. Evidently the courtyard was still thought by a few to confer status; Franks in Horton Kirby (Kent) was built in 1591 for a London alderman and Chastleton (Oxfordshire) in 1602 for a Witney wool merchant [131]. In both, the courtyard was very small, no more than a light-well and certainly not intended for circulation. It was later glazed over at Wallington and Franks.

In the Border counties, medieval peles were retained, as much for the status they conferred as for security; the halls alongside them were given a new and fashionable look, especially in the late seventeenth century. Even in the rest of England, the planning of new manor houses was dominated, for at least a century from 1550, by the medieval tradition

with appropriate modification. They had a hal[illegible]
cross-wings. The Border pele was the equivale[illegible]
plan may be represented as m, ⊓ or H (for wl[illegible]
and H are convenient), according to whether tl[illegible]
rear as well as the front and whether the hall l[illegible]
metrically. The universal modification of the me[illegible] was the provision of two full storeys with usable roof-space, best described as making two and a half storeys. They always had one framed staircase, and sometimes a second of simpler form for servants. Beyond this point, variations begin. Builders in brick and stone were more ready than carpenters to produce a strictly symmetrical elevation; houses with a porch at one end of the hall range can be found in any materials but are more common in timber-framed houses in the West Midlands. This is one of several respects in which houses furthest from London are somewhat more conservative in planning. The idea that Elizabethan houses with an E plan symbolized the queen is a modern invention. Elizabethans enjoyed allegorical and symbolical fancies of Christian or classical meaning: witness the popular overmantels in stone and plaster crowded with ornament. A Dorset house, Chantmarle in Cattistock parish, was rebuilt in 1612 with an E plan; the doorway is inscribed Emmanuel 1612, which for the owner meant 'God be with us for ever'. John Thorpe's drawings include a house forming on plan his own initials, but no indication that his fancies turned to E for Elizabeth.[18]

The readiest solution to the problem of locating the staircase in such a house was to place it in a block attached to the house, as it was in houses in the lodge tradition. This was adopted for Chastleton (Oxfordshire). Barrington Court (Somerset, 1555–69) [146] with an open U plan and a nearly symmetrical elevation, has a block in each re-entrant angle, one of them for a well-type staircase, and this was not an unusual arrangement in a large manor house; at Barrington the balancing block formed an oriel to the hall.[19] In smaller houses the stair block, if not contained within the plan, was usually attached to the rear of the house. The other new element to be planned was the kitchen. It was not thought unsuitable at Barrington to have it at the front of one wing, and it is in the same position at Great Lyth, Condover (Shropshire), built c. 1675. The U plan represented at Condover seems to have lasted longest in the west and the north. Samuel Buck, touring Yorkshire in 1719–23 to draw antiquities and mansions, made tiny sketches of small Yorkshire halls; among them the Condover type was the commonest.[20] It must have been thought to mark a distinct status; substantial houses built in the West Riding in the seventeenth century, many of which are called halls but were rarely manor houses, were much more freely designed. The hall with two cross-wings is almost unknown in Wales; one example is Old Gwernyfed, Felindre (Brecon), built in 1600–13 by an MP for Brecon.[21]

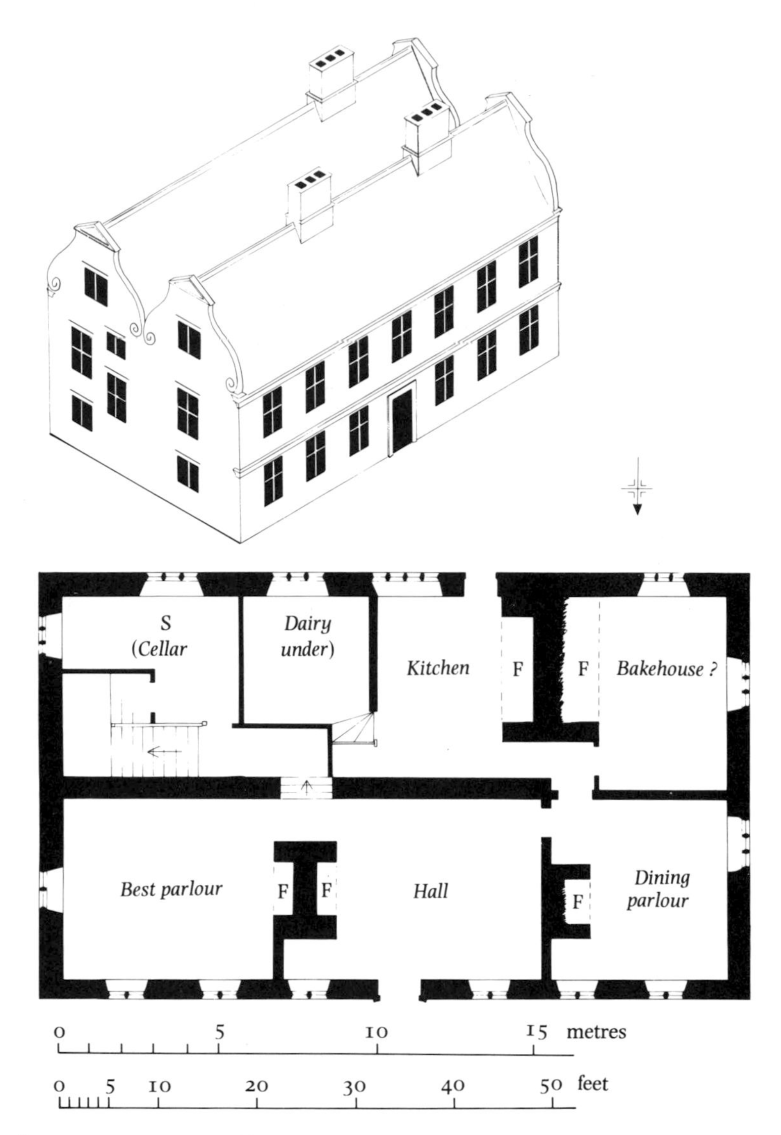

147. THE MANOR HOUSE, ALLINGTON, LINCOLNSHIRE, a double-pile house of c. 1650. The isometric drawing shows the so-called Holborn gables. *Agr. Hist.*

At the same time, smaller manor houses were being built either with a parlour cross-wing only or as a rectangular block with three units. Shutford Manor (Oxfordshire) is a good example of the latter. Its well staircase in a rear block goes up to garret level.[22] When new, the house had no kitchen; Sir Richard Fiennes who built it c. 1600 must have been content with a detached kitchen which was later replaced by a new kitchen block with servants' chambers in it, attached to the service end of the house. Shutford is a reminder that new houses of one build, whatever their design, are far more rare than what may be called multi-period houses, rebuilt or enlarged at more than one time. They are naturally more numerous in south-eastern counties, with a larger heritage of well-built medieval houses and more accessible to men with fortunes made in London.

148. The gabled design of UPTON WOLD FARM, GLOUCESTERSHIRE, c. 1660. The very compact plan was convenient because an older house (shown in outline) was retained for a kitchen and other services. *Agr. Hist.*

The double pile

The sub-medieval tradition, represented by the manor house with gabled ranges one room deep, began to give way in the seventeenth century to an even more compact plan two rooms deep.[23] Sir Roger Pratt's arguments about its compactness ('much room in a little compass') and economy of materials ('a great spare of walling and of other materials for the roof') commended themselves to the lesser gentry and wealthy parsons, who quickly adopted the design on a suitably reduced scale. Coleshill and its numerous followers had three rooms in each range, separated by an axial passage, mainly for servants and containing a back staircase for their use. The front of Coleshill was nine bays long; the norm in the manor house was five bays without an axial passage and usually having four rooms on a floor [148]. A dog-leg staircase fitted comfortably into that arrangement, either at the back of the house and facing the front door, or, less often, at one side of the house.[24]

The earliest examples were built c. 1630, and not in the south-east but in midland counties ranging from Cambridge to Hereford and as far north as Yorkshire, because the fashion absorbed two distinct medieval traditions which had been strongest there; the urban double-pile in such towns as Coventry and the West Yorkshire tradition of the single-aisled hall. These traditions influenced both the plan of the house and the

149

150

151

149. RAM HALL, BERKSWELL, WARWICKSHIRE, C. 1620.

150. HATHAWAYS, SOUTH LITTLETON, WORCESTERSHIRE, 1721.

151. THE OLD HOUSE, KIBWORTH HARCOURT, LEICESTERSHIRE, 1678, with additions.

design of the roof. The Yorkshire houses were likely to have the two front rooms, hall and parlour, wider than the rear, as they are at Low Hall, Dacre (1635), and at Huthwaite Hall, Thurgoland (c. 1748) [139], and to have a single-span roof over the whole. Cheshire halls are the same. In the Midlands, parallel ridges of the sort used in the Middle Ages were the simplest and most popular form [149], especially with brick building. At the same time, some country builders fell in with the fashion for gables on all elevations when working with brick, stone or timber. The height of fashion, however, was to have a roof hipped all round. It might be finished with a platform, balustraded round, and very occasionally a cupola. Some cupolas have gone, as at Bell Hall, Naburn (East Yorkshire) [137], but the manor house at South Littleton (Worcestershire), now known as Hathaways and dated 1721,[25] still has a tiny square belvedere on the roof [150], with a compass painted on its ceiling pivoted to a weather vane; there is just room for one person to sit and observe the view or the weather. The alternative to a leaded flat for a hipped roof was a hidden or central valley, cheaper to build but awkward to maintain; it needed a secret gutter to get rid of rainwater.[26] South-eastern carpenters evolved the M roof in which parallel ridges are separated by a valley at a level higher than the eaves; this facilitated access between

152. Plaster ceiling, c. 1600, in MANOR FARM, PAPWORTH ST AGNES, CAMBRIDGESHIRE. *NMR.*

153. Narrow windows flanking the doorway to light a narrow hall, FAIRSEAT MANOR, STANSTED, KENT, c. 1725.

152

153

the two ranges of garrets. The fashion for a double pile did not spread to the four northern counties and they are rare in East Anglia and in Devon and Cornwall. Nearly all these houses were put up by anonymous country builders; one exception was Moat House, Sutton Coldfield (Warwickshire), built for himself by Sir William Wilson of Leicester (1641–1710) who was associated with Wren.

The plan was so compact and homogeneous that it offered little scope for originality of design. The fireplaces could be located on side walls, on the spine wall or in corners of rooms (as at Hathaways); a builder occasionally tried his hand at pairs of arched chimney stacks (Hathaways) or even at gathering all the flues into one central stack. For wealthier clients the services could be in a basement, as in a villa such as Eagle House, Mitcham (Surrey) [135], or even in tiny pavilions as at Nether Lypiatt Manor (Gloucestershire, c. 1700–5); both were built for townsmen. An older house was occasionally retained to provide service rooms, as at Hathaways and at Upton Wold Farm (Gloucestershire c. 1675). Sometimes, as at Wharton Court (Herefordshire, 1659), and at Kibworth Harcourt (Leicestershire, 1678) [151], an owner soon found that a mere four-unit plan was insufficient for his style of living and added a service range to the square house.

The decline of the hall

The double-pile is part of the emergence of a design of house with a front of five bays which Pevsner called 'a standard English product for the prosperous middle classes'.[27] Behind such essentially flush fronts lay either a double-pile, an L or T plan, or one with two rear wings. Houses in Kent illustrate the change in planning behind this widespread architectural development. Fairseat Manor, Stansted (Kent), built for a John

Cox who died in 1736, has a flush front divided into three by giant pilasters. There are evidently three rooms in the front range; the windows flanking the doorway are narrower than the rest, marking the reduced width of the hall [153]. Later in the century as halls became no more than passages and there was no space for such windows, doorways were given an arched head to make space for a fanlight. At Quintain House, Offham (Kent), there are only two rooms behind the five-bay front; a timber arcade, which may be thought of as an echo of the medieval screens-passage, divides the hall from the entrance. Thorpe Hall, Peterborough, a much grander house built in 1653–6 for a judge by a London bricklayer, has the same feature. At Hendon Hall, Biddenden (Kent), the front range was built c. 1700 with three rooms of equal size; although the hall is about 4.5 m (15 ft) wide it has no fireplace. To take a midland example, Manor Farm, Wigston Parva (Leicestershire) built perhaps c. 1700 by a pretentious bricklayer, has giant pilasters yet is conservative in plan; it still has projecting wings but the hall is narrower than the rooms in the wings and has no heating.

Notes

1 *Agr. Hist.*, 4, 439.
2 *EFC*, pl. XVa.
3 Stone in *Dimensions* ..., 73–6; for further comments on those social distinctions see Stone (1984), 6–7, etc. (see page 215, note 38).
4 *Agr. Hist.*, 5, 631.
5 H. Colvin and J. Newman (eds.), *Of Building: Roger North's Writings on Architecture* (1981), 100–3.
6 Analysis of the plaster in the course of restoration has suggested that it may have been made from the waste of local alabaster quarries.
7 BE, *Gloucestershire: The Cotswolds*, 397.
8 BE, *Suffolk*, 224.
9 *Agr. Hist.*, 5, 617–18.
10 RCHM, *Westmorland* (1936), 16.
11 *Country Life*, 28 July 1983.
12 P. Smith, *Houses of the Welsh Countryside* (1975), 269.
13 *Agr. Hist.*, 4, 701, 716–17.
14 E.M. Jope (ed.), *Studies in Building History* (1961), 206–7; J. Summerson, *Architecture in Britain 1530–1830* (1953), 99.
15 The contract is in J. Hodgson, *Hist. of Northumberland* (1895), pt. 2, ii, 259n.
16 L.J. Hall, *The Rural Houses of North Avon and South Gloucestershire* (1983), 39–40, fig. 9.
17 *Agr. Hist.*, 5, 621.
18 RCHM, *Dorset*, 1, 71; Walpole Soc., 40 (1964–6), 23.
19 Barrington Court, formerly thought to have been built c. 1514 (Summerson, 13–14), is now known to be later; VCH, *Somerset*, 4 (1978), 115.
20 *Samuel Buck's Yorkshire Sketchbook* (facsimile ed. 1979), 284–5, 324 etc.
21 S.R. Jones and J.T. Smith, 'The Houses of Breconshire', pt. 2, *Brycheiniog*, 10 (1964), 88–90.
22 R.B. Wood-Jones, ... *Banbury Region* (1963), 72–8.
23 M.W. Barley, 'The Double-Pile House', *Archaeol. J.*, 136 (1979), 253–64.
24 RCHM, *The Town of Stamford* (1977), Li, fig. 7, types 9a and b.
25 BE, *Worcestershire*, 261.
26 M. Craig in *Classic Irish Houses of the Middle Size* (1976), 17, calls the secret gutter 'a fruitful source of woe'.
27 BE, *Worcestershire*, 225.

12 *Parsonage Houses*

The parsonage house is the best documented house in the village and so is a key to domestic standards and building traditions. The glebe terriers which parsons from Elizabeth's times were supposed to compile and keep up to date, as schedules of the property of the church in a parish, are at their most plentiful and explicit from 1660 onwards[1]. Widespread concern over the state of the Church and particularly over the poverty of the clergy led some enlightened bishops to compile their own notes or to carry out especially searching visitations. For some dioceses there are collections of papers, sometimes with plans, recording the process by which parsons obtained a licence (called a faculty) to demolish and rebuild. Terriers are particularly valuable in showing that the clergy were engaged in cultivating their glebe or at least dependent on tithes for part of their income; their houses were farmsteads with barns, stables, cowhouses and service buildings such as brewhouses. In the course of the four centuries they were gradually divorced from the land and most of their residences were rebuilt to the model of the villa.

The warning about problems of identifying parsonage houses (page 138) is worth repeating. The house at Hamworthy (Dorset, now part of Poole) known as the Old Rectory and a notable example of Mannerism in brick, was built in 1640–2 as a manor house. (It has recently been restored.) Conversely, the Manor House at Hale (Lancashire) with its lavish Baroque decoration, was built as the rectory. How such a change might come about is illustrated at Lamport (Northamptonshire) where the squire also owned the advowson – that is, the right to present the parson. John Isham (1525–96), a London mercer, acquired both the manor and the rectory. He bought another house for the rector and the former rectory became Lamport Hall which he proceeded to rebuild. A later Isham provided for a younger son by leaving money in his will to build a new rectory as well as presenting him to the living. The new rectory was built in 1727–30 to a design by Francis Smith of Warwick.[2]

The personal condition of the clergy changed radically when the Elizabethan settlement gave them licence to marry, but it appears that this

154. The rector of WILFORD, NOTTINGHAMSHIRE, could afford to build c. 1720 a double-pile house with a forecourt, and a range with a barn, coach-house, and stable. It is approached through a miniature park. The rector also built a summerhouse north of the church and on the bank of the Trent with a view of Nottingham. *After F. A. Broadhead.*

had no discernible effect on parsonage houses. Those of the wealthier clergy were already large enough. The poor parson no doubt took a wife without necessarily working out the consequences beforehand, but could expect her to manage the dairy and his sons to help in working the glebe, unless he chose to let it to a yeoman neighbour. Parsonage houses before c. 1700 invite comparison with houses of men of all sorts, from lesser gentry at one extreme to poorer husbandmen, if not labourers, at the other. They were invariably built in the local idiom, and it is significant that those parsons who described their houses as having walls of mud, clay, earth, loam or daub lived in those eastern counties where no medieval timber-framed houses have survived. The scarcity of timber is also revealed by the fact that many houses had upper floors also of earth – that is, puddled clay laid on reeds or straw spread across joists – or else of gypsum or lime plaster.[3] In East Anglia and Essex the parochial clergy were slow to adopt brick for building.

To judge from terriers, parsonage houses tend as a class to reflect a higher standard of living than could be maintained on the income of a single living. One reason must be that pluralism was so widespread. A pluralist could afford to build a house as good as a gentleman's or a yeoman's in one of his parishes, leaving another house for a curate, or even letting it to a farm labourer. One thing alone distinguished the parson from most of the yeomen and husbandmen of his parish: the possession of books and sometimes a study – a small room, rarely heated and usually upstairs. In a house with a through passage, the room over it was often so used; if there was a storeyed porch, it could provide a chamber for the purpose.

Piecemeal improvements

Terriers show that for more than a century after 1550, the country parson was more inclined to carry out piecemeal improvements than wholesale rebuilding since after all the house was his only while he held the living. The documents also prove, as buildings themselves rarely do, that the open hall might linger on. The Somerset parsonage houses at Combe Florey, Crowcombe and Wedmore had open halls in the time of James I and Charles I, and the rector of Churchstanton (Devon) wrote in 1680 that he had 'a great hall floored with earth, no chamber over it'. The rectory at Quainton (Buckinghamshire) was renamed Brudenell House in 1962 when it was sold by the Church Commissioners and called after an incumbent of Henry VIII's time by the historian K. B. McFarlane who purchased it. It had been given a new staircase and roof by Dr Richard Brett (1595–1637), one of the translators of the Authorised Version of the Bible, who has a monument in the church. In Georgian times what remained of the timber-framed walls was cased in brick and the house assumed a symmetrical appearance with bay windows and a hipped roof.[4] Notes made in 1672 by a rector of Clayworth (Nottinghamshire) illustrate the vicissitudes of a house belonging to a rich living. It had earlier been held by Robert Mapletoft, dean of Lincoln (as dean he held the advowson and so presented himself!) and master of Pembroke College; he did some repairs such as facing the wings with brick and he put a gypsum plaster floor in the hall, but since he did not reside he converted the Great Chamber into a granary for storing his tithe corn, with posts supporting it in the room below. His successor, William Sampson, built brick chimney-shafts for the hall and kitchen, replacing hoods of wood and plaster; he paved the hall with stone, renewed various doors and windows and ceilinged the chamber over the

155. THE OLD RECTORY, STANTON HARCOURT, OXFORDSHIRE, built in 1675. Note the dovecote and a farm building.

156. THE RECTORY, SIMONBURN, NORTHUMBERLAND, 1725.

hall to make it a more comfortable lodging chamber. The house has gone and so these reports cannot be related to a standing building. William Sampson's dovecote has also been demolished.[5]

Any series of terriers, such as that for Bedfordshire in 1706, not only reveals the diversity in size, plan and materials of parsonage houses, but it also catches the clergy in process of improving the houses they could not or would not rebuild completely. The change from daub to brick for covering framed walls and from earth to paving with brick or stone for floors, or even to boarding, is particularly evident. The vicarage at Calceby (Lincolnshire) was said in 1606 to be built of wood and thatched, with three bays chambered over and containing hall, parlour and kitchen. Before the then incumbent died in 1620 he had made a second

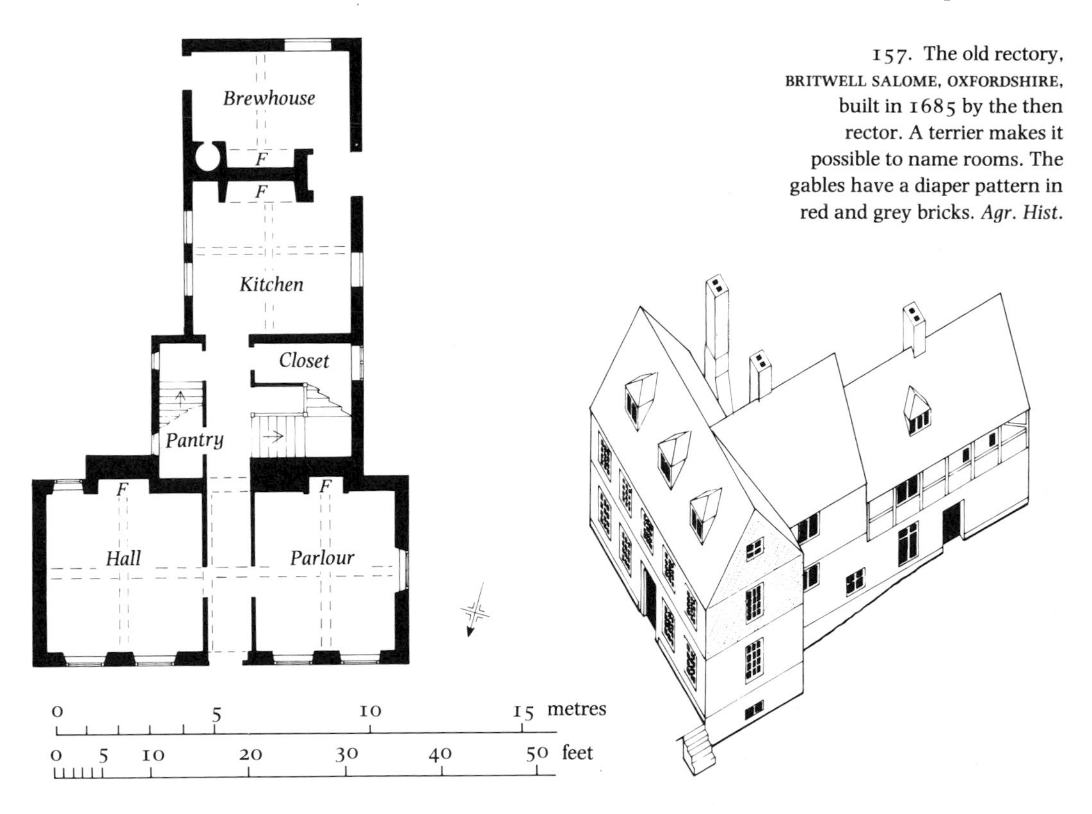

157. The old rectory, BRITWELL SALOME, OXFORDSHIRE, built in 1685 by the then rector. A terrier makes it possible to name rooms. The gables have a diaper pattern in red and grey bricks. *Agr. Hist.*

parlour, possibly to use as a study, for he had books worth £4. Although he was comfortably off, he did not use the chambers as bedrooms; no doubt he slept in a parlour like anyone else of his position. That room was usually the first to be given a boarded floor, and in the diocese of Exeter the terriers of 1679 give the earliest indications of 'planched' floors. Piecemeal improvements were not always economical. The rector of Great Hormead (Hertfordshire), having spent £103 6s 8d in that way over four years, noted in his parish register that 'a better house might have been built for the money from the ground with the help of the old materials if the money had been laid out together and the workmen well looked after'. Whether he was right or not, the Old Rectory still stands.

The parsonage house at Sherington near Olney (Buckinghamshire), said in 1625 to have been 'newly built by the incumbent now living' still stands, and an inscribed stone shows that John Martin put it up in 1607, in stone and no doubt replacing a timber house. His ideas were identical with those of the lesser gentry or richer yeomen of his time: an H plan with five bays, one for the hall and two for each wing. Of the ground-floor rooms named in his terrier, the boulting house (i.e. bakehouse) was later turned into a study and the buttery into a dining room. Sherington was a rectory; in nearly every county examples can be found of houses entirely built or rebuilt in the century after 1660 and with very few exceptions they were rectories, not vicarages. The rectory at Sutton Coldfield (Warwickshire, demolished 1938) was built as a double pile in 1701, at a cost of £239 11s 6d, the rector finding the timber.[6] Rectories were among the wealthiest livings and naturally in the hands of men the most likely to have private means. Credit for a new house must occasionally go elsewhere than to the incumbent; the parsonage of Stanton Harcourt (Oxfordshire) was leased by All Souls to Robert Huntingdon, a layman who in 1675 built a house in the latest fashion: a double pile of seven by five bays with a hipped roof [155]. Some parsons like the vicar of Blockley (Gloucestershire) kept a boarding school.

There is no doubt about the fashionable quality that wealthy parsons aspired to. Both terriers and faculties may refer to a forecourt; at Church Eaton (Staffordshire) the rector in 1702 obtained a faculty to rebuild the parsonage house with a symmetrical front and a walled forecourt; it was finished in 1712. Examination of a surviving house often shows that, as with manor houses, a fashionable front range was applied to some part at least of an older house. At Puddletown (Dorset) a fashionable wing of five bays but containing only two rooms was added to an older house to make an L plan with a stair-turret in the angle.[7] A terrier for Storrington (Sussex) for 1663 states that the house had been 'all new built of stone and stone tiled with an old kitchen serving as a brewhouse and malthouse now rectified and tiled'. At Simonburn (Northumberland), an enormous parish north of Hadrian's wall and a rich living, a rector of 1725 rebuilt in the form of a three-storey block five bays wide [156]; over a back door a dated lintel indicates some work in 1666, which in turn replaced a medieval tower house. The style of the 1725 front suggests a builder familiar with Vanbrugh's work; he may have worked at Seaton Delaval which Vanbrugh started in 1718.[8]

The former rectory at Britwell Salome (Oxfordshire) [157] provides a chance to relate an informative terrier to a house virtually unaltered. It was built in 1685 'by James Stopes our present Rector in the form of an L'; the terrier then proceeds to name all the rooms as shown on the plan. It does not refer to materials, and it is somewhat surprising to find that the front range is of brick with five bays but the rear wing of the L, containing the kitchen and other service rooms, is timber-framed and appears to be contemporary. The house is exceptional in another respect; Mr Stopes did not provide himself with a ground-floor study.[9]

The poverty of some livings and the consequent absenteeism and pluralism must have led to the disappearance of older houses and changes in the parson's place of residence. In 1649 Collingbourne Kingston (Wiltshire) had 'a very fair Mansion house in good repair'; in 1812 the vicarage (presumably the same house) was 'a ruin and tumbling down', rented to two pauper families whose 'lives are in danger every day'. When a new vicar of Weaverthorpe (East Yorkshire) was inducted in 1764, presumably without having inspected the house beforehand, he was very indignant to find it quite uninhabitable for him and his family; an old inhabitant told him that no vicar had lived in it for more than four score years past, and a tenant had kept his cow in the parlour in winter and fattened his pig in the pantry.[10] What the vicar did about his problem we do not know. Some Lincolnshire parsons faced with this problem lived in a nearby market town and rode out to their parishes to take services. What the Church did about poor livings was to initiate in 1716, under the name of Queen Anne's Bounty, a scheme for augmenting the income of poor livings, but inequalities between a good rectory and an average vicarage persisted until after 1945 and were then disposed of by uniting poorer benefices. In those counties such as Lincolnshire and East Yorkshire where the vernacular building was likely to be of mud or mud and stud, and where the legacy of the medieval economy was a large proportion of poor livings, brick parsonage houses were not built until the eighteenth and nineteenth centuries. Terriers for other counties such as Cornwall and Warwickshire suggest the same timetable there.

Yorkshire and Lancashire terriers for the eighteenth century are the most informative about curates' houses. Two in East Yorkshire, at Beswick and Kilnwick, had only two rooms in 1777 and were mud walled; one at Glaisdale in the North Riding had three rooms, earth-floored; no labourer lived in a simpler way. In the large West Riding and Lancashire parishes, the chapelries often had adequate endowments, or attracted them as the townships developed; John Scott, curate of Horbury in Wakefield parish, had in 1731 laid out for building his residence 'above 100 guineas of his own money' besides a legacy of £50 from his uncle, a Leeds parson, who also endowed the chapelry with £200. At South Owram in Halifax there was in 1764 an almost new 'messuage or farmhouse' with a barn, stable and cowhouse under one roof: a reminder that even a curate might have his stake in the farming economy.

It would be a pity to leave the country parson without a reminder that, whether or not he had a substantial amount of glebe land and farmed it himself, he was a countryman in the sense that he often kept cows, pigs, hens and pigeons; had a barn to hold whatever tithes he was entitled to and brewed his own beer. The terriers might also be used to reveal at length the great regional variations in types of house and materials and particularly the pace of improvement. The Yorkshire terriers even disclose which rooms in an eighteenth-century house had wainscotting, wallpaper or merely plastered walls, and which had ceilings 'underdrawn' or plastered. Parsons often included a reference to sanitary provision, usually as the necessary house, sometimes the jakes; that is, the earth closet outside. At Langar (Nottinghamshire) the rectory built in 1721 had two necessary houses, one for family and one for servants. Samuel Butler, born here in 1835, must have known them well.

Notes

1 *EFC*, 273–6; *Agr. Hist.*, 5, 632–8.
2 Hamworthy: RCHM, *Dorset*, 2, ii, pl. 128; Hale: BE, *South Lancashire*, 116; Lamport: M.E. Finch, *Five Northamptonshire Families* (Northants. Record Soc. 19, 1956), 20–1; BE, *Northamptonshire*, 286.
3 *EFC*, 82, 257.
4 I am indebted to Dr C. Richmond for a copy of McFarlane's pamphlet (n.d.) on the house.
5 H. Gill and E.L. Guilford (eds.), *The Rector's Book of Clayworth* (1910).
6 W.K.R. Bedford, *History of the Rilands of Sutton Coldfield* (1889), 19. Mapperton Rectory was rebuilt in 1703 at a cost of £246; R. Machin, *Building Accounts of Mapperton Rectory 1699–1703* (Dorset Record Soc. 1983).
7 RCHM, *Dorset*, 3, ii (1970), 227, pl. 191.
8 BE, *Northumberland*, 286, 292.
9 *Agr. Hist.*, 5, 635.
10 *The Local Historian*, 8 (1968), no. 2, 48.

13 *Farmhouses and Cottages*

The population of England and Wales nearly doubled between 1500 and 1700 – from an estimated 2.5 to 5.8 millions – and most of that growth took place after 1550 in spite of recurrent outbreaks of plague and a serious recession in the 1620s which caused terrible hardship and no doubt increased mortality. Population nearly doubled again between 1700 and the first census in 1801. Towns absorbed an increasing proportion of that growth but even in 1800 only accounted for a quarter of the total. The number of rural houses worthy of study grows in like manner; fortunately they are increasingly susceptible to classification, by plan and scale of accommodation. The depression of the 1870s finally checked new agricultural building. For a century before that, economic and cultural changes had diverted initiative to other industries and to towns, so that the student finds little new after about 1800 in the plans of rural houses; only improvements and better provision for labourers.

Within that enormous growth in the rural population, the economic basis of housing was transformed by the decline in the number of small landowners. Farming units and farmhouses became larger and the labourer lost his modest share in the land. 'Enclosure and engrossing were two of the most controversial topics in Tudor England.'[1] Enclosing meant extinguishing common rights over land and engrossing meant bringing two or more farms into one and allowing the unwanted farmhouse to decay or letting it as a cottage. In the two centuries after c. 1630, enclosure, first by agreements enrolled in the court of chancery and later by private act of Parliament, extinguished the remains of the midland open-field system. However much large landowners initiated the process and benefited from it, the advantages to yeomen were that in the century after 1550 the prices of agricultural products increased so much that 'no yeomen with his wits about him could fail to accumulate money savings on a scale hitherto unknown'. Those were Hoskins' words in proposing that there was a great rebuilding, especially in the Midlands, in 1570–1640;[2] it is generally agreed that yeomen fared better at that time than any other class. Labourers fared worst of all; the purchasing power of their wages fell in 1500–1650 by more than 50 per cent, and though many were not solely dependent on wages their standard of living certainly declined.

The decline in the number of small landowners was probably most rapid in 1660–1740, but that generalization conceals great variations between parishes, let alone between regions.[3] They derived from the basic contrasts between arable and pastoral farming, from variations in soil and opportunities for marketing; they were influenced even more by conditions of tenure. In one Cambridgeshire village, Chippenham, most of the small holdings disappeared in 1598–1636; the last five copyholds were bought out in 1696 by the principal landowner, Lord Orford. Chippenham now appears unusually attractive because Orford built a school for the village in 1714 (now converted as a residence) and John Thorp who acquired the mansion (Chippenham Park) in 1791 put up a row of labourers' cottages which give the village its planned character. By contrast, the parish of Yetminster in West Dorset still has more substantial farmhouses, built in 1650–1730, than adjacent villages, because the custom of the manor gave security. It was worth while for copyhold tenants to build well, and so they did.[4] In the Lake District customary tenants obtained in Elizabeth's time the right to bequeath their land by will and paid only a small money rent. The stone areas of Cumberland have a remarkable number of houses built in 1660–1715 to a stereotyped design. The explanation for the time-lag may be that after 1660 prices of livestock and dairy produce remained buoyant when other prices fell.

Inheritance customs

One factor which at every level has led to the break-up of properties has been the need to provide for the family. For the gentry it rarely led to altering a house for multiple occupation, though there are instances where a wing more or less detached seems to suggest it.[5] A large landowner could easily arrange for a widow to have a manor house, or even to build a dower house for her. Forton Hall (Staffordshire, 1669) belonged to the Aqualate estate and may have been used as a dower house though it was and is also a working farm; the same is true of the manor house at Mapleton (Derbyshire, c. 1720), part of the Okeover estate.

The peasant could only provide for his children and other close relatives by dividing his property, and it is clear that partible inheritance was widely observed in post-medieval England.[6] If a small owner divided his holding into fractions, some of them no doubt came into the hands of an engrosser but we are concerned with the effect of division on houses; instances of two houses round one farmyard. This phenomenon was first noticed in Wales, where partible inheritance, though abolished by statute in 1541, was maintained by joint tenancies. English examples are

158. Stone houses at CRANFORD ST JOHN, NORTHAMPTONSHIRE, attached at one corner and presumably examples of the unit system. Note that one has a dovecote in the gable.

uncommon but striking. Arnford Farmhouse, Hellifield (West Yorkshire), consists of a pair of semi-detached houses with mirror-image plans; it was built c. 1690–1700 at a time when semi-detached design was still very novel. It must represent a joint tenancy.[7] At Hardcastle Garth in Birstwith (West Yorkshire) are two substantial houses, one dated 1666 and the other 1703, attached at one corner; they communicate now and probably always did so. These examples of the unit system [158], as it has been called, are curiosities among the vast number of houses of normal design which must have been divided among relatives. Wormhill Old Hall Farm (Derbyshire), with a hall and cross-wing of different dates in the seventeenth century, was in 1982 divided between parents and a married son (in the cross-wing) and had been so divided between earlier generations. At Chetnole (Dorset) it was the custom of the manor in the seventeenth century for a customary tenant to transfer a holding, usually but not always to a son, and for both parties to share the house in a manner recorded in court rolls.[8] The incoming tenant usually got the inferior end.

The pace and cost of new building

Measured by the number of houses with an inscribed date, the amount of new building or rebuilding increased steadily from c. 1550 to a peak in c. 1700. This represents a continuation of a process which had started c. 1450 in the south-east and which went on until the last open fields were enclosed in the nineteenth century. A date on a Kentish yeoman's house is likely to mark an improvement such as inserting a chamber over a medieval open hall; in Yorkshire it is likely to represent a completely new house. Taking Yorkshire as a whole, building activity reached peaks in 1630–1720 and again in 1740–70. It was at its most intense in 1660–1700, but county figures conceal local variations: a peak in the Halifax area in the 1630s, in the Settle district in 1660–1700 and in the East Riding after 1770.[9]

Building accounts and contracts are exceedingly rare because small landowners did not keep such records. The few costs known, usually

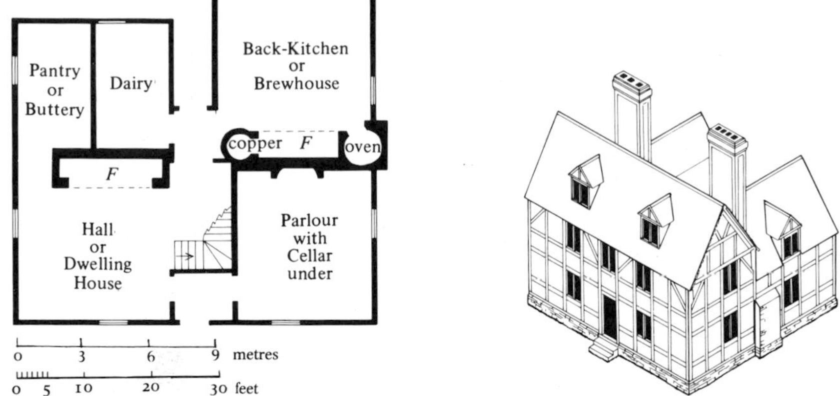

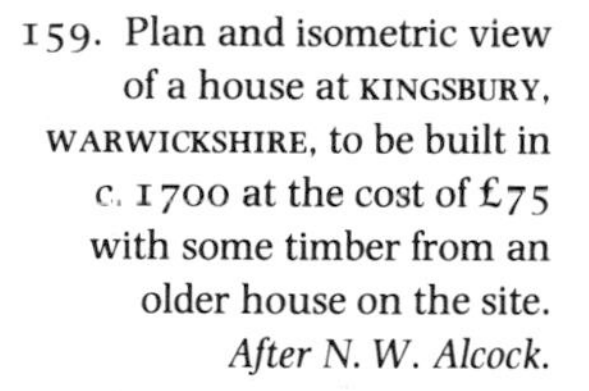

159. Plan and isometric view of a house at KINGSBURY, WARWICKSHIRE, to be built in c. 1700 at the cost of £75 with some timber from an older house on the site. *After N. W. Alcock.*

from records of improving landlords, range from less than fifty pounds to a few hundred for a new house. A husbandman of Springfield (Essex) petitioning the county justices in 1654 for help in replacing a house burnt down, claimed that rebuilding, no doubt in timber, would cost nearly £40.[10] A proposal for a framed house to be built at Kingsbury (Warwickshire) [159] for the Aston estate has both plans of each floor and a drawn elevation of the framing, so that it can be accurately reconstructed. It was expected to cost no more than £75, partly because the capenter thought that 'the timber in ye old [house] will frame four bays for a new house'.[11] The governors of St Bartholomew's Hospital, London, managed their estates very competently; their records of visitations and surveys by such professional men as Ralph Treswell include drawings of properties and in one case a plan and contract for a new house at Bottisham (Cambridgeshire) which with its farm buildings was to cost £417. Parsonage Farm, Bottisham, still stands with only minor additions and alterations;[12] so does New Deanham Hall (Northumberland) [143] for which there is a contract of 1669 and an estimated cost of £260. Not all farmhouses belonging to large estates were rebuilt by them, though they might provide materials, especially bricks from an estate kiln. The governors of St Bartholomew's Hospital were concerned to realize in the 1750s that their tenants did not insure buildings against fire. They recommended that, since tenants would not take necessary steps, the Hospital should insure and charge tenants with the premiums. The registers of the Sun Fire Office, beginning in 1729, are an almost untapped source of information about farmhouses as well as industrial buildings.[13]

The first architect's pattern book specially for farmhouses was Daniel Garret's *Designs and Estimates of Farmhouses etc for the County of York, Northumberland, Cumberland, Westmoreland and Bishoprick of Durham*, published in 1747. In it he put together the experiences of a northern practice; one of his clients was Sir William Blackett of Wallington, and drawings of some of Garrett's model farms for that estate are still in the house. It is not surprising that northern landowners should have been among the first to undertake such improvements though a few model farms of

160. Headroom contrived in roof-space by means of an extended collar (above windows) in PENDICK'S FARM, STIDCOT, TYTHERINGTON, GLOUCESTERSHIRE. *Linda J. Hall.*

161. Corn bin in garret of THE MEADS, CHILWELL, NOTTINGHAMSHIRE.

similar date are to be found elsewhere – for example, on the Holkham estate in north Norfolk, another region with a poor tradition in building.[14] We may contrast the enterprise of such men as Blackett with the inactivity of Sir Marmaduke Constable. As a Catholic he chose to live abroad in 1730–43, and to manage his estates in Lincolnshire and East Yorkshire by corresponding with his agent, a Benedictine monk, who apart from a servant or two was the solitary resident in Everingham Hall (East Yorkshire).[15] Piecemeal repairs were done, with bricks from the estate kiln, but the monk's letters show the deplorable condition of houses before comprehensive rebuilding began. A house at West Rasen (Lincolnshire) was propped up back and front; 'a wonder that it did not push down'. The tenant was an old man who had allowed some of his barn walls of mud 'to wash down to the ground'.

Farmhouse designs

Since the building of houses of this social level is very rarely documented, dating is a matter of using inscribed evidence (date panels, dates carved on masonry or woodwork, or incorporated in plaster decoration) to construct a chronology based on forms of plan and on mouldings or other decoration. It is usually impossible by that means to date a house to within less than fifty years. The archaeologist is constantly aware of the danger of applying to one region a chronology evolved for another; he also tends, rightly or wrongly, to assume a time-lag between the use of a moulding in a mansion and in a more humble house.

We are concerned with development from the simplest medieval type of plan with two or more rooms in line. This was improved so that all the space defined by walls and roof could be used for a more productive agricultural unit with a larger output and more diverse processes; changes in family habits went along with functional changes, whether as cause or effect. All the improvements, except perhaps for the most flexible features such as the position of entrance doorways, originated in houses of superior classes.

The most significant change was first the use of roof space and then the very gradual adoption of storeyed construction. Rooms within the roof space were called garrets (not attics) or lofts; in East Anglia farmers sometimes spoke of the 'vance roof' or else of the 'soler' (solar). Estate surveys show how slowly houses of one or one and a half storeys gave way to two storeys, even in some southern counties and still more in the north. In the south-east the carpenter discarded the crown-post roof in favour of side-purlins both in new houses and when a medieval open hall was chambered over. Another carpenter's device of clearing roof space is illustrated by Pendick's Farm, Stidcot, Tytherington (Gloucestershire) [160]. The extended collar, as it has been called, is common in the Bristol region but nowhere else, and goes with the multi-gabled design so popular there. In cruck territory, upper crucks planted on the cross-beams of a ground-floor room also provided clear roof space in a very small house.[16] In larger houses in the north, the development of roofs is not influenced by the desire to use the space within them because the pitch of the roofs, especially with stone slates, was too low.

162. Stair-turret of a house dated 1737 at WINSTER, DERBYSHIRE.

Garrets were used for storage; occasionally a fireplace shows that they might be used as sleeping space. There is no evidence of any industrial use, though there was light enough in those Gloucestershire houses of 1670–1700 which had a tiny second opening near the top of the gable. Farmers with large flocks of sheep used garrets to store wool. Gaythorn Hall (Westmorland), built c. 1600 as a hunting lodge, had a wool hoist inserted in a garret in 1702; there is another such hoist, as well as a cheese rack, at Preston (Gloucestershire), a timber-framed house of c. 1600 with three storeys and a row of six gables.[17] Turk's House, Smarden (Kent), is a Wealden house remodelled in the seventeenth century with an outside hoist. Garrets were most commonly used in pastoral counties to store and ripen cheeses; arable farmers stored seed corn there. There are corn bins in garrets at Ivy House, Long Whatton (Leicestershire, c. 1700), and at the Meads, Chilwell (Nottinghamshire, c. 1725) [161], in each case alongside a chimney flue. Both would have held up to ten sacks. The house belonging to Polhill Mill (Harrietsham, Kent) has an enormous bin with boarded sides that could have been made at any time after the house was built in the sixteenth century.[18]

Staircases, chimneys, chambers

A staircase to first-floor rooms and garrets could be contrived within a linear plan but only if a householder was content with a narrow winding stair alongside a chimney stack, as in a lobby-entrance plan. Away from the south-east a stair-turret at the back of the house was a common alternative at any date from c. 1600 to c. 1720 [162]. If the stairs had to reach garrets, they were made to turn round a substantial newel post, or else built on an ampler scale round a well, or in dog-leg design. As in the mansion, the quality of the staircase is an accurate measure of the pretensions of a farmer; it is also a good guide to the date of a house or of alterations to it.[19]

Chimney-stacks rising from the ridge of a house, but very rarely (if they are original) anywhere else, are a characteristic of this country easily taken for granted. They have often been rebuilt but even so it is easy to observe how many flues they contain. Stacks were tall, partly for show but partly to minimize the risk of thatched roofs catching fire. Chimneys were often separated or planted diagonally; in East Anglia they were sometimes joined with a zig-zag outline as if to exaggerate the number of flues. The hearth tax of the 1660s would not have been imposed if fireplaces had not been a matter of pride as well as easy for officials to assess. The returns have not been studied systematically or in a uniform manner as evidence for housing, but a few regional studies show that surviving houses are not a random sample of those then standing; they represent the largest and the best built. Most small and middling farmers had only one hearth, in the hall; only houses with more than two hearths are likely to have had one or more of them in a chamber. In a group of East Sussex parishes, they were homes of clothiers, tanners, maltsters, butchers and some yeomen;[20] it was men of that sort everywhere who could afford the best building, though to a diminishing extent further from London. In the Leicestershire parish of Wigston Magna only about one house in ten had two hearths or more, and the proportion was even lower in the East Riding.[21] If there was one hearth upstairs, it was most likely to be in the chamber over the parlour.

Decorative plasterwork upstairs is another indication of the status of a chamber. The distribution of such decoration, and its location in houses, have not yet been systematically studied, but it certainly percolated down from the aristocracy to the lesser gentry and to yeomen farmers. In south-eastern counties such as Hertfordshire it was most common in town houses but survives in the chambers of a few farmhouses as well as in ground-floor rooms, done by plasterers also responsible for pargeted outside walls.[22] Plasterers flourished in Devon, and at Westacott, in North Tawton, a yeoman's house built of cob and stone c. 1600, had a wing

163. Perspective views of the three floors of BROME FARMHOUSE, ISLE ABBOTS, SOMERSET, 1627, showing that the chamber and garret over the kitchen were cut off from other upstairs rooms and reached by their own staircase. *C. Carson.*

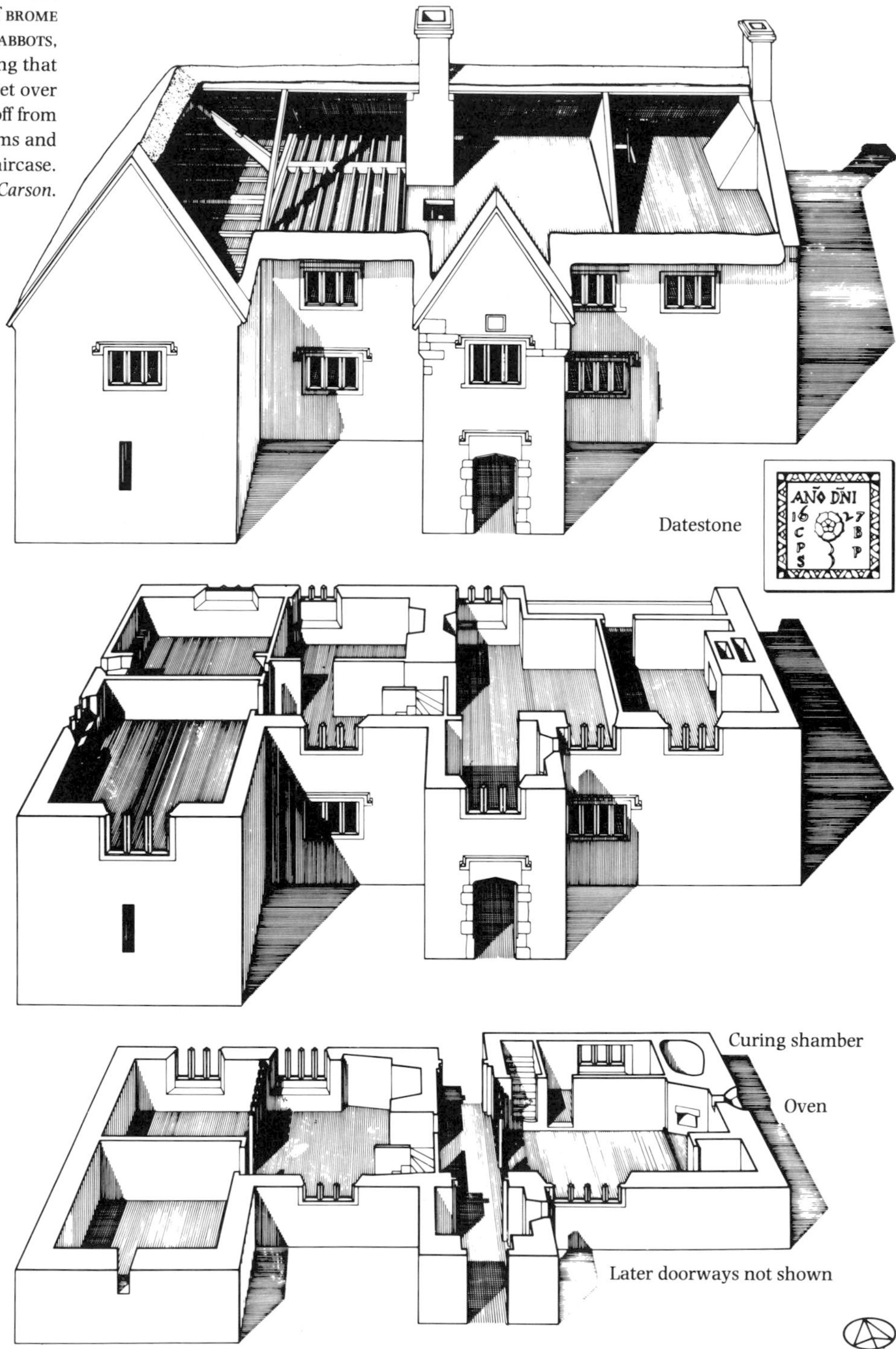

added soon after with an elaborate plaster ceiling – both in the parlour and the chamber over it.[23] Tolson Hall in Westmorland, built by a retired tobacco merchant who presumably called himself a gentleman (page 217), has plaster overmantels in two chambers dated 1638 and 1639; two farmhouses in the same parish have similar work dated 1664 and 1687.[24]

As farms grew in size they came to depend more on labourers and particularly on farm servants, unmarried and hired annually, living in the house. Servants' chambers, reached by their own back stairs or a ladder from the kitchen, were sometimes cut off upstairs from the other rooms, as they were at Brome Farmhouse, Isle Abbots (Somerset, 1627) [163], and at Manor Farm, Clipsham (Rutland, 1639). This arrangement may now be difficult to detect owing to later changes; for example, at the Manor House, Beeston (Nottinghamshire), the lower part of the winder stair from the kitchen to its chamber and the garret has been taken out and a new access made to the chamber from the hall chamber next to it. In the Fylde of Lancashire when long houses were upgraded by converting the byre into a service room, the room over it usually became a servants' bedchamber. The most ample evidence for servants living in comes from Lincolnshire, East Yorkshire and Northumberland, after the parliamentary enclosures: that is, from counties with the poorest heritage of older houses and therefore a shortage of cottages on the new farms.[25]

The plan

Every local survey of farmhouses and cottages from *Monmouthshire Houses* (1951–4) to *Rural Houses in North Avon and South Gloucestershire* (1983) included a classification of them by types of plan. Regional variations are so marked that no two classifications are identical. Any classification covering the whole country must combine structural with functional or social distinctions; it must separate plans determined by environmental and economic factors from those in which the comfort, convenience and style of life of the family are dominant. Interpretation of one house or a local type may be difficult as well as complex, since it must distinguish between a medieval plan persisting unaltered and a new one with an evidently medieval ancestry or a house built before 1550 and subsequently modified.

The dual-purpose house

The byre-house of pastoral counties of England and of South Wales is the most obvious form determined by economic and environmental conditions [164]. In Devon and South Wales new byre-houses were built by poorer farmers and on poorer land until c. 1700; they are substantially built, usually of stone; they have a hall fireplace backing on the cross-passage, and both hall and inner room have garrets or chambers over them reached by a turret stair.[26] They vary in the uses coming into fashion for both the inner room and the byre. Money was more likely to

164. Byre-house, SPOUT HOUSE, BILSDALE, YORKSHIRE, with stone walls built c. 1650 round an older cruck structure.

165. HIGHER STONY BANK, SLAIDBURN, YORKSHIRE, in the Trough of Bowland, with stable and granary attached to seventeenth-century house.

166. Laithe-house, EDGE FARM, ILLINGWORTH, YORKSHIRE, the laithe converted in 1977 to residential use.

be spent on the upper end, converting the dairy into a parlour by putting in a fireplace; the byre may become a kitchen or a general service room or, if still used for cattle, be rebuilt with a separate doorway for them. A difference of date or construction between house and byre, whatever the ultimate function of the byre end, is a clue to long-house ancestry. Some houses which by that criterion were derived from long houses appear

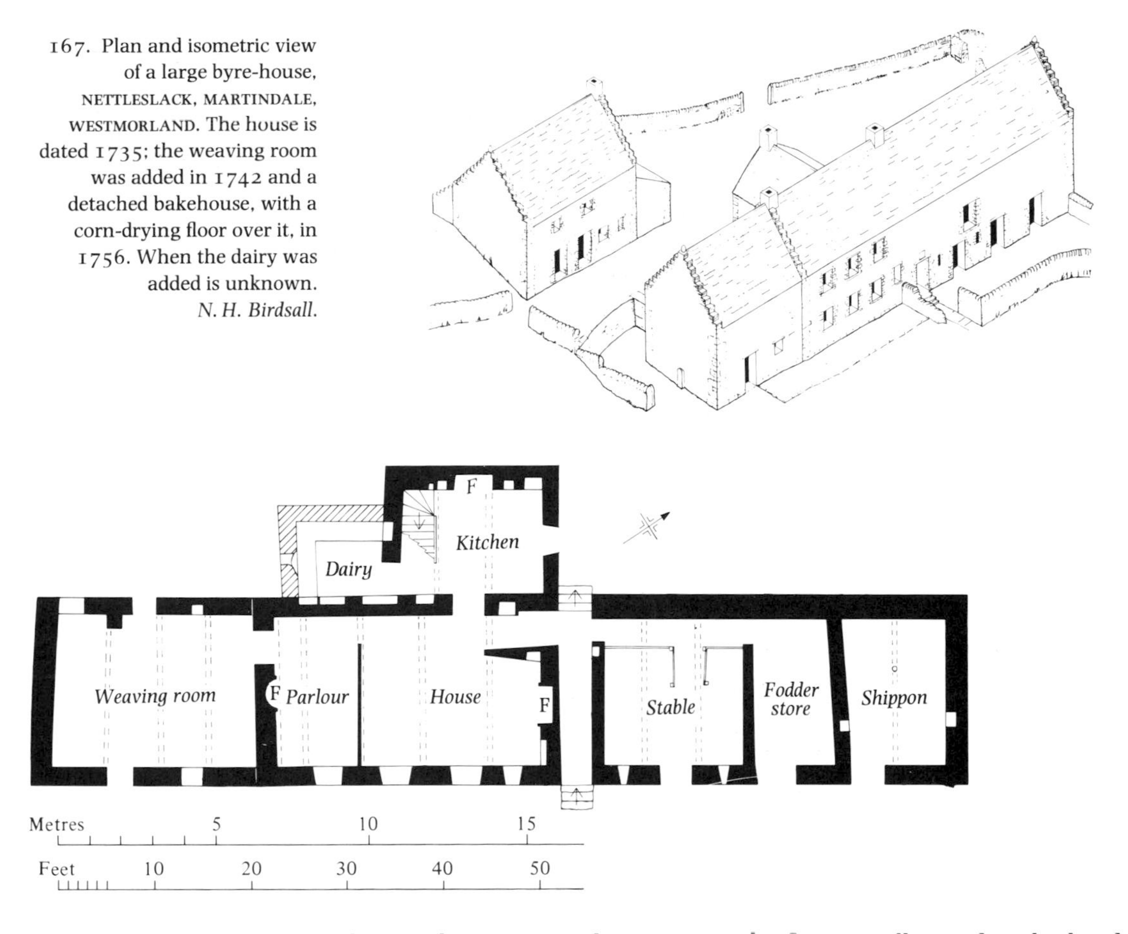

167. Plan and isometric view of a large byre-house, NETTLESLACK, MARTINDALE, WESTMORLAND. The house is dated 1735; the weaving room was added in 1742 and a detached bakehouse, with a corn-drying floor over it, in 1756. When the dairy was added is unknown.
N. H. Birdsall.

late in the seventeenth century in the Severn valley and on both sides of the Pennines [167] except for Durham and Northumberland, and continued to be built until after 1750.[27] They are in no way inferior in build or in the scale of the family's accommodation. They are more often of two storeys and the inner room beyond the hall is not a dairy but a sleeping chamber; indeed the medieval word 'bower' was still used for it in the Lake District in the seventeenth century.[28] In the north, as in the south-west, changes took the form of separating the byre from the house or converting it to a service room, the latter being commonly, as a result of alternate rebuilding, of only one storey.

Another kind of dual-purpose house was built by farmers with some arable land; attached to the end of a two-storey house and built with it is a stable or cow-house with an outside stair to a granary. There are examples in Swaledale and one at least in the Trough of Bowland: Higher Stony Bank, Slaidburn (Yorkshire, c. 1675) [165].[29] Yet another, now named the laithe-house from the dialect word for a barn, combines a two-storey house with a hay barn and a cow-house. In these types there

168. PELE HOUSE, HALTWHISTLE, NORTHUMBERLAND, C. 1610, with a watch tower. The house has been demolished. *P. W. Dixon.*

was usually no intercommunicating doorway between the parts. The oldest known laithe-house, Bank House, Luddendon (West Yorkshire), is dated 1650; most of them were built after c. 1775 as part of a colonization of high moorland.[30] They have incidentally proved worth saving when their land was engrossed since the barn made either a large living room or a garage [166]. Historically, houses of these designs are only the most enduring examples of what must have been a common sight all over England: a farm building in line with a small house.

The pele house

In a narrow strip of land along the English side of the northern border, unsettled conditions before and mostly after the union of 1604 with Scotland produced a unique reaction among farmers: they built defensible houses [168], with the animals housed on the ground floor and the family on the first.[31] They have been called bastle houses, an invented name, and pele houses would be more accurate; they are scaled down and modified versions of pele towers with an outside staircase and only one floor (hall and service room) for humans and occasionally a garret in the roof. Remains of about 180 pele houses have been recorded, built mostly after 1600 but still used until c. 1700; they were then abandoned or used solely as farm buildings.

Service rooms

The most powerful factor in the development of farmhouses was the need in the seventeenth century to incorporate more service rooms, a factor which worked throughout the social scale from the occupant of a manor house to a Cumberland statesman. The simplest way was to add an outshot at the rear principally for a dairy.[32] Even in the south this was rare before the seventeenth century, and houses there built with a continuous outshot running the whole length of the rear are likely to be after 1660 [170]. In the north outshots are more common and found in smaller houses because they descend from the single aisle of a medieval open hall, now being screened off from the hall. The strength of an aisled tradition in Yorkshire and Lancashire can be guessed by noticing that it influenced farm buildings; new barns were built with stalls for cattle in the aisles and there are even instances where an aisle was added to a cruck barn.[33] A survey made in c. 1580 of the north Lancashire manors of Lord Mounteagle of Hornby Castle describes 240 holdings of tenants at will; it does not distinguish houses from farm buildings but every property is described in terms of bays and 'onsets'. The latter can only be outshots and every single building has some.[34]

It is of course often impossible to tell whether an outshot is original or an addition, but other factors contribute to its importance in the north. One of them must be increased dairy production after 1660. It was convenient to combine the staircase projection with a service room and there are Derbyshire farmhouses such as Broomhill Farm, Brackenfield (1608), and Bothe Hall, Sawley (c. 1675), with a dairy or buttery either alongside or underneath a dog-leg staircase. The upper part of the staircase then rises conveniently under the slope of the lean-to roof. An outshot was even more important in a two-cell house such as Higher Stony Bank, Slaidburn [165], and the combination of staircase with outshot contributes to the development of the T plan with a rear wing roofed at right angles to the main range and containing a kitchen. The earliest houses in New England have only two ground-floor rooms; the colonists came from southern counties and took with them the southern plan with an axial stack between the two rooms and a staircase alongside it rather than in a turret, and the service rooms, either original or added, in a lean-to at the back.[35]

In the farmhouses of southern England the dairy or milkhouse was usually within the body of the larger house. In the home counties a wash-house becomes increasingly common after 1650; it had a sink and sometimes a furnace or copper for boiling clothes and water from a well or pump. Rich farmers in arable country had a brewhouse in a rear wing or in a separate building. In northern and south-western counties the medieval term cellar for a service room on the ground floor was still used occasionally after 1550, but in the south after 1650 cellars below ground begin to appear, especially in stone houses. Most New England houses had a cellar from the beginning because climate called for a frost-proof storage space; in this country a cellar is most commonly under the parlour, providing the comfort of a boarded floor. The parlour was

169

170

169. The front door at BOROUGH FARM, KING'S STANLEY, GLOUCESTERSHIRE, leads into what must have been a service room.

170. Original outshot at EASON'S, BARRINGTON, SOMERSET, 1715.

171. House at KETTON, NORTHAMPTONSHIRE, of one room with a canted bay-window dated 1629 – either a small house of quality or an addition to an older house behind.

171

becoming a living room rather than a sleeping chamber, and the family was withdrawing from the hall and entertaining there; for the same reason the buttery, or one of them in houses with two, may be next to the parlour.

Small houses of quality

The houses of the growing number of gentlemen living in the country on rents and investments had no farm buildings or dairies. Such gentlemen were presumably responsible for some very small but well-built houses, suitable for a bachelor or a widower [171]. Corsenside [172] was built in 1680 on a remote Northumberland fell by a retired Newcastle merchant whose goods in his house there were valued at £441 (a high

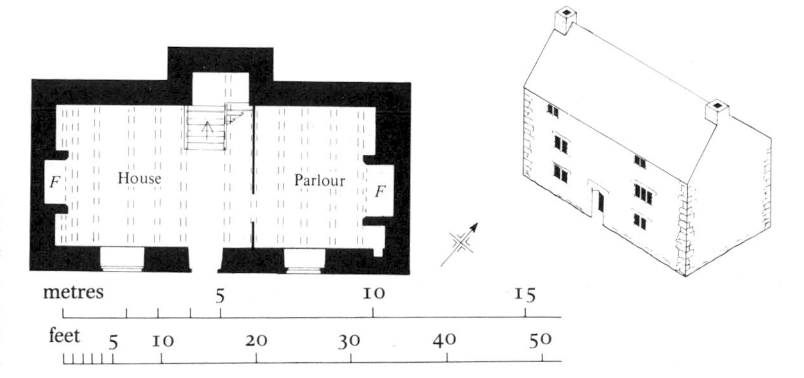

172. CORSENSIDE, NORTHUMBERLAND, built in 1680 by a Newcastle merchant. The staircase, starting in the living room, then rises in a turret to the garrets. *Agr. Hist.*

figure) when he died in 1684. Perhaps he built it for his retirement.[36] It has two rooms on a floor and three storeys, the top one lighted by small windows under the eaves and reached by a turret stair; there are no farm buildings. Among stone houses of the Banbury region are some with only one room on plan, 'built before 1700 and manifestly of fairly high social status' from the quality of the mason's work; they are usually of two full storeys and certainly not labourers' cottages. The Bristol region has examples built c. 1575–1700,[37] but none has been noted in regions of timber-framed building; all those single-cell stone houses were later extended and that sort of development is more difficult to detect in a framed construction.

The central service room

Another novel and fairly rare plan which seems alien to the needs of a working farm is that with a hall and parlour, each heated by a gable-end fireplace, and a service room between the two. It is found only in stone houses of c. 1600–1750 and mainly in the limestone belt from Dorset to Northamptonshire.[38] The largest example is in fact Borough Farm, King's Stanley (Gloucestershire) [169]. They are all of two storeys but usually modest in size. This plan defies explanation by the archaeologist but it illustrates, as does the single-unit house, the diverse social structure of the rural community.

The living rooms

The development of the ground-floor plan is more a matter of evolution than innovation, as medieval traditions were adapted to changing habits in family life. The basic distinction is between plans with three or only two rooms; eventually the distinction disappeared as the hall was reduced to an entrance passage or lobby.

The open hall of the medieval tradition disappeared only gradually. An inserted fireplace may carry a date as late as 1654, as at Lower Coombesend Farm, Sodbury (Gloucestershire), and the inventory of a Warwickshire nailer in 1613 lists beef and bacon 'at the roof'.[39] In West Yorkshire some of the lesser gentry or wealthy clothiers kept an open

173. THE HOLME, DARLEY, NIDDERDALE, YORKSHIRE, with hearth-passage plan. It was originally timber framed and in 1667 was cased in stone. Of the original eight lights of the hall, the right-hand three were a fire-window for the hearth area.

174. Derelict two-unit house at ALDWARK, DERBYSHIRE, 1686. The entrance gives on to a lobby alongside the hearth of the one heated room.

175. House at FITTLEWORTH, SUSSEX. A former smoke-bay may be detected by two main posts (over present doorway) close together, without braces. *Marjorie J. Hallam.*

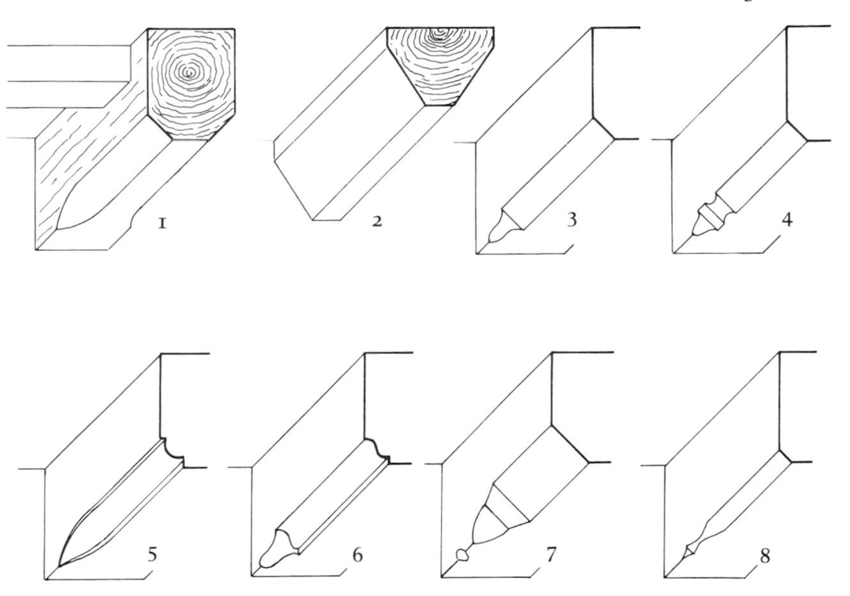

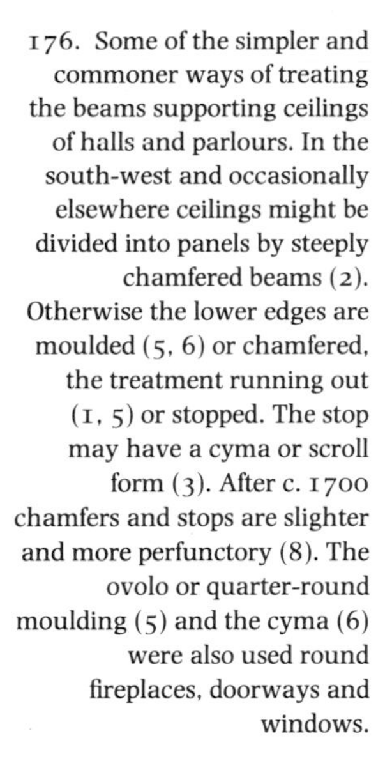

176. Some of the simpler and commoner ways of treating the beams supporting ceilings of halls and parlours. In the south-west and occasionally elsewhere ceilings might be divided into panels by steeply chamfered beams (2). Otherwise the lower edges are moulded (5, 6) or chamfered, the treatment running out (1, 5) or stopped. The stop may have a cyma or scroll form (3). After c. 1700 chamfers and stops are slighter and more perfunctory (8). The ovolo or quarter-round moulding (5) and the cyma (6) were also used round fireplaces, doorways and windows.

hall with galleries along two or even three sides of it to link the storeyed ends; examples bear dates such as 1649 (Wood Lane, Sowerby) and 1674 (Horton Old Hall, Bradford); some of them are houses of modest size and no doubt working farms.[40] In a Hertfordshire husbandman's house of 1630 the bacon was 'in the hall chimney'. There were several ways of inserting a fireplace and chimney into an open hall, or incorporating it in a new house of two storeys, without reducing the size of the hall. Farmers in Somerset, Devon and Cornwall clung to the medieval fashion for a fireplace on a side wall – that is, on the front of the house. The hearth was then shielded from draughts from the through-passage, and putting it there in an old house did not involve interfering with the roof. Much more common was what archaeologists call the hearth-passage plan, with the fireplace backing on the passage. The through-passage plan has two ancestors: the grand house with a screens-passage and the long house.[41] The former was the ancestor of the hall with a fireplace at its upper end, leaving the screens-passage intact; there are a few instances of that sort of adaptation, widely scattered in southern England. In the west and even more in the north the hearth-passage plan [173] derived from the long house; it remained the dominant type in North Yorkshire until 1750.[42]

The hall Interest in the hall and its potential for dating lie in the style of the fireplace and the construction of the ceiling; the archaeologist collects and classifies mouldings and the various forms of stop to chamfered beams. Joists were exposed, sometimes chamfered, very occasionally moulded; they were reduced in size with time and so their scantling (i.e. dimensions) is a guide to relative date. The main beam supporting them

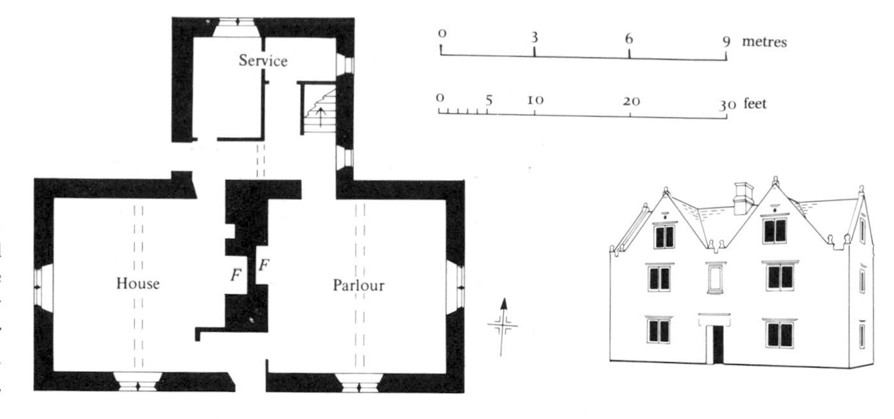

177. RAVEN HOUSE, MILLTOWN, MATLOCK, DERBYSHIRE, dated 1670, illustrates both the lobby entrance and the way the stair-turret at the rear evolves into a service wing. *After P. Woore.*

is certain to be moulded or chamfered and stopped [176], except in the poorest houses. West-country carpenters divided ceilings into compartments or panels with beams of the same dimensions running each way and steeply chamfered. The most elaborate chamfer stops were done by carpenters in the West Midlands and Wales. In stone country, interest centres on doorways and fireplaces, on which the mason could work mouldings and stops. In the north the hall fireplace, used for cooking, may be as much as 2.4 m (8 ft) wide with an arched lintel and a hood over it; the space round the fire is really a room within a room and has its own small fire-window.

Back-to-back fireplaces

A novel feature in the planning of the ground floor and therefore of the relation between rooms was the introduction of pairs of fireplaces back-to-back between rooms. This was the plan in Wolsey's lodgings at Hampton Court, built in the 1520s; it was adopted at the same time for a hunting lodge at Kneesall (Nottinghamshire), built by a court official: Old Hall Farm at Kneesall, as it is now known.[43] It has a front door opening on to a lobby at the side of the stack [177], and in this form the arrangement took such rapid and widespread hold in south-eastern England from c. 1550 that it became almost a standard plan for new farmhouses. It was economical to build and an efficient form of heating, but its popularity shows that it also met a conscious social need. A caller could be shown directly into the parlour and kept away from family, servants and the workaday business of the hall.

The two-unit plan

A significant number of houses built before 1750 have only two ground-floor rooms, the earlier ones in the south having one and half storeys with a rising proportion of two storeys as one moves north into regions of later building. Most of them are now called cottages, and it is impossible to know what proportion were farmhouses. Some have unmistakable marks of status, such as Pitfolds, Horsham (Sussex, 1673), with two lofty storeys and a storeyed porch, or Upper Farm, Bourn

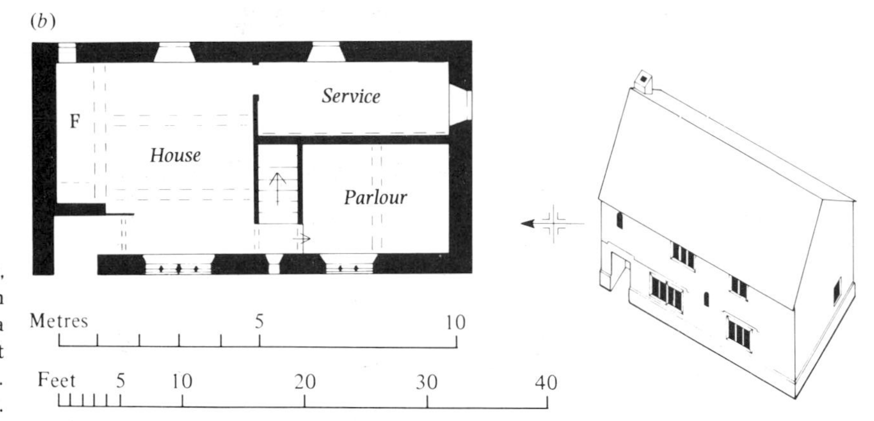

178. CLIFF FARM, HEAPEY, LANCASHIRE, dated 1696, with an end-lobby entrance, and a hearth 3.3 m (11 ft) wide at the gable end under a hood. *NMR.*

(Cambridgeshire, 1664), with only one storey and garrets but a moulded plaster frieze in one room.[44] Evidently life in two rooms, hall and parlour, satisfied a wide range of families. A small service room, either dairy or buttery, was made by taking off part of the parlour, or adding an outshot. Virtually all these two-unit houses were later enlarged still further.

Most two-unit houses had a lobby entrance plan with direct access to the parlour, but some stemmed from another tradition and represent different social conventions. The parlour was originally the principal bedroom and remained so longest in the Midlands and north where storeyed building took hold more slowly. Some two-unit houses in the Midlands with a lobby entrance can be seen to have only one fireplace, in the hall [174]; the doorway is slightly to one side of the stack and the lobby evidently led only into the hall, because the parlour was still a private room. Installing a fireplace in the parlour took hold gradually in the north and usually after c. 1650; it is small and easily distinguished from the wide fireplace of the hall, large enough for cooking to go on without dislodging the family. So many firehoods over such hearths have been dismantled and replaced by narrower chimneys that their popularity until c. 1700 has been underestimated.[45] A hood was most easily built against a gable wall, whether in a framed or a stone house [178]. It explains other types of two-unit plan. One of them, found along the limestone belt, has its only entrance in the gable-end. It has no connection with the long-house tradition since the inner room is usually a parlour and not a dairy. Yet another, found north of the Trent and principally west of the Pennines, has the entrance at the end of the side wall [178]. In both, the parlour was reached only through the hall.

The kitchen

In these developments, the role of the kitchen is the most varied and the least clear. In the south-east, a hall still used for cooking is sometimes called the kitchen in seventeenth-century inventories and terriers. In small houses it held the growing amount of equipment needed for baking,

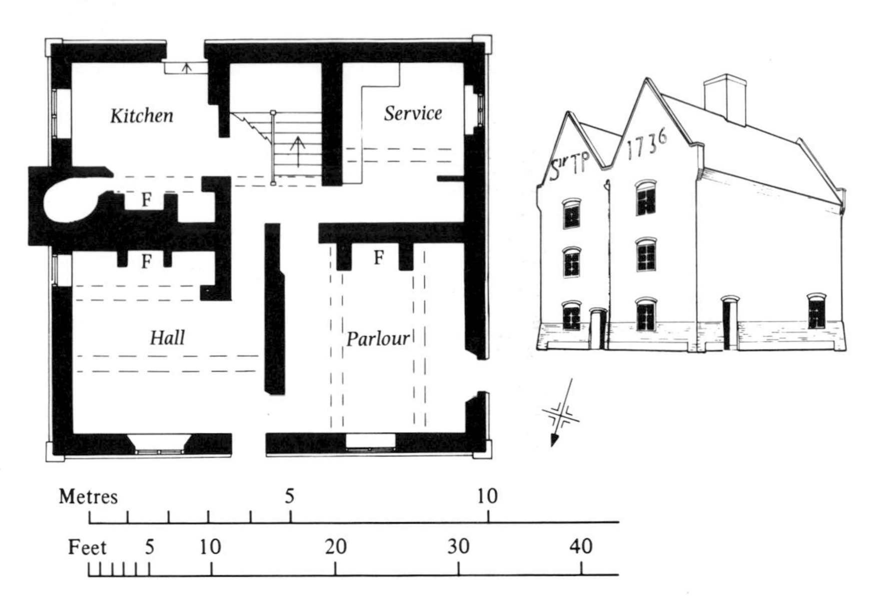

179. RANCLIFFE FARM, BRADMORE, NOTTINGHAMSHIRE, dated 1736, designed and built by the eccentric squire of Bunny, Sir Thomas Parkins, and one of several which he put up. *Agr. Hist.*

brewing, salting bacon and making butter and cheese. Bread ovens, a new convenience in post-medieval houses, are usually in the kitchen and so are the chambers alongside the hearth for smoking bacon; the latter are a feature particularly of stone houses in Somerset and of framed houses in Kent, Surrey and Sussex, where no doubt the medieval smoke-bay had been found suitable for that purpose.[46] These houses with a kitchen serving such functions have of course three rooms or more on the ground floor, and the long-house tradition lent itself to the conversion of the byre into a kitchen. In the north the two-unit house grew into the house with an L or T plan and a kitchen in the rear wing.

The symmetrical front

Eventually new farmhouses began to present a symmetrical elevation to the viewer. This is the result of a convergence of factors, brought together by the influence of what is often called polite architecture. All but the smallest farmhouses had always had both a front and a back door, and increasing prosperity and pretentions made the farmer – and his wife – make a sharper distinction between them; to separate the work of the farm and servants engaged in it from the family and its guests. The double-pile plan, as adopted for farmhouses, had only two rooms at the front and service rooms at the back [179]. In it and in similar plans, what had been the hall in the centre is reduced to an entrance space without heating or to a mere passage between hall and parlour. It has in effect assimilated itself to the two-unit plan, with a tiny service room within the rectangular plan or with an outshot or rear wing. In the north, what is called the direct-entry plan appears: two rooms, hall and parlour, the hall entered directly by a doorway not at the end or round the corner but in the middle of the front.[47] Surprisingly enough, examples have been found built before in 1650 in remote parts of the Dales. Later on it becomes common, especially west of the Pennines, its doorway having an elaborately carved head [115].

180. The central section of this cottage at STONELEIGH, WARWICKSHIRE, is known from documents to have been built c. 1570 and occupied by a labourer. *After N. W. Alcock.*

181. A typical pair of semi-detached cottages at NEW HOUGHTON, NORFOLK, Walpole's model village of 1729.

Cottages

If so many of the smallest houses built before 1775 are correctly interpreted as farmhouses, labourers' cottages built as such must be few [180]. A cottager was not necessarily landless. A survey of an estate at Syerston (Nottinghamshire) in 1724 included three farmhouses with between 85 and 189 acres and six 'cottage houses', each with farm buildings and between 1½ and 10 acres of land; one cottage had only common rights.[48] Labourers rarely made wills, but labourers' inventories made in 1650–1740 and naming rooms show that they usually had a hall, a parlour, one service room and one or two chambers: that is, houses indistinguishable from those of husbandmen. Mark Scawby of Acomb (West Yorkshire) died in 1674 in what would be classed as a long house; it had a 'fire house', a parlour and a 'lower end'.

As small farms were engrossed, landowners were likely to find themselves with too many cottages or not enough in the right location. In 1702 Lord Fitzwilliam of Milton wrote to his agent of cottages at Aylesworth (Northamptonshire) that 'they are only a shelter for poor people, who when they die leave their cottages out of repair and that proves a great charge to the landlord. My Father sold most of the cottages in

Castor for that reason.' Whether landlord or tenant was responsible for maintenance was uncertain. The agent of the Anglesey estates in Staffordshire wrote in 1739: 'in future a covenant to oblige tenants to maintain their buildings will be worthwhile'. Another landlord, constable of Everingham (East Yorkshire), was at the same time improving cottages there by raising floor levels to avoid stepping down into them, which was 'almost universal' in Everingham, and to make them 'more dry and healthfull, and last longer'. At the same time he was irritated to learn that a tenant had let one end of his house to a widow and made a new doorway for her; the agent was told to make the man rebuild the wall as before; 'one street door is sufficient for their noble families'.[49]

Improving landlords at their most active created estate villages [183]; among the earliest are Sudbury (Derbyshire) with an inn (1671) and houses of varying size built by George Vernon, and Bunny, Bradmore and Thrumpton (Nottinghamshire), with farmhouses and a few cottages. The first planned village, with ten pairs of semi-detached cottages for labourers, was New Houghton (Norfolk), built in 1729 by Sir Robert Walpole outside his park gates [181]. Some of the cottages were later

182. Mud cottage at ASLOCKTON, NOTTINGHAMSHIRE, photographed in 1950 and since demolished. The gable may always have been of brick.

enlarged and more were built but the village still looks much as Walpole saw it.[50] The estate accounts do not show how much the architect-designed cottages cost; the staircase had to be altered in the first pair, and workmen paid repeated visits to others 'about the ovens'. Walpole was not the only landowner to move a village outside a park and away from a new mansion: Nuneham Courtney (Oxfordshire, c. 1763) and Milton Abbas (Dorset, c. 1786) are well-known examples, and new housing consisted of semi-detached cottages with two heated rooms downstairs and two bedrooms. When the agricultural population was at its peak c. 1850, the Milton Abbas cottages each housed two families;[51] today some of the

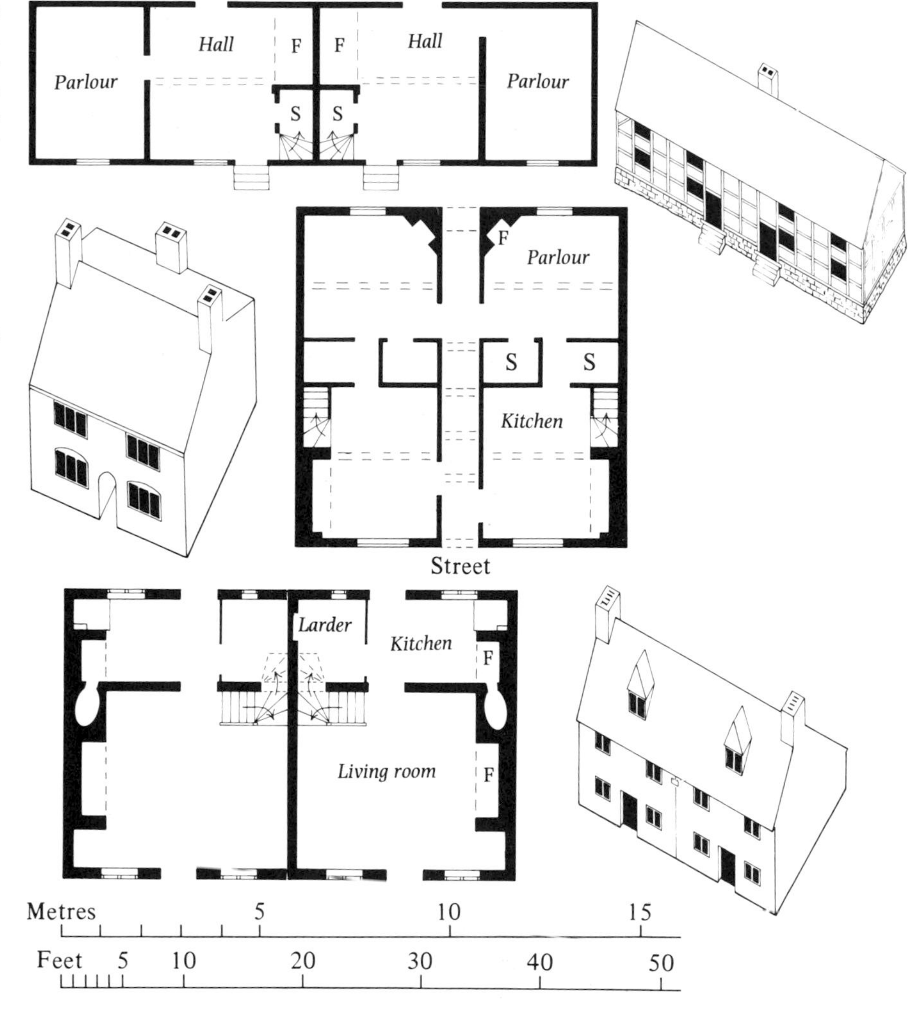

183. Semi-detached cottages at STONELEIGH, WARWICKSHIRE, timber framed, with back-to-back fireplaces for the one heated room. They were built between 1725 and 1732 for the Stoneleigh estate. *After N. W. Alcock.*

184. Semi-detached cottages at COLESHILL, WARWICKSHIRE, with entrances from a shared passage and two heated rooms. *After NMR.*

185. Semi-detached cottages at PROSPECT PLACE, HYTHE, HAMPSHIRE, may have been a speculation since one was completed in 1721 before the other, which is dated 1729. *After J. A. Reeves.*

pairs have been converted to one house. Northern standards had always been lower and remained so. Excavations in the deserted village of West Whelpington (Durham) have shown that most families lived in houses of one room, and Daniel Garrett's designs of the 1740s for new farms include single-roomed cottages, some of them without even a loft, as well as a two-storey farmhouse. The rows of such cottages built in the nineteenth century for large Northumberland farms and the miners' cottages of the same standard evidently represent a long tradition.

Estate villages such as New Houghton or John Carr's Harewood (Yorkshire) are only the most obvious mark of the improving landlord's hand. They were not all standardized in design or materials; Harlaxton (Lincolnshire) has the most extraordinary and deliberate variety in cottages built c. 1830–50, representing a conscious effort to create the diversity of an average village, the result of piecemeal rebuilding. Such work is glimpsed in the Massingberd memoranda and the Constable correspondence (pages 185–6, 246) but is largely undocumented since most landlords employed bricklayers and carpenters without generating records such as estimates and accounts. When a series of estate maps and surveys can be studied intensively, as it can for Stoneleigh (Warwickshire), it reveals that a Tudor farmhouse may now have a later cottage on its site [180].

Another solution adopted by landowners for the problem of housing labourers was to divide houses into tenements and to convert redundant farm buildings. A large and lofty brick barn at Lenton (Nottinghamshire) built in 1698 was neatly converted by c. 1750 into two pairs of back-to-back cottages, each with two rooms on plan with two chambers and a garret. Barn Cottages were demolished in 1957 for road widening.[52]

Such cottages are a minute and unrepresentative sample of the houses of men who formed between a quarter and a third of the working population in Tudor times and a larger proportion later. Many must have built their houses for themselves, with the help of family and friends. They squatted in the largest numbers on what had been royal forest, on woodland areas and sandy heaths and on manors with waste land such as roadside verges. In 1694 an agent at Downton (Wiltshire) reported that upwards of a hundred cottages had been built since the Cottage Act of 1589 and that 'every summer enlarges the number of cottages and encroachments on the waste'.[53] They used the simplest and cheapest materials – mud, clay or road scrapings; thin timber and wattling. They attracted derisory names such as Mudtown at Walton-on-Thames and Little London at Aslockton (Nottinghamshire) [182]. It is impossible to generalize about standards, though among the cottages was a large number with only one room with perhaps a small service room, and a loft or chamber in the roof.[54] When in 1686 the overseers of the poor at Saleby (Lincolnshire) built a mud and stud house for a man who had kept the alehouse there for fifty years, it cost the parish £14 14s. Another cottage of the same materials built at Dogdyke (Lincolnshire) in 1743 cost £24 5s 10d, less than one tenth of the cost of a farmhouse, one hundredth of the cost of a gentleman's residence and one thousandth of the cost of many a country seat in Georgian England.

Notes

1 *Agr. Hist.*, 4, ch. 4, 301–5, 594–601.
2 'The Rebuilding of Rural England, 1570–1640', *Past and Present*, 4 (1953), 44–59.
3 M. Spufford, *Contracting Communities* (1974), pt. 1.
4 R. Machin, *The Houses of Yetminster* (1978), 125–59.
5 J. T. Smith, 'Lancashire and Cheshire Houses: some problems of architectural and social history', *Archaeol. J.*, 127 (1970), 156–81; R. Machin and K. L. Sandall on the unit system, *Archaeol. J.*, 132 (1975), 187–201.
6 *Agr. Hist.*, 4, 9–12; Spufford, 85–7, 104–11, 159–61.
7 L. Ambler, *Old Halls and Manor Houses of Yorkshire* (1913), 93, fig. 33; BE, *West Yorkshire*, 261.

8 R. Machin, *Probate Inventions and Manorial Excepts* (1976).

9 *Vernacular Architecture*, 8 (1977), 19–24.

10 F.W. Steer, *Farm and Cottage Inventories of Mid-Essex 1635–1749* (1950), 11.

11 *Post-Medieval Archaeology*, 9 (1975), 214–18, pl. xxviii.

12 *EFC*, pls. VIII 6, XXIII; RCHM, *North-East Cambridgeshire*, 9 (no. 12). Essex estimates of similar date ranged from £220 to £275 (Essex RO, D/DRC Z27).

13 S.D. Chapman, *Devon Cloth Industry in the Eighteenth Century* (Devon and Cornwall Record Soc. 23, 1978), viii, xxvi.

14 J.M. Robinson, 'Model farm buildings of the Age of Improvement', *Architectural History*, 19 (1976), 17–31.

15 P. Roebuck (ed.), *The Constable Estate Correspondence* (Yorks. Archaeol. Soc. Record Series 136, 1974).

16 N.W. Alcock, *Cruck Construction: an Introduction and Catalogue* (CBA Research Report 42, 1981), fig. 34.

17 Gaythorn Hall is described and planned in RCHM, *Westmorland* (1936), 16, but the wool hoist is not mentioned; both it and the hoist at Preston Court (*House and Home*, pl. 45) were noticed by the author on visits.

18 *Agr. Hist.*, 5, pl. IX.

19 L.J. Hall, 'Timber staircases in North Avon houses to the mid 18th century', *Bristol and Avon Archaeology*, 1 (1982), 16–27, is the best account of staircases in small houses; another is in *Historic Buildings in Eastern Sussex*, 1, 137–59 (Rape of Hastings Archit. Survey). See also B. Harrison and B. Hutton, *Vernacular Houses in N. Yorkshire and Cleveland* (1984), 193–5.

20 *Hist. Buildings in E. Sussex*, 1, 73–104; M. Spufford in *Proc. Cambs. Ant. Soc.*, 55 (1961), 53–64.

21 W.G. Hoskins, *The Midland Peasant* (1957), 195, 299; information from Vanessa Neave.

22 M. Puloy, 'Decorative plasterwork in Hertfordshire', *Hertfordshire Archaeology*, 8 (1980–2), 144–99.

23 *Proc. Devonshire Ass.*, 89 (1957), 124–44; *EVH*, 149 (81).

24 *EFC*, pl. XVa; RCHM, *Westmorland*, 221.

25 C. Carson, 'Segregation in vernacular buildings', *Vernacular Architecture*, 7 (1976), 24–9; *EFC*, 159; *Trans. Thoroton Soc.*, 86 (1982), 94; *Vernacular Architecture*, 2 (1971), 18–19.

26 *EVH*, 37–44, pls. 28–32.

27 B. Harrison and B. Hutton, *Vernacular Houses in North Yorkshire and Cleveland* (1984), ch. 3 (The Hearth-Passage Plan Group).

28 *Trans. Cumb. and Westm. Arch. and Archaeol. Soc.*, 53 (1953), 163.

29 R.W. Brunskill in *Northern History*, 11 (1976), 120; *Agr. Hist.*, 5, fig. 25b.

30 *EVH*, 32–3.

31 *EVH*, 44; H.G. Ramm *et al.*, *Shielings and Bastles* (1970), pt. 2.

32 *EVH*, 69–73.

33 *Agr. Hist.*, 5, 670–5.

34 Chetham Society, 102 (1939).

35 A.L. Cummings, *Framed Houses of Massachusetts Bay 1625–1725* (1979), ch. 3.

36 *Agr. Hist.*, 5, 665–7.

37 R.B. Wood-Jones, *Traditional Domestic Architecture in the Banbury Region* (1963), ch. 8; L.J. Hall, *The Rural Houses in North Avon and South Gloucestershire* (1983), 20, 22.

38 RCHM, *Peterborough New Town* (1969); Hall, 17–19; Sir Cyril Fox and Lord Raglan, *Monmouthshire Houses*, 3 (1954), 130.

39 Hall, 227–9.

40 Ambler, pls. ix, xviii, etc.; *House and Home*, pl. 100.

41 *EVH*, 52.

42 Harrison and Hutton, ch. 3.

43 *Trans. Thoroton Soc.*, 76 (1972), 17–25; *EVH*, 60. This house has now been restored.

44 RCHM, *West Cambs.*, 25, pl. 124.

45 *EVH*, index, 'firehoods'.

46 *Trans. Somerset Arch. Soc.* (1976), 120; *Proc. Suffolk Inst. Archaeol.*, 35 (1982), 117–21.

47 Harrison and Hutton, ch. 5.

48 *Agr. Hist.*, 5, 677–82.

49 *Constable Estate Correspondence*, 37–8.

50 *Vernacular Architecture*, 1 (1970), 14–15; K. Pugh, *Estate Villages* (SAVE 1983); *Agr. Hist.*, 5, 645.

51 *EVH*, 77.

52 *EVH*, 75–6.

53 Wilts. Record Office, 490/909.

54 *EVH*, 75–7, 135–6.

14 *Houses in the Modern Town*

The present generation, familiar with problems of decaying inner cities caused by rapid social and economic change, should be able to appreciate what happened in towns in the two centuries or so after 1550. The Reformation had if anything a greater impact on them than on the countryside, in that buildings changed hands rather than fields: not only abbeys, friaries, hospitals and chantries but also their residential quarters and their endowments of houses, shops and the like. It has been estimated that in the city of Lincoln about one-third of the property and buildings changed hands,[1] and the proportion must have been similar in other historic cities.

The population of London grew from about 50,000 in 1550 to 200,000 in 1630 and half a million in 1700; Bristol and Norwich experienced similar growth. In addition to sucking in people from the provinces, London and eastern towns absorbed Protestant refugees from the Low Countries and France on a scale seen later only when Jews arrived from eastern Europe before 1914 and Commonwealth immigrants after 1950.

Urban castles

Urban castles were redundant, except in shire towns where they accommodated a hall for assizes and a county gaol. Ludlow Castle survived because it was used until the Civil War as the headquarters of the Council of the Marches, and its residential apartments were improved in 1581 by the president, Sir Henry Sidney. Most other castle sites were, in today's jargon, ripe for redevelopment. A rare exception was Warwick Castle which has been owned by the same family since 1604 and used as a residence; it was rebuilt to suit changing needs and fashions and now displays work of several generations. A castle in habitable condition might attract an aristocrat seeking to enlarge his territorial influence or to find a new base for power. Newark, taken from the bishop of Lincoln by Henry VIII, was leased in 1560 to Sir Francis Leake of Sutton Scarsdale (Derbyshire) and then in 1581 to the earl of Rutland (of Belvoir Castle), who certainly resided there from time to time though he also used a former medieval hospital outside the town. A fashionable wedding, of the earl's daughter to William Cecil, son and heir to the earl of Exeter (of Burghley) was celebrated in the castle chapel in 1589. Husband and wife enjoyed the rest of the lease. The castle was slighted after the Civil War and no lessee tried to make it habitable again. Marlborough Castle was acquired by Protector Somerset in 1550 and his great-grandson built a house on the site in 1620; a later descendant, the sixth duke of Somerset, rebuilt it on a larger scale in 1699. It became an inn in 1750 and then in 1843 the home of a new public school.[2]

Most castles in or adjacent to market towns were allowed to decay. Whether and when their sites were redeveloped depended on the economic fortunes of towns, the housing stock inherited from Tudor and earlier times and the amount of land available for new houses. The site of the castle at Bridgwater is now covered by King Square and streets of houses, a development started by the duke of Chandos, lord of the manor, in 1723. It is rarely possible to be as precise as that about the chronology of redevelopment. The earls of Exeter naturally acquired Stamford Castle but were content to dominate the town from Burghley House, a mile or so away. They seem to have used the castle hall for the court leet but the site remained unused until 1933; the motte was then levelled for a bus station and the bailey was sold for housing in the 1970s – after archaeological excavation. By contrast, the castles at Bristol and Southampton were used to house rapidly growing populations. Southampton Corporation bought its castle in 1617 and houses then began to be built in the bailey. At Bristol the decaying buildings were let by an Elizabethan governor and the process accelerated after the city purchased the castle from the crown in 1630; in 1673 the precinct was 'covered with little cottages piled on the head of one another'.[3]

In these changing circumstances, new provision had to be made in assize towns for judges on circuit, by acquiring an existing house such as the handsome Judges' Lodgings in Lendal, York (now an hotel), or building as at Lincoln, where the Judges' Lodgings outside the castle gate were built c. 1810. These lodgings were until recently the responsibility of the local justices and then of county councils. As houses designed for formal but intermittent use (like medieval great houses) they deserve more study.

Religious buildings

The destruction of monasteries, friaries and hospitals in Henry VIII's time and later has been called the greatest act of vandalism in English history. A few notable monastic churches have survived, adapted wholly or in part as parish churches but others were stripped of their lead, timber and fittings and sooner or later demolished. In special circumstances their residential buildings were reprieved. Henry saw the advantage of converting Dartford, Rochester and St Augustine's at Canterbury into royal

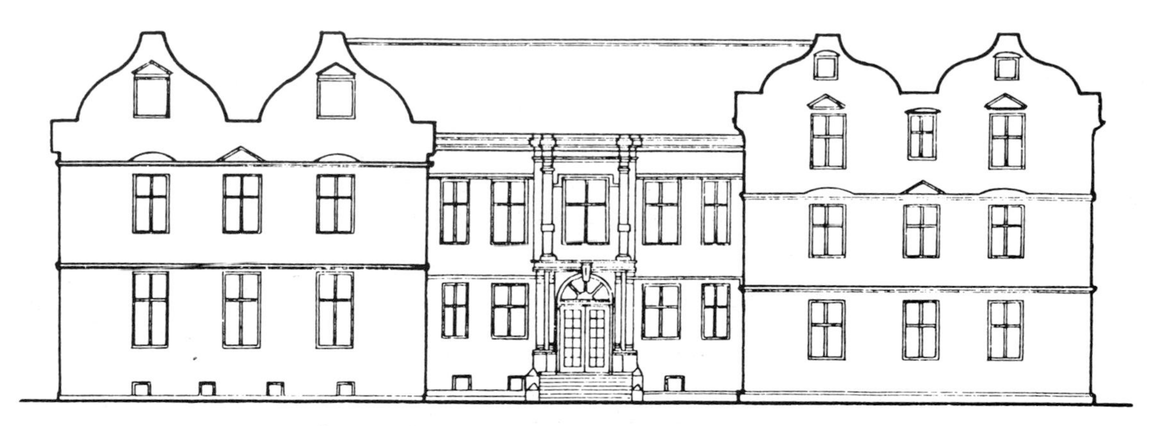

186. The front of THE TREASURER'S HOUSE, YORK, as it was c. 1700. *RCHM.*

houses for use on journeys to Dover and Calais; none of them, however, was much used after his death and little of his buildings has survived. Round the seven monastic cathedrals where monks were replaced by secular canons, and the six churches newly elevated to cathedral status (as at Peterborough), communal buildings – refectory, dormitory, etc. – were unroofed and left to decay, unless a new use, e.g. as a grammar school, was found for them. Priors became deans and monks became canons with little physical disturbance. Since the new establishments were modest – twelve canons at Canterbury, Durham and Winchester, no more than six elsewhere – there must have been room for choice. At Durham the dean, as well as having the prior's lodging, chose to take over the great monastic kitchen; his successors continued to use it until 1940 and it is now the diocesan record office. Most prebendal houses were rebuilt subsequently, but at Ely it is still possible to see how the problem of 1541 was solved. South-east of the cathedral is Infirmary Lane, flanked by residences. On each side of the lane are blocked arches, because the lane is really the nave of the long Norman infirmary which had its roof removed soon after 1541; houses are contrived in the aisles. At the east end is a house, now the deanery, formed out of the infirmary chapel and in its front is the blocked chancel arch.

Other important properties, unused if not actually redundant, were bishops' palaces in cathedral cities. Matthew Parker, Elizabeth's first archbishop of Canterbury, spent most of his time at Lambeth Palace and kept up a style not much less elaborate than his medieval predecessors and the courtiers of his time, and he also used Canterbury occasionally. The bishop of London had ceased to use his palace north-west of St Paul's churchyard; it was sold and demolished in 1661–2, and he resided either at Fulham or in a house in Aldersgate Street. The palace at Norwich was more or less continuously maintained but the great hall at Wells was demolished after 1550. A new factor in the life of a bishop was the desire to provide for his children.[4] For sons this was most conveniently done by granting them leases of episcopal manors. Thomas Young, archbishop of

187. THE BISHOP'S PALACE, LICHFIELD, now St Chad's School, built 1686–7 by Edward Pierce, sculptor and mason, at a cost of £3,972, while the archbishop of Canterbury was responsible for the diocese.

York in 1561–8, established a son in the Treasurer's House at York [186], which had been surrendered to Henry VIII in 1547 and then bought by Robert Holgate, Young's predecessor. Young removed the lead from his medieval hall to raise capital on his son's behalf and some stone from the hall may have gone into rebuilding the Treasurer's House, which remained in the Young family until 1648.[5] Bishops' palaces were sold by the Commonwealth government and returned to them in 1660 in even poorer shape, so that a preference for distant residences was confirmed. Cosin improved Durham Castle in 1663 but his successor, Crew, lived for the most part at Bishop Auckland; Winchester resided at Farnham, Lincoln at Buckden, Lichfield at Eccleshall in great style. In 1686 the archbishop of Canterbury saw to it that a new palace was built at Lichfield, presumably to encourage the bishop to spend more time in his cathedral city [187].

As in the countryside, courtiers and officials acquired most religious property in towns. Sir Richard Gresham, whose son Thomas built the Royal Exchange (1566) in London, bought over 500 houses in the city of York as well as Fountains Abbey.[6] Richard Brandon, duke of Suffolk, already through marriage the greatest landowner in Lincolnshire, became through grants of monastic land a great landowner in the city. The largest purchasers of chantry land there were Sir John Thynne, Somerset's agent and the builder of Longleat, and John Throckmorton of a Warwickshire family connected with the court.[7] In the course of generations their acquisitions were broken up and passed to local gentry and wealthy citizens. The Council of the North required premises in York and since the castle was not in good enough condition it took over the lodgings of the abbot of St Mary's outside the town walls now known as the King's Manor; as at Ludlow there was some new building. After 1660 it

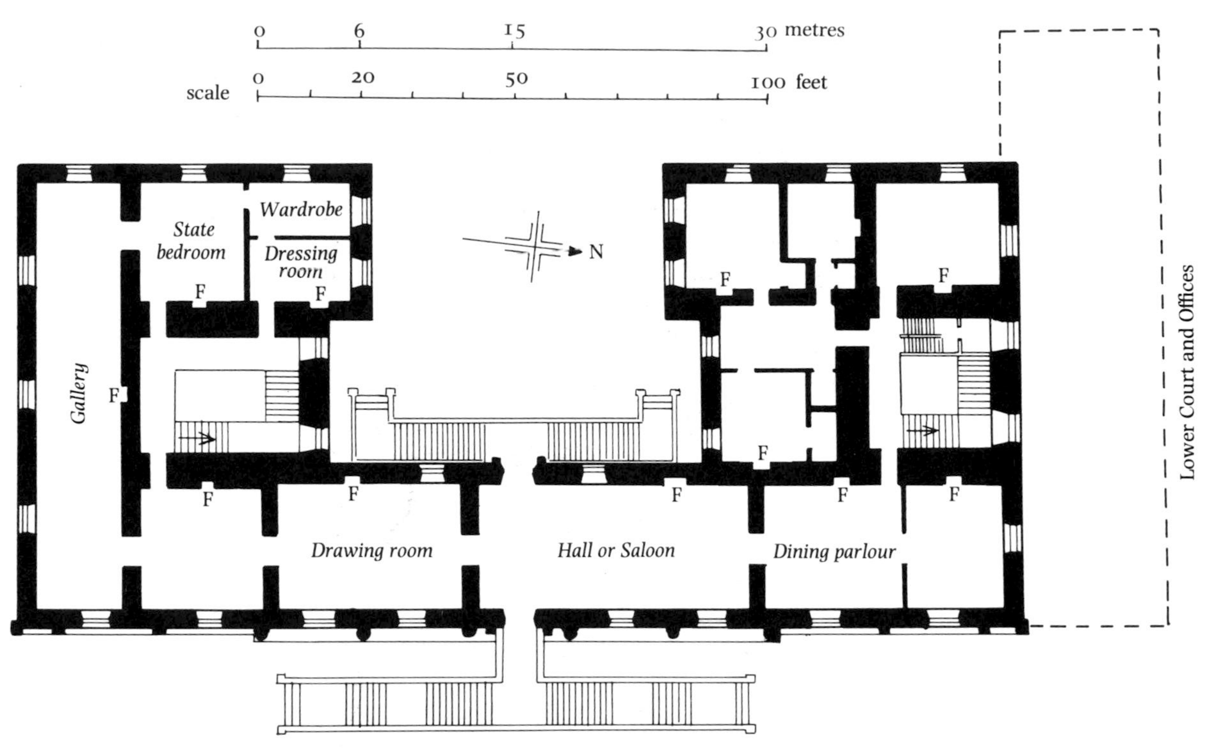

188. NOTTINGHAM CASTLE. Plan of the first or principal floor made in 1800. The uses of ground-floor rooms are not known. The service wing (shown in broken outline) was still lower down, in the castle ditch. The principal floor was approached by grand staircases removed in 1878. Rooms on the principal floor not named were bedrooms and the top floor had presumably servants' bedrooms. *After W. Stretton.*

was for a time the official residence of the governor of the city but in the eighteenth century it was divided for a variety of uses; the corporation acquired it from the crown only in 1958, and in 1963–4 it was restored, modernized and extended for the university of York.[8]

The aristocracy in the town

Courtiers when they acquired urban properties did not usually intend to keep them, except for their gains in the capital. They competed for episcopal inns in London, conveniently located on the Westminster side of the City, and for precincts such as the Charterhouse;[9] even so, they proceeded sooner or later to build new houses rather than to adapt medieval buildings.[9] In Norwich, Thomas Howard, duke of Norfolk, built a house in 1540 and his family maintained it, as a focus of power and hospitality, until 1711. Howard House, or the 'Ducal Palace' as John Evelyn called it, had a façade of c. 1690; it eventually became part of a brewery and was demolished in the 1960s.[10] The earl of Rutland, having lost Newark castle, coveted Nottingham and was granted it by James I. It was so damaged in the Civil War that a duke of Buckingham, to whom it had passed by inheritance, was ready to sell it to William Cavendish, duke of Newcastle. His two passions were architecture and horsemanship. Having inherited Bolsover castle and Welbeck abbey and having built a new house at Bolsover and riding schools at both places, he spent his last years demolishing most of what was left of Nottingham castle and building a Baroque mansion [124, 188] on the site of the keep.[11] It was finished only after his death in 1676. Like Howard House at Norwich, the mansion was a source of power until eventually another duke's opposition to parliamentary reform led to its being burnt out in riots in

189. The verger's house attached to the north side of ST BARTHOLOMEW'S, SMITHFIELD, LONDON, is all that remains of the conversion of the priory buildings to residential use.

1831; it remained an empty shell until in 1875 the corporation acquired it to open the first municipal art gallery. It is largely unaltered externally and the plan of the principal floor with its state rooms was recorded before the fire; there is also a model – an unusual survival.[12]

The gentry in the town

In a few instances, the gentry were ready to move into monastic buildings with the minimum of delay. While the London Charterhouse and Bermondsey abbey were rebuilt as noble houses, the priory of St Bartholomew, Smithfield, was granted to Sir Richard, later Lord Rich, Henry VIII's lord chancellor, who also acquired Lees Priory (Essex, page 201), and he himself moved into the prior's lodging within four months of the dissolution.[13] The history of the precinct is well documented. The choir be-

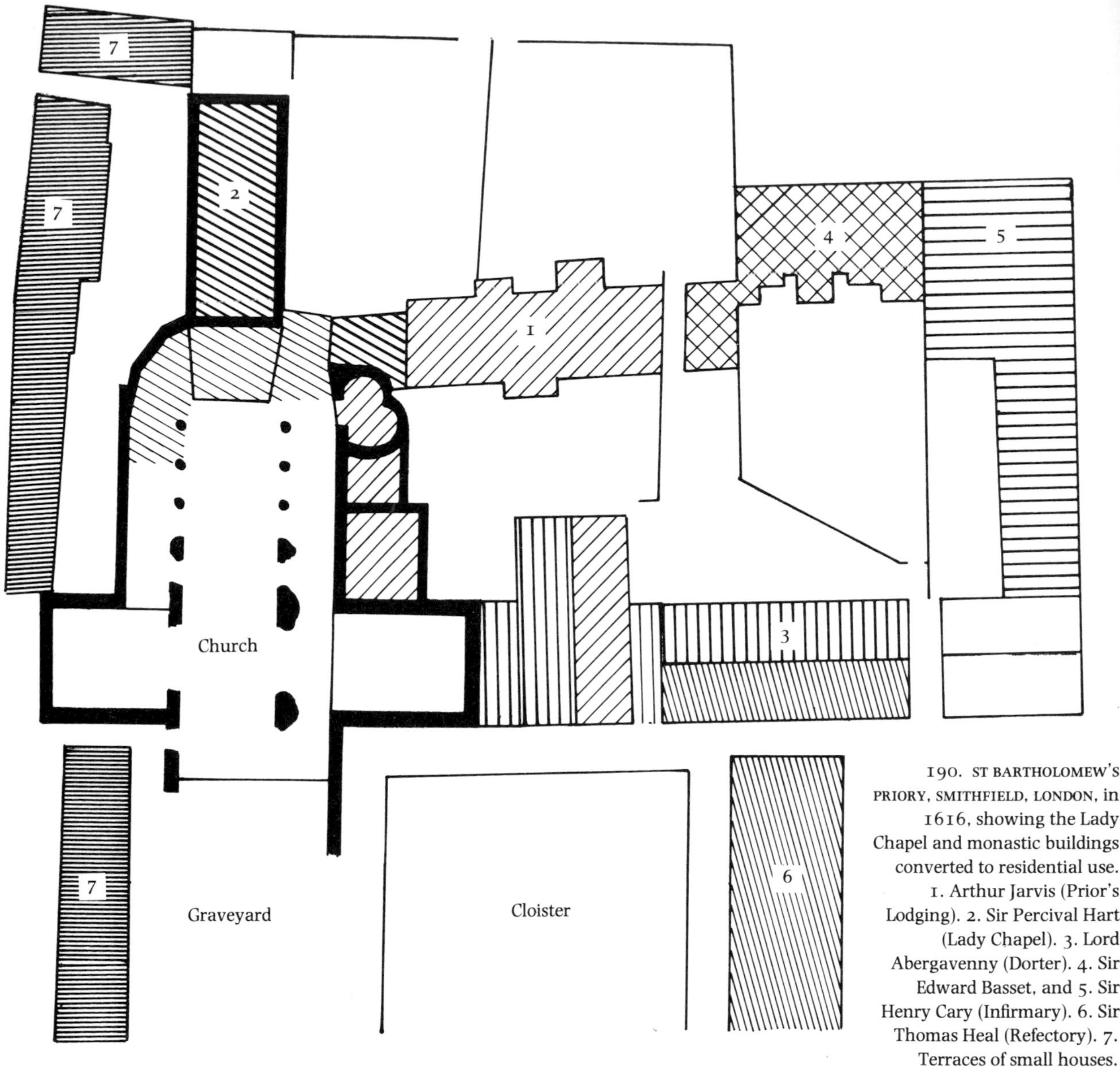

190. ST BARTHOLOMEW'S PRIORY, SMITHFIELD, LONDON, in 1616, showing the Lady Chapel and monastic buildings converted to residential use. 1. Arthur Jarvis (Prior's Lodging). 2. Sir Percival Hart (Lady Chapel). 3. Lord Abergavenny (Dorter). 4. Sir Edward Basset, and 5. Sir Henry Cary (Infirmary). 6. Sir Thomas Heal (Refectory). 7. Terraces of small houses. *After E. A. Webb.*

came a parish church and the lady chapel east of it a gentleman's house with its own access to the church. Now that the chapel has been restored to religious use and all traces of domestic use removed, it is difficult to imagine it as a two-storey house with fireplaces and the like [189]. Other gentlemen's houses were formed round the cloisters and Rich's grandson c. 1580 began to develop the precinct [190] by laying out narrow streets for small houses so that by 1666 there were 84 in the close and 177 in Cloth Fair, north of the church.[14] The church of Holy Trinity Priory, Aldgate, was transformed in a similar way [191].

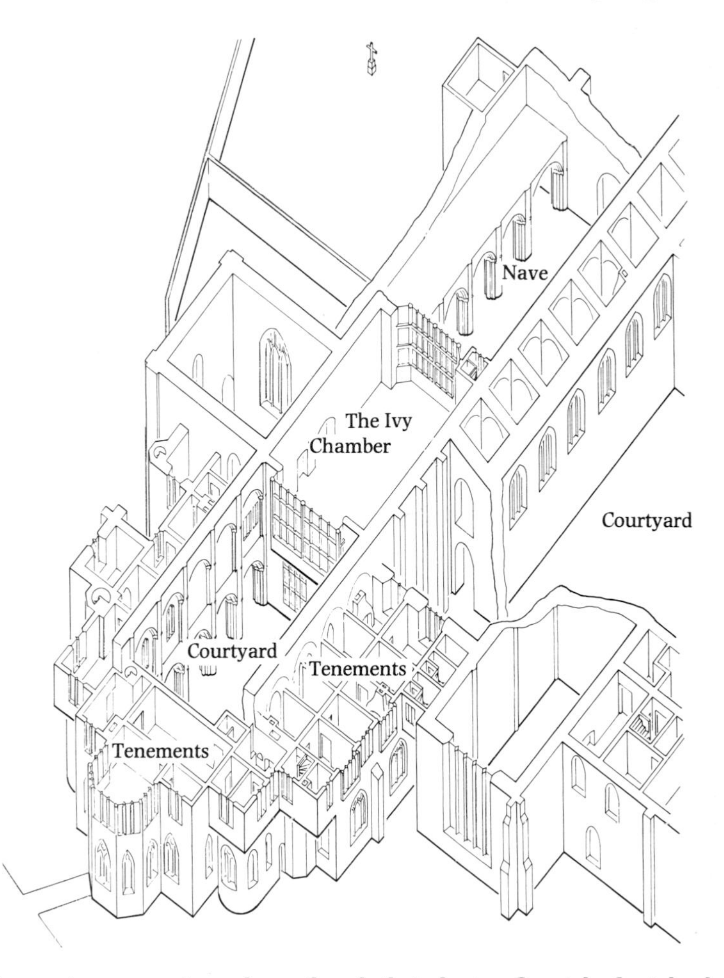

191. Axonometric view of the priory church of HOLY TRINITY, ALDGATE, LONDON, based on a survey of 1592. The priory had been dissolved in 1532 and the buildings granted to Thomas Audley, Henry VIII's chancellor, who adapted the cloisters as a house for himself. The crossing was converted into another house; the nave and choir, their roofs removed, became courtyards; the clerestory level of the choir was converted into tenements jettied out over the ground floor. *After J. Schofield.*

In western counties where the cloth industry flourished, rich clothiers saw the potential of religious sites. At Worcester, one clothier bought a hospital known as the Commandery and another the Greyfriars, in each case because there was a fine guest hall suitable for conversion to domestic use; both still stand, with Elizabethan staircases to reach upper rooms. At Gloucester the Dominican friary (Blackfriars) was granted to a clothier who converted the church (Bell's House) [192] and installed weavers in the claustral buildings. William Stumpe acquired the abbey at Malmesbury; no doubt he moved first into the abbot's lodging, for the new house (Abbey House) appears to have been built or finished only after his death in 1552. He too used the claustral buildings for his weavers.[15] This has usually been taken to imply a factory with rows of looms; certainly at Gloucester, where the Blackfriars' buildings are now in guardianship and being restored, there is no evidence that the claustral buildings were made into weavers' cottages. In most towns, friary buildings disappeared rapidly and completely, so that at the most remains of

192. BLACKFRIARS, GLOUCESTER. A. The interior of the north transept in 1946. *NMR*. B. The exterior in 1984, after the Ministry of Works had converted it back to a church. The Georgian windows are blocked.

them are encountered by archaeologists when a new shopping centre is developed at Oxford or a Georgian warehouse in York (next to the Guildhall) converted to a public house.

Monastic sites on the outskirts of towns attracted the gentry, or successful merchants anxious to establish themselves as such. At Ipswich a London merchant bought the Augustinian priory and his new house (Christchurch Mansion, rebuilt in 1675 after a fire and now a museum) was built in 1548–50.[16] A similar house in a Lincoln suburb, on the site of St Katherine's priory and built by a city family, has been destroyed and is known only from a sketch of c. 1725 by Samuel Buck.[17] Within towns, colleges of chantry priests were redundant buildings of domestic design. St William's College, York, built c. 1465 on a courtyard plan, is a remarkable survival though much altered. It was owned or occupied by local families – including the earl of Carlisle while Castle Howard was being built – until acquired in 1902 by the church authorities.[18] By contrast, St Edmund's College at Salisbury was demolished and a new house, the largest and handsomest in the town, built on the site. It was owned by one family for a long time, used as a school from 1873 and then purchased by the corporation in 1927 for use as council offices.[19]

The best evidence for the desire of the gentry to possess a town house, as well as a seat in the country, comes from Nottingham; nearly all the houses have gone but the enthusiasm of such travellers as Thomas Baskerville (1675) and Celia Fiennes (1698) is supported by documents, paintings and engravings.[20] Celia Fiennes found more people of quality in Nottingham than anywhere else except Shrewsbury, where they lived not in fine (i.e. new) houses but only in 'many large old houses, convenient and stately'. A recent observer has confirmed that there was little new building there in the seventeenth century but much enlargement of earlier houses; new houses began to be built only after the time of her visit.[21] By the eighteenth century the finest houses in provincial towns were the product of trade and commerce, of local industry and of the professionals: hence the fashionable quality of Georgian houses in Stamford and the startling size of some of the clothiers houses in Trowbridge [193, 194], both towns with first-class building stone available.[22]

The expanding town

The surge in demand for housing and pressure on space made the courtyard house out of the question for the urban middle classes. A sample of London inventories suggests that they disappeared in the seventeenth century even in suburban villages, being divided into tenements or demolished for redevelopment. On the fringes of provincial towns, houses with a wide frontage and an entrance to a yard with coach-house and stable continued to be built in the seventeenth and eighteenth centuries. Lichfield inventories frequently mention a barn in a 'backside',[23] but on the whole there is little evidence of where the middle classes – the 'carriage folk' – kept their carriages, partly no doubt because in the nineteenth century the rear of properties was filled with cottages. The study of Stamford has almost nothing to say about stables and coach-houses; there were no back lanes to provide rear access. Defoe in his enthusiastic account of the growth of greater London comments on the proportion of 'handsome large houses' in commuter villages in Essex whose owners kept a coach.[24]

Equally obscure is the history of sanitary arrangements, and the subject is hidden under euphemisms for natural processes, of which Swift's 'plucking a rose' is the most elegant; the writer has been directed by a former cavalry officer to a place for 'watering the horses'. The houses of the rich might have a piped water supply to a cistern but there was no reliable patent for a flushing water-closet until George III's time. The duke of Chandos had a flushing closet at Canons in 1725, but when as a speculation he built a lodging house at Bath for visitors to the spa, he was annoyed to find that his builder, John Wood (father of the Bath architect), could not make the water-closets work.[25] He intended the house to have ten of them, with marble basins and wooden seats; lodgers had in the event to make do with close stools in their rooms and 'necessary houses' in the back garden. There were 'bog houses' in the cellars for servants. The duke also built terraced houses on the site of Bridgwater castle, but did not attempt to instal water-closets. At Stamford the oldest bathroom and water-closet recorded were built in 1814, in the house of a rich merchant.[26] It was left to the Victorians to tackle the problem of urban sanitation.

Tall houses and towers

Since new houses in town centres now ran to three or four storeys, some wealthy townsmen sought to overtop their neighbours by building a tower, of timber or brick. One of the first was a lord mayor of London in 1536. Stow, who disapproved of this attempt to overlook neighbours, only mentions two and we do not know how common they were in London.[27] The pleasure of a view was part of the explanation; a Billingsgate merchant had in 1637 two galleries 'over the Thames'. A brick tower of five storeys was added c. 1575 to Clifton House, King's Lynn; it overlooks the Ouse. Tower House, Bracondale, on the outskirts of Norwich, has a view over the river Yare.[28] One of the turrets of Newark Castle was turned into a lofty prospect room or gazebo by one of its noble owners (page 267), and there are timber-framed examples in Shrewsbury (Park Hotel) and Oxford (Old Palace), both of seventeenth-century date.[29]

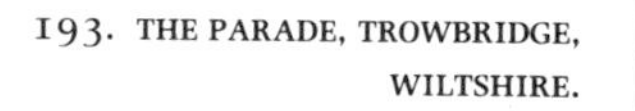

193. THE PARADE, TROWBRIDGE, WILTSHIRE.

194. ST GEORGE'S SQUARE, STAMFORD, LINCOLNSHIRE.

In city centres, the models for tall buildings were already to be seen. John Stow, writing in the 1590s, explained that in Cheapside houses consisting originally of a shop with a solar over it had become, by building 'outward and upward', some three to five storeys high.[30] His 'fair houses built for worshipful persons' on the site of St Mary's Spittle, Bearward Lane, were no doubt on that scale.

Multiple housing

The demand for houses was such that developers could think in terms of schemes for distinct income groups, regardless of professions or trades in seventeenth-century London but in some smaller towns for those engaged in a particular industry. Covent Garden, developed in 1631–7 by the earl of Bedford, was for a high class of occupant not because of the size of the units but because they were laid out for the first time round a square, contemporary with the Place des Vosges in Paris and the Plaza Mayor in Madrid. Whatever the class for which they were intended, new houses very rarely had more than one room to the frontage; their quality depended less on size than on the plan, particularly of the staircase, and on fittings and finishes. After the Fire of London, regulations were laid down for new houses other than mansions; they were limited to two storeys in by-streets and lanes, three in lanes of note and on the Thames, and four in high and principal streets. All might have cellars and attics.

London conditions imposed on the middle classes a way of life which became a fashionable norm for two centuries or more: kitchens in the basement, dining parlour on the ground floor, a parlour or saloon on the first floor and sleeping rooms above. In the eighteenth century, houses of better quality were separated from the built-up road by an 'area' with steps down to the basement and, from about 1750, a hollow space under the road for storing coal.[31] The railed-in area is to be seen in fashionable developments in Dublin, Edinburgh and such towns as Bath; otherwise the basement is half above ground and the flight of steps up to the entrance consequently longer. London builders also popularized, for the upper classes, the corner fireplace. The earliest examples known, back to back in adjacent rooms, in the lay-brothers' quarters in the Charterhouse, may be later insertions in a building of the early sixteenth century, but corner fireplaces, designed to burn coal and placed in the corner of a framed building, minimized the risk of fire and modification of the roof. At any rate, it is clear that back-to-back fireplaces either on the axis of a house or on side walls can be traced to London and to multiple housing.[32]

Inventories show that many London craftsmen with small businesses worked either in a cellar or a garret. An inventory of 1637 refers to a garret containing seven looms and eight wheels. Since such houses have disappeared there is no archaeological evidence of the form of roof, but it no doubt resembled those known by c. 1600 in both provincial towns and farmhouses. With modification of floor levels, the garret workshop turned into the 'top-shop' when silk weavers migrated to Staffordshire and stocking knitters to Nottinghamshire; in the West Riding the top floor was commonly a workshop, with a bed or beds amid the looms.[33]

Semi-detached and back-to-back houses

Other novel designs emerged as suitable for restricted sites and were employed in London and elsewhere: semi-detached and back-to-back pairs of houses. A semi-detached pair in Pembroke Street, Oxford, was built early in the seventeenth century in stone with three full storeys and a gabled roof; another pair in Beef Lane was framed with two jettied upper floors.[34] Each had only one room on a floor. By c. 1700 these casual opportunities for building in pairs were taken in hand by designers and pairs built with mirror-image plans which henceforward became standard. Back-to-back arrangements probably appeared by accident in the first place, when rows of cottages were built as infilling in yards, backing on others in adjacent properties. A pair of houses dated 1706 in George Row, Bermondsey (now demolished), marks the way an unknown architect might apply himself to a small scheme: he put together two houses back to back under a double roof, each house having two rooms with corner fireplaces.[35] Both houses were of high quality with panelling, moulded plaster decoration and a built-in corner cupboard of the sort then coming into fashion. Some such pairs were perhaps built by men who intended to occupy one house and to sell or let the other.

Urban types of plan

The most comprehensive evidence for types of plan comes from London, from provincial towns for which a full survey has been published and from parts of other towns examined in detail. They are Stamford, York and Blandford Forum, surveyed by the Royal Commission on Historical Monuments, and Frome and Yarmouth. Blandford is important because, like many other towns full of framed buildings (Alresford, Dorchester, Marlborough, Northampton and Warwick among them) it was almost entirely destroyed by fire in 1713 and again in 1731 and the houses rebuilt in the next thirty years still stand. The Rows in Yarmouth, badly damaged by enemy action, were immediately surveyed by the then Ministry of Works along with houses in Folkestone. An industrial suburb of Frome was surveyed in the 1970s when it was threatened by decay.

Frome

In Folkestone, Frome and Yarmouth, streets were filled with cumulative terraces, as a result of building houses singly, in pairs and in small groups. At Frome the prosperity of the woollen industry led in 1650–1700 to a great increase in population, as Defoe noticed; there were by the 1720s 'so many new streets of houses that Frome is now reckoned to have more people in it than the city of Bath'.[36] The town did not become, as he had forecast, 'one of the greatest and wealthiest inland towns in England' and by 1970 the Trinity district was in decay. The principal landowners had laid out streets and leased plots; each new stone house or group used one side wall of an existing house and needed only three new ones. They were of one and a half or two storeys, the best with gables: about four out of five were built on narrow plots with one room to the frontage; a few had a second room behind. Some larger houses with two rooms at the front and one or two wings to the rear had a framed staircase. There are no large windows to light weavers at work and looms must have been in detached workshops.[37]

Yarmouth and Folkestone

Yarmouth experienced a boom in the seventeenth century when herrings migrated from the Norwegian coast. Folkestone flourished as cross-Channel traffic, as well as the fishing industry, expanded. In both, new houses seem to have been independent structures, in Folkestone of stone with brick bands and in Yarmouth entirely of brick.[38] The houses were of two full storeys but there were no gables. The Yarmouth garrets had a roof system clear of obstructive cross-members and lighted by dormers. Of the three towns, the herring fishermen's houses had the highest standard of design and craftsmanship. They were invariably enlarged later at the back and sanitary arrangements added but originally they had one room on plan: a few with a wider frontage had a passage to a yard at the back.

In all three towns, the plans were essentially similar in having the fireplace on a side wall with a winder staircase alongside it going up to garret level and down to the cellar, following a tradition common to town and country and which lasted into the nineteenth century. The one distinction to be made is that staircases at Frome were in a rounded and not a square space; that is, they were really the projecting stair-turret of south-western counties brought within the body of the structure. These enclosed stair-turrets are only one aspect of the conservatism of the West Country; another is the survival of detached kitchens at the rear of properties in Bristol, Totnes and other towns.

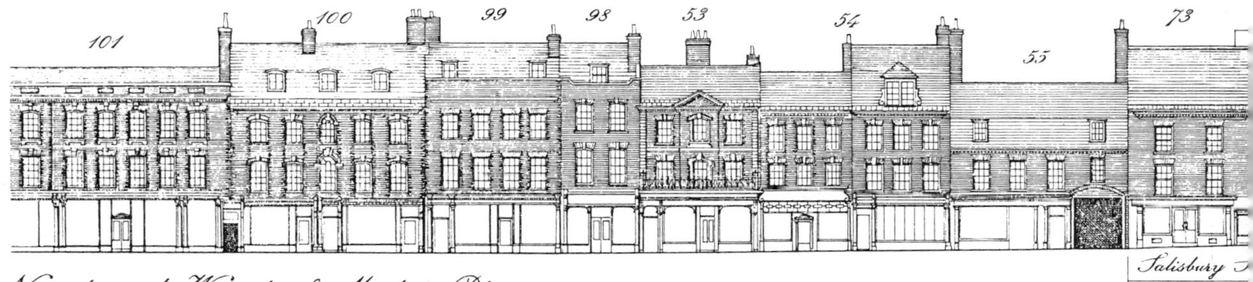

195. Street elevation of part of THE MARKET PLACE, BLANDFORD FORUM, DORSET, recorded in 1943–4. *RCHM.*

Blandford Forum

The town of Blandford, as rebuilt after the fire in 1731 [195], displays the social and cultural mixture of a market town dependent for new houses for all classes on one family firm, the Bastards, who worked for architects employed by the gentry.[39] They introduced Baroque details into the design of elevations and used good quality bricks with some stone. For the best people they provided a house with a five-bay frontage and a rear service-wing – the standard middle-class house of town and country. For shop-keepers they adopted the London plan with a narrower frontage and three storeys – taller because the front ground-floor room was a shop. For artisans they used a fairly uncommon form of semi-detached plan, with a shared service-passage from which houses were entered and going through to the rear [184].

To identify types of plan adopted for new houses reveals only the best and most enduring sorts of building, whatever the classes for which they were intended. It would be a pity not to recall housing schemes or types of dwelling which have totally vanished. One is the use made of Holy Trinity, Aldgate, London, after the dissolution.[40] More tenements were formed in the other monastic buildings. How long these arrangements lasted we do not know; Mitre Street, made early in the nineteenth century, runs the length of the church site.

Rock-houses

Another lost aspect is the disappearance of the rock-houses of Nottingham, Bridgnorth and other towns on sandstone or limestone. Central Nottingham is a honeycomb of caves and cellars, of medieval and later date and many of them still used. From early in the seventeenth century, if not before, houses were cut into natural scarps and into the flanks of roads sunk in the rock. John Taylor visited Nottingham in the 1630s[41] and said that 'a great number of the inhabitants, especially of the poorer sort', lived in such houses. He presented them as a 'do it yourself' affair: 'if a man be destitute of a house, it is but to go to Nottingham and with a mattock, a shovel or such instruments he may play the mole, the coney or the pioneer and work himself a hole or burrow for his family'. Some of the last-inhabited rock-houses were those in the industrial village of Kinver (Staffordshire) [196]. They were dry and warm but what was called slum clearance emptied them and now weather and vandalism are destroying them. Some of them belong to the National Trust.

196. At HOLY AUSTIN ROCK, KINVER, STAFFORDSHIRE, houses were partly cut out of the sandstone and partly built out in front of it. They were occupied until the 1920s and were a tourist attraction.

197. Comparative plans of terrace houses 1658 to c. 1900. A. 52 NEWINGTON GREEN, ISLINGTON, 1658. The dog-leg staircase between the two stacks is lighted by a well shared with the next house. B. 34 ESSEX STREET, STRAND, 1676, built by Nicholas Barbon. Both had basement kitchens. The massive chimney stacks contain flues for basement fireplaces and two or more upper floors. C and D. GRANBY VILLAS, SNEINTON, NOTTINGHAM, c. 1900. C has a passage giving separate access to the scullery. Both have cellars. E. Miners' cottages, PORTLAND ROW, KIRKBY-IN-ASHFIELD, 1823; the only non-parlour type in this selection. F. 116 THE MOUNT, YORK, 1840; this type with the staircase between the two rooms is common in York. The service wing is later. Only architect's design plans show the service element exactly. G. 37 PENLEY'S GROVE STREET, YORK, 1845–7. The staircase rises towards the rear of the house so that it may be lighted by a landing window. H. ZULU ROAD, NOTTINGHAM, 1879, with privy and coal-house detached, across the path leading to back doors in the row. *After A. F. Kelsall (A, B), J. Severn (C, D), G. S. Stevenson (E), RCHM (F, G).*

Innovations of plan

The enormous demand for new houses in London and its suburban villages led developers to introduce a new type of house which eventually superseded traditional plans. Building for the upper and middle classes, they produced houses with two rooms on plan, one behind the other, with a more convenient staircase than the winder type alongside the fireplace [197]. In the earliest examples there is a dog-leg staircase between the front and back rooms, dignified enough for guests being taken upstairs to the parlour. This is the plan of houses in Essex Street, Westminster, built in 1675 on what had been the site of Essex House. They were put up by 'the most daring speculative builder of his day', Nicholas Barbon, son of the fanatical anti-monarchist of Commonwealth times, Praisegod Barbon or Barebone. This two-roomed plan could be enlarged by a narrow addition at the rear and this form appears in houses of the 1680s in Great Russell Street, part of the earl of Southampton's Bloomsbury estate.[42]

The difficulty of this plan was to light the staircase and by the early eighteenth century a new version appeared with a staircase facing the front door, lighted either by a landing window or by a skylight. For a middle-class house the frontage might be as much as 7.6 m (25 ft); reduced to 3.6 m (12 ft) or less – especially by omitting the entrance passage – the design became standard for working-class terraces down to 1914. For the latter the staircase, whether between rooms or facing the front door got light only indirectly, from open bedroom doors. Apart from the width of frontage and size of rooms, the other measure of quality was whether the addition was of one storey or more.

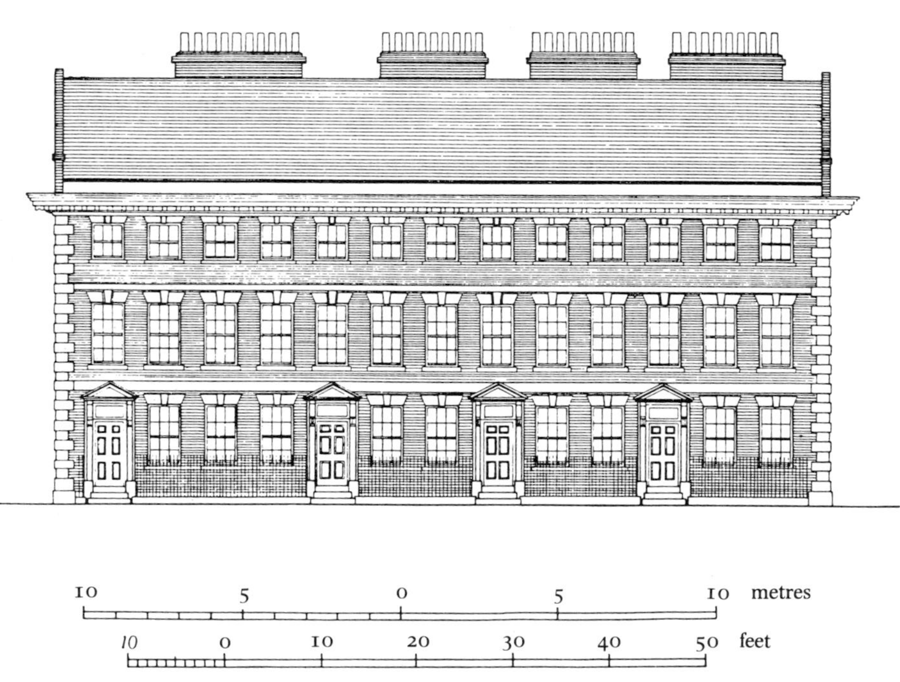

198. Reconstructed elevation of 39–45 BOOTHAM, YORK, a terrace of four houses built in 1748 by a man who occupied one of them and let the others. *RCHM.*

Industrial housing

The Industrial Revolution finally broke down the distinction between urban and rural types of house and diverted initiative away from London. The first new housing is to be found in communities created by industry in south Wales, the Midlands and the north. From about 1775 onwards and first in the Birmingham area, the better-paid and self-employed workers organized themselves for self-help.[43] Building clubs, meeting like friendly societies in an inn, enabled each member to acquire a house and then wound themselves up; they eventually gave way to permanent building societies. Freehold-land societies bought land and sold building plots at cost. The Midlands and the north led the way in this development. The most distinctive type of house was that built for the domestic textile industry [200–4], to be identified by the large window lighting a room containing looms for weaving cotton (especially calico) in Lancashire, woollen cloth in Yorkshire, silk in Macclesfield and frames for knitting stockings in Leicestershire and Nottinghamshire. Cotton weavers needed a damp atmosphere and so their loom-shops were either in a cellar or on the ground floor [204]; woollen weavers and framework knitters usually worked in an upstairs room, as did ribbon weavers [203] in Coventry.[44]

Owners of mills, mines and railways could recruit a labour force only by providing housing for it. On level sites they built back-to-back rows or else the 'blind-back' terraces with no doorway or windows at the rear – what Rowntree called 'not throughs' when in 1899 he investigated poverty in York. In Pennine valleys, new ways were found of building to a maximum density: terraces backing on to a bank, or stacked over each other [200], sometimes with interlocking plans. William Strutt built such houses in 1783 at Milford (Derbyshire) for workers in his woollen mills, and his foundry produced the hardware for them such as cast-iron window frames, gutter-brackets and even numbers for doors.[45]

Tall blocks of flats, for sale or rent, had begun to appear in Glasgow and Edinburgh from c. 1650. This involved the concept, acceptable to Scottish law, that one freeholder might live above or below another, as well as alongside. English lawyers had adopted the concept of the flying freehold for their inns of court in London, but preferred to impose the long lease on their clients and that was inappropriate for working men. The stacked houses of northern England were built for rent and not for sale, as were the blocks of model working-class dwellings in Victorian London.

Since 1919, the process of clearing away slums and houses condemned as sub-standard, in order to rehouse people on council estates, has made the study of working-class housing of the Industrial Revolution just as much a matter of archaeology as the study of medieval houses. When Lancashire cotton weavers left the loom-shops for the mill, loom-shops were converted to residential use; the stone houses remain but the large

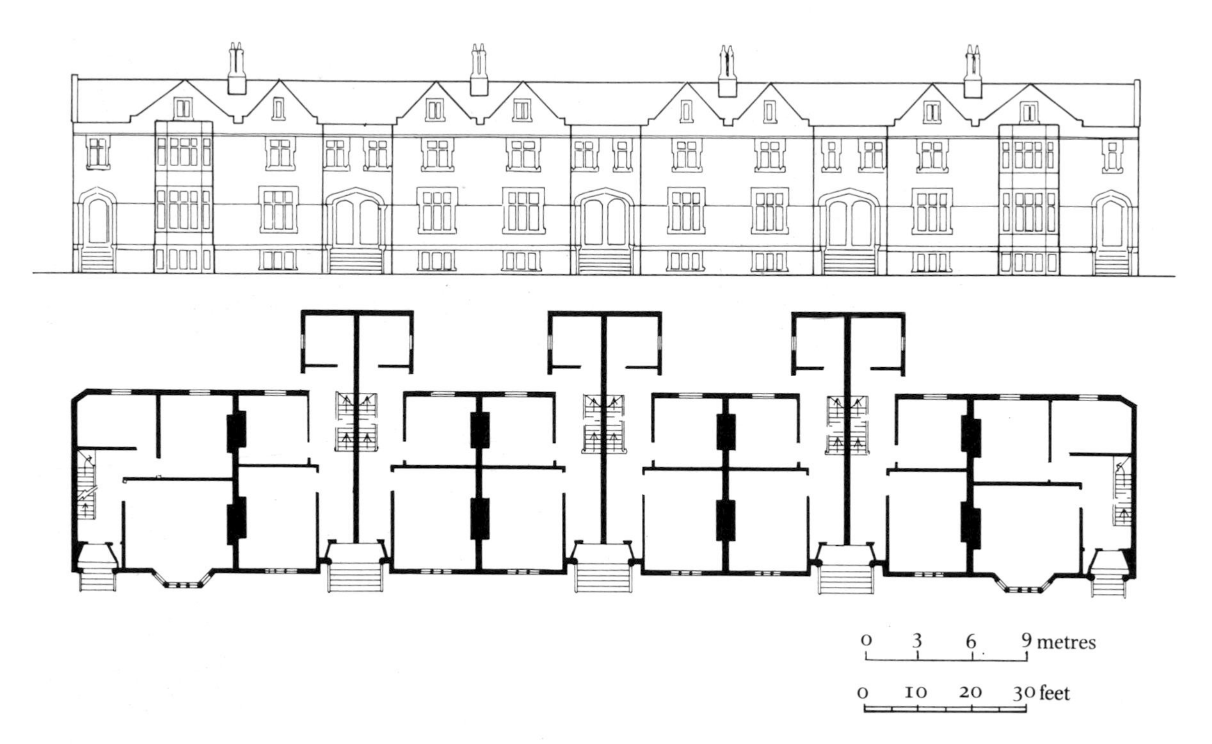

199. Ground plan and elevation of a terrace in BROOK STREET, STOKE-ON-TRENT, STAFFORDSHIRE, built in 1837 by the Brook Street Building Club, whose members included a gentleman, a timber-merchant and earthenware-manufacturers. A contemporary described them as 'a superior class of houses of the bay-window style of architecture'. They had services in the basement and servants' bedrooms in the attics. *After D. Altham.*

windows have been reduced in size and the cellar-openings blocked. Framework knitters' houses in Nottingham, built of brick, are now rare. The houses at Milford have been sold to tenants and the uniformity of the rows has been diluted as owners have 'improved' their properties. Many thousands of such houses are now listed under planning legislation and so may not be demolished without the consent of a planning authority, but alteration is not prevented. Industrial archaeologists have been more interested in pumping stations, mills, factories and their machinery than in houses; much remains to be learned about the dating and design of working-class housing, of the varying standards between regions and industries and between different grades of worker in the same industry. More assiduous field-work, and use of the ample evidence of Ordnance Survey and local maps, of official reports, census returns and the like would redress the balance between houses of the well-to-do and the poor which for earlier centuries is beyond recovery.

200A

200B

200. UPPER TEAN, STAFFORDSHIRE. The upper storey of this row (now demolished) consisted of separate flats entered from the rear. *Staffordshire County Council.*

201

202

201. EDENSFIELD, LANCASHIRE, a row of ground-floor flats and two-storey maisonettes, the latter reached by a landing.

202. Framework-knitters' houses at CALVERTON, NOTTINGHAMSHIRE, with large windows to light the stocking-frames.

203

203. Ribbon-weavers employed by J. J. Cash and Son rented a house and also a loom in the top-floor workshop. This row, CASH'S LANE, COVENTRY, WARWICKSHIRE, built in 1857, has been saved by the conversion of the lofty workshop into two-storey maisonettes.

204

204. A row of cotton weavers' houses at HORWICH, LANCASHIRE, put up by a building club, with cellar loom-shops. *J. G. Timmins.*

Notes

1 J.W.F. Hill, *Tudor and Stuart Lincoln* (1956), 62–5.
2 BE, *Wiltshire*, 337–8.
3 M.D. Lobel and W.H. Johns (eds.), *The Atlas of Historic Towns*, 2 (1975), Bristol, 18.
4 P. Heal, *Of Princes and Prelates* (1980), 255–6.
5 RCHM, *York*, 5, 69.
6 D.M. Palliser, *The Reformation in York* (1971), 17.
7 Hill, 62–5.
8 RCHM, *York*, 4, 30–45, pls. 53–76.
9 BE, *London*, 1, 50–1; 2, 51–4.
10 *Atlas of Historic Towns*, 2, Norwich, 20; BE, *North-East Norfolk and Norwich*, 271. According to Thomas Baskerville, this 'sumptuous new built house', unfinished in 1681, had already cost the duke £30,000; Hist. MSS Comm., *Portland*, 2, 270.
11 BE, *Derbyshire* (1978), 97–101; *Nottinghamshire* (1979), 366, 226–7.
12 T.C. Hine, *Nottingham, its Castle* ... (1867), 34. The model is displayed in the Museum.
13 J. Schofield, *The Building of London* (1984), 140–2.
14 Schofield, 144; E.A. Webb, *The Records of St Bartholomew's Smithfield* (2 vols, 1920–1), 2.
15 A.C. Dyer, *Worcester in the Sixteenth Century* (1973), 101, 228; BE, *Worcestershire*, 327–8; BE, *Gloucestershire: The Vale* ... 227; BE, *Wiltshire*, 327.
16 BE, *Suffolk*, 298.
17 Hill, pl. 5.
18 RCHM, *York*, 5, 62–8.
19 RCHM, *Salisbury*, 1, 48–9.
20 Hist. MSS Comm., Report 13, 2, 308; C. Morris (ed.), *The Journeys of Celia Fiennes* (1947), 227; J. Harris, *The Artist and the Country House* (1979), pls. 109, 132.
21 *Archaeol. J.*, 113 (1956), 186–7.
22 RCHM, *Stamford*, xliii; BE, *Wiltshire*, 531.
23 D.G. Vaisey (ed.), *Probate Inventories of Lichfield and District 1568–1680* (Staffs. Record Soc. 5, 1969), nos. 15, 17 etc.
24 *Tour through England and Wales* (Everyman), 1, 6.
25 C.H.C. and M.I., Baker, ... *James Brydges* ... 306–7.
26 *Stamford*, lviii.
27 J. Stow, *Survey of London* (1908), 133, 155; Schofield, 161.
28 V. Parker, *The Making of King's Lynn* (1971), 89–90; BE, *North-East Norfolk and Norwich*, 285.
29 *Archaeol. J.*, 113 (1956), 186; RCHM, *Oxford* (1939), 175 (no. 154), *Ant. J.*, 27 (1947), 135, fig. 10.
30 Stow, 1, 268, 167.
31 J. Summerson, *Georgian London* (1945), 4–5; *House and Home*, 159–60, 163–4, 184.
32 RCHM, *West London* (1925), 23; Schofield, 158.
33 *House and Home*, 169; *Trans. Thoroton Soc.*, 67 (1963), 67–92; *World Archaeology*, 15 (1963), 174.
34 *Oxoniensia*, 26–7 (1961–2), 323–9.
35 *Ant. J.*, 32 (1952), 192–7.
36 *Tour* ..., 1, 280.
37 R. Leech, *Early Industrial Housing: the Trinity Area of Frome* (1981).
38 B.H. St J. O'Neil, in *Ant. J.*, 29 (1949), 8–12 and *Archaeologia*, 95 (1953), 141–80.
39 RCHM, *Dorset*, 3, 16–40; BE, *Dorset*, 95–100.
40 Schofield, 145–8.
41 J. Taylor, *Early Prose and Poetical Works* (1888), 289.
42 Summerson, *Georgian London*, 28–32; A.F. Kelsall, 'The London house plan in the later 17th century', *Post-Medieval Archaeol.*, 8 (1974), 80–91. The RCHM inventories of the *City of York* (3, 4) contain many plans and photographs of nineteenth-century houses.
43 S.D. Chapman (ed.), *History of Working-Class Housing* (1971), ch. 6; *World Archaeol.*, 15 (1983), 173–83.
44 J.G. Timmins, *Handloom Weavers' Cottages in Lancashire* (1977); VCH, *Warwickshire*, 8 (1969), 150.
45 *Archaeol. J.*, 118 (1961), 236–8.

Index

Page numbers in *italic* refer to illustrations and captions